Praise for *Cash Grab*

If you're a show biz insider, this book will make you laugh and cringe in equal measure. If you're a show biz outsider, it'll make you happy to stay that way. *Cash Grab* is dark, funny, and will definitely piss some people off!
-Bill Martin, writer and co-creator of *The Unicorn* and *Grounded For Life*, executive producer of *3rd Rock from the Sun*

ANDY SPAIN

CASH GRAB

New York

First Printing: 2022
ISBN 978-1-954158-11-5

Humorist Books is an imprint of *Weekly Humorist* owned and operated by Humorist Media LLC.

Weekly Humorist is a weekly humor publication, subscribe online at weeklyhumorist.com

110 Wall Street New York, NY 10005

weeklyhumorist.com - humoristbooks.com - humoristmedia.com

*For my kids**

**unless they don't like it, in which case I'll dedicate this book to myself.*

1.

My newly earned media studies degree did wonders for my career when my resume rose to the top of a temp agency slush pile. I thought having a degree made me overqualified for that kind of work, but I never heard back from the TV production companies I applied to and temping paid slightly better than unemployment. The agency arranged my first assignment after a single brief telephone interview during which I wasn't asked about my past employment history. In a few days, I would begin my first post: clerical work at a staffing office. The comical recursiveness of a temp agency setting me up with a job where I would help another agency fill vacancies was apparently outside the mental reach of the hiring official to whom I pointed it out.

A few weeks before graduation, which took place in a rarely used convention center basement with all the fanfare of a shuffling line of terrified zombies being handed rolled-up pieces of paper, which could have said anything for all we knew, my former classmate and sometimes friend Chibbs Ticonderoga had already secured what he called "an industry job" at The Town Commoner, a local public access channel. The more unimpressed I acted, the more he wouldn't shut up about it.

"Buddy, you have to do jobs you don't necessarily enjoy while you keep an eye out for something better—but you have to be prepared," Chibbs said as we wielded our diplomas like sword fighters and slapped them together behind a 24-hour diner, the inside of which somehow reeked worse than the dumpster we fought beside. The school printed Chibbs's diploma and mailed it to him even though he had dropped out after getting the Town Commoner job, perfectly highlighting the institution's careful eye for detail. "You can cut corners and do the bare minimum in school, I guess," Chibbs said. "I mean, obviously, because how else did you make it through? Hypnosis? Blackmail? You skipped class so much, I'd be surprised if any of the teachers even knew your name."

"Still passed," I said and went in for the kill, crumpling my paper sword into Chibbs's chest. He moaned as I wiped the cheap ink from my hands and tossed the paper ball into the dumpster. I held the lid open and motioned inside. "Whoever comes to empty that definitely makes more money than I can make temping."

"They probably smell better, too." Chibbs shrugged and launched his paper-airplane-folded diploma into the dumpster as it closed. "Friendlier, better looking, less likely to rouse anger in others. Yeah, those garbage collectors sound like a dream compared to you." I smiled and placed a hand over my heart in feigned appreciation of Chibbs's colorful insult. "So, why are you even doing this?" he asked.

"Doing what?" I said. "Hanging out with a self-righteous egomaniac? I was just asking myself that. Well, gotta go." I waved and started to walk away.

"School, the degree, this industry; why bother?" Chibbs said.

"Working in TV just might beat the allure of sitting in a nondescript office pushing papers around all day, but I need to work a few temp assignments to know for sure."

"I've got some news for you, Buddy: making TV shows is still *work*. Unglamorous, tedious, long hours. Look, I'll let you in on an insider secret."

I laughed. "Oh ok, so a couple of months at a low-rent cable access channel makes you a TV guru? Too bad I wasted my time getting that degree. I should've just grabbed your coattails and hung on for the ride."

Chibbs snapped his fingers. "Quick, list your qualifications. Oh wait, you're already done."

I pointed to the dumpster and pulled a sad face as if regretting the fate of my wadded-up diploma.

Chibbs had prudently spent most of his college weekends assisting with any student video project that needed an extra hand, then went cold-calling around town looking for work long before our final semester was up. Serendipitously, when he made a drop-in at The Town Commoner, a video editor had just stormed out and quit. The editor alleged he could no longer handle the monotony of anything-goes public access drivel, that it had diminished his life's passion so greatly that he had nothing left to give and would "rather work on a garbage barge because at least then you're *supposed* to be around garbage," according to what Chibbs heard secondhand. That editor took with him six years of institutional memory, and The Commoner desperately needed a warm body to fill the void. Chibbs quit school that evening and started work the next morning.

"Look," Chibbs went on, "it's not like I'm that much farther ahead of you; I've barely reached the next rung. But I do know you have to put in the effort and do more than the job demands if you want to get noticed, even if you think it's a waste of time because of whatever higher skills you delusionally believe yourself to possess. You don't learn that from school—you learn that from working."

I kicked at the gravel, overturning a bent bottle cap with a cigarette butt folded into it. "Is that what you had to tell yourself when you were wrangling cables and carrying lights and setting up snack tables for other people's projects?" Chibbs nodded slowly as I shook my head. "What kind of sense does that make?"

"Uh, the same kind of sense that all reality makes," he scoffed. "What do you mean?"

I leaned against the diner's brick wall and folded my arms. Immediately feeling something damp against my back, I stood upright and tried to rub off whatever sticky grease I'd just smeared on my shirt. "What good is going to school if getting a degree doesn't prove you know how to do something?" I said and reached out to wipe my hands on Chibbs's shirt. He swatted them away and jumped back in a defensive martial arts stance, bouncing on his toes. "Where's that leg up we're supposed to have?"

"Right here!" Chibbs extended a slow-motion roundhouse kick to my head. I thrust my chin back and groaned, spitting out invisible teeth. He whirled around with a shriek and cornered me against the dumpster, fists raised. I grimaced, feeling the wetness on the back of my shirt mingling with some food grime stuck to the dumpster. "Whatever your plan is…I guess that's saying too much; you've never had a plan." He dropped his stance and bowed.

"But I did have a plan," I said, bowing in return. "Go to school and then get paid to create and produce TV shows. How else does that work?" I held my nose and scratched my back against the dumpster.

"Ha! It works the way it actually works, which is not at all like what you said, but like the way a person with half a brain could've figured out by now," Chibbs said. "A degree might show someone's potential competency—I know, I know, obviously not in your case—but proving you can do the work is a totally different thing. And beyond that, the idea of someone who doesn't play well with others wanting to work in TV is laughable. Shows are all put together by crews!" Chibbs pushed me gently toward the dumpster. "What's your hang-up with people, anyway? You think you're better than any of our classmates you refused to work with?"

"I didn't need those lesser-thans rubbing off on me, dragging down the quality of the work," I sneered. "Can you really stand there with your stupid face and tell me their projects looked as good as mine, as good as ours?"

He sighed as he checked his pockets for his car keys. "Of course not, but it's school, Buddy. That's part of the point."

"What is? To let people who are objectively bad at something pretend they're not still objectively bad at it after two years of instruction?"

"What makes you so different?" Chibbs asked with a smirk.

"All I needed was access to the equipment," I said. "I proved I know how to use it, I passed all the classes, and now I have a degree. If going to school makes me so employable, why am I begging a temp agency to give me suggestions for where I should go to be tortured?"

Chibbs grabbed my shoulder. "So you can atone for dragging down the world's average IQ," he said flatly. "It's good to see you turning a corner and working to acknowledge that."

I lowered my head and chanted like a meditating monk. Chibbs walked to his car and popped open the door.

"But seriously, what do you think is supposed to happen?" he called as he poked at some coins in the cup holder. "You get a ten-cent degree from an obscure college and The Network calls you up to ask what job you want?"

"Now you're speaking my language," I said. "Let's go live in that reality. Second thought—I'll go, you stay here. You're kind of a buzzkill."

"Keep on dreaming, Bud. Here, you'll need these," Chibbs said, offering me a fist full of coins. Before I could reach for them he launched the coins over my head. "You're so short-sighted, you can see into the back of your own empty skull." Chibbs closed the car door. I held onto the rolled-down window and stretched my legs like I was ready to run beside his moving car if I had to. "Just keep working on your showreel while you still have access to the school's equipment," he said. "That's about all you can do."

Graduates had access to the school's video editing computer lab through the end of summer and were encouraged to cobble together a minute-long showreel—a montage of the least embarrassing moments of our school projects that could be used as a calling card when applying for media industry jobs. My showreel mostly consisted of dry cinematography and editing exercises along with experimental "video art" from my courses, the only highlight being a clip from a short documentary piece Chibbs and I had worked on together. I sent a copy of my showreel to every relevant company in town, hoping one would be inclined to gamble on the potential of a self-proclaimed jack-of-all-trades with no real credits or career history.

"Maybe fortune will smile on me and dish out a dead-end job at a public access channel like yours," I said.

Chibbs revved the engine and flitted his hand for me to move. "Sorry, we're all staffed up right now. But hey, if there's ever an opening, maybe I'll tell your staffing agency to hire someone else because I never want to see you again." We grinned and shook hands. Chibbs stomped the gas, spraying dirt across my back as I turned away. I reached behind me to brush it off my shirt but, along with the sticky dampness from the diner wall, it was already congealing into a thin layer of gritty sludge.

.....

Lacking the credentials necessary to qualify as the pioneering TV producer I knew to be my destiny, my only means of gainful employment was the temp agency. Money wasn't that big of an issue yet because my foster parents had hooked me up with a cheap apartment and a mostly functioning car so I could focus on studying instead of having to work through college. Since I'd graduated, I didn't want to keep being a drain on them, regardless of how cool they were about it. The problem was I wanted to make things of my own, not huddle and wilt in a cubicle the way I saw most adults doing.

Over the course of a year of soul-depleting temp work in exciting fields like accounting and telecommunications, I noticed a common thread: most small offices only had one or two people who knew what they're doing and cared enough to keep things running smoothly; the remaining employees were empty-headed stooges whose eyes glazed over while they stared at the clock like pagans worshipping the sun. The staggering number of worthless bodies I had the misfortune to work beside effectively schooled me in the disheartening reality of the modern workplace and left me daydreaming schemes to get rid of them.

The month I spent at a healthcare provider's billing office was a supremely regrettable yet enlightening experience thanks to Winda, a prickly old hag who was so irate at the inconvenience of being alive that her only means of catharsis was to offload that suffering onto every person around her. Her pasty, puckered jaw always hung open in a demented trance, as if Death were constantly staring her down. It was a wonder how she held herself upright without her fleshy folds and pillowy cheeks melting and dissolving into the carpet.

I walked into the office five minutes early on the first day of my assignment. Winda sat in a heap behind the front desk, her head lolled down and cushioned by her third or fourth chin. I coughed quietly into my fist to get her attention. Her eyes blasted open as her jowls tightened into a vicious snarl. "Who're you?! Why you in here?!" she screeched.

"Good morning," I said with the flaky enthusiasm of a used car salesman.

"Don't you make me get up out my seat and throw you out here, mister smiley boy! Whoever told you, you could stroll up in here this early in the morning all unannounced? Whatever it is you tryin' to sell..." She must have been accustomed to people fleeing the office by the time she reached that level of verbal thrashing. I stood and awaited her tirade's crescendo, but the flexing of her colossal jaws must have fatigued her because she halted it there.

"The agency usually contacts the office manager before I start a new assignment," I said. "Maybe there was a mix-up. My name is Buddy Buppsen, and I'm here—"

"That agency don't tell me nothin'! I *am* the office manager, and they don't tell me nothin'! Always sendin' people over here like we a daycare and we have time to hold your little hands and walk you around. This ain't no hospital. I ain't got no wheelchair to push you around in." Winda had accumulated an impressive glob of slobber around the edge of her bottom lip. She clutched a heavily used tissue and dabbed the edges of both nostrils, sniffing laboriously. In the process, the remainder of the hanging slobber smeared itself onto the sleeve of her sweater.

"Well, I'm sorry they didn't mention it to you," I said, glancing at the mail piled in her inbox. "But I'm here to help out however I can, so just...you know, show me the way."

"Boy, what makes you think I got time to show you anything at all? Who you think you are to come in here and make demands like that?"

"Well, that's exactly why I'm here. The agency must have heard just how overworked you were and they sent in the reserves." I expanded my smile until the corners of my mouth verged on splitting open, then held out my hand. "I'm Buddy Buppsen. The agency sent me here to help you. What do you need help with today?" I cocked my head to one side like an expectant puppy.

Winda stared with her mouth hanging low, drool collecting again on her lip. "Lord help me. My name's Winda, and I run the show. You forget that, you'll be out of here quicker than the last one." Winda threw her hands up, slapped them on her desk, and heaved to lift her quaking five-foot frame. "Lord help me, not today," she whispered. "Come on, let's go then."

I followed Winda through the door behind her desk and past some recklessly overcrowded bookshelves. She edged sidewise by the shelves, but still her baggy midsection skimmed a few overhanging notebooks, sending one to the floor with a thud and scattering its contents. Winda cursed quietly and flapped a hand at the strewn papers in abject dismissal.

"Now, those doctors think they know so much, but I'm here to tell you, they ain't so smart. I seen their paperwork and don't none of them code nothin' correct. I seen their pay stubs too, and I know I do as much work as them day in and day out, but I don't get paid but a tiny fraction of what they get. They sit up in their offices writin' down incorrect codes for services they say they did, and down here we got to decipher them things, Lord help me." Winda rambled in a breathless sermon during our walk down a muggy, low-ceilinged hallway. We passed several small offices, each housing an elderly employee gaping at an obsolete computer monitor like some sort of exhibit in a history museum. One man in a floppy fishing hat was fully asleep in his chair, head tilted back at an impossible angle, audibly gargling the saliva streaming down his throat. At the end of the hallway, Winda quickly knocked twice on a closed door and opened it before awaiting an answer. A smartly dressed woman in her early forties with dark brown hair and kind eyes sat at a computer station, typing rapidly with one hand and drinking a mug of tea with the other. She glanced in our direction, then did a double-take and removed her headphones.

"Jamsin, this is Eddy. Agency done sent him over this morning," Winda sputtered as she turned and left us. "Hi, Eddy. Welcome aboard."

Jamsin extended her hand, and I shook it, quietly saying, "Nice to meet you. My name is Buddy, by the way."

"Buddy. Got it. So Winda showed you the ropes?" Jamsin smiled and continued to type as she sat back down. "Sorry, I have to finish this one statement. Just a moment, please," she said and pored over what was on her screen, mouthing the words to herself. A moment later she said, "Ok. That's that. So Winda showed you the ropes?"

"Well, no, actually. I think she's busy," I said. "And honestly, she didn't seem too happy that I'm here."

"Oh no, that's too bad," Jamsin pouted, scrunching up her face. "I'm sure everything will be just fine. Don't worry—it's Monday, it's early, you know how it goes. So, what can I help you with?"

"Well, the temp agency sent me here for a typical one-month assignment and today's my first day," I said. "My last assignment was answering phones at the sewer maintenance facility down the road. I guess that doesn't really matter. Are you the manager here?"

Jamsin snickered. "Me? Oh no, no. I'm outranked by everyone else. I just do the grunt work. But hey, somebody has to."

"Oh, I was under the impression… So, are you new here, too?" I asked.

"Nope, six years," she said, nodding and glancing back at her screen. "I'm sorry, Buddy. I don't mean to cut our chat short, but what can I do for you? Did Winda want you to shadow me? I don't know if I'll have time to teach you much."

"No, no, I… Look, I'm only here for a month, but I'm willing to work and all that. I just need the money. And the work. I mean, I just graduated, and I need a job while I sort things out. Does that make sense?"

"Yes, of course!" she beamed. "We've all been there. I'm so sorry I can't be of more help, though." She motioned to her computer. "I have an absolute mountain of work to get through today. I got in at six, and I've still barely gotten started. Oh! But here." She whirled around in her chair and riffled through a stack of red and blue folders on the shelf behind her. She selected four blue folders and handed them to me. "Tell Winda the two on top have been correctly adjusted and the other two are still missing information. Thanks so much, Buddy!" Jamsin smiled and waved. Before I could react, she put on her headphones and was busy typing with a fierce concentration.

I made my way back down the corridor, past the sleeping fisherman whose head was now slumped forward on his chest. As I rounded the corner at the end of the hall, I was startled by Winda, hinged over in a half crouch trying to reach the folders she had knocked over.

"Pick those up, mister helpful," she snarled and continued swiping.

I gathered all the papers and rotated them into a uniform orientation. "Let's see, this one appears to be an intake form, and the note attached says 'erroneous code—should be zero-zero-two-zero, not zero-two-zero-zero...'"

Winda snatched the papers from me. "Don't you go readin' no personal information! Who you think you are?" She grabbed a notebook, stuffed the papers haphazardly inside, then stood and returned it to the shelf with no regard for its proper filing. She pointed a twisted, chipped-nail finger at me. "Lord, help me. You want some stranger readin' all your personal information? Imagine you done had gonorrhea or some such and then some smiley boy mister helpful run up into the clinic and start readin' off all your information to a pack of pretty girls waitin' outside. That what you want?" she growled. Down the hall, I heard the fisherman briefly gag and smack his lips, then begin to snore.

I shook my head furiously. "No, what? Of course not. I thought you'd need to know where it should be filed."

"Boy, that's the third time you tried to be helpful and failed. You ain't even gonna last as long as the last one." She retracted her finger and shook her head slowly, wheezing deeply. "Best stay out other people's business, hear? Now, I took you to Jamsin so you could help her and stay out my way. You go bother someone else, or I'll ring up that good-for-nothing agency and tell them to come down and throw you out on your ear, you got that?" She waddled off and kicked the remaining folders under a shelf.

My days were mostly spent filing small batches for Jamsin and arranging the notebooks and folders on the shelves so they were flush with the edges and therefore clear of Winda's girth if she sauntered through the halls, which, fortunately, was rare. If I found a misplaced or incomplete file, I would take it to Jamsin for guidance but quickly learned that only added to the ever-increasing pile of work that forced her to stay late most days. The other employees filed in and out of work at odd hours and either napped at their desks or stared at their monitors for the bulk of the day. I envied their drab tomb-like offices; anything was a step up from my warped plastic chair in the corner of the dim hallway from which I could hear Winda's heavy breathing.

Coming back from lunch one afternoon, I rounded the corner by the shelves and abruptly stopped, astonished to see Winda berating Jamsin, who stood rigidly, dewy-eyed and trembling.

"You people are all exactly the same! You don't do nothin', and you take all the credit!" Winda shrieked, dabbing the sides of her nostrils with what may have been the same crumpled tissue wad I saw her holding every day. "You some kind of big shot? What gives you the right to parade around like you own the place? You come up in here every single day makin' all kinds of trouble for me, and I'm supposed to reward you for it? Has the whole world gone crazy?"

Jamsin shuddered, her lips quivering. Winda slapped a typed memo onto a shelf and pounded it with her pruney fist. I leaned in and read what I could while Winda continued her tirade. It was a letter from the head office recommending a promotion for Jamsin, citing her constant attentiveness and good deeds over the preceding year. Jamsin took a deep breath and held up her hands. "Winda. I assure you, I had nothing to do with this and I didn't know a thing about it. I wouldn't dream of—"

"Oh, here we go again with the lies," Winda bawled. "Save it for your diary, girl. I ain't got the time." Winda noticed me and rolled her eyes, which made her jiggly face stretch like a kneaded lump of dough. "I swear, I don't know how we keep the lights on with the two of you here. Lord, help me." She pushed past me, snatched the letter, and returned to her office. Jamsin rushed down the hallway to her office, heels clicking in a brisk even tempo.

I knocked on her door once Winda had left for the day. "Buddy, I appreciate your concern," she began as she slowly dunked a tea bag into a stained mug. "When any two people have worked together a considerable length of time, it gets to where…Well, stress shows itself differently depending on the person. All interpersonal relationships deal with this from time to time. You understand what I'm saying?"

I shook my head vehemently. "What are you talking about? How could you defend a sociopath like that? She's a monster and doesn't do anything around here. If there was any justice in the world, you would be the office manager," I said.

Jamsin visibly shut down and pulled a solemn, condescending face. "Buddy, I don't think it's within our professional interests to engage in a closed-door conversation about one of our co-workers," she said. She put down her tea and pressed her index fingers together. "You've only been here a few weeks, and that's insufficient time for understanding, much less mastering, all our operations. Please don't assume you know what's best for us." She threw away the tea bag and strapped on her headphones.

On the final morning of my assignment, I had no illusions about any sort of cheery farewell from Winda or the elderly staff members hibernating in their office dens, but to salvage any possibility of a positive standing with the agency, I hoped to smooth things over with Jamsin. As I walked to her office rehearsing my apology, a bleak revelation struck me. I jogged down the hall and threw open her door.

"You turned down the promotion, didn't you?" I said. Jamsin had removed her headphones when I walked in but immediately thrust them back on when she heard my tone. "Why? To make Winda happy? You don't win points for being a nice person in the face of insurmountable idiocy." Her placid non-reaction enraged me further. "Do they have dirt on you? Did you kill a patient by filing their chart incorrectly, and now you're shackled to this depressing job for all of eternity while Winda gouges you with hot knives? Otherwise, why would you do this? Who would willfully inflict on themselves such a thankless life?"

She ignored me and continued working. I fought the urge to slam the door, outraged that someone like Jamsin could torment herself in a lowly position that made a complete waste of her personal and professional skills.

On my way out, I was surprised by Winda's satisfied cackle. "You see, boy? You see what Jamsin does to us sometimes?" She narrowed her eyes and dabbed her nostrils with the same old tissue. "She gets all high and mighty and needs to be brought back down to earth. Can't nobody in the office think they better than any other person. A team don't work like that." She snorted harshly and cleared her throat, then turned back to her computer screen and opened a sleeve of saltine crackers sitting on her desk. "Now I know we ain't benefited from you being here, but I pray maybe you at least learnt something." She plucked out three crackers, tongue flicking like a dying lizard, and crammed them into her mushy jaws, launching a spray of slobber and crumbs across her desk as she chewed. She waved toward the door, presumably informing me the lesson was over and it was time to leave.

.....

I returned to my shabby apartment confused by Winda's resumption of power and morose at the prospect of calling the agency to request another assignment. To my surprise, I had a message on my answering machine from Tom Geiger-Beef, station manager of The Town Commoner. Tom's woozy drawl made him sound like he was drooping into a toilet bowl after vomiting.

"Buhhhhdy. So, yeah. Your showreel. Wound up on my desk this morning." He whistled low and slow like a lonely train at night. "I think it was this morning. Was it this morning? Could've been over the weekend, you know. Or even Friday for that matter." Air softly escaped his lungs in a calming breeze. I stared at my refrigerator, suddenly hungry and tired. "Think you should come by. Meet the team." After another long pause he said, "Ok, then," and abruptly disconnected.

Chibbs had told me if I ever received an incoherent message from Tom, it probably meant another position had opened at The Commoner. When I reached for the phone to call Chibbs and get the full story, it rang, displaying the number of the temp agency.

"Hello?"

"Buddy. Is this Buddy?" asked a clipped and controlled voice.

"Speaking," I said, trying to hide the confusion in my voice.

"Buddy, listen: you can't yell at people. Appropriate behavior is classified under 'the bare minimum' when it comes to workplace etiquette. I assumed any qualified personnel seeking job placement would appreciate that and compose themselves accordingly."

My increasing heart rate and sweaty palms fought to counterbalance the elation I had received from envisioning future job prospects outside of a grubby cubicle. Jolted by the profound absurdity of my recent temp experiences, I suffered a psychic break wherein the temp agency no longer held significance for my future.

"Let me guess," I said. "You're from the agency and you heard about what happened today."

"Yes, Mr. Buppsen. That is correct."

"You want to congratulate me, I assume."

"Pardon?"

"For making it out alive! What a crazy ride. It was almost exhilarating, in a way. I suppose any near-death experience is."

"I'm sorry, is this Buddy Buppsen? There seems to be some confusion," the agency rep said.

"Yeah, pal. I'm confused, and it sounds like you are, too. How do they do it?"

He sighed. "How does who do what, sir?"

"How do those people clock in every morning and have nothing to do? They sit and stare and die slowly, draining the universe of precious resources, and they're paid for it? It's outright anarchy, and we can't let them get away with it."

"Buddy, we're not talking about them, we're talking about you. The performance of other employees is hardly your concern, but you seem to think working there for a few weeks makes you an authority. Most people would agree that's barely enough time to get the general feel for how a particular office is run."

"So, what you're saying is, you don't know about Winda? How is that possible?" I laughed. "She got kicked out of her coven for being too ornery, and when she was flying away, her broom stick snapped and dropped her into that office where she makes everyone's lives worse with her verbal lashings."

"Wow, yeah, I'm relieved you're gone, as I'm sure those poor people are." The rep's voice dropped to an abrasive grind. "I normally have a substantial well of understanding and compassion for recent graduates who find themselves lost at sea when they first come face-to-face with the reality of a daily work life," he said, "but this is pathetic. Instead of meeting the future head-on and adjusting your expectations and attitude to conform to the standards set before you—which is part of every job—you decided to let your cynicism get the better of you. You made the mistake, sir. A valuable career experience has been wrecked by your indiscretion and irreverent regard for workplace standards."

"If I didn't know better, I'd say you're mad at me," I said. "Back to Winda, the most worthless office manager I've ever come across. She constantly berates Jamsin, who does all the actual work, then tries to take credit for everything in the office running smoothly, which is completely insane because she can't even catalog anything correctly. I don't mean she doesn't know the correct medical codes, I mean she doesn't even understand how filing physically works. She drops folders everywhere like a blind farmer scattering seeds."

"Well, that's the first I'm hearing about any of that, and guess what? I don't care. It's not my job to care because I don't run that office and whoever does can structure it however they like," he said, his voice distorted as if he were pressing the phone against his teeth, threatening to eat it. "But here's the hilarious thing: you just said Jamsin does all the work. Is that the same Jamsin you yelled at today? How is anyone at the agency supposed to take you seriously? You verbally berate a co-worker, then turn around and defend them. Are you bipolar or psychotic or just stupid?"

"Woah, now who's berating someone? Cool it, pal. Pots and kettles and all that."

"Nice try, but it's up to me whether you receive another assignment, and it looks like I'll be forced to change your status to 'suspended.'"

"No!" I shrieked. "The secrets of the universe are slowly being revealed to me through my suffering; I just need one or two more temp assignments before I can die fulfilled. Don't take this away from me. I don't know what I'll do!" I pounded my fist against the wall and sobbed theatrically. "Oh wait, I *do* know what I'll do: literally anything else."

"Good luck with that," the rep hissed. "You wouldn't have come to us if you had anything else you could do! We've connected you with employment opportunities for over a year, and that's your reaction? You needed help, and now having a job is somehow beneath you?"

"Yeah, you helped me learn life's too precious to waste scurrying around under fluorescent lights like lab mice."

"Oh, please. Go cry to mommy with your prissy Sisyphean hissy fit. That's life. The only thing you can change is your reaction to it. If you want to survive in modern society, a job is a necessary inconvenience. You're young, and you don't know what your true calling is yet, and once you think you've figured it out, it'll change on you. You think this is where I saw myself when I was your age? Not even close. But I get to help people, and that's more satisfying than—"

"Go meet Winda, and then tell me all this high-minded garbage about you helping people."

"Good luck," the rep said. "That's all I can offer you."

"Well, I suppose it's in our mutual interest to burn this bridge down and move on with our lives," I said. "Thanks for the memories."

"You supplied the gasoline, Buddy. Remember that."

.....

The Town Commoner's dingy cinder block studio sat on the eastern edge of downtown, an area somehow more rundown-looking than where I lived. A commuter train path extended through an adjacent block; you could see the wrong side of the tracks from the parking lot. A dense clutch of browned grass near the crossing signal formed a mound where a family of groundhogs had made their home. They were rooting in a nearby garbage pile, completely ignoring my presence. "Well, at least there's live entertainment," I said to myself. A shaded valley on the far side of the mound overflowed with litter, mostly glass bottles and candy wrappers, but also the remains of a weather-beaten couch, torn and spilling sun-bleached foam.

I overestimated the importance of my first day and waited over an hour before another person showed up. I had my hands in my pockets and yawned fiercely when a heavily bearded troll appeared at the corner of the building. He froze, ashen-faced and wide-eyed. I recoiled, then leaned forward and spoke just as my powerful yawn concluded, sounding as if I had just been socked in the gut. "Woah, hey there, I'm Buddy," I said, extending my hand.

His downturned mouth gaped in an expression of astonished horror. His nostrils flared.

"Yeah," he said. "Ok." He stared blankly for a moment longer without noticing my handshake offer, his shaggy head trembling slightly, then turned and unlocked the door. He shambled inside and left the door open behind him. I took that as my cue to follow but had to wonder if he would have left the door open regardless.

The water-stained ceiling in the dimly lit building should have been a foot or so higher. The cramped lobby gave the impression of the entrance to an underground bunker. In a flash, I pictured the last television station left on earth after a totalitarian apocalypse, secretly transmitting counter-regime programming to rally the few remaining dissidents. The reception desk sat behind a sheet of acrylic glass and could hardly be seen through a smeary, yellowing film covering it. I walked into the main hallway where the ceiling was somehow even lower, straining my lower neck and shoulders from the unshakable urge to duck.

In the first office I came to, I saw the troll-man sitting in a plastic pool chair facing an oversized wall calendar covered in sticky notes. He had put on a small white cap with an embroidered ship's anchor on the bill. The calendar listed what I assumed were the titles of Town Commoner shows: *The People's Person, Eye on I, All Access Progress, Live Healthy! with Veena Chumbley*, and *Too Much Truth Under One Roof.* The floor was mostly hidden under piles of outdated industry magazines and filing boxes full of video cassettes. A hand-drawn novelty caricature tilted against the back of a broken television monitor was undoubtedly the troll-man's likeness, depicted holding an acoustic guitar with a hacky sack resting on its neck and his name bulging above in puffy balloon letters.

"Tom," I said brightly, causing him to tense up and turn toward me, stroking his beard. "I'm Buddy. I got your message." I extended my hand again.

"Buddy, I'm sorry to tell you this, man," he said, briefly dampening my spirits at the prospect of being told that I did not in fact have a position waiting for me at The Town Commoner, "but I can't shake hands, man. Nothing personal. Just a rule of mine." He hacked dryly into his closed fist and peered over the top of his wiry glasses at a point just to the side of me. "I don't really believe in rules as an ideology. I mean, I'm no anarchist. I may lean towards one side, but it's not…You know, rules are rules, but people are people, so what can you do? My ex was a real taskmaster—you see where that got us." He propped his head back and coughed again, then swallowed with great effort as his throat bulged grotesquely. He grimaced and readjusted his captain's hat. "What can you do?"

I nodded sympathetically. "I guess we can just wave at each other. Ahoy there!" I said triumphantly and waved broadly. Tom nodded steadily. "Whatever floats your boat, brother," he said with a trace of a smile before turning back to the calendar and twisting his beard into a coil. I stepped forward to attempt to restart the conversation just as I heard the front door open.

"Well, if it isn't my arch nemesis, Bloody Buttstain," Chibbs said, raising his eyebrows rapidly as he walked in.

"Hey, that's mister arch nemesis to you, pal." We shook hands and saluted each other.

Chibbs cuffed my shoulder and cocked his head toward Tom. "You meet the top brass already?" he asked.

"Uh, yeah. I guess technically I did." I lowered my voice, squinting at Tom. "Are you sure he knows who I am and why I'm here?"

Chibbs glanced at Tom, who was still transfixed by the calendar. "Oh yeah, he saw your showreel. I made sure it was at the top of the applicant pool. And you don't have to keep your voice down; I'm pretty sure he can't hear you unless you're standing right in front of him. Isn't that right, Tom?" Chibbs bellowed, projecting his voice with an open hand next to his mouth. "I learned the hard way he couldn't hear me from the editing room when I shouted questions to him. Come on, let me show you around."

The editing room was roughly half the size of Tom's office but with twice the number of video cassettes lining the walls in ramshackle, military-surplus aluminum shelves. A dusty folding table had been sawed in half and bolted to one wall, serving as a makeshift desk. An ancient computer monitor sat precariously on it, completely covered in stickers for extinct punk bands.

"So, here's your new home," Chibbs said. "This computer is ten years old, as is the editing software on it."

"So, it's state-of-the-art compared to what we had in school," I said.

"Only the best for you, Bud. No food or drink in here because if anything got spilled, the whole station would have to shut down. Seriously, I can't overstate that." He grabbed and shook a jumble of wires and plugs covering an antique switchboard. "The way this machine is plugged up to the hardware and monitors—nobody knows how it works or how the cables should be routed, so for the love of all that's sacred and electronic, please never unplug anything. Treat everything in this room like it's your own." He placed a hand on my shoulder and smiled with a kindly, benevolent face. "Wait, I forgot you don't know what it's like to actually have anything. So, imagine what it's like for people who have things, and then try to treat this stuff the way they would treat it if it was theirs."

I exhaled and widened my eyes. "Wow, that's a lot of pressure, Chibbs. I may go ahead and trash the place, just so I don't have the threat of an accident hanging over my head."

Chibbs motioned around the room. "This is it. Aside from the computer in Tom's office that runs the scheduling software and the ingest computer down the hall, this is all we've got." He lightly hammered the keyboard, which sat on an upturned cinder block, to wake the computer from sleep mode. "Look, I'm sure this beats whatever your last temp assignment was," he said, thumbing through a stack of papers on the desk as the computer monitor pulsed a gentle low-end buzz I felt in my throat. "It was all so disorganized when I got here. Every day seems like Tom's first day, and he runs the place. He never knows where anything is, who sent him what, what airs now versus what used to air," he said and handed me two pages of printed spreadsheets. "So, I started printing logs—oh yeah, there's a working printer in the ingest room. Who knew? I started printing logs of every tape we ingest, where it goes on the server, what show it's part of, and which tape to find the finished episode on."

"They didn't do that before? Before the war, I mean, when retreating into this underground shelter was their only means of survival," I said.

"Laugh all you want, pal, but consider yourself lucky. If you had walked into the cluster bomb situation I did, all the snarky comments in that mediocre brain of yours would have helped you accomplish a nice pile of goobley squat. I imagine you would've said something like, 'Hi, Tom, I'm new here, and I don't like the way you do things, so instead of working I'll just squawk like a terminally ill sea bird until you politely ask me to leave.'"

"Sea bird; that's great. Tom and I also had a nautical-themed rapport going on earlier," I said.

"Hey, good for you, that's nice to know. Except instead of being nice to know, it's actually made my life so pointless I may just go home and kill myself." Chibbs pretended to slit his throat with a stack of papers.

"Finally, you've started reading my notes in the suggestion box," I said.

"You know what?" Chibbs said, pointing to the front of the office. "I should just go outside and get one of the groundhogs to do the editing work. They're sure to perform about as well as you, and they probably wouldn't stink up the place as bad."

"Guys..." came a voice from the hall. Tom shambled into view, rubbing his face. I momentarily panicked, assuming Chibbs had set me up and Tom could hear everything, including our leisurely insult bonanza.

"Hey, Tom. How goes it?" Chibbs said. "You need anything? I'll have those schedule updates this afternoon, just so you know." I nodded in assent, as if I had anything to do with that or knew anything about it.

"Guys...What day was it when...Tuesday?" Tom asked distractedly. "It was Tuesday, right?"

"Well, Tom, it's Monday now," Chibbs said with confidence. "Does that help?"

"Ok, so it was probably last Tuesday. Phew. Man, that's a relief." Tom sighed loudly and bent over as if he were undergoing extreme intestinal pain. "Alright, then. I'll leave you jacks to it." He stood upright and cracked his back as he left the room, his oblong belly protruding like he was hiding a front-strapped backpack under his shirt.

I looked at Chibbs for analysis on that brief and confounding spectacle. "That's it," he said. "That's an average morning here. We likely won't see him again today."

"Yeah, that's probably for the best," I said dubiously.

Chibbs leaned his head back and sighed. "Ok, look. Tom's a really nice guy. You could do much, much worse, and I know you know that. The hours are whatever you want them to be, you get paid on time, and you're doing actual editing work, so shut up about it before I go grab a groundhog." Chibbs picked at a fingernail, then turned his hand over slowly, flexing his fingers. "Oh, you'll meet a few random freelancers, too—people, not groundhogs. They're all on the level, but if they were any more laid-back, they'd be in coffins. They're just Tom's friends, and he throws a little money their way for smaller jobs. I never know when they're coming, but they bring their own laptops and sit at the empty table in the ingest room while they work."

"Maybe they're just ghosts of soldiers who died in the war, haunting their old bunker until some brave person listens to their story and helps them move on."

"I'd rather listen to a hundred wailing ghost troopers moan about their unresolved affairs than deal with you any day, Buttstain," Chibbs said. "Anyhow, they mostly do low-level editing for one of the potpourri shows like *Video Gumbo!*, just taking what someone sends in and finding a place for it. Some of it's so unsalvageable, I just slap a Town Commoner logo on the end and move on."

"You're saying there's more than one potpourri show?

Chibbs laughed. "I think we're up to five now. Finding a home for scattershot material people send us is most of what we do here, and potpourri shows are the easiest answer. I even created one myself from all the educational-type videos people send in—raw footage of lectures, seminars, stuff like homemade intelligence games and brain teasers. I packaged that up and called it *Brainy Miscellany*. Pretty sweet, huh?"

I saluted Chibbs. "You really outdid yourself with that one. I think you deserve to take the rest of the day off and relax a little after all that effort." He returned my salute, then rested his head on a pile of tapes and pretended to fall asleep.

.....

I cataloged tapes in the morning, adding the pertinent information to the spreadsheet, then took a two-hour lunch while Chibbs edited shows for me to add to the scheduling server later in the day. Tom rarely left his office but always made time in the afternoon to play hacky sack with his friends in the parking lot. The motley conclave comprised the freelancers Tom sometimes hired for side work, and they used the hacky sack diversion to hit up Tom for work when they were desperate to stave off their various debts and obligations.

Metch Mullins, a freelance editor who specialized in color correction, had the look of a speed freak coming down from a month-long bender. His stringy black hair was constantly sweat-plastered to his temples underneath a stained bandana, and his voice never surpassed a crunchy grumble. He wore the same faded denim jacket and threadbare commando boots regardless of the weather. His color correction skills were off the charts, but the extremely low visual quality of most Commoner programming made his efforts seem futile, as there was only so much polish that could be applied through the magic of computer technology. Metch intermittently found his way to the office and would color-massage a pile of tapes we had prepared for broadcast in the coming month.

"Tom and I go way back, man," Metch rumbled like an over-revved engine. "Good guy, understands the importance of harmony, you know? Cosmic balance." I nodded sympathetically, having not the least idea what he meant but impressed by how he continued working whenever we talked, seemingly without looking at the computer. I imagined he had a backup brain which assumed control over basic operations to self-preserve its host body whenever his drug binge hit its peak. "Tom's been good to us, man. I see this as my car payment job, and the camera op work I do as my house payment job, you know? Otherwise..." Metch glanced at me with one hand raised in helplessness while the other clicked and adjusted color settings on his laptop. "How're you settling in so far, man? You been here about a year now?" It was our third meeting during my first month.

"Yeah, just a little shy of that," I said. "It's been cool so far. It sure beats the alternative."

"Oh yeah? What's that?"

"You know, working in a cubicle or something. Sitting at a desk all day staring at number tables and stuff. I knew pretty early on I couldn't do that for very long before I'd go crazy, and doing temp work only confirmed that."

"Right on. I gotcha, man," Metch said, half-turning his head toward me. "But you're still sitting at a desk all day."

"Sure, but any type of creative work doesn't have that...*lifeless* quality of regular-people jobs, you know?"

Metch coughed a crusty laugh. "You're one of those, huh? Sure, man. What we do is so much more important than what other people do because we're 'artistic.' Why does it have to be us versus them?"

I threw my head back and groaned.

"Nah, look," Metch said. "You're young, I get it, but everybody has a different path that works for them. I mean, look at Tom," he said, throwing a hand over his shoulder toward Tom's office. "Guy had everything, especially money, but he bailed because it wasn't right for him."

My eyes bulged in disbelief. "What, was he some kind of entertainment mogul or something? And he walked away at the peak of his power to open up the airwaves for regular folks at The Town Commoner?"

Metch laughed harshly again. "Nah, man. Not Tom. He and his ex-wife ran a charter boat company. Six locations out by the coast, man. I don't mean family fishing trips with Bobby and Susie, I'm talking top-tier yacht excursions to private islands, secluded estates and all that. Very hoity-toity, very expensive." He clicked a few final settings, closed his laptop and stood up. "Alright, man. Done for the day. So yeah, Tom, man. Tom's a guy who knows himself, man." Metch smiled wistfully, patting his heart. "That's important, and it ain't something they teach you in school, right?"

"Yeah, that's for sure," I said.

"Tom knows. And there's a lot to be said for that." Metch stretched his arms wide in the dinky ingest computer room. "You're still in a cubicle, you're still at a desk, but so what? Does that matter? And if it does, what are you still doing here?" He squeezed my arm and pushed passed me, hoisting his laptop bag over his shoulder. "Until next time, brotherman."

.....

Chibbs and I eventually caught up on logging and finding homes for all the tapes The Commoner had received. As we managed the steady flow still arriving, Chibbs granted me actual editing work, freeing himself to focus on creating more polished artwork for the on-air station branding. My first assignment was to remove all the dead space from a new episode of *Too Much Truth Under One Roof*, a freeform anti-government tirade delivered by a paranoid doomsayer beseeching the populace to "wake up, rise up, and giddy up," a tagline he screeched multiple times during each rant. The program was allowed a half-hour time slot, so each two-hour tape had to be whittled down to the most vital points of the unnamed patriot's ravings. He sent in two tapes per week.

The first *Too Much Truth* tape I watched began with five minutes of emptiness. The host could vaguely be heard mumbling to himself off-screen. Various faded flags overlapped on the wall behind a wooden chair covered in patchwork fabric. A shredded-veneer desk in the foreground held a chipped coffee mug filled with ink pens and miniature flags next to a microphone that resembled the scorched scrap of a prototype space shuttle. The host shot into view and slumped into the creaking chair. He had begun his rant before he sat within range of the mic, causing his voice to drastically ramp up in volume as if to ambush the audience with his bombardment of truth. If he'd hoped to allay the viewer's fears that he was just a garden-variety ranting weirdo, he failed simply by his unkempt desert-wanderer appearance. As he gesticulated ferociously, his ring of wiry storm cloud hair thrashed about his balding dome like strings barely maintaining their hold on a rowdy puppet. His black and gray mustache drooped savagely at both ends of his mouth, highlighting his constantly pained grimace, and, along with his inordinately high angular eyebrows, he gave the impression of a man being tortured by having his face stretched in two opposite directions at once. His eyes seemed to pulse horizontally as they constantly scanned the room.

As I squinted and tried to focus on his disjointed blanket-accusation meaninglessness, he suddenly screamed, "Wake up, rise up, 'n giddy up! That's all they're after. Authority. Control. Dominance. Supremacy!"

"Those are all synonyms," I said as Chibbs crept into the room at my side. He pointed to the monitor with one hand and waved the other in my face menacingly.

"You're in on the conspiracy now, Buddy! There's no turning back. They'll be coming for you next!" He punched my arm while I rewound the tape to find a good starting point. "Oh, no, no, no," Chibbs said. "With these I usually scan forward to at least the thirty-minute mark to find a good opening bit. You'd be here all day if you tried to digest all this and actually package it up nicely."

"But there hasn't been a suitable break in his flow," I said. "It's just one tangent after another. Do you at least try to put it in some sort of order?"

"Nope, this show is jump cut city," Chibbs said. "Splice and dice, it's twice as nice. You can cut him off mid-sentence for all I care. Nobody's ever complained, and he keeps sending in tapes."

"The epitome of quality; that's The Commoner way."

"You know it, and with you as our new secret weapon, it's only downhill from here."

"Big shoes to fill, but I'll see what I can do, boss," I said. "Why didn't you name this show *Dope on a Soapbox*?

"Isn't that already the title of your autobiography?" Chibbs said. "Anyhow, we didn't have the chance—the tapes were always pre-labeled with that title. The oldest one I've found is from six years ago, and it's labeled 'Episode Forty,' so there you go," Chibbs said, shrugging. He clapped and turned to leave. "As pleasant as it is dumbing myself down to your level, it's probably time for me to rise up and go do some real work. Good luck keeping all that truth under this roof, Buddy," he said, reaching up and tapping the precariously low ceiling in the ingest room.

"I'll get a structural engineer out here next week and see what we can do about adding more vertical truth space," I called.

"Attaboy!" Chibbs shouted from down the hall.

The potential tedium of a full plate of Truth was thankfully disrupted when Chibbs coached me in editing *Live Healthy! with Veena Chumbley* and the "personal stories" show *Eye on I*. The latter mostly consisted of finding a home for viewer-created material, but Veena, acting as host and sole crew member for her healthy cooking show, set up two cameras and a bank of lights for her shoots, immediately exhibiting a higher production value than anything else on The Commoner. Cutting between wide shots of Veena, usually in zebra-print yoga pants and a puffy orange vest, and close-ups of food cooking offered more elaborate cutting choices than the other shows.

This was a more satisfying experience as an editor because there were actual strategic decisions to be made for the timing and flow of each episode. Veena produced one show per month, and each tape was delivered with concise notes on which take to use from which angle and where to find it in the tape. The unmistakable contrast between Veena's professional commitment to her craft and the rest of the sludge we slogged through was staggering. By Town Commoner standards, Veena's show was actually watchable.

.....

After a year, I reached cruising altitude at The Commoner and was content with my competency in finding a home for any ramshackle abomination we received. I was essentially the lead editor, as Chibbs spent most of his time fine-tuning the graphics and credit sequences for each show, adding simple touches that punched up their look from the archaic artwork that had been used for who knew how long. Chibbs came by the ingest room one day to ask how things were going while I logged tapes for a special *Live Healthy!* episode about the history and benefits of lentils.

"Looks like you've got it under control, Bud," Chibbs said as he propped his feet up on an overturned cable spool that doubled as a table. He rested his hands behind his head and yawned. "Nobody believed in you, but somehow you pulled through. It's obviously thanks to my prowess as a mentor and leader. I don't want to take all the credit, but it would be wrong not to."

"It would be wrong of me to disagree with you, but I'm ok with being wrong." I stacked some tapes, cradled them under my arm, and stood up to take them to the edit room, but Chibbs raised a hand to hold me back.

"Like I said, it looks like you've got it all under control here. Which is why I'm confident things will keep running smoothly when I'm gone."

"Oh no, Chibbs," I said in dramatic hand-wringing worry. "How long did the doctors say you have left? Weeks? Days? It's obviously eaten away most of your brain, but you can fight this!"

Chibbs smirked and bit his lip. "So… I put together a showreel of the graphics work I've done here and sent it to The Sports Channel a couple months back. Didn't hear anything, which is what I expected. I figured I'd be here another year or two." I nodded my head unconsciously. Chibbs leaned forward and rested his elbows on the spool table. "But apparently, they're expanding this year. New shows, more markets, and they need some people. So, there you go."

"Hmm…I'm still not seeing where you fit into all this," I said.

Chibbs looked down at the spool and thumbed a splintered strip of wood. "A producer over there got in touch with me a few days ago. I gave Tom my two weeks' notice this morning. I was worried; it's always hard to have those conversations, but honestly, he was happy for me."

"Who knows what it would've sounded like if he'd had to raise his voice," I said. "I'm accustomed to the temp agency method: you get a fresh whirlwind office romance with an automatic break-up after thirty days. It really removes the 'we need to talk' anxiety from the equation."

"Seems like a good practice for you; just cut and run before they can complain about your lackluster performance. It's win-win. They get rid of some deadweight, and you're spared the embarrassment of a humiliating exit interview."

I shrugged. "Like I said, it sure takes the pressure off. But speaking of awkward conversations, tell me this: were you just grooming me to take over this run-down rubbish-fest so you could move on? Was that the plan the whole time?"

Chibbs shook his head vigorously. "No, no, no. I didn't plan this at all, at least, not like this. The times we've shared together in this bomb shelter have been the best days of my life, except instead of the best, they've been a total nightmare of regret and disaster."

"Ok," I said. "It's fine, it's fine. I like it enough here, and it's cool to have a job, you know, an actual production job. With as aloof as Tom is, it's shocking how on-time the paychecks are. Anyhow, I'm a little blindsided, but it makes total sense."

"I know, man. I know. But hey, you should take this as an opportunity to put your own stamp on The Commoner. Do something crazy. Make your own program, host a variety show, cook up an original conspiracy theory and yell it at people. Bring in your own team of freelancers and hack some sacks around, brotherman. Make it your own."

.....

Every new tape we received felt like a truck dumping sand onto a pile I had almost shoveled away, only to find myself buried up to my neck again the next morning. After Chibbs had been gone for a few months, I found no humor in the psychotic prattle of *Too Much Truth*, and Veena Chumbley's healthy dishes only stirred my cravings for fast food and soda. The suffocating monotony gave me flashbacks to my temp experiences where I had fantasized about having the power to fire people like Winda at-will, as if being upset at one job reminded me of when I was upset at other jobs, providing the only continuity across my scant work experiences. Before collapsing under the burden steadily accumulating on my shoulders, I resolved to take Chibbs's advice and produce some fresh content of my own.

I arranged to borrow Metch Mullins's camera and sound recording equipment for an hour while he color-corrected some tapes one afternoon. Outside, I attached the camera to a tripod and swiveled it to face the groundhog burrows. I clipped a tiny wireless lapel mic to my collar, pressed record on the camera and stood in front of the mound.

"Hey, friends! Are you fed up with the mindless drones in your office receiving a paycheck in exchange for having no discernible skills? Do you feel like anyone, and I mean *anyone*, could do their job better than them? Well now's your chance to test that theory and get those slackers sacked! Welcome to a whole new reality television experience: *Your Job in a Week*! We select one unemployed person from a pool of applicants to join your office staff and learn the ropes. After one week of training, if the rookie can out-perform the deadweight in your office, they get the job and the worthless wonder gets the shaft! It's win-win for your office and fun for the whole family! *Your Job in a Week.* Coming this summer to The Town Commoner!"

I nailed the pitch in the second take. I hadn't scripted it beforehand but was able to breeze through thanks to my firmly rooted post-traumatic temp disorder. Before returning Metch's camera, I shot a variety of close-ups of the groundhogs toiling aimlessly in their makeshift pyramid.

"Get everything you need, brotherman?" Metch asked as I packed up his gear in the ingest room.

"Yeah, I think so," I said, snapping the lid on the scuffed bazooka case that housed his camera.

"So, what is it, a nature show?"

"What is what?"

"I saw you out there with the groundhogs. Figured you were one of those amateur animal lovers or something." He coughed like a garbage disposal full of ball bearings and whacked himself on the chest. "Gotta start somewhere, man. Might as well do something fun, and animals don't forget their lines."

"No, it's not that," I said. "It's more of a creative exercise, so to speak. I'll let it be a surprise."

When Metch left for the day, I ingested the footage and started editing my commercial. I kept myself on-screen for the first bit, then cut to the groundhog footage while my voice continued. I cut between shots of one groundhog working furiously, popping out of holes and piling up brush and rocks, and shots of a second groundhog sleeping. I laughed out loud when I saw how well it worked in juxtaposition to my description of the show. At the end, I cut to an extreme close-up of the first groundhog panting frantically and overlaid a graphic of the show's title along with The Town Commoner's phone number. I copied the finished thirty-second commercial onto the scheduling server and routed it into the playback schedule, overwriting an ages-old public service announcement on the dangers of some obscure sort of plastic. The plastic had been banned for use in baby bottles years before, but the spot still aired at odd times overnight and in the early morning.

Coming back to the office after a late lunch, I had to tramp over the groundhog mound to avoid the hacky sack squad who were mostly leaning and swaying in a triumph of nonchalance. I had become so accustomed to ignoring their awkward little gatherings that I walked into the building and nearly shut the door before I realized Tom had spoken to me. I yanked the door back open and leaned my head out.

"You say something, Tom?" I asked as he stared intently, juggling two hacky sacks in one hand. The freelancers casually strapped on their bags and gear, limping and shuffling away. "Buddy…Yeah, man. Let's, uh," Tom said tensely, pointing inside. I followed him to his office, where he plopped down in his pool chair and wheezed heavily.

"Buddy, man. I thought maybe somebody had left the building unlocked. Vagrants came in, made a mess of things, you know? Tinkered with the schedule and promos," he said, miming buttons being pressed. He glanced around the room and twisted his tangled beard. "I didn't know what it meant, these phone calls, people yelling—*yelling*, man—about where they work and the people they don't like there. People trying to get their coworkers fired?" He rattled his head like he was trying to shake off his constricting eyebrows. "Heavy stuff, man. Then I thought maybe you were working up a new psychiatry show, trying to help some people, so I looked into it to see what you were up to." As our eyes met, he looked desperately confused. "It's a prank, right? I know you have that sense of humor—Chibbs did, too—but is it really funny?"

"Well, yeah, I do think it's funny," I said. "Look, I've worked with some real losers, and you wouldn't believe what they get away with. It's like every office has just one person who does all the work while the others—"

"No, man. No," Tom interjected unexpectedly, waving his hands side to side in some sort of fly-swatting semaphore. "How could you want to do that to somebody? Some people, they can't work as hard, but that doesn't mean...You can't expect...Would you want someone doing that to you?"

"Of course not, Tom. That's half the reason I get stuff done instead of just freeloading around here. Tell me I haven't worked hard in the time I've been here."

"Nah man, that's not..." Tom slapped his hands on his thighs and rubbed them. "When you've worked for someone else your whole adult life, you want to look back and think, 'Gee, I wish I had seen more people get fired?' Look, some people can only manage doing what the captain asks and nothing more. That's all. And if it works for the captain, what do you care?"

"They know someone else will do the work for them, which turns those people into enablers. Look, I know you're a laid-back guy, but this is all yours," I said, motioning around the studio, "and you didn't get it by sitting around and wasting someone's time and money. Do you not find it insulting that some people take advantage of situations like that? Getting paid to do nothing?"

"You can't assume those people are deliberately...That's between them and their boss." Tom cleared his throat like a car backfiring and shuffled some papers at his desk without looking at them. "But 'taking advantage of' is a funny phrase to use. I mean, didn't you take advantage of Metch's generosity by borrowing his equipment under false...You know...Now he's complicit in your scheme. You didn't give him the chance."

"Yeah, but it's Metch. Do you think he'll even notice?"

Tom balled up a stack of papers and stared at his fist, breathing shallowly. "I copied over your commercial and put the old promo back in its place. I can look past all this as a goofy prank, but don't use Metch like that, man. He's a good guy. You don't know what he's been through. Don't lump him in with those people you'd like to see get fired."

"That's exactly what I'm talking about! Metch is talented." I leaned forward and tapped a finger on Tom's desk to accentuate my points. "He works hard, he works fast, and he never complains. That's a good employee. None of these other losers I'm talking about—"

Tom bounced the paper wad on his desk and threw it into a garbage can. "Sorry, Buddy. I got to bail out. Don't do that again." He turned to look at the schedule on his wall calendar. "Rules, man. I don't like...I shouldn't have to, you know?"

.....

"How did you expect him to react?" Chibbs said. I could hear a steady buzz of sports talk and keyboard clacking around his desk at The Sports Channel.

"I didn't think he'd notice," I said. "You switched things up and changed graphics and added new programming all the time without telling him."

"Oh, come on, you know that's different. I made things look better, and the programming stuff—I made executive decisions a couple of times and told him after the fact. Never anything earth-shattering, just repackaging content, mostly."

"Content that nobody watches," I seethed. "I wasn't even planning on going through with the show. It's not like I have the resources to do it, anyway."

"Then what was the point?"

"I thought at the very least, I would get some funny stories from viewers that I could do something with, like, documentary or prank call style, or a forum for complaining about co-workers."

"Uh-huh, and who would watch that?"

"Me! Are you serious? Everybody complains about people in their office. What are you talking about?"

"I don't know, isn't that going too far?" Chibbs said. "It's like that group project all over again."

For our final semester film project, Chibbs and I had been placed on a production team with six other students, none of whom seemed bright enough to know a camera from a tripod. I thought it best to just do the work ourselves—scheduling, lighting, recording, all the audio and editing work. So, without Chibbs's knowledge, I convinced the other students to sit back and get an easy A while Chibbs and I did all the work. It was the only way to ensure creative control and maximize our time with the school's limited resources.

Being randomly assigned to the same team as Chibbs—the only obvious stand-out student in the class who might actually make something of himself—was the best lucky break I could have hoped for. I knew our work would look professional compared to anything the other students could produce.

Chibbs only found out about my plan when he arrived at the location on our first day of shooting. For our short documentary profile project, we were interviewing a local retired farmer who split his time between raising llamas and building a lavish doomsday bunker big enough to accommodate the eight wives he planned on procuring. Chibbs was irritated that I had essentially fired the other students before they had a chance to prove themselves, but he quickly realized to have any hope of finishing on time, we would have to keep moving forward with the schedule we had drawn up.

Chibbs felt bad about robbing the other students of the opportunity for hands-on work and creative decision making, but, like most of the other students and temp workers I had been around, they seemed thrilled about getting credit without having to work for it. I was willing to look past that in exchange for not having to deal with the potential pitfalls of ignorance they would have invariably brought with them.

Of course, we got an A, and by then Chibbs had dropped out, anyway. So, in the end, what difference did it make to him?

"I'm willing to go there and beyond if it means getting viewers," I said through gritted teeth. "I'm making an effort, like you're always blathering on about. What's the point in anything I do here if nobody sees it? If a tree falls on The Town Commoner, does anyone ask, 'What's The Town Commoner?'"

Chibbs chuckled. "If a tree falls on The Commoner, it's probably because some junkie scurried up there to fetch a hacky sack."

I waited for my heartrate to settle into a stable cadence. "You suggested I make something my own. I did that, and nobody got hurt. My spot aired a few times, and Tom aired his grievances. So, what?"

"Well, I got you a decent job, and since we're friends, I assumed you wouldn't make me regret that."

"Friends? Since when? Chibbs, this is all happening so fast. I don't know what to say."

"Yeah, that would be a first. Maybe if you didn't know what to say more often, people wouldn't hate you so much."

"Why are we doing any of this if we can't make something original?" I said. "Why call it a creative job if you can't actually do anything creative? Are your hands completely tied at The Sports Channel, or do you get to do your own thing?"

"Well, I have a lot of creative flexibility, but we obviously have corporate guidelines."

"And they brought you in to make better graphics and whatever within those guidelines. How am I not doing the same thing with pitching an idea for a one-of-a-kind show on The Commoner?"

"You have a twisted point, but you're still wrong," Chibbs said. "Look, I can't talk much longer, and—"

"Just tell me this: should I assume Tom's looking to replace me? Possibly with one of those burnouts from his freak closet?"

"He would've made those guys full-time years ago if he wanted to. I think he knows them well enough to know that giving them free reign at the station might be disastrous. Maybe he doesn't want to be an enabler."

I dug my thumbs into my eyes and rubbed, cradling the phone against my shoulder. "I didn't think it would be that big of a deal to him. I didn't think he'd even notice."

"Look, the commercial aired, what, maybe ten times? In four days? I can't imagine Tom holding a grudge over that. If anyone saw it, he can say it was a computer error or something. Maybe just don't do anything like that behind his back again," Chibbs said. "You can still use the opportunity there to make something of your own without making Tom regret hiring you."

.....

I brainstormed ways to use my groundhog footage in a nature show format. Half of my mind insisted on devising something subversive with it, compensation for dealing with the doldrums of the viewer-submitted waste of airspace I couldn't escape. I settled on a comedy series format with a typical mismatched roommate situation. The idea seemed to have potential as something uniquely loose for The Commoner and likely wouldn't force me into another awkward conversation with Tom.

I combed through my footage to find any usable material and was instantly pleased with what I had captured. Each of the three groundhogs' specific mannerisms and twitches lent themselves to distinct personified characteristics. I mouthed dialogue for the shots I chose as I replayed them.

"Has anyone seen that moldy plastic bottle?" I said over a shot of one groundhog popping out of a hole and glancing around worriedly. "You know, the one with the white label?"

"Do you mean the one with the label that's actually white or the one with the label that looks like it used to be brown but turned brown in the sun?" I said as another groundhog barely raised its head and opened one eye while resting. "The one that still has some liquid in it?"

"That one, that one, that one," I said as the first groundhog popped in and out of the hole three times in rapid-fire succession. It plopped out with its paws down in a determined expression. "I was going to use that as part of a retaining wall for the new kitchen. What did you do with it?"

"Who says I did anything with it?" I said for the second groundhog in a shot where it leapt forward on two paws and looked around suspiciously.

"Buddy! What's got you laughing so hard?" Metch startled me as he slid into the editing room.

I paused the footage and rubbed the stinging tears from my eyes. "Well, I thought about what you said the other day and decided that maybe I should do a nature show after all," I said.

Metch twisted his neck to look at the monitor, then back to me. "That's great," he said calmly. "So, look, man. When I loan you my gear, you know…? We're still cool, but man, that commercial wasn't exactly the sort of thing I want to be associated with."

I threw up my hand dismissively. "It won't happen again. I was trying to do my own thing, and it wasn't well received." I gestured to the computer. "With this nature show idea, I can definitely use the footage I got the other day, but I'll need to borrow your mic again to do the voiceover."

"Uhhhh...yeah. I don't think I can do that, Buddy. See, when you take something of mine and use it to do something behind Tom's back, you make *me* do something behind his back. I smoothed it over with him, but this is my livelihood, man." Metch shook his head. "Look, I get it, but trying to get people fired from their jobs is just plain mean. Keep trying, brotherman, but remember, you gotta think about what's acceptable to most people—not just yourself."

"Whatever you say, Metch." I swiveled around to my monitor and scrubbed through the rest of the groundhog footage.

I zoned out while looking for a good starting point in a new *Too Much Truth Under One Roof* tirade. The host suddenly sat bolt upright with his mouth open as if struck by lightning. "People...people, it's not too late!" he gasped, sobbing. He stood and kicked his battered chair to the floor, clenching and rattling his fists. "They can't stop us all! We'll choke their rivers with our truth!" On a whim, I copied the audio portion of that section and imported it into my groundhog project. I selected a slow zoom of a groundhog sleeping atop the mound. As it filled the frame, the groundhog jumped, startled by something I didn't hear, and twisted around in a nervous spiral. It stood on its hind legs and reached its paws high before slamming them repeatedly on the dirt, then scampered to a creek bed full of shredded garbage in the valley on the far side of the mound.

I cut the audio from the Truth rant into three short pieces, then timed them with the groundhog's bizarre performance. It all lined up perfectly. Starting with the slow zoom, as the groundhog jumped and spun around, the host said, "People..." and then, "People, it's not too late!" as the groundhog slammed the dirt. The synchronization culminated in the host yelling about choking the rivers with truth as the groundhog ran into the creek bed.

I found a few more gems from the tirade and copied the audio to develop my new nature-conspiracy crossover program. I shifted the pitch of the ranter's voice up a bit so one of the groundhogs had a squeakier tone, giving the impression of two separate groundhogs yelling at each other while scampering around their truth mound.

I opened the show with several shots of the groundhogs running and abruptly stopping, over which I placed a wealth of spastic breathing and wheezing from the Truth host. It felt like the groundhogs were ramping up their energy levels to the appropriate velocity before launching into their tirades.

I was shocked that it was dark outside when Tom popped his head in the room.

"Red sky at night. Midnight oil is being burned, man," he said and punched the wall beside him. I stared at him dopily while he rocked from heel to toe. Tom held his gut and laughed. "Oh brother, I've seen that look before. It's got its claws in you." He waved gingerly and left the room. "Do what you gotta do, man. See you on the other side," he said from the lobby as he left.

Once I had a full thirty-minute episode ready, I selected a shot for the show's opening title screen where two groundhogs pop in and out of burrows in opposite intervals. I borrowed the title screen from the *Too Much Truth* project files and altered the text to read *The Hole Truth*. I copied the finished episode onto the scheduling server, overwriting a program where an elderly woman offered cutting-edge macramé advice. It aired once per day in the early morning hours, where I assumed no one would notice.

.....

The phone ringing caught me in the deepest realm of sleep. My face twinged with a numb soreness when I reached for the receiver. "Hi's, Buddy," I barely forced out between my tingling lips, straining to open my eyes.

"Buddy!" growled a sinisterly low voice. "Praise the holy netherworld, I don't have to talk to Tom again. How do you ever get work done with a dope like that traipsing around? And he owns the place?"

"Who's'iss?" I breathed laboriously.

"Cliff. I'm a producer at The Independent. We're a public access channel on the prowl for new programming. Edgier stuff, anything goes. We want to grab people by the face and bite their lips off." I lay face down, baffled by how such a deep voice could chatter on so rapidly. "Long story short, we want *Your Job in a Week.*"

"Ohyeah?"

"Buddy, shut up and listen. We saw the commercial. I called up Tom Goober Slobber over there and said, 'Look man, hand it over. You don't know what to do with it. It's mine.' He's all, 'No, no, that was a mistake,' and I'm like, 'You're the mistake, you half-wit, nitwit, no-wit. Hand it over.' He said talk to Buddy, so I'm talking to Buddy."

I sat up gradually and held the phone closer. "You like the idea? For the show?"

"Didn't I just say that?" A tinny ring in the receiver told me Cliff was banging his phone against something. "Who was I talking to before if it wasn't you? How many clowns does it take to answer the phone over there in your reject clown enclave? Come on, try to keep up."

I chuckled. "No, I got it, I got it. That's great news, Cliff. So, what—you want the show? We could arrange that," I said, feigning confidence.

"Just shut up and come by the office. Now. Tell Tom you're taking a late breakfast and an early lunch and a year's worth of cigarette breaks at the same time. Who cares." Cliff hung up as he spoke. I slowly rose from my bed and stretched my back, unsure whatever our conversation had meant and what he expected from me.

I stood outside a nondescript pale stone building eight blocks from The Town Commoner, holding a scrap of paper with ink-smeared directions I hastily copied while eating a piece of toast. I cleared my throat and walked up a crumbling brick staircase to knock on the door, but it flew open as I approached, slammed against the outer wall by a stocky man-child in a black shirt and black jeans with matted black hair covering his arms, head, and somehow his neck.

"Buddy!" he rumbled with a demonic grin. "Right this way." He walked back inside without holding the door open for me. I followed, slightly hunched over, my body accustomed to the hazardously low ceilings of The Commoner. The overhead lights seemed to be reduced to the maximum dimness without being off. I stood upright and looked to my left, where Cliff sprawled on a faded faux-leather couch behind a wrought iron table, both of which I assumed had been rescued from a dumpster. He kicked a tiny backless swivel chair toward me.

"Sit and shut up and listen," he said as he picked at dead skin on his fingers with an exaggerated air of self-importance. "*Your Job in a Week* is exactly what we're looking for at The Independent. Edgy, in-your-face, we do what we want whether you like it or not. If you have more ideas like that, we can talk hiring. If that's all you've got, we'll buy it from you and you can retreat back to Tom's dungeon of mediocrity." His woolly black unibrow rippled with bitter suspicion.

"Oh, I have ideas," I said, masking my distortion of truth with enthusiasm. "Yeah, plenty. I just need the right environment to—"

"Great, fine." He smashed his fists on a stack of year-old magazines and stood up. "Let's go talk to my worthless boss about yanking you away from your worthless boss," he said and lumbered down the hall. He opened a door as he pounded on it.

"Arbie, here's the guy. Buddy." Cliff shoved me into the office. Arbie had the lopsided haircut of a used thrift store doll and the same empty eyes. His tan suit jacket was a size too big and severely outdated but not in a hip, self-aware way. The amped-up brightness of his room contrasted immensely with the low-light vibe of the lobby and hallway. As I approached his desk, he turned toward me with a quizzical look, then muted the television he had been watching and folded his hands, arching an eyebrow. Cliff stood behind me, breathing like an eager bloodhound and humming a deep, nearly inaudible drone.

"Buddy," Arbie said, screwing his mouth up to one side. "Speak of the devil's advocate, and whom shall appear. Arbie Darman, creative director."

"Arbie, thanks for your time," I said, extending a hand, which he shook limply. He cocked his head to one side and twisted his mouth around to the other.

"Buddy. So..."

I waited an appropriate duration for him to finish his thought, then decided it would be an eternity. "Heard you liked my idea," I offered. "*Your Job in a Week.*"

Arbie popped his lips and nodded. "Yep. Sure do, sir. And I imagine Tom over there at The Town Commoner didn't bite, hmm?"

I shook my head and snorted. "Not at all. He thinks the idea is just mean."

Arbie shrugged and exhaled. "Nobody watches their programming, so who cares what they think?"

"Total freak show. Bunch of grimy little sewer rats," Cliff fussed from behind me. "Brain cells all squished up and bled out. Subhuman. Inferior. Just totally, utterly inferior."

Arbie smiled mirthlessly. "Cliff's the cheerful one. It's hard to keep up sometimes." Cliff grunted and kicked the wall behind him. "Anyhow, we're looking for ideas," Arbie continued. "Ideas viewers might actually tune in to watch. Being a public access channel, we enjoy the same creative freedoms as your current employer, but we'd rather create watchable content. A penny's worth a thousand words, as they say. How does that grab you?"

"It grabs him just fine, Arbie," Cliff groaned. "It grabs him by the horns and slaps a saddle on him."

Arbie held up a hand without looking at Cliff. "I need to hear it straight from the gift horse's mouth."

I nodded fervently. "Anything's better than what I'm doing now. I have exactly the kind of ideas you're looking for. *Your Job in a Week* is just the beginning. I think I'm a perfect fit."

"Wouldn't have called you if you weren't," Cliff murmured.

Arbie's face writhed into a bizarre mocking smirk that may have been his natural smile. "That's the spirit," he said. "Go break the breaking news to Tom and come back this afternoon."

Cliff grabbed my shoulder and yanked me out of Arbie's office. He flung the front door open against the outer wall and led me outside.

"That's all he does—talk. He thinks he's good at it, but he's not. He waits for someone else to do the work so he can take credit for it. If that's a skill, then he's a wizard. A level five necromancer." Cliff let go of the door and turned to go inside, but then shot back out and slammed it open again. "Look, Arbie's an idiot. How he hasn't accidentally walked in front of a bus is a total mystery. He has no real abilities and no justification for how he got the position he has here, but he lets me do what I want, and we need ideas so we can branch out. That's where you fit in." He waved me off like a gnat. "Go. Just come right back so we can get started."

.....

Tom stood alone by the front door, juggling two hacky sacks, his face drawn in a desperate strain. I was surprised to see him approach my car as I got out.

"Buddy. Look, man, I thought we were done with this. I can't be the boss, it's just not...I mean, authority, man." He shook his head and exhaled wildly, looking around the parking lot. "If you want to insult me, go for it. I got a thick enough skin. But the public relies on us, man. We don't ask them to send us tapes just so we can chop 'em up and ridicule them. Where's the fun in...What kind of...I mean, who does that?" Tom glanced at me and rocked back on his heels, still juggling the bags.

"Tom," I said with the calm indifference one gains when arrangements for a more suitable job have been made and the risk of being fired is no longer a serious threat, "whatever it is, I don't care." I snatched one of his hacky sacks and whipped it in a high arc over a twisted wire fence. It bounced off a rotted board and startled a groundhog by the creek. "The Town Commoner holds as much interest for me as drinking swill from that creek bed. In fact, the time I've spent here feels like I've been gulping it down until I blacked out and now my face is being nibbled by those mascots of yours while they wait for the interior of my corpse to provide a new home."

Tom's face knotted into an anguished scowl. "*Too Much Truth Under One Roof* may not have been your cup of tea, but man, that doesn't mean you had any right to overwrite the entire program. All the time slots? If you only aired the groundhog thing once, maybe nobody would've gotten hurt, but what do you have against Jeremy, anyway? He's just trying to rattle people's cages and help them expand their minds, man."

As Tom prattled on, I realized my mistake. When I copied *The Hole Truth* to the scheduling server, I had been exhausted from working a double shift. I had instinctively punched in the schedule code number for *Too Much Truth Under One Roof* instead of the late night macramé program I had meant to bump. That meant my nature-conspiracy crossover show aired somewhere around fifteen times over the weekend.

"Wait, Jeremy?" I asked. "That's his name? Not Sergeant Scream or Captain Cuckoo? *Jeremy*?" I laughed until my spine hurt and I hunched over, unable to speak. Tom stared at me in total bewilderment, then threw up his hands and plodded down the embankment to fetch his hacky sack. I got back in my car and left The Town Commoner for good.

2.

Cliff Montagna skidded into The Independent's pothole-checkered parking lot, nearly sideswiping me and spraying forth a shower of dark gravel I shielded against with one arm. He wriggled out of his rusted-gunmetal hatchback as he shifted into park, orchestrating a symphony of gnarled metal and screeching belts. On one end of the rear bumper was a red and blue sticker that read "MY POLITICAL BELIEFS ARE MORE SENSIBLE THAN YOURS AND THIS BUMPER STICKER PROVES IT" and on the other end, a black sticker with a red circle and diagonal line over the silhouette of a Labrador with the text "NOBODY CARES ABOUT YOUR DOG." The driver's side door scraped and clicked as it swung closed. He immediately launched into a verbal strike that was his default mode.

"Can't get lunch for under ten bucks anywhere in town anymore," he moaned. "They're obviously all in on it together. 'Hey, let's even make cold sandwiches cost ten bucks, and nobody can do anything about it.' 'Yeah and let's make the sides cost extra. If they don't like it, they can starve.' Total racket, but what can you do?" he said, under-handing me a paper-wrapped hoagie the size of a baseball bat. "That's your signing bonus. Don't expect lunch again on my dime." He glanced at his watch, then pointed his sandwich at the building. "Better get in there. Guess these guys will have to watch us eat." He plodded up to the door and flung it open.

In the waiting area sat three professionally dressed consultants who may as well have been three duplicated heads on the same body. Their faces were indiscernible from one another, down to identical tinges of two-day beard growth and scalp-cropped haircuts. I blinked rapidly, overtaken with a pang of vertigo, then leaned against a wall. All three stood and extended hands to shake with Cliff, who sat and unwrapped his sandwich on a stack of magazines without looking up. He wolfed a large bite as he spoke.

"Guys, Arbie says you have ideas, so let's hear them." The clones sat rigidly on the hand-me-down couch. Two of them stared at each other, open-mouthed, while the third drew his shoulders back and leaned in, spreading his hands dramatically. "Ok. It's the distant future..."

"Nope," Cliff said, pushing a handful of lettuce and mayonnaise back into his mouth. "What kind of budgets do you think we have here, you bobblehead? Look around you. Or at least ask your puppeteer to turn his wrist side to side so you can take in the full view. Next."

The first clone continued speaking anyway. "Ok, a routine police procedural—a cop show, if you will. But the star witnesses at every crime scene are two lowly street performers—mimes—and in accordance with the statutes of their profession, they must act out the wrongdoings they witnessed without speaking. They are *Prime Time Crime Mimes*." He sat back, folded his arms, and pursed his lips. Cliff looked over at me and shrugged. "I won't say it's the worst idea I've ever heard, but on second thought, I *will* say it because it's true, you useless human focaccia."

Another consultant spoke up hesitantly. "Here's an edgy one. *HEIST*, a game show where contestants break into a bank without getting caught by the guards, who are also contestants."

"Whoa, you mean we give people body cameras and actually follow them to a bank while they try to rob it?" Cliff asked, seemingly interested.

"Well, no. That would be illegal," he backpedaled. "I meant...Well, we could possibly use a real bank as the stage, but it would still be a game show. The whole thing would be set up like a real robbery. The contestants would be given a directive, supplies, maps—"

Cliff waved his sandwich at him. "Beh, no. It's still a routine game show, plus remember what I told your friend there about budgets."

The consultant flapped his hands. "But if the objective was difficult enough to only be attainable once per season or so, the payout wouldn't break the bank. See what I did there?"

Cliff hid behind his sandwich and grinned menacingly. "Yes, viewers might tune in for the vicarious thrill of it, but we have neither the time nor the resources to get something like that off the ground. Ergo, my earlier comment to your dimwitted crony over there. You!" He snarled, pointing at the as-yet silent third consultant. "Give me something."

"Ok. Two rival drug cartels—"

Cliff slapped his sandwich on a magazine. "No!" He sunk down and rocked his head from shoulder to shoulder, then looked up with a satanic smirk. "Let's start over. Arbie says you're all known for having good ideas, so let's hear some. We'll go clockwise this time. You." He said and pointed to the one who pitched *HEIST*. "I'll even help you out. Give me something that would make viewers laugh. Go."

"A children's cartoon show where criminal birds are taken to the highest court in the trees: *Owl Be the Judge of That*. You see, the owl—"

"Cartoons? Are you serious?"

"No, how 'bout this," the second consultant cut in. "A madcap comedy about an overactive baby who constantly gets into trouble, every day driving his parents to the brink. The title of the show is also that baby's name: *Whydee Doodat*. You see—"

"Did you say whitey?" Cliff asked. "What's wrong with you?"

"No, no. WHY-DEE. It's like asking 'why did he—'"

Cliff stood and brandished his sandwich with both hands like a sword over his head, then slowly lowered it to within inches of the final consultant's face. He leaned in and shook the sandwich gravely. "Imagine you're about to be split in two, each half of your body ready to trickle forth whatever modicum of guts you still possess, and the only thing that can save you is—"

"A sandwich," said the first consultant brightly, snapping his fingers. "A show about sandwiches?" Cliff facepalmed him out of the way and climbed onto the couch, squatting over the trembling final consultant.

"An idea! A good one. Your best. You dive deep into the crumbling caverns of your hazy mind and retrieve that one outlandish idea you were too scared to ever mention to anyone because you don't know where it came from or what it says about you. You grab hold and yank that idea out from underneath a moss-covered stone, heave it high over your head and with all your might you proclaim—"

"What makes you think you're so special?" the consultant said with an eerie calmness.

Cliff's eyebrows jumped up as if to thrust his forehead into the ceiling. "What's that now?"

"A reality show. *What Makes You Think You're So Special?* We send out a call for people with a long-standing grudge against someone they know. We follow them as they track that person down and then film the confrontation."

Cliff clenched the remainder of his sandwich in his teeth and clapped loudly. He ripped off a large bite, spraying bits of mustard and lettuce across the table as he bellowed, "Finally! Something we can all get behind." The consultants looked bewildered, especially the one who pitched the idea. Cliff reached forward and patted his head, ruffled his hair, then lightly pinched his cheek. "Good boy. You might have what it takes to actually accomplish something in this business. Unfortunately, an idea like that would probably be deemed unacceptable by a general television viewing audience. Thanks for trying, though. Go home and give yourself a cookie, or whatever nutrient pill the scientists raised you on. You two," he said, pointing to the others, "go start your cars and suck on the exhaust pipes until the ideas start flowing, you miserable junkyard rejects."

Cliff threw open Arbie's door while knocking on it. "Ok, they're gone," he yelled inside. He turned to the consultants who sat dumbfounded. "Did you not hear me? I said you're gone. Get out." They gathered their notebooks and left. Cliff waved me into Arbie's office. Arbie muted the late-night talk show he had recorded and was watching on a screen next to his door.

"Arbie, we met with those idiot friends of yours, but they didn't have the kind of ideas we're looking for."

Arbie scrunched up his face and looked at me. "Buddy? In for a penny, in for your thoughts."

"Yeah, I have to agree."

Arbie pulled a sad adolescent face. "Well, I thought they could help us, but maybe they've been doing this too long and the wishing well's run dry. Anyhow, hindsight's always a catch twenty-two." He clasped his hands atop his desk and half closed his eyes. "So, what next, gentlemen?"

"I'm thinking a reality show is the way to go," Cliff said. "Minimal overhead, small crew, not much investment. I have an idea I've been fleshing out."

Arbie smacked his lips. "Let's hear it."

"We send out a reality show casting call looking for people who haven't gotten over some grudge from a long time ago. We help them find that person and shoot the encounter. It's called *What Makes You Think You're So Special?*"

I bit my lip and stared at the framed diploma behind Arbie's head. It was an ornate and frilly number from a correspondence college I had never heard of.

Arbie slapped his desk. "Do it. You could probably shoot something in what, three days? Don't forget to sign out the equipment and fill out time cards for the crew."

Cliff nodded slowly and rolled his eyes. "I know that, Arbie. With this one and Buddy's new show, we'll have a load of new programming in a couple weeks."

"Just get out there and do it, Cliff," Arbie said. "Remember: actions speak louder than a thousand words."

Cliff smiled sarcastically and pulled me out of Arbie's office, nearly slamming the door on my foot. He grumbled an unintelligible mélange of curses and gripes as we walked down the hallway to the equipment room. "He's so stupid. He watches late-night shows all day and says he's doing research. What a joke. I can't figure out how he even got that title. I saw his resume once, and it's like he basically slid right out of a phony college into a creative director role. Excuse me, but aren't there like four or five rungs you skipped on that ladder, you malignant lump? Did you use other people's bodies as your footholds and physically slither up their backs? And yet he has the audacity to remind me to schedule the crew first. That useless jumble of quivering entrails." Cliff slapped a spreadsheet onto a clipboard, filling in names and crew positions.

"Well, I'm thrilled to hear you have such a high opinion of him," I said. "But what does he actually do?"

"I just said he watches shows all day; I meant that. If you ever see him actually get up and walk around the office, I'll give you a thousand dollars." He opened and closed a few portable light cases, then stacked them in one corner. The equipment room was immaculately organized compared to any space at The Town Commoner.

"The good news is, as long as you don't mind him taking all the credit, we can pretty much do whatever we want. You saw my whole pitch meeting, right? He just says, 'Do it.' I've been pushing him and pushing him the past three years. He said he wants edgier content, so I held him to that, and I've been surprised how far we've come. Again, as long as he gets the credit." Cliff grabbed the pen from his clipboard and inked something into his hand. "I forgot to ask—does this number work for you?" I looked at his palm for a moment before I realized it was a salary figure almost twice what I made at The Town Commoner. I narrowed my eyes to mask my excitement and pretended to consider the offer. Internally, I was salivating over the prospect of upgrading to a new apartment, a nicer one that my foster parents weren't paying for. With that kind of money, I could afford a place one level above humiliating, somewhere between tenement and hostel.

"Yeah, I think I can handle that," I said.

"Your title is Producer-slash-Editor. That ok?"

"Definitely. Thanks," I said. Cliff shook his head, spit into his hand, and smeared the ink on his pants. "Don't thank me, thank that idiot," he said, tilting his head toward Arbie's office. "Or better yet, don't thank him. He's an idiot. But he comes through with the money somehow."

Cliff had started out as a contract camera operator on one of the Indie's roundtable political discussion shows where he constantly berated the guests for their clothing choices and the crew for their lackluster interpretation of quality. Arbie appreciated Cliff's no-holds-barred approach to voicing suggestions and offered him a full-time position as producer, overseeing three programs and allowing him the latitude to create his own. His first undertaking was an overhaul of *Collision / Decision*, a point-and-counterpoint program where two individuals with opposing viewpoints would discuss their differences while a mediator attempted to craft a mutually agreeable resolution. It was filmed at a table in the Indie's equipment room. Cliff ditched the name and mediator, opted for panelists who were more interested in violence than peaceful settlement, and renamed it *Face-to-Face With Hate* (stylized *face2faceW/hate*).

"I found a stack of casting call responses that had been tossed out because the people sounded too angry on the phone; those were my first choices for panelists on the new show," Cliff told me as he gathered equipment for a shoot. "I brought together every combination of homicidal freaks I could find and only considered an episode successful if we had to call the cops to get them off each other. Man, those were the days. All of the crew refused to work on it after I changed the format, except Todd Gherkin. He's not the worst. We handled the cameras, mics, and set up lights by ourselves. I screamed questions and rebuttals at the panelists to stoke the flames. I almost got knocked out probably ten different times."

Cliff switched a few microphones on and off, then wound them up with cables and zipped them in canvas bags with extra batteries.

"That ad for *Your Job in a Week* told me you want to push things up to the next tier, too. I assume you'll work hard for the right payoff, and you obviously have no love for unproductive deadbeats in the workplace."

"Guilty as charged," I said. "Let's round them up, fire pistols at their feet, and make them dance."

"That's the spirit. I wish we could actually do that—shoot at them. Just line them all up and open fire. *Guh guh guh guh guh,*" Cliff grunted, wielding a microphone stand like an assault rifle. "Maybe you can do that for your show's finale. *Your Job in a Week* presents a very special episode: *Your Life Before Your Eyes.* You run a highlight reel of some doofus's greatest workplace blunders, then their old boss shows up, faces them against a wall, and brings out the firing squad."

"If I ever see you putting a blindfold on Arbie, I'll know what's coming," I said. "All I ask is you at least wait until our checks clear on payday."

Cliff grinned wickedly and scratched his back. "As long as he stays out of my way and keeps paying us, he gets a free pass."

.....

The Independent ran an altered version of my *Your Job in a Week* commercial to find applicants with workplace grievances. I didn't have access to the files at The Town Commoner, but luckily Cliff had recorded the spot when it aired once. We made a copy, cutting my voice out before I mentioned The Commoner, and ended with the Independent's contact info. My first shoot for *Your Job in a Week* was an interview with Martin, a software developer at a tech-industry company called Bladoodle. He had scrawled frustrated details of his co-worker John's uselessness in every possible edge and margin of the questionnaire he mailed us. Cliff scheduled Todd Gherkin to help me shoot Martin's backstory interview. Martin invited some other co-workers over to his apartment to watch and, because they were all so eager to badmouth John, we wound up with another four talking heads to use in the episode.

"So, I'm completely up to my eye sockets with projects and crazy deadlines, and a manager comes over, 'Hey, I know you got a lot on your plate, but John really needs help. He's slammed.' I'm like, dude, we're all slammed, but this guy gets special treatment? I sure didn't when I started here," Martin said on camera. "I go to John, he's like 'I'm slammed, I got too much going on, I need somebody to wrap up this one project for me and I'll be ok.' He shows me what it is. It's so rudimentary it took him longer to explain it to me and show me where to find the project files on the server than it did for me to finish it. I roll my eyes, 'Sure, John, I'll help.' Took no time at all, then I'm back on my regular workload, speeding through best I can. Couple hours later, I'm eating lunch at my desk while I tear through this stuff, I get up to get some water, and I look over and see John playing ping-pong in the breakroom. I even hear him saying 'Come on, come on, one or two more games, best of seven.' I was blinded by rage. I seriously forgot where I was for a second. But I didn't have time to think, I had so much work to do that week. I honestly assumed he'd get the ax in another week, anyway."

Martin mostly ignored John until he noticed him becoming friendly with someone in middle management.

"This guy, Wiley, he means well but he's way too impressionable," Martin said. "If you talk passionately enough about something, he assumes you know what you're talking about, and John, he's basically perfected this hollow, meaningless techo-speak that makes him sound smart, so he pitches these impossible ideas to Wiley, and Wiley's like 'Yeah, we should be doing more of that.' So, they started giving John project director duties on different jobs, and that's when it's a red flag field day for me, man. I can't let this happen. We've all been shouldering his responsibilities for months now while he whines and plays ping-pong, and it's getting worse. Jobs that should be going to him are piling up on our desks instead and now management's trying to implement these absurd, stupid ideas that John just rips off from other firms without knowing how much effort actually goes into them. It's got to stop, or there'll be a coup."

Martin collected thirty signatures from co-workers asking to allow *Your Job in a Week* to film at Bladoodle and potentially terminate John. Each petitioner included a page or two of incriminating stories that established a motif of John's negligence. I hadn't asked Martin to do this, but it removed some potential obstacles from our first shoot. The CEO, a tanned and bleached titan with an indefinable accent named Chürles Thway, surprisingly agreed to the proposition because Martin had so easily built a case against John. Chürles worried company morale would rapidly deteriorate if John's issues weren't addressed in some manner.

I drafted a second casting call inviting applicants to a week-long 'working interview' where they would be taught new skills on the first three days, then work on real projects for the remaining two days before engaging in a skills-based competition. I hung fliers with the details in a few staffing agencies, including the one where I had worked my first temp job, and was quickly overwhelmed with responses. I selected Arthur, a retired physical therapist and occasional substitute gym teacher. As I explained the nature of the job to him, I had prepared to ease him into the idea of tackling the sophisticated nuances of coding language and software architecture, but he shrugged it off. "If all those young lollygaggers can make millions off it, I think it'll be a gas to figure out what it is they're actually doing," he said on the phone.

Todd and I hauled our gear to Bladoodle. The building interior was a hodgepodge of creamy white edges and glittering glass-encased rooms with exposed ceilings and ductwork, like a half-finished spacecraft. Arthur had already been in the office for thirty minutes chatting up the two front desk receptionists who were laughing hysterically at some outrageous anecdote Arthur had told with a straight face. Martin materialized beside me, clasped my shoulder, and whispered, "They already like him better than John." He winked and went to his workspace amongst the multitude of nondescript cubicles rooted below the front desk mezzanine.

"Just so you know, I'm heading out when we break for lunch so I can meet up with Cliff for his shoot," Todd said as we unpacked and set up some overhead lights. "The story for his first episode sounds pretty crazy. One of the panelists from an episode of *face2faceW/hate* got in touch with him, this fat, squishy banker type who talks out of the side of his neck like '*mrrr mrrr mrrr buh buh buh*' and hates everybody. He heard about the new show and actually came down to the studio and demanded Cliff help him confront this girl he knew in high school. He was in love with her and she rejected him—big surprise. Cliff dove in and found out she had a restraining order against him that lapsed a few months ago. She and her husband live about an hour away."

"Well, that's bound to be uncomfortable for everyone involved," I said. "I just now thought of the legal logistics for Cliff's show, though. There's no way he'll get anyone's consent to be on camera for something like that."

"Pffft, just blur the faces. Who cares; they can't stop him. The action is still the same and that's all people care about. Slapping, punching, hair pulling, maybe a knee connecting to a groin." Todd pantomimed the latter action with a tripod. "Should be a good time, but it's a one-chance-only shoot for the encounter, obviously. We'll be out there late tonight getting everything we can for coverage; Cliff wants a rough draft tomorrow."

I squinted into the eyepiece and lined up the camera for an establishing shot of the cubicle area when a broom-handle-thin figure bent into frame, grinning idiotically. His barren egg-shaped head reflected the overhead lights into a concentrated beam that sent the camera's light meter into a spasmodic hysteria. "Can I help you?" I asked.

"Nice camera. Really good optical components on those babies, right? I'm John Klemchky, one of the project leaders here," he said, extending a bony hand which I ignored. "Saw you setting up and figured I'd come get the lowdown, see if you need anything. You guys shooting film or digital?"

I recognized him from the employee database photo Martin had shown me when we first met. His beaklike suck-up face alone was grounds for termination. "I don't want to bore you with the technical details. Plus, I'm busy and you're in my way, so can you move and leave me alone?"

John glanced back and forth, springing his neck up and down. "Yep, yep, yep. Establishing shot, right? Got to have those. I used to dabble in filmmaking myself, so, you know..." He scanned the room with a serious face, then draped his arm across my shoulders and pointed to the main stairwell. "Here's what I need you to do: go to the bottom of the stairs there and pan up to the people coming down to work. It'll look great from that angle."

"Actually, John," I said, shrugging his arm off my back, "a pan is side to side and a tilt is up and down. I appreciate the advice, but on second thought, I don't appreciate it at all."

John smiled and leaned his head toward me at a preposterous angle. "Maybe I can grab you a coffee; help with those morning groggies," he said, pointing over his shoulder to the break room. He elbowed me gently and chuckled.

I nodded cheerily. "Yeah, that should do the trick. Bring me a hot coffee so I can toss it in your face. That's sure to provide the perking up I need." I looked into the eyepiece, pushed him aside, and reframed the shot. "Well John, it's been a thrill talking to you, but I'd honestly rather be doing anything else."

John snorted and waved. "Well, I'm here if you need anything. Just ask." I mirrored his doofy smile until he reached the stairs.

Todd eased up to my side. "Wait, so that's the guy? John? He was here earlier trying to tell me how to set up the lights. I figured he was an intern or something. He came up to shake my hand, so I let him grab the thousand-watt light I was holding. You can still smell the seared flesh of his palm."

"Shameless yes-man suck-ups like that," I said. "They think if they're friendly enough, the boss won't fire them. I can't wait to see how this week goes. But more importantly, while we're here, I want to get to the bottom of what Bladoodle means."

"Oh, that's easy," Todd said, coiling an extension cable around his arm. "It's what you say when you uppercut a cashier instead of paying them. 'Sir, that'll be three-hundred dollars.' 'Nah, I don't think so—Bladoodle!'" he said, heaving a spinning punch into the air. The front desk workers cleared their throats and pretended to shuffle papers.

Todd and I set up a few shots around Bladoodle to establish the layout of the office, then I split my day between following Arthur around as he learned the particulars of the working interview and secretly catching shots of John, who mostly spent his day doing nothing. In the most incriminating shot of him I captured, he stood by a water cooler with an empty glass. When an employee rounded the corner, he would start to fill it, then turn and ask, "Hey, has anyone asked you about helping out with a client package we're pitching tomorrow? Strategy, databasing, design; it's a big one. Here's what I need you to do..." Three times I saw Bladoodlers push past him and fill their glasses without responding. John would wave, then return to his post at the cooler. He rocked back and forth on his heels practicing his smile for a full minute before giving up and strolling back to his desk.

John clocked thirty minutes at the ping-pong table, then sat at his desk for five minutes of complete inactivity before returning to the pong-pong table for another thirty minutes. I picked up bits of conversations between John and the other workers, who would only play a single game before returning to their tasks. The real game was John attempting to get a feel for how busy everyone was and whether he could maneuver them into assuming a portion of his workload. Most of the back-and-forth ended with John winning the match and saying, "Yeah, I feel you. I'm slammed too," but a few younger and lower-ranking employees were duped by his ruse and agreed to help out with projects they hadn't been previously assigned.

.....

I drove to The Independent early the next morning to start combing through my Bladoodle footage, and I was surprised to see Cliff's car already in the parking lot. On the front bumper was a homemade sticker with a picture of an overturned bicyclist covered in tread marks above the words "I'LL SHARE THE ROAD—WITH YOUR FACE!" Next to it was a chipped and faded sticker reading "WHEN THE GOING GETS TOUGH, JUST KILL YOURSELF." I hustled into the building to find Cliff and Todd jittery, ashen and slack-faced, deliriously yelling at each other from the editing and ingest rooms.

"Then he tries to run up to the camera and she, no, then fatty holds up the picture and then he, no, he holds up the picture, no, he—let's start over," Todd said, squeezing the bill of his ball cap with both hands.

"Shut up, shut up, shut up, I have it, it's fine, shut up," Cliff snarled back. "I went back to the way we had it, just shut up, it's ok, it looks great. We're trucking along, trucking along, trucking along, *chugga chugga chugga*. Next stop, slap in the face!"

"Have you guys slept?" I asked, peeking into one room and then the other. Cliff feverishly clicked and banged at his computer station like it was infested with beetles while Todd hummed to himself. Cliff finally looked up, recognition barely registering across his sunken face, and shrieked, "What?!" before abruptly reverting to his computer smashing delirium. "These stupid fat fingers are slowing me down, they're numb and all stuck together like webs, like one big hand, like a penguin flipper, it's so annoying I can't…" He jumped up and tried to grab my shirt sleeves with both hands, furrowing his thick thumbs into my arms. "Buddy! We are gold, we are platinum, I need a breakfast burrito." He stumbled out of the room and knocked me against the door jamb.

Copious handwritten notes arranged around his computer suggested he had edited an entire thirty-minute episode of *What Makes You Think You're So Special?* hours after filming it. "You're a surgeon," I said. "You could be a walk-on at the clinic, I'm sure. Go down there and show them how you slice it up." In the lobby, I spotted Cliff sprawled on the couch, eyes closed, head slumped back and drooling on his shoulder. His car keys were gripped in one raised hand as if he had blindly caught them in a show-off no-look move. "You look like a hairy baby that fell asleep while eating din-din and playing with mommy's keys," I said.

In the ingest room, I patted Todd on the back. "Todd, hey."

A guttural moan accompanied his distant stare. "Hey, Todd, you're Buddy," he mumbled. "I mean, Todd's buddy. You're Buddy, Todd."

"I'm so glad we had this talk," I said. "I feel like our friendship has finally leveled up." I smacked the side of the monitor and snapped my fingers. "And we're back. Tell me everything. What did he drug you with? Do you feel any organs missing?" Todd blinked slowly, prying his eyebrows up with his thumbs. He swatted his face rapidly on both sides, producing some sort of ascending xylophone scale through his pursed mouth.

"Buddy," he said as he inhaled deeply and stretched like an animal napping in the sun. He twisted his neck to two opposite extremes and rolled his head around, whimpering softly. "Man, what a long day. Long night. It's still morning, isn't it?"

I nodded. "When did you last eat?"

"'Have you eaten? Have you slept?' Yeah, mom, we had some midnight pizza and curled up with our binkies." He closed his eyes and mimed sucking his thumb, but momentarily seemed to fall asleep again. I kicked the wall to snap him out of it.

"Cliff's passed out in the lobby. Did he seriously finish the first draft of the episode?"

"Yeah, but we should watch it to be sure," Todd said. "We were talking about whale sharks at some point, and he said he was going to start cutting in random whale shark footage to make sure people were still watching. But he was joking. I think he was joking. Anyhow, I was in here ingesting all the Bladoodle footage I shot yesterday." Todd swallowed arduously and wiped his slobbered thumb across the edge of his cap. "I wanted to see some of the footage we got from his thing—it's really good—and then I stayed here with him while he worked on it." He rubbed his eyes, started to stand up, then plopped back down. "The Bladoodle stuff looks good, too. You've got plenty to work with."

"I thought you were going back there with me to shoot more today, but you're obviously in no shape to do that."

"Oh, so now I'm gonna hear it from you, too?" Todd leaned forward like a confused drunk. "Look, I ingested the footage and got your project all set up. It's all right there, I'm not gonna do it for you."

"Cliff and I worked out a schedule for our two shows, and it's kind of tight with the resources and only the three of us."

Todd wheezed a laugh and clapped slowly. "You think he's not looking out for himself first? I don't think he can physically stop himself. Like a boulder. So, you have to roll with it, otherwise, what?" he said, discharging a barrage of finger guns in my direction. "I'm here to work and he's my boss, so I do what he says and you can figure out stuff on your own, Big Boy Buddy Buppsy."

"Got it. Thanks for nothing." I leaned back toward the lobby. Cliff was gone. "I suppose the insatiable allure of that breakfast burrito finally awakened his senses."

"Huh?" Todd said in total bewilderment and stumbled out.

"That's pretty much all he ever eats. They're his Achilles' meal," called Arbie from his desk. I spun around in opposite directions, then vaulted toward Arbie's office, stumbling over a broken tripod case in a dark corner. "Well, besides pizza and sandwiches. All the major food groups, I guess," he added.

"When did you get in?" I asked.

"I've been here," Arbie said, shrugging.

"But you weren't…Forget it."

"Already forgotten. How was the first shoot?" he said, using a remote to switch on the monitor next to my head. He queued up a late-night show.

"Good. Great, actually. I think I can get by shooting half-days the rest of the week, maybe a full day Friday for all the fireworks."

"Well, if that's all you think you need to put into it, I guess," Arbie mumbled.

"I have enough context coverage for the full episode. I only need some day-to-day stuff with Arthur and John to round it out, maybe a couple more interviews."

"Hmm…" Arbie said, twisting his mouth around in fluid circles. "Maybe that's enough for a decent episode. But if it were *my* show…" He swiveled around and stared at me, raising a stern eyebrow and clasping his hands together on his desk. I returned his stare as he arched his neck side to side, probing me with half-masted eyes in an attempted appearance of thoughtful interrogation.

"Maybe…I should be there all day? In case anything interesting happens?" I offered.

"I would spend full days there shooting everything I could, just in case...You know."

I stared at Arbie, stifling the urge to ask him what else he saw himself doing if he ever got up from his desk. "But with all the ingesting, cataloging, editing…I don't see how I'd have time—"

"Look, take it with a grain of your own medicine. All I'm saying is: it is what it is." He waved the remote and pressed play. Todd appeared at my side, stretching both arms above his head. "Arb, I'm heading out."

"Where to? Buddy's shoot?"

"I'll tell you later." Todd yawned, crashing his collarbone into the door frame as he left the building.

Arbie turned back to me and shrugged. "It is what it is."

.....

On the far side of the Bladoodle office, past the cubicles and breakroom, rose an enormous bank of windows and elevated viewing platform. It overlooked an immaculately manicured pine grove next to an open greenspace with park benches and a jogging path most Bladoodlers were too overburdened to ever utilize. From the lower level just outside the breakroom, I had an unobstructed vantage point for a prime Slacker John experience.

He stood on the platform, gazing toward the greenspace, scratching his chin. From the floor below, I quietly set up a tripod, tilted the camera up, and recorded five minutes of John thoughtfully staring into oblivion. Eventually, a senior developer climbed the platform steps and passed John, who stopped scratching his chin and snapped his fingers. "I've got it," he said.

"Doubt it," said the developer, laying a shoulder into John's back as he walked on. John rewound himself back to his meditative posture as if nothing had happened.

Minutes later an unsuspecting junior programmer walked by. John launched into the same ploy. "I've got it," he said, snapping his fingers.

The programmer abruptly stopped, removing her headphones from which blasted a blisteringly loud industrial metal piece that was so fast and violent it blurred into white noise from far away. She plucked a carrot stick from a snack bag covered in cartoon skulls and raised it to her mouth. "What's that?" she asked.

John turned toward her as if he had just noticed her presence. "Jan," he said, moving to place a palm on her shoulder. She pivoted away, avoiding contact. "Jan, you're the only one who can help me. I've been standing here basking in the glory of creation, hoping the right solution would reach out to me through thoughtful contemplation."

Jan rolled her eyes and ate another carrot. "Uh-huh."

He wiggled his hands as if spirits were entering his fingertips. "You won't believe this, but as the answer came to me across the ethos—"

"Ether," Jan said through a mouthful of half-chewed carrot.

"You see, we understand each other." John nodded sympathetically and narrowed his eyes. "The voice that spoke the answer told me to turn around. I turned, and there you were. Is that not ironic?"

Jan stared blankly. "It's not…It's not? Was that a hypothetical?" she asked.

"Isn't everything? When you really look at it?" John smiled, shaking his head. "Here's what I need you to do..." He guided Jan back down the platform from the direction she had come, out of range of my microphone. After they left, I climbed up and filmed two minutes of slow pans and zooms on the greenspace so I could cut to a sweeping nature montage as John eloquently described the genesis of his remarkably incomplete ideas.

In the management wing of the building, Wiley and the CEO were embroiled in a fierce back-and-forth outside Wiley's office. Chürles noticed me from across the hall and thrust his imposing chin in my direction. Facing Wiley, he firmly smoothed down his suit, ran his fingers through his golden hair and left. I raised my hand to knock on Wiley's open door but hesitated when I saw him hurriedly brushing items off his desk into a large plastic bin. My hope for an interview was instantly dashed.

"Might as well go ahead and put all of John's stuff in one of those while you're at it, am I right?" I said, winking and nudging the door with my elbow.

"I don't know what you're talking about," Wiley mumbled without looking up.

"Seriously? You aren't going to stick around to see what happens with John?"

Wiley sighed and threw an inflatable potted cactus wearing sunglasses into the bin. He looked up at me, his face slumping into a melted gloom. "I don't know what you're talking about."

"I've been here two whole days," I said, "but I only needed thirty seconds to see how worthless and expendable he is. Just because he reports to you and you've given him responsibilities beyond his job description—none of which he seems able to fulfill by himself—that doesn't mean you have to go down with him."

Wiley clenched his teeth and breathed heavily through his nose like a bull ready to charge. "I'm in management, you idiot. I delegate work based on skill sets and availability, and what I saw in John…Look, John likes to take his time and probe issues from oblique angles, to get a better sense of the big picture, you know?"

"Yeah, he's a dreamer all right; he fantasizes about how to get other people to do his job for him."

"He has that 'gift of gab' thing that rubs some people the wrong way, but clients love it," Wiley said. "He inspires their confidence."

"But why promote someone and give them higher-level duties if they couldn't perform the duties they were originally assigned? If John constantly relied on the assistance of others to complete his work, why would you reward that and put him above other employees here?"

"How is this any of this your business?" he asked, standing inches in front of me. "You've been here two days, and now you're an authority on, what, our entire operation?"

I twisted my neck around to look down both ends of the hall and threw my hands up. "Yeah, pretty much. These places are all the same, regardless of how many ping-pong tables and free snacks they have."

Wiley stared me down for a moment, then reared back and pushed me with both hands. I tripped over the bin and shimmied against a wall.

"Hey, who put that there?" I asked incredulously, pointing at the bin. "Oh wait, you did because you're leaving before you get fired. Now I remember!"

Wiley pushed me out the door and slammed it closed.

John wrapped up a ping-pong match and attempted small talk with a group of Bladoodlers who stood silently in the breakroom, waiting for him to hand over his paddle so someone else could play.

"Guys, I know we're all slammed here, but this project is one of those once-in-a-lifetime, career-making deals. I want you all to be a part of it. I've got chills," John said and giggled maniacally, fanning himself with the paddle. I set up my tripod just outside the door, anticipating another great John moment. "We'll look back on this day and—"

"I feel you, John. Thanks, but can we get that paddle back?" said a twitchy overweight developer in black boots and a flat-topped military-style hat. "We need to finish up this week's tournament."

John gaped at the paddle in his hand as if it had been planted there by magic. He sucked in his bottom lip and patted himself on the head with it. "You know me. Head's always up in the clouds."

"Your head's always up in—" one programmer began before the twitchy one kicked him in the shin. "Just the right place. One step ahead. The next frontier. Thanks."

John tossed him the paddle and lurched by me. "Hey, Buddy. What are you working on these days?"

"I'm working on minding my own business, John. You should try it sometime." I flashed a broad smile and winked.

John winked back and cocked his head to one side. His body always seemed to start walking away before his head turned to catch up.

I shook my head and walked into the breakroom. "I was hoping you'd let him keep talking. Every day here is a goldmine of John's semi-articulate gibberish."

"That's great, Buddy," said the programmer who had been silenced, "but you weren't here a minute ago. He walked in and took the paddle right out of my hand, mid-game," he said, face tightened in outrage. "I said, 'Woah, grabbin' hands. What's the deal?' He starts playing like he didn't hear me, squawking all this nonsense about some overly complicated project none of us have time for. I swear, you can't get him fired soon enough."

"Trust me, I'm with you on that one," I said as I packed my gear up to leave for the day. "I had him pegged the second I met him. He walked up and tried to give me advice on where to set up the camera. It was ridiculous."

"Trying to be your friend so he can exploit you somehow. He'd have been better off as a grifter or one of those illusionists who don't do illusions," said the twitchy military hat developer. "Never had me fooled once. He's a slacker, plain and simple." He readied his serve, rocking his hips side to side, and resumed the game. I grabbed my gear and started toward the door.

"And you forced us all to choose sides," one Bladoodler at the edge of the room said to me through clenched teeth. "You don't work here, so you don't have to care, but I'd rather look like a team player that doesn't spend all day bellyaching about what the other guy is doing. If Wiley catches wind that we're even talking about it—"

"First off," I said, "the only wind Wiley's catching is from the front door slamming behind him on the way out. He's done. I just came from his office, he's packing up his cactus and moving on."

The Bladoodlers' faces went limp with sudden discord. "But he's not even…" one began. "Yeah, he isn't to blame," said another. "Why would Chürles…" One extremely tall but hunched Bladoodler with comically large facial features raised a pale arm and slowly extended his finger accusingly. "You," he said in a contrastingly high-pitched voice. "Wiley leaving—that's on you."

"Go ask him yourself whose fault it is; there's probably still time," I said. "If you want people like John gone, there have to be some concessions, right? If Wiley was sucked into John's cyclone of nonsense and lies and—"

"But we all like Wiley. There's a difference," said the angry programmer at the ping-pong table. "You don't have to take everyone down with him. Wiley may have helped him get promoted, but—"

"Then he's also part of the problem, right?" I said, leaning on the tripod. "What would happen if John kept his job and together they promoted some other inept twerp to lord over you? Trust me, I've worked enough temp jobs to know that's basically what it's like everywhere else. Instead of making all the talented people quit out of anger, just purge a few lesser-thans and move on."

The angry Bladoodler threw his paddle on the table and stormed off. The military hat developer shrugged and sucked his teeth. "I'm comfortable with whatever happens. Wiley, honestly, wasn't all that great as a programmer, either. He was super enthusiastic when he first started, what, two, three years ago? We all like him, he's always upbeat and never complains, but…I mean, he kind of did what John does, you know?"

"How can you say that?" shouted a hoarse voice. "How can you even compare them?"

"Just hear me out." The developer retracted his fingers into claws before facing the small crowd of Bladoodlers. "Buddy's sort of onto something. Wiley, man, he's cool, but if you really think about it, that's it. He's cool. He's good for keeping morale up, but when he landed the manager gig, he still sort of looked to us to steer the ship. I mean, I know I've had to take the lead on several projects under him, and it's getting worse." A few Bladoodlers nodded, a few shook their heads. They all stared at the floor. "So, I guess what I'm saying is, it *is* kind of us versus them. I mean, would you rather have a cool job with a sucky boss or a sucky job with a cool boss?"

"With people like John and Wiley running the show," I said, "you don't have an option. It sucks all around."

.....

Cliff commandeered all of Todd's availability for *What Makes You Think You're So Special?* and they shot stories for three episodes by Friday.

Cliff also assumed control of the editing room and said he would be finished when he was finished. I wrapped up the Bladoodle shoot and planned to sort through all my footage over the weekend to arrange a few options for how the episode could be structured depending on the outcome of the Monday morning 'trial by fire' with John and Arthur. I watched the completed pilot episode of *What Makes You Think You're So Special?* while I ingested footage.

Herb, the corpulent and endlessly furious "banker-type" drives Cliff and Todd around his hometown at breakneck speeds to show them places of interest in his deranged story of unrequited obsession. He incoherently describes how Mitzi, the love of his high school life, disastrously rejected his romantic advances, tormented him relentlessly and made his young life unbearable, none of which he ever succinctly explains. He claims to have been so distraught that he was urged by his parents into a rehabilitation facility for acute emotional disorders and forced to switch schools to escape the irreparable damage Mitzi inflicted on him.

Herb weaves the car spastically as they approach Mitzi's modest two-bedroom bungalow, his screeching oratory becoming indecipherable. He yanks the wheel to one side and skids into the driveway, narrowly avoiding a muddy drainage ditch by the mailbox. He stomps through the yard and bangs on a loosely hanging screen door as Cliff shouts, "Go in there! Open the door!" A shadowed face briefly appears around the edge of a curtain, which is quickly drawn as the front door opens.

Dunn, Mitzi's meek and non-threatening husband, comes out with palms raised. "Herb, you know you can't do this. It's a bad idea, and you're only making it harder on yourself. If you leave now—" As Herb lunges forward, snarling and pointing an index finger accusingly, Mitzi flies out from behind Dunn at an inhuman speed. She double-slaps Herb with one hand before grabbing his jacket collar, jumping into a tight knee-tucked ball against his chest and toppling him over. She then unleashes a hail of knuckles and elbows, quickly transforming Herb's verbal assault into a piercing banshee wail.

The episode cuts to an interview after the attack where Dunn says, "Mitzi was always worried about Herb coming back. I'd say, 'No, no, no, honey, why would he bother? It's ancient history, he's moved on with his life. He's a big deal now, he doesn't care about us.' Shows what I know. Cold-hearted as it sounds, I'm glad all those kickboxing classes paid off." Cutting back to Mitzi's blitz, a gory close-up shows Herb gurgling and spitting, his hands feebly raising and falling as he submits to the punishment and finally stops screaming. Mitzi, spattered with dirt and blood, collapses in tears, her face a horrendously smeared butterfly of mascara.

Cliff whips his close-up camera around to Todd, who maintains a safe distance, and screams, "Dude, he might be dead!"

Later, Dunn explains their side of the high school saga. He and Mitzi had been dating for two years when Herb crashed one of their dates and violently accused her of rejecting his devotion and humiliating him. Mitzi didn't recognize him from class and claimed to have never seen him before that night, which is what jump-started his course from a few late-night peepings all the way to the restraining order. Herb's family moved when he was in twelfth grade, the rumor of his psychological torment as catalyst being less exciting than the reality of his father's promotion to daytime supervisor of a water treatment facility two counties away. Years later, Herb ran a sizable regional bank and Mitzi was a teller at a tiny local credit union he was in the process of acquiring. Looking through personnel records may have given Herb the information he needed to track down Mitzi and Dunn.

"You know, regardless of what he felt in high school and all that..." Dunn says. "Well, I wasn't exactly popular, either. I was co-captain of the chess club, not a star quarterback, so of course I had some negative feelings towards a few people we knew back then. That's typical for everybody, and it's not like I had to go to therapy to get over it. I just got over it, you know? Isn't that part of growing up?"

"Apparently not!" Cliff growls. "Herb only got fatter and angrier. How's that for life being fair, huh?"

Dunn smiles faintly. "I just hope it's over. At first, I thought I'd be angry with you for bringing this to us, but at least—"

"I'll kill him," Mitzi sobs, looking directly into the camera and slowly scratching the nails of one hand against her forearm. "Next time, I'll kill him." Dunn reaches up to massage her shoulder and she flinches, shrugging off his arm. She looks at him desperately, then pulls his arm back over her shoulder and kisses his hand before looking into the camera again. "Herb, you need to get help. It's like you're trapped in your own head and you make up reality based on how you think things should be instead of how they are. Then you get mad when the real reality doesn't line up with what you imagined. That's not normal, and it's never going to be normal. Please get help before you do damage to yourself that can't be undone." Over a freeze frame of her flushed face, Cliff's voice cuts in. "Speaking of damage…" The credits roll over a montage of the attack with many of the blows sped up, slowed down, zoomed in, and replayed in rapid-fire succession, complete with over-the-top sound effects.

I was astonished that Cliff, even with Todd's assistance, could have edited such a cohesive episode within a day of completing filming. My skills as an editor were no match for whatever dark compulsion drove Cliff past the threshold of a humane workday. I walked out to congratulate Cliff, but he was sleeping on the couch in a sitting position with his keys held in his upright hand. Before shouting a sarcastic wisecrack at his expense, I paused, then jogged back into the ingest room and slightly rewound the episode. At first glance, I hadn't noticed that the credits scroll included at least twenty names for crewmembers besides Cliff and Todd. I remembered Cliff bemoaning how understaffed The Indie was, but he'd never mentioned soliciting freelancers for shoots, nor had I seen any. I considered bringing it up to Arbie, but I didn't want to invite Cliff's wrath or jeopardize my newly acquired creative freedom.

.....

Cliff finally relinquished control of the editing room on Sunday afternoon. As Todd left, he told me their next two stories involved child custody encounters that "don't work out as planned." He chuckled and said he originally assumed they'd be faced with unwilling participants and possible restraining orders, but Cliff seemed to have risen above the laws of man; once the confrontations began, the players mostly forgot they were being filmed and never asked to have the footage destroyed. I worked on my edit through the evening and by 2 a.m. had a reasonable foundation for the story. I slept fitfully on one of the lobby couches, worried Cliff might show up early and seize all the camera gear before I could take what I needed for the Monday Bladoodle showdown. In my exhausted state, I still somehow woke up before the antique alarm clock sounded in Arbie's office. I wrestled with the jammed controls to turn it off, then rubbed one side of my face, which was sore and creased, plastered with damp couch stuffing. I grabbed all the equipment I could fit in my car and raced with jittery-eyed double vision to Bladoodle, hoping to make it in time to film an entrance shot of each of the major players. Arthur, the eager challenger, was already in the parking lot wearing a new track suit, leaning against his paint-chipped pickup, cracking his knuckles.

The first episode of *Your Job in a Week* begins with Martin describing the frustrating backstory of dealing with John, juxtaposed with shots of John's stupidly blissful face staring out the window overlooking the greenspace. Twice he turns to initiate one of his ploys for help before realizing the person coming toward him has reversed and gone a different way. Other Bladoodlers explain their experiences with John's ineptness and their worries over the unfair potential for him being promoted. John plays ping-pong in the breakroom and talks excitedly about projects he needs help on because he's "slammed," and each time he says "slammed" it cuts to a shot of him acing a serve across the table.

Arthur, whose wise-but-youthful face looks like that of a paid actor in a drug commercial, toils endlessly to learn not only the proprietary software used at Bladoodle, but also the fundamental concepts leading to advanced computer programming. He speaks eloquently to the usefulness of possessing a diversity of experiences to draw on for rational thinking, relating to others, and general problem solving. Shots of Arthur's excitement and satisfaction in his preliminary evaluations during the week are counterpointed by images of John aimlessly sneaking around the office, staring at the outdoor greenspace while practicing his smile, and abruptly bumbling away when he notices the camera on him.

"Bladoodlers are totally committed to helping each other out," Arthur says. "It's heartwarming and overwhelming, the response I've gotten when I've asked for help sorting out some of this stuff." He continues describing niceties he experienced during the week over a montage of Bladoodlers rolling their eyes when they see John. The sequence ends with one programmer flinging a ping-pong paddle across the breakroom and kicking over a trash can after losing to John.

On the day of the final assessment, Chürles meets with John and Arthur independently of each other and tasks them with their challenge for the show: they have six hours to rough draft the framework for a sensor-based application that monitors brake pad thickness in automobiles and displays dashboard alerts when the pads are low. Completion of a full working application isn't expected, but a detailed outline for the essential team, number of hours, and mock-up of the software will be peer reviewed.

A large countdown timer overlaid in the lower-left corner of the screen displays the time of day for each shot of Arthur and John as they approach the assignment. John sits at his desk, rubbing the back of his head and staring at a blank page in a notepad for twenty minutes, spasmodically looking up to check the time. The single shot gradually speeds up into a jittery time-lapse, giving his fitful neck gyrations the appearance of a confused chicken. John then sets out to ensnare any unsuspecting helpers he can get his hands on, taking with him a large plastic dodecahedron that sits on his desk. His last-minute scheme is to stand at the base of the staircase, holding the dodecahedron contemplatively while rubbing his chin and squinting. When a Bladoodler walks by, John feigns surprise, as if being shaken from a deep meditation. He holds out the plastic dodecahedron like a holy relic and asks, "What does this look like to you?" Not a single Bladoodler stopped to offer an observation, save for Martin, who turned and said over his shoulder, "It's a Platonic solid, you dodecadingus." Each time John is passed by, the screen smash-zooms toward his dejected face, overlaid with a giant red X and the sound of an obnoxiously loud cartoon buzzer.

John attempts the dodecahedron tactic for nearly an hour, then stares at the greenspace for thirty minutes while not a single Bladoodler walks by him. He plays ping-pong during his lunch break and defeats every Bladoodler he plays, even though they all talk loudly and interrupt John every chance they get. John then visits six senior members to straightforwardly request help on the sensor project. He is thoroughly rejected.

Arthur, however, sits quietly and drafts a rough sketch of the overall project immediately after his morning meeting with Chürles. He presents the plan to a few senior programmers to ask if they would do anything differently, two of whom commend his effort in constructing a simple but highly effective solution to the assignment. By noon, Arthur has finished and spends his remaining time assisting a few younger Bladoodlers who need help meeting a deadline. A split-screen time lapse compresses the last hour and cuts to black when the clock hits 4 p.m.

Arthur walks into Chürles's office, where a panel of eight Bladoodlers wait on stools with notepads and pens, dramatic tribal drums pounding and punctuating the tension like the earth's own distressed heartbeat anticipating the trial's outcome. Chürles straightens his tie, shakes Arthur's hand, motions to a dry-erase board, and hands him a green marker. In ninety seconds, Arthur succinctly describes the minimum necessary number of sensors in various styles and functions and suggests an approach for balancing the total available man hours versus those crucial for programming and development in the project. He outlines a schedule for how the project could conceivably be finished in two weeks without adversely impacting other projects currently in the pipeline. He then unveils a poster board schematic of the sensor components communicating with an automobile's dashboard computer using Bladoodle's proprietary software. Chürles spreads his arms wide and asks the panel for questions or concerns; there are none. The Bladoodlers clap and congratulate Arthur. He waves, says, "Thanks, this was fun," and exits.

In the next shot, John enters holding the dodecahedron at his back. When he reaches the center of the room he extends one hand with slowly undulating fingers, like a magician teasing the crowd's curiosity, then dramatically hoists the dodecahedron. "Fellow Bladoodler extraordinaires, I'm here this morning to ask a simple question with complicated answers." He holds the dodecahedron higher, like the cup of life, and rotates it slightly. "What do you see when you look at this?"

Chürles clears his throat and glances at his notepad. "Chon," he says soberly with his stilted pronunciation. "That is a type of polyhedron, specifically a dodecahedron. It's very interesting to look at and ponder over, yes, but it holds no relevance to this sensor project we are all here to discuss. If you please."

John suspensefully lifts a finger and his eyebrows, gearing up to suggest some meaning for his diversion, but is cut short by Chürles. "No, no, Chon, we have no time for these shenanigans. This is business, you know. Let us all hear what it is you have decided for this project, please."

John holds the plastic structure behind him, bouncing it with both hands, and tries to mask a tense gulp with a thoughtful grin. "You see, when I first started ruminating over this project, I was really taken aback at how far technology has come, even in the past five years. Sure, you could say that at any time in any era, but truly, the time in which we find ourselves—"

Chürles slaps his notepad against his thigh and seems to consider throwing it at John. "Chon, no, you see, this is not..." He runs his fingers through his hair and breaths carefully. "Chon. We have gathered to hear your idea. We are all waiting. We are not investors for you to butter up and indulge in poetic waxings. So please, you mustn't waste time; you must tell us of your plans. Understand? You have thirty seconds."

John blinks rapidly. "First off, the team. Any project with a magnitude as vast as this one can only come to fruition—successful fruition—with the right team. Here at Bladoodle, we are so profoundly fortunate to have—"

"We are done," Chürles says, turning to the Bladoodle developer panel. "We are done. I am sorry for wasting your afternoon with this...this...foolishness. Chon, you may go." For the first time, worry shadows John's face. He tries to smile, seems to think of saying something to salvage the meeting, then turns abruptly and leaves.

Nobody knows where he went. His car sits in the parking lot at the end of the day, but no one sees him after the pitch meeting. He neither returns to work the following day nor contacts Bladoodle regarding his disappearance, making his termination as breezy as it always should have been. Martin and his allies host a raucous party in the breakroom anchored by a double-elimination ping-pong tournament, ostensibly in honor of Arthur's hiring but undoubtedly a derisive send-off for whom he replaced.

"I think he went out to the woods by the greenspace to build a treehouse," Martin says near the end of the episode. "He's probably out there staring off into space, wrestling with his deep thoughts, trying to save the world by staring at dodeca-what's-its all day."

The twitchy military hat developer, after a few celebratory drinks, stews in his anger, saying, "I'm thrilled at the prospect of something like this show spreading the fear of failure throughout workplaces everywhere. We have to admit as a society that a job isn't a right granted to someone simply for being alive. You have to work for it, earn it, and own it. People should be clambering over each other for jobs, not sitting back and looking for ways to get comfortable with stagnation. Don't reward them for it—put them on the chopping block, sharpen the blade and then drop it."

"I will endeavor to be diplomatic in the saying of this," Chürles says in an interview after John leaves. "Perhaps Bladoodle is not the right environment for John's potential to thrive. During brainstorming sessions, he could be very abstract where I am one-hundred percent details-oriented; you know, facts-based. Tell me the cold hard truths of what you mean without all of this metaphysical pandering. He irritated me somewhat, but I don't like to micromanage or to always be second-guessing the various department heads I have put in charge. His managers seemed to like him, and the projects he led were always achieving timely completion. In those regards, he kept the clients happy, so I say, 'Ok, no problem then.' But now I realize the problem in terms of a domino effect, a bad apple spoiling a bunch of other apples."

Chürles adjusts himself in his towering naval commander's armchair and leans forward to rest his elbows on his knees. "When I founded this company, I never considered Bladoodle could be something for people to laugh at. That is what worries me—that a single person such as John could bring ridicule to this company. People saying, 'Oh, Bladoodle is nonsense, they have no ideas, they can't write code. They are like kindergarteners, you know, they play in their little sandboxes all day and never develop anything substantial.' Bah. I have struggled for years to maintain a lead over my competitors, and I have overcome obstacles far more distressing than a simpleton loafer like this Chon. So I say, good riddance. Let the big boys handle the business now." The episode ends with a delicate piano piece playing over a slow-motion montage of John's doofy spellbound face. He gazes at the outdoor greenspace where I graphically inserted an enormous dodecahedron gracefully spinning amongst the trees, resonating a comforting and harmonious whirr. I had hoped to include a glowing spaceman in the center of the shape mysteriously beckoning John, but with Cliff's stranglehold on The Indie's editing machine, I had to table the idea for the sake of time.

After working through the night to finish the final draft, I slumped forward on the computer monitor sometime before lunch and dreamed that both of my feet had been painlessly amputated at the ankle. The editing room telephone woke me on its last ring. As I stirred and flexed my numb toes confusedly, my jaws involuntarily chewed a non-existent breakfast burrito, assumedly given to me by an attendant nurse after the operation. A small trail of saliva escaped over the edge of my open lips, and I caught it on the back of my hand. In the same motion, I reached for the phone and sent it ricocheting off a wall into a waste basket.

"Too bad about that dropped call," Arbie shouted as he sat at his desk with a plastic box of cheap chicken stir fry. I mumbled a snide response and flexed my brow to force my eyes open as I pressed play on the message machine. It was Martin, laughing deliriously and offering his profuse thanks, assuring me I had a slew of humanitarian awards coming my way for getting rid of the Johns of the world. I chuckled and deleted the message, then woke my computer so I could copy the final cut of my episode to The Independent's scheduling server. The file was already there, so I slumped over to Arbie to tell him where to find it.

"Arbie, I got to go sleep some, get some sleep," I said, rubbing my strained eyes. "I put the file up—"

"Yeah, you told me," Arbie said through a mouthful of noodles. "This morning. I watched it. It's good. It's...yeah, it's good. It works." He shrugged casually and put down his fork, then affected a thoughtful face and stroked his chin as his eyes scanned the room gravely. "It just needs..."

I bit my tongue, chewed my lip, and ground my teeth but couldn't leave his comment unfulfilled. "Well, I guess it...It could...uh, move a little faster, maybe? I could, I don't know, add a few more shots here and there, tighten it up, and throw in some quick zooms to keep it kinetic?"

Arbie extended a finger and thrust it slowly in my direction. "There you go. Kinetic. It needs more energy. I think that'll do it," he said as he swung his attention back to his chicken and late-night show. "Best get to it now before Cliff comes back from his shoot, or you'll never finish by the deadline. Noon tomorrow."

I winced and breathed slowly. "Yeah man, I haven't really slept, so...What do you mean, tomorrow? It's due *tomorrow*? Who said—"

"I'm saying it now," Arbie said and turned up the volume. "Make those changes, and we'll be good. Then you can move on to something else."

I stared at the side of his empty head. "It is what it is, huh, Arbie?"

"Sounds like you're finally catching on, Buddy."

I limped back to the editing room and stumbled over a potted plant, knocking it over twice more before I correctly balanced it upright. I spent another two hours making small changes and adding every usable shot I could find, cursing Arbie's stupid ragdoll face. In the end, I had watched the edit so many times, I couldn't tell if I had made it better or worse, so I decided to leave it alone. When Cliff tore into the editing room and demanded every available resource, I asked him to watch my episode and give me feedback, then hobbled to a corner cantina to fulfill my nagging breakfast burrito dream before heading home.

My answering machine blinked with Cliff's reaction as I dragged myself into my apartment—the same place as always, as I still hadn't found the time to look for a new one. "It's not terrible. It's fine," he said. "But never show Arbie anything, or he'll ask for changes just so he can say he did something. How else would he justify being the boss? Idiot. Him, not you, but also you. I'll go ahead and schedule it to run after the first episode of *What Makes You Think You're So Special?*"

On Friday, I met up with Todd and Cliff at The Independent to eat pizza and watch our new episodes as they aired. I asked why they hadn't invited Arbie, but they looked at me like I had nonchalantly asked to see them both naked. The first episode of *What Makes You Think You're So Special?* was somehow more brutal than I remembered. Cliff had found the time to tack on an epilogue where he and Todd awkwardly wait for a taxi to pick them up at Mitzi's since they had ridden there in Herb's car. After the attack, Herb must have regained consciousness and walked off while they filmed the post-incident commentary inside the house. Cliff left a time-lapse camera recording for two days to catch Herb returning to pick up the car, but it simply disappears between two frames.

Todd's reaction to my first episode of *Your Job in a Week* made the entire struggle worthwhile. He roared laughing at all the "Thoughtful John" montages and was quickly outraged when he saw how much time John wasted trying to bait Bladoodlers into helping him. "How did this guy ever last there? It's senseless," he said.

"Good job, Todd. That's the whole point of the show," Cliff said as he slapped him with an oily napkin. When the episode ended, Cliff rolled up a slice of pizza, stuck it between his teeth like a dog bone and stood up clapping. He tore the slice in half and gnawed savagely. "Now that's what we pay you for. Line them up and shoot them down. Same time next week?"

I choked on a bite of cheese, the rest of which insisted on sticking together and landsliding off the crust. I chewed laboriously until I'd swallowed enough to speak clearly. "Uh, I have a few calls out to potential subjects. Plus, well, it takes a whole week to shoot, plus the final day showdown, so—"

"So, you should've set up another story to start filming last Monday as well as the next—that's 'so.' I have two more episodes of my show done, two more rough drafts, and another two more lined up to start shooting next week," he said. "Look, we're out for maximum exposure. We just gave people a taste of what's coming; now we want them to crush it up, snort it, and run around their homes with lampshades on their heads. Constant entertainment; something new every day to keep them hopped up on their brain mush high. Your show takes a little longer to make—big deal, just hire another camera operator and start a new shoot each Monday," Cliff said and swallowed, the bulbous pizza chunks visibly travelling down his throat like a mouse inside of a snake. He scratched the back of his neck with the crust. "Try to keep up, or we'll find someone who can."

He handed me the half-chewed pizza crust and smacked my shoulder, then picked up a rolodex and thumbed through it, licking his fingers. "Here. Arbie earmarked a few college kids for non-paying apprenticeships last year before I told him where to cram that idea. Of all the idiotic...Which of us has time for babysitting? That feeble-minded baboon." He ripped a card from the file; it was immediately spattered with tomato sauce. "Three options: two jerks and a moron, most likely. Call them up and see if they can handle some basic camera work without asking to be murdered. If not, I can handle the murdering part."

.....

The pilot episodes of *Your Job in a Week* and *What Makes You Think You're So Special?* made regional headlines. Arbie soon spent most of his days fielding phone calls. Because I often waited for Cliff outside the editing room door like an anxious family in a maternity ward, I overheard countless Arbie-sided conversations, most of them ending with a flat, "It is what it is." His changeless tone offered no clue as to whether we'd just received praise or threats from the viewing public. Some callers might attribute his unshakable poise to a deep reservoir of self-confidence, whereas I would suggest additional pieces of evidence that point to a lack of basic emotional faculties. He never shared the results of those calls, waving me away with his remote the one time I asked, so I assumed the good and bad were equally balanced. With the customer service aspects of the business taken care of, and with Arbie finally fulfilling a duty that could be described as "doing something," Cliff and I were mostly free to operate however we pleased with little oversight or guidance. Cliff maintained an average of two new episodes per week whereas I could barely eke out one in five, so to help with that, Arbie arbitrarily demanded I create one per month. It was what it was.

The volume of phone calls spiked whenever a new episode of *What Makes You Think You're So Special?* aired but also leveled up a bit with each new installment of *Your Job in a Week.* Cliff swore those instances were just callers asking why his show wasn't on and heaping contempt onto Arbie for allowing anything so inferior on the air. I took an outdated editing room availability spreadsheet and drew lines on the reverse side with black marker, one column for each of our shows. Listening in on Arbie's conversations for keywords proving which show the call was about was like trying to translate a language you'd only had one class on, but I drew an X for each show whenever his responses made it semi-apparent. It was the closest system we had to monitoring ratings, and Cliff's show was certainly the big winner.

I slumped into an unintended nap in the lobby one morning and dreamt I had absentmindedly pressed too many digits on an ATM when making a withdrawal. I was desperately thumbing the bills, which were brand new and sticking together, to separate them and determine how much excess cash I had accidentally withdrawn. When I fully woke, I saw I was picking at a hole in the plastic couch and discolored fluffs of foam were wedged under my fingernails. I had reserved a few editing room hours to finish up a twist episode where an RV salesman gets fired for going behind his boss's back and trying to use my show to get his co-worker fired, but Cliff had locked the door and showed no signs of slowing his work. I growled and limped through the lobby, kicking over a stack of old magazines. I had been looking forward to editing the RV lot footage because it was the first shoot I'd done that didn't feature cubicles, those boxy reminders of the interchangeable temp cages I'd barely escaped from.

"Buddy, let me bug you a second," Arbie said as I huffed past his office. I made sure to finish rolling my eyes majestically before turning around. "Yeah, what is it?"

"Buddy," he said, arching one eyebrow in concern and folding his hands over his desk, "I heard you groaning just now. And you've been groaning a lot lately. We don't need a groaner, we need a…a…person who doesn't groan so much." He further arched his eyebrow in villainous suspicion. "So, what we should do is…" he said and left it hanging in the air between us.

"It's fine," I said. "Cliff's got seniority, and he's juggling a lot at once. He puts a ton of stress on himself and honestly, it's admirable in some sick way."

"That's a high horse of a different color," Arbie said. "If you have a problem with a co-worker, you should feel comfortable voicing that concern to me. I still call the shots."

I laughed softly and scratched the back of my ear, shaking my head. "No, no, it's not like that. I've learned a lot from Cliff, and his skills are nothing short of prolific. I guess I'm still adjusting to the routine here. He logs a lot of hours in the editing room, but—"

"That's neither here nor high water. There are still hours available, right?" Arbie said, craning his neck to look past me. "I can see the schedule next to the door from here—it's got oodles of empty slots. It's like swish cheese over there."

I swiveled around confusedly and only saw openings in the early morning hours, mostly between midnight and 5 a.m. "But that's not…Why did you call me in here?"

Arbie shrugged. "I see holes. All I'm saying. So stop groaning. What's the big deal?"

"Yeah, but...are you saying I should—"

"It is what it is," Arbie said, shrugging again. "Sometimes you have to do what you have to do."

"Right."

"And sometimes you have to do what you don't want to do."

"Got it," I said, breathing deeply in hopes of suppressing the elaborate and delectable obscenities spinning around my mind's nucleus. "Because sometimes you can't do what you can't do, and you can't want to do what you *can* do." I cocked my head to one side and chewed my tongue.

Arbie's eyes constricted in puzzlement, then slowly came to rest. "Yes. I suppose that's true." He switched his late-night program back on and waved me away with the remote. "Best get to it, then."

I surrendered to Cliff's suggestion of contacting Arbie's internship recruits and offered each an on-the-job trial run as secondary camera operator on *Your Job in a Week*. One candidate never showed up to the site, one showed up an hour late to the wrong site (a business with a similar name two towns over, even though I had explicitly sent him the correct address and directions), and one showed up for two days but may as well not have, his only accomplishment being the baffling destruction of a brand new tripod before storming off and crying. I had to include footage of his bizarre tantrum because it occurred just as the slacker employee in that episode had been fired. The only usable shot of the episode's climax was from my camera, so when I whip-pan from the boss waving sarcastically to the terminated loser pouting away, my intern can be seen colliding with the former employee as they both walk through the exit at the same time. They start elbowing each other and seem to refocus the blame for their respective outcomes. The boss nudged me and asked, "So who's replacing him? Were you just filming a show within a show?" I winced and couldn't help but imagine Cliff appearing in the parking lot to film those two fighting for use on his show.

I shelved the assistant idea for a few more months and determined to power through on my own, but the punishingly long days were made worse by the wealth of drab office dungeons I had to shoot in. Seeing hundreds of different employees densely packed in indistinguishable compartments white-knuckle typing their lives away had a detrimental effect on my attitude toward the show. Their bodies began to blur together in my mind, each of them scarcely displaying any details that could qualify as distinguishing marks. They fluttered around their hives in some invisible but predictable pattern of work and non-work. I wondered how anyone could be drawn to those jobs in the first place, much less entire billion-dollar industries built around monotonously pressing buttons in a prison cell. I couldn't sift through the hours of footage without feeling contaminated by it, as if showcasing those companies somehow illustrated my approval of whatever their operation sought to suck out of those people. I worried the purpose of the show might be lost if it wasn't clear to me which was worse: working one of those jobs or getting fired from one of those jobs.

Thirty minutes late for the final day of shooting on a new episode of *Your Job in a Week*, I shuffled across the Indie parking lot loaded down with all the equipment I could carry. As I tilted to one side to keep a tripod from slipping off my arm, I nearly shoulder-tackled a perky but sunken-eyed young woman standing with her hands clasped diplomatically in front of her. Startled, I lunged backward and tripped over a light stand I had dropped. I dusted the loose gravel off my knees and braced for being served the inevitable subpoena papers signifying the end of my show's run.

In an over-practiced but pleasant cadence, she identified herself as Megan Brambles, recent graduate of a local community college business school and future Indie employee hopeful. I may have drooled on my shirt in confusion instead of responding or introducing myself. She pulled a stack of green index cards from her bag and read aloud her qualifications and references, all of which made her sound like an award-winning producer compared to anything I had accomplished. It made me wonder what kind of elaborate scam she had concocted and how it could even be worth executing at The Indie.

"Sure, sure, that all sounds great, but do you know what this is?" I pointed at a camera as I packed it into a case which I snapped shut and shoved under an oil-stained blanket in my trunk.

"Of course. That's a Dekon 24-4s with the upgraded lens and shoulder harness package that allows for an external microphone attachment." She sorted her index cards and double-checked one, pumping her fist at having remembered the correct answer.

Dumbfounded, I looked up and nearly slammed the trunk on my thumb. "Uh, the answer I was looking for was 'camera,' but that'll have to do. Are you free right now?" She nodded quickly and agreed to ride with me to the site of a *Your Job in a Week* showdown.

In a double-twist episode, a fed-up manager of a government benefits office set two petty suckup employees against each other, both of whom thought the other was in the running for an undeserved promotion. Unbeknownst to them, two entry-level additions to the team were learning the duties for both soon-to-be-vacated positions ("two-for-one special," the manager barked multiple times throughout the preceding week, always jabbing my ribs with a pencil he kept behind his ear and only seemed to use for poking people). I alerted Megan to none of this, but, having seen every episode, she knew what to expect and performed stunningly. With no direction from me, she set up the camera and instinctively captured an admirable variety of coverage for me to use in the edit, from intense close-up reaction shots replete with streaming tears and sniffling nostrils, to a glorious high-angle zoom of one terminated employee hilariously attempting to vent his anger on a revolving door which, unsatisfyingly to him, would not slam like a regular hinged door.

Megan insisted on being shown the ingest process back at the office. This was only doable because our shoot was cut short when a higher-up rushed into the government office and shut down the production, citing some nonsense about public sector privacy laws. We had just enough time to get back to The Indie before Cliff or Todd requisitioned the computers. I gave Megan a crash course on the editing software basics, and she was off and running, cutting together a decent framework of the episode's interviews by end of day. I was exhausted, but she wanted to learn more.

Cliff rushed into the ingest computer room where I was showing Megan how to copy finished episodes to the scheduling server. "Oh, this is exactly what I need," Cliff bellowed. "I'm a half-day behind as it is, and now you bring in an intern to slow things down even more? If you think for a second I'm going to forfeit my life's work so you can hold her hand and show her how a computer works, I'll burn the building down just to prove you wrong. Move. *Now*. Get out."

Megan stood and held a finger up to Cliff as she rummaged through her bag. She plucked out a purple index card, then put it back in favor of a bright red one. With eyebrows raised in a deliberately cheery fashion, she read, "Hi. Since we are meeting for the first time, it's in our mutual interest to start things off on the right foot. My name is Megan Brambles," she said, pointing the index card to herself, "and I'm new here. It's a pleasure to meet you..." Megan shot out her hand as if she were trying to surprise Cliff with a magic trick.

Cliff's eyes narrowed; he must not have been breathing, because I could normally hear it when he did. His brow and jaw gradually sunk into the most confused expression I had ever seen on him, or even Arbie, for that matter. Megan's fight-or-flight response seemed to have been rewired to approach every human interaction as a business proposal with a high potential for success. Cliff murmured his name without moving his mouth.

"Cliff," Megan said, and, tapping her temple, repeated twice more. She continued reading from the card. "Truly a pleasure, and I look forward to working with you here at—" she broke off and looked around the room—"The Independent. Unfortunately, for me to get up to speed and become an effective asset worthy of your team, I will need to hold off on getting to know you better and continue learning the ropes from—" she broke off again and looked at me—"Buddy."

Megan flipped the card over, but before she could read any more, Cliff backed out of the room like a puppy failing an etiquette class. "I hope to continue our conversation later, Cliff," she said as she shut the door gently behind him. "Ok," she said, "we've copied the finished episode to the scheduling server; now how do we schedule it to air?"

I yawned and pointed to a computer. "That's on this machine here."

Megan's eyes suddenly took on a horrified expression, as if she were witnessing her own death in the reflection of some kind of cursed witch's mirror. She didn't move. I clapped my hands and waved them in front of her face, making incoherent noises usually reserved for getting a baby's attention. She continued staring at nothing, frozen in terror. A gravelly sound came from deep in her throat, like a sick bear.

Just as soon as it had happened, Megan snapped to attention and said, "We've copied the finished episode to the scheduling server; now how do we schedule it to air?"

"Gah!" I shouted and recoiled, shocked by her demeanor's sudden switch flip. "Did you just fall asleep? With your eyes open? I think you were snoring."

Megan twisted her lips around and looked in her bag.

"Uh, I don't think you need an index card to explain that one," I said. "You're probably just tired. Maybe we should call it a day."

Megan rubbed her face and pounded her index cards against her head. "No, there's way too much to learn and too much to do, and I'm too excited to sleep." She wheeled her chair over to the scheduling computer. "Life won't stop and let us catch up. Come on, let's keep going."

I wasn't able to leave until I had shown her how the scheduler operated and let her practice scheduling shows until she could effortlessly do it on her own. Her nonstop willingness made me worry I was the target of an episode of *Your Job in a Week.*

Other than her unpredictable bouts of narcoleptic catatonia, which were obviously the byproduct of constantly learning and never sleeping, Megan was intuitive, ambitious, and, best of all, had her own computer. Arbie worked out an entry-level position for her to help out on my show, and her index card-laden over-preparedness proved to be a venerable match for his fill-in-the-blank conversation style.

"So, Megan," Arbie said after she signed the contract and spun it back around to him, lining up the ink pen in the exact middle of the paper and clicking it closed. "What you're bringing to the table is…" Arbie raised an eyebrow and clasped his hands together.

Megan held a blank poker face, slyly glancing at a card in her lap. She pointed. "This contract is a mutually beneficial exchange of skilled labor for appropriate compensation." She nodded.

Arbie nodded back with a fleeting trace of a smile, softly bouncing in his chair. Megan high-fived herself. "Exactly. Working together," he said. "That's the key word: together. Call it what you will, but it's six of one, a dime a dozen of the other. Working together." He rapped his desk in a rainfall of knuckles and pointed at me. "Best get to it, Buddy. Maybe she'll have your job someday."

I gave him my best lip-curled moronic smile and said, "It is what it is, Arb." With the comfort of much-needed support in sight, I finally began sleeping full nights and actually had time to shower before work most days.

3.

While pulling an all-nighter studying for her business school exams, Megan saw the original *Your Job in a Week* commercial I had made at The Town Commoner. Stirred by the audacity of its inventive premise, she called The Commoner's office and tried to speak with Tom Geiger-Beef about the possibility of an internship, only to be confused and discouraged by his forking-path stammering and stop-start interjections. His befuddled behavior led her to believe the commercial was some sort of prank beyond his control. She told me the absurd groundhog shenanigans of *The Hole Truth* were also a big hit with students and much easier for them to have seen since the episode aired multiple times, giving ambitious viewers ample time to record and share the episode. When I asked her if she thought it was funny, she simply said, "There seems to be a market for that sort of thing, considering its popularity on campus."

By the time Cliff and I were churning out material at reckless speeds, ramping up by exponential degrees the baseline of broadcast acceptability, The Indie had become a local sensation and inspired Megan's determination to become part of our team. She was drawn to the business side of the unrestricted television landscape being carved out by innovative content like ours. She had assumed a large crew was likely required for the full output of The Indie's original programming and was shocked to hear the true size of our team. "We wear a lot of different hats here," I told her as we finalized the edit of our fourth co-produced episode of *Your Job in a Week* that month, "and all the hats say 'Arbie's an idiot.'"

Without missing a beat, Megan shrugged and said, "It is what it is." I chuckled and clapped politely at the perfect timing of her Arbie jab.

She opened her bag and riffled through to find a pink index card with a puffy flower sticker on the back. She read from it as if giving a presentation on her future life story. "In an entry level position such as this, I will meet each demand head-on, including the unforeseen obstacles occasioned by ineffectual management. Gaining experience on the ground floor and throughout all facets of production will grant me deeper knowledge of the inner workings of television production, making me a more suitable and well-rounded candidate for a higher-level Network job in the future."

I squinted and wondered how any person could be so certain of their future. "Yeah, but these are glamourless behind-the-scenes jobs," I told her, "and we still technically report to Dorkus McDoofus, so maybe you'll want to put your dignity on hold for now."

To assist her in pursuit of that goal, but mostly to avoid admitting I had no idea how The Indie operated, I suggested we meet with Arbie to hear about the station's deeper business practices. I was shocked she didn't nod off once.

Arbie put on his serious face—the one that made most people think he was tired—and folded his hands. He told us because The Indie fell under the public access classification, the station didn't rely on advertising for monetary support and therefore had no clients to appease or ratings performance numbers to satisfy. The Indie was instead funded by "franchise fees": money the local government collected from national content providers like The Network and The Sports Channel in exchange for local airwave access. Public channels like The Independent and The Town Commoner received grant funding from the city's community media budget and had to reapply every five years. It was the ideal setup for new shows like ours to be given air time since we were immune from advertisers' complaints and shareholders' concerns.

Arbie went on to explain how he thought it best to hand over lump sums to producers to pay their staff and cover their own expenses for each episode produced, granting them more flexibility over how the money was spent. I don't think he understood how lazy that sounded, and on hearing the system explained, I suddenly realized Cliff's money-making ploy. The credits in his show included many fictional staff members, so he was accepting payment for multiple jobs he performed himself. This likely amounted to him receiving four to six times his actual salary every year at The Indie. I was simultaneously surprised but not surprised. The breakneck pace I pushed for in trying to keep up with Cliff was sufficiently consuming, and I had never cared where my salary came from. I got paid for my efforts every two weeks, and that's all I had time to consider. When Arbie handed me a check to cover my *Your Job in a Week* expenses and Megan's first two weeks as assistant, it was astonishingly obvious how easily I could have swindled her and just how colossally ignorant Arbie was when it came to judicious business practices.

Megan then asked about how The Indie tracked viewership numbers, verified a show's popularity, and determined optimal resource allocation, all metrics Arbie never felt obliged to follow even though rudimentary software for doing so may have been attainable within the station's budget. The unfortunate flipside of our artistic independence was the total lack of data to evaluate the viewership of our shows. "I looked into it once," Arbie told Megan, throwing up his hands and shrugging.

"Yes, you looked into it, and you found..." She prodded him in a mirror of his own fishing-for-sentence-completion routine, only to receive a token "It is what it is" before his attention shifted back to his recorded late-night show. I nudged Megan and pointed at the door.

The next afternoon, reps from three data analysis vendors lined up at the Indie's door to showcase their companies' viewership tracking solutions. Megan, with her smeared mascara and twitchy eye lids, had obviously stayed up all night researching TV ratings and invited the vendors to make their presentations. She looked like she wouldn't blink if she was tear-gassed. Cliff called the young and eager salespeople the "Dream Team Dweeb Tweens" and during their presentations openly scoffed at the suggestion of numbers tracking at The Indie.

The only affordable service came from Viewsful, some sort of multi-armed research company. Their jumpy rep handed out a business card each time he opened his mouth. I wound up with enough of them to build my own flimsy cubicle. The Viewsful package required upgrading the Indie's archaic analogue signal transmitter to a digital feed so that the bits and bytes entering viewers' homes could be reliably aggregated and parsed before sending reports back to the signal source. When the rep finished and walked out, leaving a stack of business cards on the lobby table, Megan beseeched Arbie to fund the Viewsful upgrade. Arbie gave her the thoughtful eyebrow treatment and exhaled. "Our margins are thinner than air. We can't afford to pay for both the signal upgrade and the tracking software. If some small group of dedicated individuals can pony up for the digital signal, I think I could see my way to working the Viewsful package into our budget," he said with a smirk.

Megan stood rigidly, teetered a little, and nodded toward me. "Ok, it's about a thousand dollars for the initial setup—"

"I'll do it," Cliff said, rounding the doorway from where he'd been hiding. After his first run-in with Megan, whenever Cliff entered a room in which she was present, he would stand against a wall with his hands behind his back and stare at the ceiling, rocking on his heels and moaning softly.

"Look at this guy, dropping eaves," Arbie said.

"I said I'll do it, so shut up and let me do it, and also—shut up," Cliff sneered. He snatched a business card from the pile on the lobby table, then flicked the remaining cards onto the floor.

A week later, we had an operational digital signal, and two weeks after that, The Indie finally began aggregating viewership data with Viewsful's software package called DataScrute. The same nervous rep came back to train the office on the software's various functions and components, but he was forced out of the building by Cliff. "You clicky on things and they show you things, right? I think we got it, champ," Cliff said, ruffling the rep's shaggy hair and pinching his cheeks with enough force to flush them dark red. "Who's a good boy? Now go back to the quiet-time corner so you can finish your juice box and cookies."

Megan became an expert DataScruter in about thirty minutes, minus two of her brief daymare naps I'd started calling "eye-openers." She initiated the tracker and scheduled DataScrute to return reports ("InsEYEghts," according to the software) every twenty-four hours. We waited two months to accrue enough data to accurately reflect viewer patterns before we ran it through the "AnalEYEzer." The first summary showed that *What Makes You Think You're So Special?* achieved numbers close to routine daytime programming on The Network, which was simply unheard of for an operation as miniscule as ours. We also learned that eighty percent of those viewers also watched *Your Job in a Week*, but only forty percent tuned in to *face2faceW/hate* (which Cliff had somehow found the time to continue producing while ramping up its violent content and minimizing the discussion portion), and any show featuring physical violence was sixty percent more likely to be viewed by young adult males but only twenty percent by young adult females. Young adults seemed to like us, but viewers over sixty-four practically didn't know The Indie existed.

Arbie reviewed the reports with us in his office. "So. All this wonderful data tells us…" he said and glanced around the room with one eyebrow stretching like an archer's readied bow. Cliff and Megan both spoke over each other. Arbie raised a hand, then pointed to Cliff.

"We have to double-down on the young adult males. They're the ones really watching, so let's keep them watching," he said. "The rest can set fire to their TVs and die slowly for all I care."

"While I agree that viewers over forty are well outside our reach for now," Megan said, "the numbers for young adult women are promising enough so as to not neglect them." She pulled out a stack of index cards from her bag. They appeared to be color-coded for variations on how our conversation might go.

"And that means we should…" Arbie said and shimmied side to side while trying to scratch a spot in the middle of his back.

"Grant me the bandwidth to create and run a show of my own," Megan said, "under Buddy's supervision, that caters more directly to the young adult female demographic." My eyes shot open at the word supervision, not because it sounded like more work for me, but in fact the opposite: aside from how to log episodes in our system, she'd picked up everything she knew on her own, so the idea that Megan needed any assistance from me was laughable.

Cliff snorted. "Yeah, great. What's next, the—"

Megan flipped a number of yellow cards to the top of the stack and read. "We secure a more diverse cross section of viewers and thereby increase the popularity and viewership of every Indie show, reaping a return that positively impacts the station's overall prestige and opens doors to any manner of broader possibilities. That's what's next, and that's only the start."

Arbie turned to Cliff. "Let's free up some air time for Megan."

Cliff held his hands behind his back and stared at a flickering light. "Oh sure, now that we have numbers proving our popularity, let's cancel something just for fun and clog the empty spots with whatever wonderful cutting-edge malarkey this inexperienced infant can drool onto a page for us."

Arbie's goony smile and cowlicked clump of shiny hair made him look like a mischievous mole that had been yanked from the ground and thumped on the head. He locked eyes with Cliff but slowly raised a finger and pointed it at me. "Buddy, shake up the schedule a bit and see what falls out. Cancel *face2faceW/hate* and make room for Megan. Now that's killing two birds with one in the bush." He held up his hands like a moderator officiating a successful peace accord.

Cliff shook his head wildly and slapped himself on the cheek. "Hey, idiot. Let's head to the library and grab a dictionary so you can look up the word 'I was joking, you moron' before I crush your feeble skull with it and file you under the letter D for 'dead!'"

Arbie patted the table, seemingly oblivious to Cliff's threat. "It's settled, then," he said. Megan gathered her index cards and left to begin developing her own properties.

Cliff edged towards Arbie's desk with his hands in his pockets, rocking on his heels. "It is what it is, huh Arbo?"

Arbie picked up a remote and switched on the screen next to him. "Couldn't have said it better myself, Cliff. Best get to it, then."

.....

Approaching my second anniversary at The Indie, I had almost forty episodes of *Your Job in a Week* under my belt. Only one showdown resulted in the target employee not getting fired, but he quit and started his own company after the episode aired, so I still counted it as a win.

Megan created two promising shows that were performing admirably: *ManDates*, a reality-based program where women attempted to find friends for their husbands by arranging blind meetings for them with like-minded men, and *Zero's Sum*, a scripted drama about a widowed man named Frank Zero who inherited his father's estate after his death. The backstory involved something like Frank using a portion of the money to pay off his deadbeat younger brother's mortgage and debts with a stipulation that he not allow his immature trophy wife to have a credit card or access to a bank account. This apparently teased reflections of the late family matriarch and her ability to haphazardly drink up their father's paychecks, but I usually nodded off halfway through each episode and could never remember why the characters were always at odds with each other. To fill out the ten-character cast, Megan enlisted her college drama troupe friends who were enthusiastic about performing in the show for free as a means of broadcast exposure. This kept the budget low enough for Megan to fund the show from whatever was left of her *ManDates* allotment. Most of the show took place in one of two locations in the same neighborhood, so, with her drama friends assisting with script writing, wardrobe, and set dressing, Megan was easily able to produce a new episode every week for the first summer of the show's run and two per week after that.

Each *Zero's Sum* installment was rife with conflicts over money, pride, reputation, and other routine melodramatic fodder. It often felt like a quest for the precise number of face-slaps per episode that would most appease the average viewer. The whole affair was a bit sappy for my taste, but it steadily garnered a large following in Megan's target demographic and eventually became the first Indie show to receive a sponsorship. Pure&Purer, a regional organic shampoo company, contacted Megan directly about cutting to a commercial break mid-episode to showcase their products. When she asked Arbie about the legality of doing so on a public station, he simply wriggled his hands and said, "I'm sure it's fine." Thus, Megan set into motion a means of additional revenue that no one at The Indie had ever considered pursuing. Pure&Purer's parent company Z.B. Trihandle was pleased with the return on their sponsorship and paid for a series of marketing moments in *ManDates* for their boutique male fashion line of military-style boots and jackets called Barracks. Some of this revenue Megan funneled back into *Zero's Sum*, affording her the ability to hire local actors of higher repute than her college friends. Suddenly, a wealth of Frank Zero's distant relatives appeared on the show to offer unsolicited advice and slap faces. Arbie never asked Megan what she did with the marketing dollars she brought in and neither did I.

In the same period, Cliff produced one-hundred eighty episodes of *What Makes You Think You're So Special?* and was looking to branch out, as if the idea of Megan running multiple shows provoked him far more than some internal creative motivator. He had been kicking around ideas for a new show where he would film street fights and package them as a program, which basically sounded like *What Makes You Think You're So Special?* without any backstory or structure. Whenever Arbie scoffed at this idea, Cliff would casually suggest he and Arbie go out back and shoot the pilot right then and there. Eventually, Arbie said he had looked into it and concluded that so long as The Indie didn't pay anyone to fight, the law was probably on our side.

Megan used DataScrute to discern what types of shows might help The Indie win numbers in the daytime hours alongside *ManDates* and *Zero's Sum*. DataScrute's InsEYEghts detected patterns for when target viewers were likely to tune in, helping Megan devise ways to steadily build the maximum number of viewers throughout the day. No data analysis was necessary to know the most popular early show in the country was Network's *Firth Thing This Morning (with Fay Firth)*,due to the overwhelming number of Fay fashion clones walking the streets. Trying to compete with Fay would've been futile, but viewers who switched channels after her show would rush straight past The Indie because we lazily aired reruns of a severely outdated financial advice discussion program called either *The Current-Sea* or *The Annuity Table*, depending on how old the episode was. Broadcasting anything livelier than the visual manifestation of down-time seemed like an opportunity worthy of pursuit.

The results from the AnalEYEzer led Megan to brainstorm ideas for a mid-morning stopgap to carry viewers to The Indie before *Zero's Sum*, which aired two hour-long episodes starting at noon. In a search for on-air talent, she came across Veena Chumbley, who still self-produced and hosted the *Live Healthy!* show on The Town Commoner. Their personalities were impeccable counterparts of business acumen and fashionability. Together they developed a light and fluffy morning lifestyle program showcasing people and their exceptional pets, offering advice on being a more loving and responsible pet owner. After two weeks of shooting, they had six episodes of *It's the Leashed You Could Do* ready for broadcast. Veena also brought her healthy cooking show over to The Indie, starting with repackaged versions of old episodes since they'd probably gone unnoticed on The Commoner, anyway.

DataScrute immediately returned favorable results with those new daytime additions, and The Indie garnered unprecedented numbers. With Megan's refreshing approaches to data analysis and sponsorships, the upward trend for the station began to sharpen aggressively. She slept less than I did but accomplished three times as much. The final missing piece was to develop properties that could retain viewers across the afternoon and primetime slots, carrying them into the late night hours where *Your Job in a Week* and *What Makes You Think You're So Special?* were steadily building a strong following. Megan deferred to my judgment on that issue, which meant nothing got done.

I had originally hoped to hand over control of *Your Job in a Week* to a different producer so I could move on to something fresher and less demanding. Cliff never stopped moving, Todd wasn't interested, and Megan was tied up with her shows, so I had gone back to shooting on-location by myself and editing at night. Worse than the exhausting routine was that I had become completely desensitized to the excitement of helping companies toss out their bad eggs. Like a junkie building up an alarming tolerance, I speculated what next-level action could restore that lost thrill and began losing sleep over having to generate another idea for a watchable show.

I didn't have to worry for long because The Independent's public access grant funding ran out, or, more accurately, was foolishly squandered by an incompetent nitwit.

I was surprised to see Arbie in the Indie lobby early one morning as I stopped in to grab some lights on the way to a location. Cliff and Megan fidgeted on the worn-out sofas, each the embodiment of impatience. Cliff propped his feet up on the stack of magazines covering the lobby table, kicking some onto the floor as he looked from me to Arbie. Megan riffled through her index cards, one half of her face seeming to fight an impending eye-opener. I stood and stared like a frightened animal awaiting a predator's sudden movement that would initiate a chase.

"Ok, he's here now," Cliff said to Arbie and slid a few more magazines off the table with the heel of his boot. "Let's get it over with. We were counting on you to screw it up somehow, so I guess there's some relief knowing we were right. Did you trade the station for some magic beans? Or did you bet all the grant money on a horse, and now some mafia goons are at the door?" He lifted his leg to shotgun more magazines across the room, but Megan firmly grabbed his pant cuff and dropped his leg to the floor.

Cliff sat up and leaned back. He waited a beat, then with both hands thrust the remaining magazines across the table and onto Arbie's shoes. "I always knew it would come to this," he said, "and I guess it's good to get it out of the way before we're all one-hundred percent invested in our jobs here, but—oh, wait a minute—*we are*! This is our livelihood, you thick-headed twerp." Cliff breathed furiously, rubbing his palms over his face. "You have about five seconds before—"

Megan, after succumbing to a brief eye-opener and nearly falling off the couch, twisted a magazine between her hands like she was inviting a puppy to shred it. "We can only stop holding our breath if you let him speak, so either do that or go ahead and pass out so the grown-ups can speak, Cliff." She said his name like coughing up shards of broken glass. Cliff looked ready to charge through a cinderblock wall, fists raised to absorb the impact. Megan frowned and flipped through a stack of dark blue index cards clearly marked "apologies" but fell asleep again while doing so.

Arbie gently placed his hands together and explained how he had allotted an excessively generous portion of the five-year grant money to the development and production of our new shows. He had hoped that if he spent money upfront on the quality of new properties, it would attract fruitful deals with sponsors. Megan's sponsor deals were only a drop in a bucket compared to what the station required to keep running, plus the money was funneled back into Megan's shows anyway, making it a typical double-play of stupidity for Arbie. He had become so fascinated with monitoring our positive feedback from DataScrute that he not only lost track of the station's budget, but also neglected to re-apply for the five-year government grant that was essential to the station's existence.

"Usually my guy calls to remind me," Arbie said.

"Who does?" Cliff and Megan asked simultaneously.

Arbie shrugged. "I have a guy over there in the grant office. He calls me sometimes, but maybe he's gone. Who knows?"

Arbie realized he wouldn't have enough money to pay the Indie's next energy bill. Instead of warning us of the potential for massive change in our employment statuses, he sat and did nothing. One day, he answered a chance call from a vice president at The Network named Breff Kholkers. The station had been family-owned for decades but was on the verge of going public. The family and executive hopefuls sought to make their initial public offering value soar by teasing the addition of radical new programming in the coming year.

"Breff tells me Network is interested in our properties. I tried to sell him Buddy's show, but he teased it out of me that we're bankrupt," Arbie said.

"He teased it—" Cliff nestled his face into his forearm and stuck his thumb in his mouth. "Oh, Mommy, Mommy, when will the police catch this awful man and bury him alive for all his terrible transgressions? Everyone will hold hands and cheer, and there'll be fireworks and ice cream."

Suffocating under the force of sweaty-palmed anxiety, I surfaced just enough to ask, "Why my show?"

"The numbers." Arbie shrugged. "It is what it—"

"What numbers? What numbers are you..." I started in a shaky near-whisper, then ramped up to a roar, grabbing at my hair as if to split my head in two. "Arbie darbie doobie dumbo! Say what you mean for once, you malingering dingus!" I kicked the lobby table and fell onto the couch, sinking back into the disorienting sensation of raw nerve panic which had only been intensified by my outburst.

Cliff picked up the magazines he had knocked to the floor and piled them into a precise stack on the table. He stood stiffly and cleared his throat, then picked up the stack, cradled it under one arm, and flung the top magazine into Arbie's chest.

"I was going easy on you. What a sucker I was." He hurled a second and then a third magazine. Arbie flinched, but otherwise his expression was unchanged.

Megan pressed her hand against her forehead and closed her eyes. "Buddy, your show. It needs to be retooled." She reached for a stack of index cards, but I held up my hand and winced. "The DataScrute reports show it's starting a gradual decline," she said. "It doesn't seem to be fresh enough anymore. Or maybe you visit too many similar offices. Some episodes are almost identical, and viewers might not know which are reruns. The new episodes aren't having the same impact as the first season, and Arbie and I have been discussing what to do about this. That's all." She glanced at me sympathetically, then quickly looked away.

"So, then he offered to take the whole station," Arbie said detachedly, like a funeral director telling the bereaved where to find pizza after the burial service.

"Who…Wait, Network bought us?" Cliff jumped up and sunk his stubby fingers into his own cheeks, kneading the bristly flesh like a worn-out clump of dough. "Tell me you didn't say no, you…you…heinous misuse of otherwise valuable molecules."

"I invited Breff to stop by tomorrow and oversee the transition. Try to be here by eight. He'll want to meet you all and see if you pass mustard and cut the muster." Arbie made a nonsensical scissoring gesture across the side of his hand.

Cliff slid his palms down his face, leaving sweaty crimson streaks. "Look, I know you haven't reached the stage of cognitive development where you can distinguish between good and bad, so it's unfair for us to have expected you to accurately prepare us for this last-minute meeting. But this sounds like a good thing, Arbo. We'll all be better off with the backing of regular cash flow, and the three of us non-morons will enjoy the additional benefits of working for any upright human body that doesn't have your extraordinarily punchable marionette head lolling around on top of it. So, let's try to do better next time and not terrify the healthy colon tracts out of everyone for no good reason, ok?" Cliff gathered all the magazines from the floor and pressed them against Arbie's chest. He seized his hands and forced him to steady the stack in his arms.

Cliff spun around to Megan and me. "Who wants to celebrate?" he shouted, clapping his hands. "Me either! Because we all have work to do!" He grinned and patted Arbie's shoulders, then brought both hands down on the magazines, spraying them across Arbie's shoes. "Do me a favor and pick those up and pile them on top of your phone so you'll never have contact with the outside world again. Just let the grownups handle everything from now on, ok?" Cliff said as he picked up one magazine and turned it over to read the back cover as he left. After slamming the front door, he opened it, threw the magazine at Arbie, and left again. I was surprised Cliff wasn't more hostile about any new management coming in and potentially discovering his ploy to drain money from Arbie and The Indie; maybe he had covered his tracks well enough to plod around undetected, or maybe, thanks to Arbie's lack of serious bookkeeping, the money had successfully hidden itself without Cliff's involvement.

Arbie asked us to 'dress appropriately' for the meeting with Breff, which for me meant scrounging for my one collared shirt and for Cliff meant wearing his standard dirty black t-shirt with black jeans and black boots. Arbie, as per usual, looked like he had slept in his dress shirt and hastily found a thrift store blazer on the way to work, forgetting he had hair to comb. Megan dressed so impeccably that a casual observer may have assumed she was the station manager, unless they noticed her passed out with her eyes open staring at the floor like lava was bubbling from underneath it.

Network Vice President and Chief Marketing Officer Breff Kholkers was pencil-thin with a perfectly round head, giving him the appearance of a foam ball atop a paper towel roll in a child's craft project. His flushed and mottled cheeks had the greasy violet sheen of salmon skin stuck to a broiler pan; his low narrow shoulders bowed back to front like a warped wire hanger that any coat would slide right off of.

"Thanks for the invite, guys," Breff said with the mock enthusiasm of a field reporter at a state fair. We filed shoulder-to-shoulder into Arbie's office. Arbie sat in his chair staring blankly at the remote control on his desk while Breff stood behind him, gripping the seat back as if he might spin him around at any moment and demand a confession. "Arbie tells me you're the trailblazers we have to thank for these spine-tingling new programs. I'm sure you'll be juiced up beyond words with how our team builds a devoted viewer base and furthers each show's legacy." Breff's bowl cut and bristly mustache exuded the vibe of a timid cartoon street sweeper, but that pleasantry was fully diminished by his narrow, red eyes that constantly scanned the room like a malevolent cyborg while the bottom half of his face was continually frozen in a demented grin. "Us Networkers are over-jazzed about the future of bold content like these Indie shows—especially the new frontiers of marketing experiences we've been thinktanking. Watch out! We're grateful for how you got the ball rolling, so thanks!" He leaned forward and tilted his spherical head slightly back, less of a bowing motion and more like he was showing off his larynx. It strangely seemed to signal the end of our meeting.

"Glad to hear it, Breff, and there's more where that came from," Cliff said, edging his way past me to fully encompass Breff's field of vision. "What you've seen us do at The Indie is only the first crack of the chasm we're going to rip open in this miserable world's backside."

Arbie cleared his throat. "Cliff, Breff is a busy man, and there's a mountain of a molehill of issues for us to discuss in private."

Breff's unholy smile tightened as he patted Arbie's chair. I imagined one being a puppet and the other a puppeteer, but in truth they both seemed to be controlled by some external force not present in the room. "No sweat," Breff said, "I don't mind talking shop before we part ways. We're indebted to Arbie's wisdom that's steered this ventureup until now, and since he won't be joining us at Network—"

Cliff whooped and laid his face on the desk, shaking with laughter. My mouth hung open long enough for my soul to have escaped. "Arbie's wisdom?" I asked. "I mean, where's Arbie going?"

Cliff slammed his hands on the desk, then slid them lightning fast across the surface, scattering coffee mugs and magazines to the floor. "Don't you see? He's that ruthlessly stupid. 'And for my final performance of the evening, I will initiate a deal that leaves me jobless and destitute,'" Cliff said in a stage performer's dramatic incantation as he rose. "Ha! You yard-sale-prototype buffoon. You got yourself fired!" Cliff rocked Arbie's desk so vigorously his computer monitor's plastic stand twisted violently like the neck of a dead bird. Cliff picked up the screen by its wires and swung it onto Arbie's lap, then placed a hand on his shoulder. "For all your service, dedication, and hard work. A little something to remember us by."

Breff pursed his lips like he was bracing himself for a needle injection, then nodded rapidly, as if the motion would help ease the pain. "Well, with all the overlap at Network, Arbie's position—it's unfortunate for sure, but what can you do? Restructuring inevitably leads to redundancy, and even the most fruitful transactions can have undesired consequences, you know?" Breff said as if reading from a script and addressing no one in particular. "But don't take that as a negative view of your worth or Arbie's worth."

"Breffie Boy, you missed your calling as a comedian if you can keep digging up and polishing off gems like this blockhead having wisdom or worth," Cliff whined derisively. "You're sitting on an embarrassment of riches right there—and Arbie should be embarrassed that you're rich and not him! Ha! Getting himself fired is a great punchline to go out on, though. I'll give you guys dual credit for that one." Cliff snapped his fingers and clapped, skipping side to side gleefully like a troll under a bridge after spotting some chunky kids with untied shoelaces. "Wait, wait, wait, I've got it. Arbie offered to sell *Your Job in a Week* to Big Breff here, and Breff says, 'No, in fact, you're so dumb that gives me an idea: let's put you on that show and see how well you do.' Right? So, where's the chimp you're going up against? Or is it a chihuahua? A chicken? A chipmunk? Any animal will do. I'm sure DataScrute will support the addition of animal contestants in your show, Buddy."

"Cliff," Arbie said absently.

"No, this is too good. You're not getting off that easy." Cliff twisted his neck with both hands and cracked his knuckles. "Let's see, what's in the news today. Ah yes, Arbie Darmin, the human stink, capped off a lifetime of mediocrity by successfully shepherding a telecommunications merger and was duly compensated by having his own position deemed unnecessary, resulting in his immediate termination. A real gold star of human performance. What's next? His—"

Cliff paused in full terror when Megan's hand touched his shoulder and laid there. It may as well have been a two-foot-long wasp. "Cliff, you don't understand. We're all getting let go." Cliff turned slowly toward her, mouth agape, his system-shocked brain awaiting a total reboot. Megan held a thick black index card with a large red dot in the middle. "Network wants our properties, but they already have their own team in place," she said. "We were blinded by the prospect of larger budgets and increased visibility. Of course they don't have to buy us; they can just take it all. Our shows are public and owned by no one. It seems like Arbie was also confused and only realized the full details of the arrangement this morning, so he didn't have time to tell us. I'm upset too, but we shouldn't waste our time—"

Cliff suddenly tore through the room with his elbows up, pushing Megan and me out through the door. He grabbed two armloads of magazines and launched them into Arbie's office. Then he removed the leaf from the center of the lobby table (revealing to me for the first time that it was in fact an old dining room table whose legs had been sawed down), stacked it over the other two sections, and slid the entire unit across the room, twisting it into Arbie's doorway.

"Cliff, look," Arbie shouted. "This is only a temporary setback. Every cloud has a line of fire, and this could be a blessing in sheep's clothing. Sometimes you have to—"

Cliff shot across the table heap and thrust his finger sideways between Arbie's lips, shaking them up and down. "Bluh bluh bluh bluh bluh! I've heard enough of this joke, Arba Darba, and it ain't funny anymore!" He grabbed Arbie by the ears and hoisted him up, pressing their noses together. "I'm gonna seal this room up like an oak barrel and see if some cellar aging can dilute the impurities and render a more desirable product, like a vintage pile of dust and bones that were once somewhat human." Cliff dropped Arbie and crawled off the table. Breff stood in a corner, smiling that demented smile, nodding like a realtor awaiting a couple's decision on buying a house. *Is he tuning this out or enjoying it?* I wondered. *Is this how people usually act at Network?*

I jumped out of the way as Cliff shoved one of the lobby couches over to Arbie's door, tipped it up on one side, and heaved it end over end onto the disassembled table. He grabbed the couch cushions and lobbed them into the office, yelling, "Incoming!" with each toss, then slid every piece of lobby furniture in front of Arbie's door. Cliff turned to Megan and me, flashed a goofy toothpaste commercial smile, and left without slamming the door.

.....

Two weeks into my sabbatical of cheap junk food, naps, and daytime game show reruns, I felt as if my ratty couch had untethered itself from the space-time continuum and transported me back to my foster parents' house, where every day was so quiet and predictable it was like living in a painting while watching the paint dry. People would usually apologize when they heard I had been in foster care my whole life, but I had no complaints and it was all I'd ever known. My foster parents, although really nice people, were pretty old and didn't talk much; the easiest way to keep me happy and out of trouble was to leave me in front of a TV for hours. Game shows were my favorite because they were always upbeat, glittery, and exciting, but best of all, they aired all day across multiple channels. That made it easy to spend most of the day lost in a state of low-stakes bliss instead of becoming disenchanted by the quiet reality of my monotonous confinement inside a small bungalow in a boring neighborhood with no other children around.

Since watching TV was the only activity that consistently held my interest, finding a job in TV was the only viable option I ever considered as a career. I might have dropped out of high school if not for discovering a few grant programs that helped foster kids pay for college. A local commercial I often saw for a community college with a media studies program was the only motivator that kept me in class. I fantasized about making TV shows and then sitting at home alone to watch them. I applied for every grant I qualified for, and the money I received, though not enough to cover tuition at a reputable state university, was plenty to launch my community college plan.

Disillusionment with the media studies program set in on the first day when I realized how many of the other students had nowhere else to go career-wise and didn't take class seriously. Even at the college level—willfully paying for more school after high school, which still sounded preposterous to me—they slept through class, talked on their phones, and put in the minimum effort toward the projects we were assigned, if any effort at all. I did the work on my own and kept away from them; I skipped class a lot to stay at home and watch game shows.

I remembered how meeting someone like Chibbs legitimized the program a bit, even at the times when his cheerful non-stop work ethic irritated me, then remembered how we hadn't kept in touch since I started working at The Indie. During a commercial break at the end of an old knife toss game show called *Happy Throw Lucky*, where blindfolded contestants got to throw knives at trained performers who almost always got hurt, I called Chibbs and begged him to meet me for lunch. I'm sure it was obvious things had turned sour at my job and I was looking for work, but I knew if I didn't make a move in some direction I would just stay on the couch and repeat all the weekends of my school years, still, embarrassingly, in the same apartment.

"So how did you screw it up this time?" Chibbs asked as he crushed a lime wedge over some fish tacos. Most of the two-hundred-plus Sports Channel staff were eating from one of the six food trucks parked behind the building in a paved area that was covered in line markers from every sport. "More groundhog videos? Or did someone blow up your building after getting fired on *Your Job in a Week*?"

"My boss sold the station but forgot to keep our jobs in the deal," I said.

"Yikes, some deal! Well, at least you mixed it up with a twist ending this time," he said, sucking some lime juice off his thumb and eating half a taco in one bite. "I'm sure your usual routine was getting stale, you know, trying and failing at every job and having to move on out of shame and everyone hating you because you're worthless and—did I mention you fail at everything?" Chibbs seemed to inhale the rest of the taco without chewing. "Wasn't that your whole temp experience? I think you're better off when a job has a natural end regardless of your performance. But now you're starting a new trend of temporary employment even at full-time jobs."

A bald, smirky thick-lipped jock in a Sports Channel muscle shirt lumbered past the wooden benches where we sat outside. "Fishin' Chibbs! How you doin', brew?" he said and slapped Chibbs square on the back. "Better than you!" Chibbs cried. They both laughed goonishly. Chibbs sat up straight and twisted one arm behind him to massage his spine. "Oof. You remember Warp, right?"

"Who, the walking bottle of protein powder who called you brew just now?"

Chibbs choke-laughed and wiped his mouth. "Warp Dewhitty, from class. From school. You fired him from that group project?"

I sat up and looked around, feeling faint. "Oh, was that him? That was so long ago, I guess I didn't recognize him. Small world. He works here?"

"Yeah. I doubt he remembers you, either," Chibbs said. He winced as his watch beeped softly. "Anyhow, speaking of getting fired, what's your deal this time? Oh, please tell me Tom Geiger-Beef was inspired by your show and bought The Indie just so he could fire you! Mandatory hacky sack and captain's hats for everyone. The irony is more succulent than this tilapia."

I took a small bite of a vegetarian empanada, the cheapest food truck option, and looked up, shielding my eyes from the intense glare. The Sports Channel complex was a modest and tasteful engineering marvel shaped like a half soccer ball stuck in the side of a hill, but it looked more like a contemporary art museum than a sanctuary for sports lovers. Pentagonal panels in the ball design were windows fashioned from some sort of pale green space-age thermal glass that absorbed heat and funneled it into the company's private energy grid, the edges covered in spray-on solar cells to harness more power.

"Impressive, right?" Chibbs said as he tore into his third taco. He matched the rapid wolfing speed of everyone around us; it churned my stomach to watch. "That's the desired effect: total hypnosis. State-of-the-art energy efficiency, ridiculously souped-up computer stations, twenty-four-seven gym on-site, free fitness classes daily, endless variations of protein smoothies in the kitchen, probably some sort of free childcare prison I never looked into." Chibbs balled up the paper from his tray and tossed it into a garbage can behind us that had four different holes for a diversity of waste I couldn't discern. "They're all gimmicks that only work on people who are the ideal combination of young, eager, and stupid. Dangle some yarn in front of their eyes and distract them from how little they get paid." Two thick-necked bruisers in knee-high Sports Channel socks leaned across our table from either side and high-fived overhead, both shouting, "What's the ha-ha, brew?" A third cruised by for a running high-five and shrieked, "Drive-though, brew!" They all laughed like delinquent children and scattered.

"Is it really that bad?" I asked. "At this point I'm willing to—"

"No, no, listen. It's great here, in a way. You feed off everyone's energy, and the shows are exciting, but, well, take the food trucks for example. They bring the food to us, so we don't have to leave for a lunch break. Having pizza delivered every day is boring and unhealthy, so let's have a mini food truck rodeo every day and watch everyone's eyes glaze over." Chibbs glanced at his watch as it beeped obnoxiously. He shook his wrist and wiped his hands on his shorts. "Smoking is strictly prohibited not because of the health risks, but because it's a time-waste that encourages people to gather and collectively time-waste." Chibbs's watch beeped again in shorter bursts with more urgency. He motioned toward the building as most of the crowd stood up and began funneling back into the office. I folded up my mostly untouched empanadas and slaw in their paper tray and tried to delicately slide them into my pocket but only smeared an oily stripe on the side of my pants.

"Every possible article of clothing and knick-knack with the company logo on it," he said. "It's all propaganda and brainwashing, but these people can't get enough of it."

"Wow, Chibbs, I'm starting to think you actually like working here," I said and wrapped a few napkins around my food before tucking it tenderly under my armpit. I freed my hands to carry the folder full of DataScrute analytics I brought to show him but didn't have time to mention.

"Look, I have to get back to it, but send me an updated showreel and I'll see what I can do. No promises." The other Sports Channel employees seemed to follow Chibbs's lead back to the office, tossing or gorging whatever food they had left before hoofing it down the path in a jerky speed walk. "Honestly, when you called the other day, my first thought was you were bringing your show here to fire someone, and my second thought was it better not be me. I don't know, you're only as good as your last project here, and if that was more than a week ago, then what have you been doing with your time? You know?"

"No, I don't," I said. "My last job was at an insane asylum where the warden turned out to be patient zero. Anything is more appealing than sinking further into the swamp that was under this trapdoor I fell through."

"Now there's an idea for a show: *Trapdoor Sanitarium*. They're always losing their patients." Chibbs grinned and looked at his watch again, shaking his wrist. The beep's frequency had steadily accelerated into a solid flatline. "Thirty seconds, I can make it," he whispered to himself and quickened his pace. "All I'm saying is I worked my way up to middle management pretty fast, so I must have done something right, but nobody here ever seems to shake the feeling that someone's breathing down your neck and waiting for you to screw up. And since screwing up is the one thing you're good at..."

"They'll make me CEO in record time, I can feel it," I said.

"Fishin' Chibbs! Zap, brew?" whooped a lanky doofus who high-fived Chibbs and held the door open for us. As we entered, he matched our pace and walked alongside Chibbs, who ignored him. The door holder gave me a "zap, brew" and slapped my back with enough force to propel me two extra steps forward, making me crush the empanada under my arm. I raised my elbow over a trash can and let the mess drop in, trying not to look at the stain under my arm.

"Showreel, no promises, you're a failure. Did I hit all the salient points?" Chibbs stopped in front of his tiny glassed-walled office and clicked a button on his watch. Two caretakers sprayed hoses on an enormous wall of plants and flowers across from us, coating the outer glass of Chibbs's office with a fine sparkly mist.

"Well, I'd say it's been nice to see you, but I hate to lie," he said.

"Too true, brew," I said and waved halfheartedly.

As Chibbs turned to sit down, I noticed the back of his yellow Sports Channel T-shirt featured a large black oval with the words "PACE CAR" inside. Underneath in a smaller font read, "If you don't keep up, you won't win the cup."

I snuck into the Indie office, which had been predictably left unlocked, and sifted through hours of *Your Job in a Week* clips to include on my new showreel. Every episode basically looked the same regardless of the office where it was shot, making it hard to show off any advanced editing or cinematography skills. I cut and recut clips throughout the night, trying anything to make the work look more exciting. In the end, my showreel was a minute of *Your Job in a Week* highlights interspersed with a few quick shots from *The Hole Truth*'s groundhog antics for comic relief. A part of me felt embarrassed at having so little to show for creating and running a television program for over two years, but another part of me told that part to shut up and move on because I needed money.

I constantly looked over my shoulder while I worked, worried the ghost of Arbie Darmin may appear to rattle chains in his vacant office, and checked all the rooms every few minutes even when I hadn't heard anything. I fled when I was done and locked the door behind me so I wouldn't have the option of going back.

Chibbs asked me to come back to The Sports Channel two days later. He had been too busy to discuss anything on the phone, but having a second meeting so soon gave me hope he had lined up a position for me in his department. "Since you were last here," he said, "two people got fired and two moved on—one without telling us. He didn't show up and his phone seems to be disconnected."

"Yeah, goodbyes can be hard sometimes," I yelled. We stood on the edge of the office kitchen where a half dozen roaring blenders thundered together like airfoil testing in a wind tunnel, punctuated by obnoxious wild animal laughter and skin-slapping high-fives from the spirited "brew" crowd.

"So, we have a few jobs that need to be filled, like *today*. I already regret asking, but if you're interested…"

"Hey, work is work. I think I could set aside our blood feud to do something great, or at least mediocre, or at least not illegal," I said as the blenders wound down, emphasizing the increased volume of my last few words. "So, what have you got for me? I'm cool with learning graphics work if that's what you need. I'm sure I can get up to speed pretty fast."

"Oh, Sharin from HR will fill you in. I didn't have a chance to watch the reel you sent, but I'm sure it's fine. The openings we have are, well, beneath you, but it's a foot in the door and one more day you won't starve, unless you forget to eat because you're really that dumb. So please don't forget about the food trucks, you hopeless idiot." Chibbs patted my back and looked at his watch, then pointed down the hallway toward the managers' area as he walked away. "Here she comes. She'll fill you in."

Sharin Billevits had a face that was so plainly generic it seemed like the template placeholder for an actual human face. She was perfectly nice and helpful, but if she robbed a bank in front of thirty witnesses, the police sketch artist would be driven psychotic before being able to render an acceptable facsimile of her appearance. Every time I glanced up at her while signing the standard employment forms, whose numerous pages I spent no time reading, it seemed like she'd been replaced with a lookalike. Even later, I would walk by her and think, "Wait, is that her? Is that Sharin?" I realized asking that question meant that yes, in fact, that was her.

I had been so preoccupied with the bowel-loosening relief of starting a new job that my brain halted when I was signing the last page. My new title read "Junior Editor," and the starting salary was slightly below what I had been making at The Indie. Sharin didn't mention that, and I never thought to ask, but I'd previously created and produced an inventive TV show that succeeded in taking people's jobs away from them; what was junior level about that? I closed my eyes and considered tearing up the papers I had signed, showering Sharin with a confetti blast of dissent, but then remembered I had rent to pay and no other job prospects available. I absentmindedly chewed the inside of my cheek and scribbled my signature one final time.

Once we wrapped up the red tape free-for-all and an hour-long session on how to correctly log hours in the timesheet software (of which I retained nothing), Sharin walked me to the editor's room. It was a blindingly fluorescent chamber of six cubicles and seemed to be the only space in the entire building without natural light in view. "Feel free to settle in at either of the two empty desks; the other station will be used by interns. Warp will be here in a moment, but is there anything you need while you wait? Smoothie, energy bar, bottled water?" I shook my head and smiled; surely someone with the name Warp was a step up from Arbie, I thought, but then remembered what Chibbs said about me firing Warp from a school group project years before. Hopefully my new boss was as forgetful as I was.

Sharin handed me a Sports Channel messenger bag, the final transaction officializing my employment, and left. I opened the bag and checked all the finely stitched interior compartments and mesh pockets, wowed by the prospect of having such a nice place to put things but at a total loss for what those things would be.

I sat down and scanned the room, counting the Sports Channel stickers affixed to every available surface: computer towers, walls, trash cans, shelves, monitors, phones, ceilings, and floors. The four editors sat rigidly, entranced by their computers, and didn't seem to notice me or Sharin. Only their hands and mouths moved as they operated at atom-splitting speed and engaged in a confusingly deadpan exchange of insults, ideation, and non-sequiturs, all at maximum volume.

"A new show where we combine fishing and football called Bait and Tackle."

"Pass."

"Go long!"

"Fishing line, linebackers; I'm sure there's a joke in there somewhere."

"Yeah, it's your face."

"Gadoosh!"

"Catch a pass, catch a fish."

"Catch a cold."

"Catch the fever!"

"A new show where we combine volleyball and football called Bump, Set, Hike."

"Stop trying to combine things!"

"How about I combine my knuckles with your jaw?"

"Gadoosh!"

"Split the uprights."

"I'm a nonviolent person, but for you I might have to make an exception."

"I'm a lover not a fighter, but I love to fight."

"Are you a passive activist or an active pacifist?"

"More like an old-fashioned gas-passist."

"Perfuming the room with his noxious fumes!"

"Hahaha, farts!"

"Too many cooks in the kitchen, and they each brought their own recipe."

"Eels: they're not just for breakfast anymore!"

I found myself grinning, inspired to participate in the swirling vortex of nonsensical babbling, when I suddenly heard, "Warp Dewhitty!" I turned to face a prototype superjock wearing the epitome of frat boy couture—a baggy Sports Channel jersey over a crisp Sports Channel polo shirt whose collar looked sharp enough to slice a melon. His neck and shaved head matched each other in width, lending the impression of a tin can stripped of its label and wedged between two humps of shoulder muscle. He stood with perfect posture and his hand extended, fingers splayed at the ready to connect knuckle on knuckle. "Mr. Bupp, right?" A silver referee's whistle hung from his neck on a blue cord.

"Buppsen," I said vacantly, finding it difficult to shake the fever-dream quality of the editors' deranged conversation. "Buddy." I shook Warp's hand limply. He crushed mine and then slapped my shoulder.

"You made the roster, brew. Let's get to work." He slapped my shoulder again, and I forced a smile.

All morning I ingested endless reams of raw footage from various sporting events. I routed the files to their appropriate homes on the corporate server, navigating a six-level-deep folder framework with an incomprehensible naming convention determined by project number, sports code, client code, day of the week, time of day, and camera number.

The editors linked their software to the files they needed for their projects and ignored me.

At noon the floodgates opened, and the employees raced to the food trucks while most of upper management met in the kitchen to mix gruel-colored protein shakes in the ear-splitting blender orchestra. Warp Dewhitty stood with his arms crossed, nodding like a stern android, in front of a statuesque behemoth who I assumed was the CEO. I was dead last in line for the food trucks because I refused to sprint like everyone else.

Ten minutes later, I heard the synchronized beeping of a few watches, one of which blared frighteningly like an air raid siren. Those who had made it through the line gulped their food, intently eyeing Chibbs and five or six others in Pace Car shirts as they wrapped up their abbreviated meals and headed back inside. Those who hadn't placed an order hung their heads and jogged back, unexpectedly leaving me first in line for any of the trucks. I leisurely ate two fish tacos with extra cilantro and gazed around the sudden ghost town, wondering how someone could possibly take a fifteen-minute lunch break without being overcome by severe indigestion. "The lines for the bathrooms are probably as long as the lines for the food," I said aloud. A mustachioed cook wielding a scorched fryer basket popped out of one truck's sliding windows and shouted, "What? What you say?" I smiled and held up the last bite of my taco as a salute to his prowess.

The moment I walked back inside, Warp emerged from nowhere and blocked my path, fingering the whistle around his neck. "Buddy. Brew. Enjoy your lunch? Prime bonding time with the star players, am I right?"

"Actually, I didn't have a chance to introduce myself to anyone, and then..." I motioned to the outdoor seating area in disbelief. "It's like some invisible piper blew a beguiling melody on his flute and led everyone back inside."

Warp's shaggy dark unibrow yanked itself up by the middle like a dying caterpillar. "The flute with the who now?" A painful expression of primordial fury momentarily breezed across his face. He shook his head and slapped my shoulder. "Don't let them bother you, brew. They love to beat each other to the punch. That doesn't mean you have to go to the mat, too, but I bet pretty soon you'll be racing out there to set the new record for wolfing down lunch and getting back to work."

"Wow, you don't know me at all," I laughed. "I mean," I added quickly, immediately attempting a shaky backpedal, "I, uh, prefer to bring my lunch and eat at my desk. While I work." Warp turned his head and glared one narrow fish eye at me. I recoiled slightly.

"Change the game on 'em," Warp said in a sagely tone, squinting his eyes as if staring into the sun. "That's how you go the distance, brew. If you can't beat 'em..." He held his palms up, patiently awaiting my astute contribution to his maxim.

"Uh, avoid 'em?" I said, raising and lowering my eyebrows in a pouty nod which Warp mirrored flawlessly.

"Something like that. But here's what I'm getting at, strawberry brewbarb pie: nobody's breathing down your neck, nobody's watching the clock, and nobody's keeping tabs on you. As long as you come out swinging and meet your deadlines and fill out your timesheets, you're off the ropes and we'll keep you in the game." Warp slid his arms and feet side to side in an elegant but confusing grapevine shuffle of some sort. I nodded and fluttered a jazz-hands semicircle between us, hoping it was an adequate enough response without full-on dancing. He slapped each of my shoulders, about-faced, and scampered off in a stiff-legged butt-clenched march. A few steps from the editor's room, I could already hear another spellbinding group tirade in progress.

"A new show called Inverse Bowling where you try to knock down as few pins as possible without getting a gutter ball."

"That's right up my alley."

"Spare me your puns."

"Somebody write these ideas down on a piece of paper."

"Then tear up the paper and throw it away."

"Ashes to ashes, gadoosh, gadoosh."

"A new show where we combine volleyball and bowling called Bump, Set, Strike."

"You're starting to repeat yourself."

"Say what?"

"You're starting to repeat yourself."

"Say what?"

"You're sparring to defeat yourself."

"Say what?"

The editors' ceaseless babble became the white noise that eclipsed all other interference as I scanned and catalogued a mind-numbing assortment of sports footage, hunched over an unnecessarily expensive computer that looked better than it performed. I would often blink and briefly see images from two different sports merge into one unholy abomination before me, a subliminal residue cloaking my vision as I rubbed my eyes and chuckled along with the delirium of our sequestered enclosure.

.....

Three months into the job, I hadn't learned the editors' names, but I learned not to address them directly. Warp had left an extra pile of tapes on my desk one morning, each from a separate event but with underlined instructions that they be made available on the server for rough drafting by 3 p.m. that day. I feverishly ingested, copied, and catalogued the footage per the needlessly specific official Sports Channel corporate guidelines, but the last tape on the pile had no identifying writing on the label. The tape felt like a twenty-pound weight as I slid it into the drive and pressed play. Two bare-chested opponents squatted on opposite sides of a lightly dirt-covered ring. With their hands up, they orbited around each other along a white circle painted on the outer rim. One would suddenly charge forward, screaming, and grab a medicine ball from the center which he would throw straight up into the air. At that signal, the other player would attempt to run a full circle around the ring before the ball landed. Or at least, that's what they appeared to be doing in the thirty minutes of raw footage I scrubbed through before leaning over to ask the nearest editor for help.

"What in the world is this?" I asked. "It's like a combination of jump-ball and sumo wrestling played to the tune of ring-around-the-rosie." The editor stared straight ahead, his lips repeatedly pooching out like he was blowing bubbles.

"Hey… sorry, but hey," I said. "Do you know what I should do with this? Where it should go on the server?" I pointed toward my monitor and scrubbed back and forth through one play, the ball rising and falling in sync with the players intensely focused expressions stiffening and releasing. Meanwhile, the delirious babble swarmed around us.

"A new show where we combine football and sumo wrestling called Fumble Thighs."

"Everybody wears diapers and helmets and pushes each other out of the huddle."

"Goo goo ga ga gadoosh!"

I glanced at the clock; two minutes to go. Despite Warp's frequent pep talks, an oppressive and relentless standard of productivity was reinforced by every Sports Channel employee, rendering it irrelevant whether a prime directive from upper management had decreed it so. The tangible corporate vibe suggested that, at its inception, The Sports Channel had exploded in every direction as fast as possible without anyone ever asking why, where, or how. The endless pile of tapes secured my desk to the floor with a force more powerful than gravity. New tapes were added, and the stack was fully replenished every evening after I left, like a sadistic hourglass with painted-on sand. I was often told, "Thanks, but I needed this five minutes ago" from various editors and producers, never discovering if the phrase was an inside joke or meant as a condescending jab.

I finally got the editor's attention by casually rapping his desk and snapping my fingers in front of his face. He blinked rapidly and turned toward me, horrified. His eyes abruptly narrowed their focus and his expression turned grim. "Why? *What*? Sumo *who*-mo? Whatever the...You can figure it out, you big baby! You brew bah ba-doo bah!" He swatted me away and turned back to his monitor, rubbing his eyes vigorously and snorting like his sinuses were clogged with sawdust. He slapped the side of his monitor as if to kick-start an outboard engine and resumed working. He offered up a new line of crowd-participation gibberish, like tossing out a fresh bucket of chum for swirling sharks.

"I want to hear athletes respond honestly to stupid pre-game questions. 'Did you come here to win today?'"

"'Well, I didn't come here to win, per se. That's unrealistic. I only came here to score a few points and raise my field goal percentage slightly.'"

"'But we don't stand a chance at actually winning this thing.'"

"'What will it take to make tonight a victory for your team?'"

"'Well, according to the rules, whichever team scores more points, wins.'"

"'So, I guess we'll have to make a concerted effort to score more points than the other team, unless there's something I completely misunderstood about this sport.'"

"'We'll leave nothing on the field.'"

"'There won't even be a field left when we're done.'"

"'We'll load the fans on the buses and take them with us.'"

I tiptoed back to my seat as the mock player interviews continued. I opened a drawer at my desk and slid the unlabeled sumo jump-ball tape under a stack of dusty papers. At lunch the next day, I looked around for the editor I had disturbed in hopes of offering a half-hearted apology, but when I found him he was eating a kale and apple salad with such manic intensity, I worried any attempt at communication would be met with growls and deliberate projectile vomiting. He returned to work before any of the Pace Cars' watches announced their impending departure.

Four more months passed before I successfully scheduled a quick check-in with Chibbs that he didn't have to cancel last-minute for a more important meeting. He constantly monitored his watch like he was reading lines off a tiny teleprompter. We met outside a conference room where his next meeting would take place; upper echelon managers filed in, each wearing a perfectly cut suit that was worth more than my life.

"So, the editors have their own rhythm and dialect and no time to help me with basic questions—fine," I said. "That doesn't bother me as much as being hired on as the bottom-rung flunkey who catalogues footage all day for the people who do the real work."

Chibbs held up a finger and tapped a few buttons on his watch. It beeped a low off-kilter pulse as he looked back up at me. "So, what's the problem? Have you really tried talking to them? Those guys are all—"

"Look, I assumed you were bringing me onto your team to do something higher-level, but now I'd settle for routine editing work. Not this embarrassing gophering garbage."

"I never promised that. And besides—"

"Fishin' Chibbs!" yelled a voice from down the hall. Chibbs smiled and threw up his hands in a "You got me!" pose, which immediately dissolved as he turned back to me. "I told you the job was beneath you."

"It's so entry-level, it might as well be the birthing room where the doctor pulled me up and slapped me," I said.

"How I envy him. But I thought you were born in a test tube? No wait, you were scraped from a cankered petri dish outside an illegal lab the feds had to shut down."

"From humble beginnings." I bowed theatrically. "Regardless, you know where I've worked and what I can do. I was running my own show! Why would you stick me here? I didn't mind when I thought it was a short-term deal to get me accustomed to the whole Sports Channel vibe, like maybe for a couple of weeks, but now I'm starting to worry this is it for me."

Chibbs clicked a steady tempo of four beats on his watch, paused, then shook his wrist. "That's all up to Warp, and I also assumed you would've moved up to bigger things by now; but I think the problem is...Well, you've put up with ingesting and cataloguing longer than the last few people in that position, so to Warp, it's probably not a question of what else you can do; it's a matter of not disrupting the workflow when it's running smoothly."

I leaned my head back and moaned like a lonely animal. "So, if I'm good at one thing, I'm stuck there? There's no room for growth? What's the point of ever being good at something?"

"I didn't say that, and I also didn't say you were good at anything. With all the brews clambering over each other to get attention, you really have to do something special to stand out." Chibbs held the door open for a manager who marched in and frantically ran his fingers over his necktie, pinching and smoothing it to flatten some invisible wrinkle. He turned and sneered at me briefly, as if I were the source of his tie problems, then showered Chibbs with finger guns as he walked in.

"But I'm not doing anything!" I seethed. "I'm just copying files. A machine could do that! I don't have anything to show for my time here. My showreel at least—"

"Yeah, about that. I never had time to watch your reel before we made an offer, but Warp did, and he wasn't impressed. He said something like, 'Really, brew? This guy's a producer?' No offense, he's only impressed by a person's retention of football stats and how tight they can wear their pants without cutting off circulation. I assured him you were a solid hire, and then I watched your reel. All the footage from your show was pretty boring, honestly, and then there's the groundhog stuff. I mean, what's a serious employer supposed to think about that? 'Oh great, he has no real skills but a dynamite sense of humor?' I vouched for you."

I tried to offset my increasing heart rate by clenching my fists and massaging my knuckles. "Wow. Any more compliments, and I might start thinking you're interested in keeping me here." Chibbs held open the door to the conference room for a tall, prickly-haired manager who bent over and whispered, "How you doin', Chibbs?" as he passed. Chibbs responded quietly, "Better than you." He sighed and stared at the floor as his watch hummed a guttural croak.

"I think that baby might need a new battery."

"No, actually," Chibbs said slowly, "it's charged by the simple kinetic motion of your arms moving as you walk, like constantly winding an old clock." Chibbs rotated the outer metal ring on the watch slowly to the right, then twisted it quickly in the opposite direction and pushed a button. It made a gleeful high-spirited chirp. He jiggled his wrist in front of me. "The Sports Channel has specialty ones custom-made for us, so they can track different things. That low groan was informing me I've spent nearly fifteen minutes being unproductive."

I convulsed with unintended laughter and put a hand to my mouth to force it back down. One team leader walking by raised a quizzical eyebrow at me. I wanted to yank it down like a window shade. "'I'm constantly being warned about the serious ramifications of my performance—not that anyone's watching,'" I joked. "Do you hear yourself?"

Chibbs leaned in close and waved for me to stop, grabbing my shirt with his other hand. "Look, don't talk like that. Some people here are paranoid for no reason, but I'm telling you: nobody's watching you behind your back." He let go and smoothed out my shirt.

"I know—they're doing it out in the open!" I nodded in the direction of the suits in the conference room. "With the full complicity of every employee! 'Remember the good old days under that tyrannical fascist when all of our decisions were made for us without our input and everyone was constantly being whipped and prodded and stomped into the ground?'" I gestured with my hands like two mouths talking. "'You said it, brother—those were the days.'"

"Fishin' Chibbs!" called a humorless robotic voice from inside the conference room. Chibbs stared me down with an expression that was equal parts angry and sad. "You needed a job—I got you a job. Last time I'll make that mistake." He spun around into the meeting, closing the door in my face. As I sulked off, I could hear muffled variations of Chibbs's nickname echoing across the room.

I took a late lunch break to see if anyone noticed, seducing fate and testing Chibbs's assertion that no one cared how I spent my time. I relished eating three fish tacos with extra cabbage as slowly as possible. It seemed keeping employees healthy and productive would be more easily achieved by not encouraging them to choke down food like malnourished pirates. I was chuckling to myself, imagining public service posters around the office showing how many times an adult should chew each bite of food, when a suave gentlemanly voice sauntered up behind me. "That taco just tell you a joke? Say what, friend; I'll give you a hundred bucks for that sucker if it's tellin' jokes. The dirtier the better. Con carne, you know what I'm sayin'?" I turned to see the high forehead and glossy pompadour of Sports Channel lead anchor Buck Tarstick, the popular guy in high school you constantly trash-talked but deep down wanted to party with. His jaw was chiseled like a rustic log cabin, and he had the disposition of a cartoon in fast forward. "Boy, I'll take that act on the road and make my first million."

"Tell you what," I said, holding the taco to my chest and twisting away from him like I was protecting an ancient treasure, "you show me the cash first, and I'll get the taco to tell you one about Warp Dewhitty blowing his own whistle, if you know what I mean."

Buck threw his head back in a silent roar, mouth open wide like a baby chick catching rain in its beak. "That's too good. But you better hope this watch of mine ain't recordin' all these here proceedings," Buck said, lifting his Sports Channel watch into view and winking suggestively.

"Oh, right," I said. "I heard those things can even detect early warning signs of cancer, but they're also the cause of it, so it kind of evens out." Again, Buck threw his head back, this time releasing a full-body guffaw like he was summoning all the animals of the forest to mobilize at his side. "Partner, where they been hidin' you?" He grabbed my hand and shook it once as if to wring the last drop of water out of it. "Buck Tarstick: on-air talent, but the jury's still out on the 'on-air' part."

"Buddy. I've been here six months. Eight months? I thought I would be editing and maybe doing some graphics, but I'm just sticking tapes in a machine and punching buttons all day."

"Well, sir, somebody's gotta do it. Truly the Lord's work." He clicked his heels and saluted me solemnly. "Thank you for your service. I'll see you down at the next veteran's club shindig. Bring that talkin' taco of yours, and we'll have us a grand old time." One of the food truck cooks leaned out a dirt-streaked window and shouted something unintelligible to Buck. "Ok, yessir. Got it," Buck shouted back, hoisting a big thumbs up. "Buddy, you discovered my little secret: let everybody else rush out here and huddle up to eat like pigs at the slop. I'll take my own sweet time, thank you very much." Buck stood piously and brushed his shoulders. "Now, if you'll excuse me." He turned in place, took two straight-legged military steps, then shuffled off toward the food truck in a ridiculous pantomime of musical theater dancing, replete with knee-tuck jumps and flailing limbs. He landed perfectly in front of the order window and straightened his tie. I nearly choked on my last bite of cabbage and wondered if the compound stress of ceaseless work and full-scale unfulfillment had caused me to hallucinate the whole thing.

A blurry month or two later, I was shocked to see a vacant seat at one of the editing stations as I walked in. Three interns had come and gone from the station next to mine, failing to simply log and copy footage with any routine success, but none of the editors had arrived late, left early, or taken a sick day in my time there. "Woah, where's the other guy?" I called out, referring to the editor I had once interrupted. I crept to my desk, glancing over my shoulder. The remaining editors ignored me, continuing a maelstrom of cheese-related metaphors in some sort of rhyming slang prattle. I dropped my mostly empty Sports Channel messenger bag and jogged to Warp's office. He circled his desk pressing a football-shaped phone against one ear and a red, veiny hand against the other. He looked like he was attempting to make both hands meet in the center of his skull and merge his brain with the ball.

"Not today, cowboy," he said into the phone. "You come down here talkin' that jibber, and I'll show you some real jabber, mister honkytonk jukebox rodeo star. I'll hog-tie you one real good. Why'nt you come on down and see? Bring your buck-toothed sister, and she can herd my sheep. Baahhhhhh." He tossed the football phone in a perfect spiral against a wall-mounted cork board with a yellow goal post in the center, then pushed his knuckles full force on his desk as if to prevent it from hovering away.

"Uh, Warp." I waved limply from the hallway, noticing clusters of dents and scratches littered across the cork board.

His head slowly swiveled toward me, his hairless dome perfectly capping the psychotic cyborg look. "Buddy. You lost, brew?" He gently placed the tip of the whistle between his teeth and danced his fingers across an oversized desk calendar covered in football field lines.

"No, of course not, I...What was that all about?"

Through the whistle he said, "Client," and shrugged without breaking his stare. "Sometimes you gotta talk their kind of talk, brewbie doobie."

"I was just wondering what happened to the editor. The one who isn't here today."

Warp puffed himself up and crossed his arms, massaging his collarbone. "Haven't heard from that glass-jawed featherweight since he threw in the towel in the middle of a big project last night. Look, brew—everybody in this place can talk big, but you got to back it up and keep on backing it up every day. That's the name of the game. Take the gloves off and show no mercy. What's so hard about that?" Warp stared through me, ruminating on something deeper than I cared to engage with.

"Well, if he's gone, can I—"

Warp stretched backward and wheezed through the whistle, nearly touching his elbows behind him. "Brew, look at you. The ref hasn't even counted to ten yet. Sure, tee up and show me what's what. But I ain't gonna be your caddy. Ball's in your court." I dashed back to the editing room to seize the opportunity and finally do some real work.

The one positive aspect of The Sports Channel's relentless workflow was the streamlined standardization of project management. A list of daily tasks appeared and auto-updated itself on each editing computer, so jumping right in was seamless. I imagined being a hero to the other editors since the no-show employee's workload would've fallen to them, but they didn't seem to notice he was gone or that I had taken his place.

A few weeks later, I had taken over a portion of the editing duties, and I was compiling a montage of the season's standout second-base steals when I involuntarily started a verbal discourse that bypassed my brain entirely and shot straight out of my mouth. "There should be two leagues for each professional sport: one where no performance-enhancing drugs are allowed, and another where drugs are mandatory." I looked up, momentarily terrified of what I had carelessly blathered for the whole room to hear. The other editors latched on like ants ravaging a piece of sticky candy.

"Deploy the 'roids!"

"Give the fans what they really wanna see."

"Freak show, freak show, freak show!"

"Pill-poppin' and show-stoppin'."

"No chance of survival without drugs on arrival."

"Show up for practice with more needles than a cactus."

"Gadoosh!"

"Can't have too much of a good thing."

"Moderation is the enemy."

"Too much moderation is bad for you."

"'In my professional opinion, he died from an excessive amount of moderation.'"

"'He died from an excessive amount of GADOOSH!'"

I was equal parts dismayed, confused, and giddy. From then on, I was as close to being an active component of their hive mind as I could ever expect to be.

.....

The next eight or nine months bolted past me in a total blur, the sole instance in my employment history where I neglected to count down the days until my first anniversary. I begged Sharin Billevits to hire interns at double-speed to take over my ingest and catalog duties while I focused on editing. I never spoke to them and couldn't estimate how many had come and gone.

Toiling deep within a perpetual fog, I experienced a bizarre synchronicity. For a golf tournament montage, I loaded an extreme close-up of a sun-lit golf ball resting on tee and pressed play. At the moment the club came into frame and made contact with the ball, I heard the unmistakable *thwop* of a tennis racquet blaring from another editor's computer. In a microsecond of concentrated alertness, I heard someone saying, "A new show where we combine tennis with golf," but when I pulled off my headphones, the room was abnormally silent. I looked back at the paused image of the teed-up golf ball; I momentarily saw the fuzzy hyper-yellow corona of a tennis ball superimposed over it. My eyelids jittered and twitched in a frenzy as the image lingered briefly, then vanished.

I rested in a bathroom stall during lunch with a warm damp rag over my eyes to combat my daily razor-slashed eyeball strain, overwhelmed by the constant onslaught of energetic sports footage. Back at my desk, I queued up the golf ball footage I had seen earlier, then scoured the company's video archive for similar shots from other sports. I strung together the best close-ups I found and raided the Sports Channel sound effects library. After an hour's work, I leaned back, placed the warm rag on my forehead, and played my ten-second creation.

In extreme close-up, a golf ball is struck and immediately becomes a tennis ball spinning in slow-motion in the center of the screen. It then seamlessly becomes a basketball, a bowling ball, and finally a soccer ball, each perfectly centered in the same position and accompanied by game-specific sound effects. In the last cut, the soccer ball zooms back and becomes the O in The Sports Channel logo. The clean simplicity of the piece gave it a professional sheen I wasn't expecting, and, with modest resources, I felt I had created something worth showing to Warp in hopes of upping my status at the brewhouse.

The next morning, I rushed into Warp's office to find him blasting offensive frat rock music from a comically oversized boom box while setting up an inflatable basketball hoop. "Hey, Warp!" I shouted over the music.

"Can't hear you, brew!" he shouted back without looking at me. He turned and briefly held a rubber ball toward me as if I had passed it to him, then spun away, executing a triumphant windmill dunk. He turned up the music and gyrated his hips in a slow-jam victory dance. "We'll have to talk later when I'm not intentionally blasting tunes to drown you out." He squatted low and shuffled backward, quickly pushing me out of the office with his rear end. "Box him out, box him out!" he said as the door closed. I kicked it with the frustrated futility of a pouting child.

I jumped and flattened myself against a wall as the prehistoric roar of the blender brigade suddenly fired up in the kitchen. As I glanced around to make sure no one saw my humiliating reaction, I noticed Chibbs talking with the CEO, who swirled the dregs of a smoothie into a glass. I jogged down the hallway and waved. "Fishin' Chibbs!" I shouted despite myself and winced. The CEO looked up confusedly and smacked Chibbs on the shoulder. He pointed in my direction, then feigned a gut punch and strolled off. "That the CEO?" I asked, shamefully out of breath after a twenty-yard run. "Still haven't met him."

"Yeah, Cheebie's a busy guy, as you can imagine. He does as much work with his real estate deals as he does with the channel, so, you know. He isn't around all that much." Chibbs exhaled curtly, clearly irritated at my having scared off the CEO.

"You call him Cheebie? Or is it Mister Cheebs?"

"No, his name's Chedster Baulhog. I shouldn't have to tell you this; it's all in the orientation." Chibbs clicked his watch the exact moment it beeped, then dragged his finger back and forth across its blinking face. "Anyhow, Cheebie—it's a childhood nickname, and he insists on everyone calling him that. It helps the atmosphere stay loose and organic, I guess."

"Chibbs and Cheebs; what a delightful combination. You guys should start your own brand of nachos," I said, awaiting a lighthearted snicker that never came. "Sorry, did he just tell you he's dating your mom? I'm sure it'll be hard at first, but you'll get used to it. Hey, you can bond with him over your new nacho franchise."

"No, he just promoted Warp and me," Chibbs said and narrowed his eyes. "That's another thing you should've known; it was in the feed this morning."

"Feed? What feed? Is management going to hang burlap bags around our necks so we can eat like horses and never miss a second of work?"

Chibbs raised a hand as if to throttle me but was thrown off by his watch beeping again. He rotated the outer ring and tapped it twice. "Your brain is like a pellet rattling around an empty bucket," he said before looking up. "In the bottom left corner of your computer screen, mixed in with the project to-do list, there's the company news feed. News appears in olive green, tasks in hunter green. All other questions about basic day-to-day stuff should go to Sharin."

He turned to leave, and I grabbed his shoulder. "Shouldn't you be happy about getting promoted? What am I missing?"

Chibbs threw up his hands. "Corporate restructuring—that's what. Last month, Cheebie said we had to focus on squeezing in more projects, even if that meant sacrificing a little bit of the quality; this month, he says everything we do has to be the epitome of quality, even if that means doing fewer projects." Chibbs clenched his fist and shook it in phony anguish. "He just gutted middle management, leaving me with twice the number of employees to manage and six times the number of projects, not to mention the absurdly unrealistic numbers we're supposed to meet this quarter. But in a month, they'll realize how understaffed we are and go on another hiring frenzy, leaving us no time to vet anyone! That's how we wind up with people like you here." He patted my chest. "No offense, but still, you should absolutely take offense." His watch squealed in triple bursts. He slapped at it like it was a giant insect trying to burrow into his arm. "And last but not least, I have to go tell forty people there's somehow no money for raises this year. That's what Cheebie was really telling me—that I should be happy he likes me enough to keep me around to be tortured for the foreseeable future."

A low-end murmur droned quizzically from his watch like a drunk robot having its car keys taken away. He sighed and rubbed the watch's face in circles, breathing deeply and methodically. "I can do it. I've done it all before, and that's just the way it is. I can do it, do it, do it again. But you," he turned and elbowed my ribs, "good luck, Godspeed, and gadoosh!" He yanked a protein shake from the hands of a baby-faced employee walking by and chugged it in three massive gulps before handing back the empty cup and sprinting down the hall.

A note from Warp was stuck to the lower left corner of my computer screen. "Bud Bud, swing on by for some eye-to-eye," it read. I snatched the note and crumpled it. As I stomped off to Warp's office, I noticed something odd on my screen the note had covered: all the text in my feed was bright red and flashing.

In his office, Warp slid a Sports Channel sweatband over his head and checked its evenness in a mirror, shooting a satisfied smirk at his reflection. He cinched up the Sports Channel sweatbands on his wrists and plunked a touchscreen computer monitor on the desk between us. "Bud Bud, let's do this thing," he said and spun a rolling chair toward me.

He opened a video and slid the timeline back and forth with a flamboyant flourish, scanning for a specific section. "Here we go. Check the playback, Bud Bud." I watched a ten-second clip of a beach volleyball match, then held up my hands. "Yeah. Volleyball's considered a sport now, so we air it sometimes here at The Sports Channel."

Warp rewound and played the clip twice more. "Something's…not…right...here." He paused on a close-up of two hands reaching for the ball.

I snorted. "Sorry, Warp. Ol' Bud Bud here's not seeing—" But then I did see it: the two hands were reaching for a football. In the back and forth of the match, a close-up from the wrong sport had somehow been spliced in. Warp waltzed around the desk and shimmied his eyebrows around, delighting in my sudden recognition of the problem. "Nothing gets past Warp Dewhitty. Swattin' layups like little mosquitoes. Get 'em outta here!" He pushed the monitor to one side of the desk and leaned back, resting his wrists on his head and fingering the basketball net behind him. "That aired three days ago, and we got a few complaints. Then we got complaints about another messed up show. Then another. Even Cheebie himself noticed one and called us into a huddle. But here's the thing—you didn't edit any of those, so why did I call you in here?" His mouth curled slowly into a fiendish grin, deadening any hope that I wasn't to blame.

"Because…you want me to fix them?" I asked.

Warp shot forward onto his elbows and fixed a hexing stare on me. "Airball. Second attempt. Why did I call you in here?"

I opened my mouth, and Warp pounded a fingertip drumroll down one side of the table. He reverse-slammed the goal behind him, pretending to swing from the net. "You've been ingesting the wrong footage for weeks, brew." He yanked the computer monitor back to his desk and tapped his foot frantically as he clicked around and pulled up my stats. "The DataScrute AnalEYEzer says one in three shows this month could be corrupted based on all the mistakes tagged so far." In the magnitude of the moment, I had no time to process one baffling development: next to my name was the title "Senior Editor."

"What are you talking about? I haven't used the ingest computer for months. The interns are responsible for—" The realization flattened me into the chair like a deflating balloon. "No," I said meekly.

"Can't blame the interns, Bud. My screen here clearly says you've been logged into that machine every day for almost two years. Buddy Buppsen. Swish." He hooked the plastic ball behind his head, bouncing it off two corners toward the goal. To my complete irritation, he made the shot. "Can't argue with DataScrute, chicken cordon brew. These records are official. Gadoosh and good night."

"No, the interns were the ones doing it, regardless of who was logged in. You could check security camera footage and see that. What do you think they've been doing? What do you think *I've* been doing? Hundreds of hours of editing work—that's also in the DataScrute analytics. One of the interns must've been incorrectly cataloging—"

Warp stood and crossed his arms. "Brew, I don't think you heard me. Clock's run out. Game's over. You're gone."

A surge of blood flooded my ears until they swelled and burned. "Are you just getting me back for..." Warp pointed toward the door, then made a two-handed broom sweeping motion. I stepped toward the hallway, but the second Warp turned away, I snatched a large pair of scissors from a Sports Channel mug on his desk. I yanked down the end of the basketball net and started cutting across the top.

"Ice cold, brew!" he shouted in total moronic dismay.

"Touch me and see where these scissors go next!" I screamed, my voice grinding like an angry demon scratching at a door.

Utterly dejected, Warp plopped down in his chair and pulled his headband over his eyes. "Ice cold, brew," he mumbled. I yanked the net free and ran down the hall with it held high over my head. As I rounded the corner to the editor's room, I saw a new body occupying my chair, already working robotically and contributing to the black hole of chatter. I had intended to take my Sports Channel bag home with me but realized I never carried anything in it, anyway, negating the sole purpose of a bag. So, I left it behind with the rest of the hazy unreality of whatever it was I had failed to accomplish in my time there.

4.

The wrong footage debacle was an accidental grand slam hole-in-one for The Sports Channel. Word spread like gangrene, and sports fans tuned in en masse hoping to catch some nearly subliminal mix-ups. The Sports Channel senior management team rushed head-first through the short-lived window of opportunity and cranked out their own bloopers recap show with the botched footage: *Game Changers*, executive produced by onceagain newly promoted Warp Dewhitty. It was hosted by Buck Tarstick and Pete Pamselle, a dry-witted field reporter with a preternatural proclivity for esoteric sports statistics. The show compiled all that week's mishaps while Buck and Pete provided deadpan play-by-play. Viewers were encouraged to call in and vote for their favorite, awarding the selection with the *Game Changers* ultimate seal of approval, "Bloops, That's on Us!" It was an instant hit. By my own negligent duncery, I had increased The Sports Channel's viewership by an untold factor, which felt akin to the channel giving itself a severance package for firing me. In a few weeks, the interns' cataloging mistakes dried up and everything went back to normal. *Game Changers* stayed on the air and, in addition to actual sports bloopers, began featuring Buck Tarstick's goofy pre-game interviews, where he asked players ridiculous questions like, "If you score more points than the other team tonight, do you think you'll stand a chance of winning?"

In a sadistic invitation to my own pity party, I stuck a flyer for the temp agency on my fridge. Every morning, I let the bleak reality sink in while I scoured the bitter wasteland inside for meager scraps of semi-edible material. The depleting food supply was like a timer counting down to doomsday. I imagined my life up to that point reversing back on itself, through the temp agency and school, back to the solitary stillness of my foster parents' house and my years of innocent TV obsession, only to loop back again and start once more from the same place.

I removed the final items from the fridge for what would have to pass for lunch: two warty, medium-sized pickles, one with week-old bologna wrapped around it. As I strained to swallow the final bite, I held my phone at arm's length and trembled as I dialed the agency. I took two deep breaths, blew a stale vinegar cloud, and pressed the phone to my ear. I heard nothing but the beat of my throbbing pulse. I looked at the buttons and mashed them wildly, slowing as I realized the phone had been disconnected without my notice. I had sold my car—an old sedan my foster parents had given me that they hadn't used in years and smelled like a crawlspace—for a sum that covered one month's rent and a bounty of bargain store food, but I hadn't accounted for monthly bills. I was lucky the lights were still on. I glanced overhead, assuming they were the next to go and would most likely black out while I was thinking about them.

After an uncharacteristically brief two-hour couch nap, I instinctively turned on my television. In the soft grip of waking amnesia, my thumb mistakenly pressed the channel number for The Indie instead of The Network. I grunted and waited for the static to load before I could switch channels again. A deafening shout caused me to jump and kick a stained cinder block propping up the tattered old door I sometimes referred to as a coffee table. I growled and squeezed my toe as I grabbed the remote and stabbed the down arrow on the volume button fast enough to numb my finger into an immediate cramp.

I leaned back and fully absorbed the shock of the harder blow: on the screen, a bony, bug-eyed service station attendant sprayed gasoline at a cherry-red sports car that looked like a giant toy. He shrieked variations of "You think you're tough?" and "Who's tough now?" The owner of the car jumped in and floored it, darting across the parking lot and abruptly squealing to a stop as his front bumper was nearly shredded by a garbage truck that had barely swerved in time to avoid a collision. Smoke poured out of the front tires of both vehicles. The driver rubbernecked side to side, throwing the car into reverse as the nozzle-wielding psycho chased as far as the hose would allow. The car peeled out backwards, hopping the curb and narrowly cutting off a minivan, before swerving and jumping a median. It lurched into drive and blasted off down the road. The shaky handheld camera swooshed to one side to catch the exhaust trail as the deranged worker ran into frame and yanked the nozzle forward for maximum distance. As he squeezed the handle, the hose stretched to its limit and yanked him back, twisting his feet comically up into air before he dropped flat on his back with a drizzle of gasoline showering his face.

I rose and placed my hands on the back of my head, eyes bulging dangerously, when I noticed the watermark in the lower-right corner of the screen: a grisly, jagged logo worthy of a death-metal band that read "Cliff's Edge." There was no questioning who would air something like what I had just seen, so my synapses fired chaotically to discern how he was doing it, settling on some sort of untraceable pirate signal the federal government was working round the clock to pinpoint and eradicate. The show's logo ruptured on screen with the shrill clank of a blacksmith's anvil: *So You Think You're Tough?* The end credit scroll consisted of a single line reading "Created by Cliff Montagna, whether you like it or not." Another episode immediately cranked up. Recoiling like a scared child, I turned it off and shot the remote at the screen in one flinching motion. I wiped my hands on my pants and went for a walk.

Instead of clearing my head, my sullen jerky-paced hike across town simply filled it with the unknown terror of what could possibly be worse than temping again. Going back to school? Returning to my foster parents' house and watching the same game show reruns? Playing hacky sack with Tom Geiger-Beef in hopes of snatching some scraps from his freelance table? I stopped short on a street corner as the answer hit me, forcing a large woman in an electric scooter to side-swipe my ankle and curse at me as she puttered away. I massaged my foot and considered the worst possible agony I could force myself through: crawling back to someone who had fired me and begging for a job. Since the Sports Channel termination was still a bit fresh, I opted to make a surprise appearance at The Network for a humiliating attempt at groveling and bootlicking, hoping at the very least I could be a contestant on their version of *Your Job in a Week.*

I sold my TV to buy a new dress shirt and tie, hoping they would distract from my two-inches-too-short thrift store pants. I took an early bus across town to get to The Network office before they opened but completely overestimated the length of the trip and waited forty minutes before anyone showed up to open the building. An expressionless custodian told me most people didn't show up for another hour but I could wait in the lobby if I promised not to root through the trash cans.

"You have a problem with that before?" I joked.

"Last guy asked me the same thing," he said curiously as he shoved off behind a hallway-wide mop that looked like a speared alien insect.

I sat for an eternity in the confoundingly beige lobby, then decided to stand, hoping it would ease the impression that I was the kind of person who had that kind of time to kill. I suddenly brimmed with worry over what to do with my hands; I hadn't thought to bring anything, even a tape of my showreel, so I panicked and snatched a magazine from the lobby table and curled it into my first, patting it against my leg. That probably made me look more anxious than I had hoped, so I started across the lobby to look for another prop, when I heard the revolving door whoosh open. I took a deep breath, forced a fake smile, and readied my hand for shaking, when around the corner walked Megan Brambles. She stopped still in her down-to-business makeup and power suit, neither confused nor surprised. "Buddy. Come up to my office."

"Your office?" I asked as I followed her to the elevator.

We got off at the fourth floor. Next to her door stood the custodian, propping his sweeper inside a closet and grabbing a wheeled bin full of supplies. When our eyes briefly met, I said, "Everything's still in the garbage cans. Feel free to check." His steely look told me my joke fell flat and that he may have even thought I had in fact rooted through the cans, now daring him to discover what was out of place.

Megan's office was barely wide enough for a small desk and two chairs. A large white wooden spool hung from the ceiling, cleverly utilized as a circular bookshelf to make up for the lack of floorspace. Through the center hung around an enormous antique light bulb. The desk surface was covered in perfectly stacked spreadsheet decks from DataScrute. I pointed toward them as I sat down. "Woah, now there's my personal nightmare. I wouldn't wish that on anyone. I wouldn't wish that on Arbie, partly because he'd screw it up."

Megan pulled a laptop from her bag and opened it atop the spreadsheets. She nodded off twice in the time it took her to do so. "But learning DataScrute did so much for me; it's the whole reason I'm here." She refiled a few index cards that had become stuck underneath the laptop lid, flipping a green one over to read the back again before nodding and straightening her stacks of cards.

"Seriously? You took a DataScrute position? I thought you wanted to do real work."

Megan's sunken cheeks looked horrifically angry for a moment, but then I realized she was just bracing against another quick eye-opener. She suddenly smiled and spread her hands over the DataScrute reports on her desk. "Well, of course, Buddy. Learning DataScrute has really made me valuable to them, and who knows where that will take me next." Megan went on to explain that Network Vice President and Chief Marketing Officer Breff Kholkers had in fact come looking for her. While making cold calls with her index cards and searching for a new job, Megan was workshopping new show ideas with Veena Chumbley, when she got a chance phone call from a senior Viewsful team leader looking for who had overseen DataScrute analytics at The Indie.

"Breff assumed we had brought in one of the Viewsful managers to run the queries and suggest programming decisions. He was shocked when he heard I had done all that myself, and that's why I'm here now." She merged two stacks of DataScrute gibberish and stored them in her bag, bringing out another stack of reports carpeted with multicolored index cards paperclipped to the sides. "They hired me to learn all the advanced

DataScrute functions, and now I offer powerful data-driven insights to the executives here—directly to Breff and Murk. It's great; they trust my suggestions for programming needs and new show concepts." Megan smiled, nodded off briefly, then smiled again.

"Cool, so I guess you might've found a backdoor into real work again," I said, timidly motioning to the thin line of drool trickling from the corner of her mouth.

She dabbed at it with a tissue and tucked it into a tiny garbage can at her feet, then gazed up in total panic at the overhead spool. I flinched, thinking it might fall, then heard her snoring. I read and reread the incomprehensible title of one DataScrute report until she came to.

"Oh, you'll love this," she said. "Arbie actually applied for a job here, maybe a year ago. He walked in smiling and waving—they hadn't responded to his application or offered to interview him. I can't imagine what he thought might happen." Megan picked up one stack of reports, started to file it away in the overhead spool shelf, but then put it down and selected a different one, fanning through the color-coded pages. "And yet I can't convince Veena to develop properties here full-time," she mumbled. "She's a natural but has to be her own boss." She grabbed some blank yellow index cards and a red pen.

Before I could make a plea for sympathy, Megan said, "Buddy, I'm sorry, I can't offer you a job." She looked at her calendar and wrote on an index card. "Seeing you dressed like that, I assume you're desperate for work, but all I can offer you is a routine pitch meeting. No promises, other than I promise to listen to your ideas for new programming until the allotted ten minutes have expired."

"That's a good idea, we should do that." I scratched the back of my head and tried for a sheepish expression, which she completely missed in a five-second blackout where her head tilted forward and clinked against the antique light bulb. "The thing is, though," I said, "I was hoping there would be some sort of low-level editing job to start with. I'm over-qualified, I know, but The Network seems to have so many shows. Don't they always need some lackeys to run tapes around and do simple rough cuts?"

She dropped the card and pressed the pen firmly on top, rolling it back and forth. "Buddy, it's all I have the power to do. Since you created *Your Job in a Week*—and I have DataScrute proof that it was successful over its original two-year run—that's enough to get you a pitch meeting. Here's a time and date." She glanced down, snored briefly, and buzzed her lips. "You might want to buy some new pants first."

She wrote down the meeting details as I rose to leave. "Oh, just the other day I came across Cliff's Edge," I said. "I guess he found a creative outlet aside from coming down here and shooting the place up for retribution."

Megan threw up a hand and snickered. "That's one way to look at it. Oh, and I've overheard some chatter about Network receiving threatening calls about copyright issues, and there's been a sudden increase in viewer complaints over the lack of decency in some programs. Doesn't take a genius to figure out who might be behind that, but I'm too busy to do anything about it. Plus, his attempts at being menacing and just kind of goofy." She exhaled softly and gently spun the spool shelf above her. The color-coded tabs on the edges of the spreadsheets and index cards whirled by in kaleidoscopic waves. She stared at the passing data rainbow, and her eyes seemed to sparkle before she briefly blacked out and gargled. She snapped awake long enough to wave goodbye, then coughed into her elbow.

I left the building already in anguish, knowing I would squander the next four days in a frenzy of anxious, sweaty hopelessness instead of actually trying to brainstorm new ideas.

In school, we were taught to always bring three ideas to a pitch meeting: two half-hearted ones likely to be shot down, and the third, the actual idea you're passionate about and committed to. I tore a flyer from a wholesale lumber company into tiny pieces because it had the most blank white space for writing notes. I scribbled furiously with five different pens before finding one with enough ink to write legibly. After brainstorming for two days, I couldn't tell which were the joke ideas and which were real. "A pile of money in a room," read one note. "A show where we combine exercise with karaoke singing, ha ha," read another. "People fight each other?" was crossed out. I couldn't remember why "Something about horses for girls" was underlined and circled. My supposed opus appeared to be "Sassy redhead waitress starts her own bakery." I sighed and decided to take a break, which regrettably turned into a deep thirteen-hour sleep. I awoke to the hammering insistence of the rational sliver of my brain telling me, "You counted wrong, dummy; the meeting was three days later, not four."

I bought a cheap pair of pants and my first ever necktie on the way to the pitch meeting. I luckily remembered to remove the tags as I pushed through The Network revolving door, with just enough time for the custodian to glance at me suspiciously while I struggled to get the brand name sticker off my finger and into a trash can. I smiled and shot him a thumbs-up. He folded his arms and stared me down until the elevator door closed.

Megan stood in the hall as the door opened and waved for me to follow. She stopped outside a closed door and, as she grabbed the handle, looked at me and raised her eyebrows. I checked my tie once more for any remaining stickers or tags, then nodded, and we went in.

"Everyone, this is Buddy Buppsen, creator of *Your Job in a Week*," Megan announced. She sat down at the head of an enormous table that nearly encompassed the entire conference room. I held up my hand to wave but had to use it to shield my eyes from the blinding white laser beam of light shining directly at me from a modern overhead chandelier in the shape of a regal swan. A few people clapped when Megan mentioned my show, but I was unable to mask my horror at the sheer number of bodies in the room. Twenty, thirty, forty I estimated before realizing Megan was politely gesturing for me to sit next to her. "Buddy has a few fresh ideas he'd like to share with us. Buddy?"

I gulped and fingered my shirt collar, realizing I hadn't washed it since I last saw Megan. "Hi, everyone. Thanks for your time." I fixed my nervous gaze at the far wall slightly above the sea of heads. "So, let's get right to it." I immediately forgot the order in which I had organized my ideas from worst to best, then wondered if I had picked up the wrong stack of notes.

"Ok, so I'm envisioning a scripted comedy about a sassy redheaded waitress named Barbara. She's tired of being put down by her boss and decides to strike out on her own. She opens a bakery where she calls the shots—*Strawberry Rude Barb's Pie.*" I bit my lip the moment I finished speaking. Hearing it out loud, I realized it may have been the worst idea I'd ever heard, from myself or otherwise. A flurry of synchronous discussion erupted.

"Animated or live action?"

"Is she a strawberry?"

"Could be funny."

"Could be terrible."

"Could be a hit. Or not."

"Is she a pie?"

"And her hostess sidekick Revenginger—the spice that fights back!"

"An animated strawberry or a live-action pie?"

"The fast-walkin', sass-talkin'—"

"—sly pie in thigh-highs?"

"So, she *is* a pie?"

The jabbering continued for a full minute, then abruptly stopped. Every face turned back toward me in unison. Megan elbowed me and wiggled her eyebrows.

"Ok. *Ahem.* Next, we have *What's The Holdup?*, a game show where contestants watch actual crime scene surveillance videos and try to guess—"

"Pass!" came a call from the end of the table. It was echoed on both sides.

I fidgeted and clutched my tie. "I…but it's not—"

"Pass!" roared the original voice with alarming force. I adjusted my collar, immediately regretting doing so as my wet fingers signified how drenched with sweat I had become. I looked to Megan; she nodded off with a strained grimace and throaty wheeze, then sat up with a pert mannequin smile.

"And finally," I began, hoping to sound excited but instead forcing it out on a dejected down-note, as if to say "finally I'm almost done," "a high-energy game show where we combine weight lifting and karaoke. Contestants attempt to complete a thirty-minute strength training routine while belting out hit songs. Points awarded for pitch accuracy and showmanship. Last one standing wins." I held my hands out and scanned the slowly nodding heads; they all stared silently as if waiting for me to finish. Megan gathered her spreadsheets and index cards and opened the door for me.

I turned to wave goodbye as she whisked me through the door and down the hallway. "Well, they actually discussed the first idea, and that doesn't always happen," she said.

"So, they liked that one?" I said, looking at my twisted, damp tie.

"When they get so worked up they forget they're in a pitch meeting, that sometimes means they might move forward with the idea. No promises, though." She patted her DataScrute spreadsheets, suggesting the data's potential approval held more sway over ideas that got greenlit.

"Why'd the holdup idea get shot down so quickly? They didn't even react to the last one. I don't even know if I meant to pitch any of those ideas," I said. "All the bad ones seemed good yesterday, or the good ones seemed bad. I don't know anymore."

"Who knows, but it's normal for most pitches." We stopped outside Megan's office, and she stood in front of the door, glancing in to check the time. "I understand—it's intimidating. But I promised I would listen for ten minutes, and you have three remaining. What other ideas do you have? I can run them through DataScrute now if you want." She walked in and sat down. I leaned against the door jamb and lazily picked at the wall.

She sorted two stacks of index cards and glared up at me. "Buddy, come on. That's it?" she said. "Where's that spark that led to *Your Job in a Week*?"

"I think it fizzled out with the reality of how much work it was."

"So, you want a job, but you don't want to work? There's your scripted comedy right there."

"No," I said and slowly punched the wall. "I worked myself crazy until I didn't care about the work anymore, and then I had nothing to show for it: no job and no material worth putting on a showreel. Of course I want to work, it's just hard to find the right..." I trailed off and stared at a small metal Viewsful paperweight on her desk in the shape of a dodecahedron. Its vertices connected to a single point in the center, a small sphere with the letter V repeated around it. I imagined it spinning, glowing, and sucking up the data from the reports, carrying it off into the sun to be incinerated.

Megan sat back with her hands on the data pile. She held up a finger, then sorted through a drawer and pulled out a gray index card. "Ok," she said and cleared her throat. "This is a creative thought exercise. Try to put yourself in the same frame of mind as when you last had a good idea you liked. Where did it come from—a place of joy, or fear, or excitement, or pride? Were you sitting or standing? Were you hungry or had you just eaten?" She spoke gently and went on like a teacher explaining to a hurt child that not everyone wants to be your friend. She put the card away, then slumped face-first on her desk for a full minute, eyes open the whole time. She suddenly sat up and grinned; her eyes were ringed with tiny red dots and squiggles. "Maybe you should try to relax when you get home tonight and search your inner self for the motivation that led you to *Your Job in a Week*. That might help." She shrugged, blinking her eyes rapidly.

I covered my face with my hands to keep from shouting the truth: the idea only came from routine juvenile anger. I hated working monotonous temp jobs surrounded by incompetent zombies; I hated the people who showed up and did nothing and still got paid; but mostly, I was terrified by the alarming potential for being cornered into accepting a mediocre life like those people had: used up, worn down, and finally ignored like broken pencils in the back of a drawer.

I shuffled down the hall. "Well, thanks for your time, Megan. I'll throw myself out." I expected her to call my name sympathetically, but as the elevator door closed, I saw her frantically thumbing through spreadsheets and marking them up with a pen.

I loosened my tie and snarled at the back of the custodian's head as I stomped through the lobby. Pushing through the front door, I ran chest first into Chibbs Ticonderoga, beaming in an expensive tailored suit. He stutter-stepped back and nearly lost his turtle shell briefcase in the revolving door.

"Buddy!" He cocked back for a high five, but I folded my fists together and shook them at him.

"Fishin' what's-his-name. Of course, you landed a job here! This vengeful universe has something to prove, and I'm so stupid, it has to keep pounding me into the ground until I get it. Here, rip out my rib cage and pluck it like a thumb piano while my innards gush out." I undid my necktie and launched it at him; it barely made half the distance between us and limply flopped to the ground.

"Buddy, look, man," Chibbs said. "The Sports Channel shook things up again, and basically the rest of middle management got the ax. I'm in the same spot as you. I mean, you saw how tense things were, and look at what they did to me: I had to break the news about no raises to my whole team, then a week later, they made me terminate twenty of them. And my only reward for that was getting laid off in the next round."

Chibbs's genuine play for sympathy completely enraged me. "Oh man, that's terrible. Yeah brew, I so feel for you." I pushed my fists into my cheeks in dramatic glumness. "It's so awful the way you were able to make so much more money than me and work on lots of cool stuff that you could put on your showreel to help keep you employable. Yeah, totally, brew, we are definitely in exactly the same boat, except mine is full of holes and never left the harbor."

Chibbs held his briefcase behind him with both hands. "So, I'm supposed to feel bad about being good at my job? *Pfft*. Sounds like you. You know what? You should start a show where you have real people get fired from their jobs because you're a bitter insignificant nobody who can't stand to share the world with regular people. Oh wait! You already did that!"

I picked up my tie and wound it around my knuckles, feeling the circulation slow. "Chibbs, you should put all these motivational speeches in a book, and then set fire to the book while you're writing it and let your house burn down while you sit there writing your awesome motivational book."

Chibbs backed toward the revolving door, slowing it with one hand. "Sounds like a plan. Maybe the first chapter will be about how I pitched programming ideas to Network and became a successful showrunner while all the inconsequential trolls whose names I forgot died alone in pools of their own salty tears." He winked and clicked his tongue, spinning cleanly into the revolving door. I grabbed the end of my tie to throw it again but only over-tightened it into a knot around my hand, squishing my fingers into a tiny purple claw. I growled and bullwhipped the tie against an enormous potted shrub as I marched away.

.....

At some point, I decided it was best to condense my daily food budget into a single meal. If I could fight the morning hunger pangs with a black tar dose of caffeine and spin around my apartment warbling nonsense to keep my mind distracted while watching game shows, I could slowly eat a larger meal at midday and coast through the evening, drinking plenty of tap water to feel full. It's difficult to accurately account for how long this period lasted; the funny thing about hysteria is your mind automatically fills in the inconsistent gaps to fashion a stable reality. The worse it gets, the less you notice, and in that context, it might be true to say it's good Cliff found me when he did.

I barely registered a knock at the door during a mid-morning wall-stare space out. I was drooling on the cover of an old magazine, letting the spit trail circle a celebrity's face while I chuckled dopily. I smiled at the perfect bullseye, congratulating my effort with a shaky thumbs-up, then went to the door. I had never seen a look of honest concern on Cliff's face before, and in the moment, it was hilarious. His eyebrows clenched together in a V of massive uncertainty. He reached out and gently pushed me backwards. I giggled and teetered back to front like an inflatable punching bag, but then overcorrected into a neutral stance and stumbled back a few steps. I took out a lamp as I flailed around. Cliff stepped in, closed the door, and picked me up by my shirt front, ripping the already torn collar until it hung threadbare. He held me close and gazed deeply; noticing the drool spanning the hole in my shirt, he dropped me and wiped his hands on his black jeans.

"You seriously still live here? Phone's disconnected, dummy." He walked around the room and kicked over anything that wasn't already spilled on the floor. "I'd say you look worse than ever, but that would imply you ever looked better than terrible, which is an outright lie and if you're calling me a liar, I'll torch this place right here and now."

"There's drool and crumbs everywhere; I don't know which is worse," said Todd Gherkin, who seemed to have materialized beside me. He hoisted me up by my armpits and pressed me to the wall, then rhythmically tapped my face with the bill of his ball cap like a bird pecking at the ground.

"Todd, hi. Glad you could make it. Come on in, have a seat." I rocked back, bouncing my foot against the wall until he grabbed my shoulders. "Have you heard from Cliff?" I asked. "I feel like I just saw him." My eyes darted to one side, then my head sluggishly spun in the same direction. "Don't look now," I whispered, "but I think he's been here the whole time."

"Look, Buddy," Cliff snarled. "I'll murder you if you say no, and I'll probably murder you if you say yes, so what's the real choice you're mulling over—how quickly you want to get it over with?"

"Say no? Cliff, brew, I have no I do...you have no idea...I have no ideas. I have no more ideas." My head sank. I grasped and released the air like a magician releasing doves, looking up as they scattered skyward. "I have no idea what you're talking on about."

"Told you he blacked out," Todd said as he snapped his fingers by my ear and pinched my cheek.

"Todd, hi," I said. "Glad you could make it. Come on in, have a seat."

Cliff spun me around and slapped my face with the drool-circled magazine. "Idiot, I just offered you a...Oh, please kill me now. How could it possibly have come to this? Did you hear anything I said?" Cliff steadied the magazine in front of my nose until I stopped wobbling and focused on it.

"Hey, Cliff. Come on in, have a seat."

It was three months before I fully recovered from my sequestered dementia. Once I could routinely keep down ordinary portions of food throughout the day, I was able to stitch together my fragmented recollections into a linear coherence. After the Indie implosion, Cliff furiously rampaged in every direction, first trying to sue The Network, then Arbie, then the lawyers who represented The Network. Unfortunately, Cliff only learned what Megan had tried to tell us—that all content produced by The Indie fell under the domain of public ownership, the legal property of local citizens whether they ever watched it or had even heard of it. Cliff asked himself, "Who would bother creating anything original for a bunk deal like that?" He realized the answer was probably nobody, meaning the grant money was likely still up for grabs, as well as the empty channel space that once broadcast The Independent. Because he had paid for The Indie's digital signal upgrade himself, he outright owned the new broadcast antenna and, utilizing his own trio of computers with editing software, only needed to purchase a master control switch board to broadcast content over the air. Cliff easily secured the government grant money to do just that. "It was less complicated to legally obtain the airwave rights than to break into The Indie and steal everything and burn the building down and salt the earth to cleanse whatever malevolent hoodoo hullabaloo Arbie invited to that place," he said.

Cliff set up a small corporation and placed all the grant money into its account. He maintained a meticulous ledger for how the money was spent, mostly by paying Todd to produce public service projects and local-interest documentaries for the daytime hours. All other shows were registered under his own personal copyright and designated as "rebroadcasts" in the station ledger as a quasi-legitimate means of validating the ownership of his content. The grant money also covered the lease of a locale in which to situate the broadcast antenna, a squalid half-demolished industrial building across the creek and down the hill from The Town Commoner. I had always assumed the site was infested with squatters, if not groundhog-worshipping cult members. Cliff occupied the ground floor and basement, as the upper three floors were decimated through the middle with the corners still raised in defiant peaks, like devil horns rising before the apocalypse. The unwitting local government had granted Cliff an unencumbered five-year dominion for the channel he christened Cliff's Edge, an innocuous public access channel that by night morphed into a powerhouse exhibition of demonic pleasures.

Cliff saw the Sports Channel wrong footage bloopers and loved their subtle subversiveness. When he found out I worked there, he assumed I had done it all intentionally. He tried to contact me about working together to bring down the whole channel from the inside, but apparently my phone was disconnected while I still worked there, meaning even when I had the money to cover the phone bill, I still didn't remember to pay it. Cliff later discovered I had lost my job and knew I'd be desperate for work, unwilling to decline any offer he could make me. He propped me up at one of the Cliff's Edge computer stations and had me ingest tapes for him and Todd to edit; I only stumbled home when I was told to leave. My fourth media industry job had me working essentially the same position for less pay and longer hours. Looking back up the ridge from Cliff's Edge and seeing The Town Commoner always shook me with a fairy tale horror, like I had slipped into the dark forest that parents warned their children about, magically barred from returning to my former reality whose once-detailed remembrances were quietly fading.

In the late afternoon, Cliff would sneak in with a box full of new tapes and spill them over my head as I worked, like the celebratory showering of a coach after winning a big game. After a few cloudy weeks of twelve-hour days engulfed in ingesting and cataloging swaths of preposterously reprehensible footage, a great deal of which had yet to be packaged into actual shows like *So You Think You're Tough?*, he allowed me start on rough cuts for his live music program *Shut Up and Listen!* Local bands from every stratum of talent and preparedness performed live-to-tape in "Cliff's Cellar," the leaky exposed-wire basement of the half-demolished building.

The most entertaining act by far was Snake Karma, a two-man psycho thrash punk group featuring a perpetually sweaty and barefoot weirdo named Randy Rain. His wispy sorcerer's beard and rat tail seemed to flick around according to their own rules of physics and air resistance as he flailed about during songs. He rarely came close enough to the microphone for any lyrics to be made discernible as his face contorted into a look of colon-cramping agony. In one episode, Randy Rain punched a hole in the wall with the head of his guitar during the song "Nobody Wants to See You With Your Shirt Off." What lyrics I could make out went something like:

Walkin' your dog / Mowin' your lawn
Put a shirt on
Bikin' to work / Don't be a jerk
Put on a shirt

He attempted to continue singing six feet from the microphone as he angrily writhed around kicking at the wall in hilarious futility. The drummer threw up his hands, tossed his sticks at Randy, and kicked over a crash cymbal as he stormed off. Randy screamed and cursed as he pummeled the wall with his forehead, managing to hammer out bits of sheetrock and streak his face with a fine white powder.

"Oh man, this guy," Todd said in a rare daytime sighting as he stacked some tapes into towers on my desk, blocking my view of the hallway. "Third time they've played on the show, but that's the fourth drummer he's had, if that makes any sense."

Randy finally removed his guitar from the wall, but then smashed it into three pieces on the cement floor, wrapped the dangling strings around his neck, and pretended to asphyxiate himself. He reached off-screen, picked up a barely functioning guitar, and plugged it in. With the old guitar still suspended from his neck, he crooned childishly:

Everything I do is wrong
Ba dum dum
I can't even finish this...
Tuuuuuuune

He then smashed that guitar as well, spending an inordinate amount of time ensuring each piece was as thoroughly smashed as possible. Once finished, he kicked the pieces to one side and thrust an album cover at the camera, saying, "All them songs and then some gonna be on our upcoming full-length release, called *This Album Contains No Mitsakes.*" The camera held focus briefly before he tossed the cover aside; the album was upside-down and from a different band entirely.

From behind the camera, Cliff screamed, "Told you, you couldn't peddle your junk on my show, Randy! Just play your asinine rubbish and get out!" to which Randy casually retorted, "Randy don't care." He snorted and hocked a discolored glob of something awful past the camera before it cut to black. Cliff insisted that I let every performance for *Shut Up and Listen!* play out in its entirety. "The rapport I have with these hopelessly unprofessional idiots is half the fun," he said, "so leave it all in, or I'll kill you in your sleep. But you have too much work to do, so if I catch you sleeping, I'll kill you anyway."

The show frequently featured a once semi-famous blues musician named Howlin' Jowls. Even considering the man's frail agedness and local notoriety, Cliff pulled no punches, hurling insults while he played. At the beginning of one tape, Mr. Jowls slowly shuffled across the cellar with his guitar strapped to his back. As he reached a folding chair in the center, Cliff shouted, "*Today*, grandpa. You're so close to the grave, anyway; what's a few more steps?" Jowls slumped over the microphone and sat down to adjust it. He slung his ancient guitar forward and, as if he were completely alone, quietly played the touching unrequited love song "You Are the Flaming Trash Barrel to My Cold Hobo Hands." He sang:

I traded my coat for some pickled beets
Now I'm lonely and cold, wanderin' the streets

Cliff moaned, "Borrrrrrring! Gah, just kill yourself already." Nothing phased Jowls. When he finished the song, he wiped the accumulated slobber from the side of his slack mouth with a red handkerchief and heaved the guitar onto his back by deftly yanking the strap down. He whispered into the microphone, "Thank you so much. I'll see y'all next week." He ambled away, dragging his worn loafers across the dusty cement.

"Here's what you should do someday, if you ever actually develop some skills," Cliff said as we watched my first draft of an episode with Howlin' Jowls. "I want you to airbrush out the studio around him and put the entrance to a cave back there, so it looks like he comes out of hibernation to play his songs and then goes back in there to sleep. Or we'll film some gravediggers in a cemetery and superimpose them around Jowls, so it looks like his reanimated corpse crawls up out of the ground after they bury him just so he can torment the people he left behind with his terrible songs. What a rotten tub of entrails that guy is."

Working on the music show was a welcome palate cleanser to the footage Cliff had me ingesting for his other programs. The vicious name-calling, threat-shouting, and fight-picking essence of *So You Think You're Tough?* was tame compared to the raw footage of burglaries, arsons, explosions, and other atrocities I tried to ignore while combing through tapes whose origins were completely obscured from me. I seldom saw Todd, who I considered the legitimate side of the business. He worked tireless hours six days a week, expertly producing shimmery daytime shlock. He landed a modest sponsorship from Pure&Purer for an elder-care line of shampoos and skin creams. Their commercials ran on Cliff's Edge during a fluffy lunchtime variety show with the pandering name *Well I Just Think That's Great!* Its shrill unseen narrator was most certainly Cliff's voice pitch-shifted up to that of an intensely delighted old woman, gleefully commenting on footage of sunsets, dogs playing in parks, and families going for walks in leafy suburban neighborhoods.

In the never-ending ingest pile, I would sometimes come across unlabeled tapes featuring a camera operator hiding out-of-sight at public events and launching firecrackers into the crowds. He would scream like he had been seriously injured as people scattered. Regrettably, the footage did make me laugh out loud once, when an older man in a dark aquarium shrieked like an infant and ran nose-first into the glass wall of a shark tank, then screamed again and fled in the opposite direction, doubling over into a waist-high cylindrical pool full of circling manta rays.

"I'm thinking about anchoring a new show with these clips and calling it *Here Come the Fireworks* or *Head's Up, Dummy*," Cliff told me. "Or maybe not using it at all. People usually don't get hurt, so it's kinda boring." When I asked where the footage came from, Cliff responded with what became his go-to reaction to any questions about his sources: he growled like a dog and chewed his arm as if restraining himself, then backed out of the room.

Cliff spent several hours each week calling in voice-altered complaints to The Network, condemning the wanton perversions in their programming. He specifically targeted the lewd innuendo in *ManDates* and *Zero's Sum*, the fundamental inappropriateness of *Your Job in a Week*, and the outright barbarism of *What Makes You Think You're So Special?* He argued that certain commercial breaks were "unethical" because the products advertised didn't appeal to him, meaning many viewers might also feel unjustly left out. His frustration was obviously rooted in having his old properties wrested away from him and receiving no credit, but since he was now running his own station and creating new programming, I couldn't understand why he wasn't willing to let it go.

"Maybe if you ever created something better than worthless, you'd understand," he told me through mouthfuls of breakfast burrito as a clip of the firecracker bandit tossing M-80s from a gas station roof played on a loop behind him. "They stole everything from me, and they can't get away with that. I don't care who they are; what's mine is mine."

"It's still public domain, though," I said. "If everybody owns the shows, it's like *nobody* owns the shows, so you could legally do your own version of those shows, too. Their new version of *Your Job in a Week* feels more like a corny game show, anyway, so I could even—"

"Nah, I've moved on," Cliff said without a trace of irony, using his teeth to remove every glop of melted cheese from a foil wrapper before balling it up and tossing it over his shoulder. "We're doing our own thing, and it's completely ours. Next time, if they want to steal any of it, they'll have to pay up or die. Plus, we've got the secret weapon."

He pointed to the computer in his office that auto-refreshed every minute with DataScrute reports for every show currently airing on The Network. It also displayed intermittent reports on viewer habits and offered algorithmic suggestions for the creation of new shows based on other successful properties. I falsely assumed Cliff's devious proficiencies included high-level computer hacking, but the answer was far simpler. When we worked at The Indie, Megan Brambles had shared her Viewsful username and password with us in case we needed to run DataScrute reports. She still used the same login at Network, allowing Cliff easy access to every analytic report she ran in the program. "Touch that computer, and I'll kill you," Cliff warned. "But since I've told you about it, I'll probably have to kill you anyway, so let's go ahead and pencil in some face time for that." He picked up a pencil nub and tapped the outdated calendar on his wall.

For months, the late-night lineup on Cliff's Edge was *So You Think You're Tough?*, *Shut Up and Listen!*, *Heads Up, Dummy*, and *Over the Edge*, a potpourri program showcasing all manner of illicit behavior but mostly teenagers using aerosol cans to start fires. Even with four shows airing new episodes regularly, we had hundreds of hours of unaired footage stockpiled in a video vault looking for a home. One evening, after combing through two tapes of literal ambulance chasing, I searched for Cliff in the half-demolished building before creeping down to the basement, pursuing a trail of faint, ghostly echoes. I closed my eyes in the frantic hope that it was only Cliff and not something worse. "Hey, I have a stupid idea for some of this unused footage," I called across the dim cellar.

"Mm-hmm, and the only thing stupider is you thinking I'm gonna stand here and listen to it," Cliff said, chucking empty pizza boxes down a three-foot-wide brick-trimmed hole in the middle of the basement floor. One box had half a slice left; he curled it up and ate it in two bites. The empty boxes landed seconds later with a dull *whoosh*.

I kicked at a rock lodged in the muddy cement floor. "Some of that footage we have is really insane, but then some is just people running around with cameras in the dark. So, I'm thinking, let's splice some of the bad with the good and call it *Looking For Trouble*. If we cut it right, it'll look like one continuous story. Imagine some first-person footage of punks running the streets—shaky, lots of jump cuts—and it builds up to one of the abandoned house fires from a different tape. Then we pad the ending with a few minutes of them driving away or graffiti-tagging stuff. It'll give it a verité feel and really freak people out, I think."

Cliff launched stacks of unopened mail into the hole. "Why are you standing here talking about it instead of just doing it, you idiot?" The envelopes fluttered softly into the darkness, plunking into a puddle I hoped to never see. "Does your contract say you get paid for talking gibberish instead of working?"

"Contract?" I asked, shaking my head. "Look, I just thought...Ok, sure, you know what? I'm on it." I shouldered an enormous load of damp magazines, crammed them into the hole and stomped them down with my heel. "And after that, maybe we can send Randy Rain down to the bottom of this pit for a new concert special—*Snake Karma: Live from the Center of the Earth*."

"Now you're talkin'!" Cliff shouted. He walked off and kicked a brick loose from a sagging window sill.

.....

Cliff demanded "something shocking" for the *Looking For Trouble* intro sequence. I sat an old camera on a creaky wheelchair I had fished out of the creek and tied its handle to a wall anchor in the basement, leaving a few feet of slack. I pushed record and wheeled the camera slowly toward the hole in the floor until the chair tipped, dropping the camera down. I filmed the move at a high frame rate, so I could start slow and ramp the speed up as the chair surged forward, accelerating into a sudden drop. As I hoisted the camera back up, I winced, expecting an infestation of germs and debris to come along with it, but only found a blind beetle-like insect clinging intently to the lens. Its feelers tapped the outer ring in a steady double-time rhythm.

"Give you five bucks if you eat that." Cliff held out the money and wiped his nose on his shoulder, smearing coarse dust and mucus across the seam of his shirt. I shook the camera vigorously to no avail, finally having to pry the bug off with a tree limb that had blown in through a broken window during a storm. The bug scuttled off in a tight zigzag and climbed back down the hole.

We used a worn-down crowbar to carve a rudimentary *Looking For Trouble* logo into the cracked black asphalt behind the building. At dusk, we launched clear balloons full of watery raspberry jam at the logo with the camera hanging overhead. In the finished shot, the dark ground bursts alive and red like a ruptured blood vessel. Cutting to the logo after the rushing wheelchair shot gave it the morbid quality of someone running head-first into the basement pit and splattering gruesomely on the ground as the logo appeared. The intro ends on a black screen with stark white text in colossal frame-filling font reading "WE DARE YOU TO WATCH THIS SHOW."

The *Looking For Trouble* pilot episode contains one of my proudest editing hoaxes and established the approach for future installments. The first three minutes follow a group of teenagers on the prowl in a mostly deserted inner-city neighborhood as they casually toss bricks and bottles through windows, cursing and lighting fire to anything that will catch. The tempo of the jump cuts steadily increases as a booming heartbeat sound effect pulses faster and louder. When the camera operator grabs a makeshift fire bomb to hurl at a boarded-up bungalow, the episode cuts to a different tape where an enormous fire consumes an entire city block. The footage is sped up and treated to appear darker, shakier, and grainier. It's accompanied by the sounds of horrific screaming from a third unlabeled tape, a recording of an amateur theater production of some sort of staged cult ritual. The end effect is that of a horrifying explosion caused by a savage group of young anarchists who subsequently flee and avoid apprehension.

In the original footage of the gang, a hunched and lanky older man emerges from behind a hedge and wallops the camera operator with an aluminum walking stick. He tears the bottle bomb from his crony's hand before he can throw it and complains about children needing to be raised correctly, bemoaning his lack of hope for future generations. The suddenly infantile teens scatter like dust in a tornado, scared out of their underdeveloped wits. The footage of the fire is really the viewpoint of a camera attached to a man's bicycle helmet as he tours a completely different part of the city during a later-contained four-story factory fire from the summer before. The episode ends on a slow zoom of the shimmering flames but cuts before the fire department extinguishes the blaze. With a little editing magic, it was simple to refashion contexts and suggest our city was constantly under attack from unimaginable urban terrors.

The pilot aired after a particularly great new episode of *Shut Up and Listen!* that introduces Power Cream & Jive, a twenty-member funk band—including a horn section, two tambourine players and six backup dancers—all in matching purple sequins jumpsuits. The band barely fit into Cliff's Cellar; the drummer teeters on a square of plywood balanced over the hole in the basement floor. Given a ten-minute slot to play a customary three or four songs, the band opts for a single song: "Improve the Groove," a never-ending dancefloor burner built on inane tropes like:

Don't lose the groove
Improve the groove
Be real smooth
Improve the groove
Let's get loose
Improve the groove
You've got to move
Improve the groove

When a perpetually smiling and impossibly petite dancer launches into a flying somersault, the drummer ducks to provide clearance. This offsets his balance enough to tilt the plywood riser into a slow slide off its axis. The drummer bangs the crash cymbals furiously to get the attention of the singers, but his pounding only seems to suggest they sing louder and dance harder, which they do until the entire drum set collapses in shambles behind them. The band catches on and stops playing; one singer whimpers a falsetto "improve the groove" and finally looks behind him. He jumps back when one of the blind beetle-bugs scurries angrily across the floor and into the pit underneath the fallen drummer. Since Cliff doesn't scream insults at them while they perform, I assumed he had set up the unstable plywood ploy for his own amusement.

The episode abruptly shifts gears with the inclusion of Thimble Skins, a dementedly mellow folk singer. His tweed vest and wingtip shoes evoke a university professor at open mic night. Gently fingerpicking a battered acoustic guitar, he softly sings tunes from his new album *Songs About Violence for Kids.* The song "Retribution" begins:

When you are down, and you don't know what to do
Because your dear friend was untrue
Make them pay for what they've done to you
And it wouldn't hurt to harm their families, too

The catchy refrain goes something like:

Retribution, retribution
When you've had more than you can stand
You'll feel so much better when you take
The law into your hands
Retribution, retribution
Vengeance tastes so sweet
You'll reach Zen only when
Your foes lay at your feet

In placid detachment, Thimble Skins gingerly sings two more songs that suggest children seek out and hurt people they don't like. He stands up from his stool, picks up a flat patchwork cap he had been sitting on, and wriggles it onto his head. As he walks off, it becomes apparent he's wearing a gray wig and convincing fake mustache, which led me to believe he was another of Cliff's puzzling jokes I couldn't understand or prove.

The episode concludes with a supremely classic Snake Karma breakdown. Wearing an amateurishly screen-printed shirt reading "SNAKE KARMA IS REAL!" Randy Rain sets up a cheap drum machine on a stool in the back of the cellar. He presses various buttons on the machine while shaking his head and murmuring for the first two minutes of his set. Finally, the tinny drum beat kicks in, which he immediately pauses, whispering, "Easy, sister." He straps three cheap guitars over his chest like bandoliers and bumps the microphone teeth-first as he says, "This here song's called 'Horse Onomatopoeia,' and I done wrote it to go like this." As the cheap drum machine taps out a shrill one-two march, he gallops in place, whipping the top guitar like driving reins. He shrieks wildly into the microphone:

Starts like a squeal, ends like a snort
Reee hurner, reee hurner, reee hurner, REEEEE!

He repeats the lines and flaps his lips with increasing intensity for five minutes, then the drum machine skips a beat and throws him off. He grips the neck of his guitar and hammers the machine off the stool. "Can't even *buy* a decent drummer these days!" he growls as he slings the topmost strap off his shoulder and tosses the guitar. He cranks the volume on the next guitar as he drops it in front of his amplifier, producing an ear-splitting, pulsing noise loop. With the third guitar, he pounds the neck into the amp and strums ferociously over the feedback swell, screaming, "Horse onomatopoeia!" over and over until his voice is nearly shot. Finally debilitated by the flood of sweat stinging his eyes, Randy heaves the last guitar onto the mess of broken equipment, grabs the handle of the amplifier, and topples it over as the feedback crescendos and eases into a high-pitched whine. He yanks the microphone from its stand and sits on the amp, panting.

"Look, now here's the part where I got to tell you folks 'bout my new enterprise. Phew. So, everbody knows you get hungry on the road and you don't always have healthy options what to pick from. You ain't got to be in a band to know all that; it's pretty near obvious if you think about it. So, I aim to fix that, and here goes." Randy checks each of his jean pockets, bewildered, until he finally removes a speckled plastic-wrapped bar that looks like it's been dug out of the ground. "You heard it here first, folks. This here's Randy Rain's Righteous Rockin' Roadies. It's one of them organic superfood deals everbody's been talkin' 'bout, and I'm tellin' you, it's the real deal." He bites down hard on the side of the bar and manages to wrench off a small piece. "It's got kale, oats, maybe some chia, dates or somethin'," he says out of one side of his mouth as he chews laboriously, his eyes swelling with sparkly tears. "So, come on down—"

The camera suddenly shifts to one side as Cliff's shoulder appears in the corner of the frame. "I thought I warned you," he roars, his voice reverberating monstrously between the cellar walls.

Randy twists an elastic hair tie into the lower half of his beard and stands up straight. "I keep on tellin' you, Randy don't care."

"What did I tell you last time? What have I told you *every* time? You try to sell anything on my show, and you're done, you backwoods bonehead!"

"Hey, fatty—come and get some," Randy says calmly, under-handing the bar directly into Cliff's chin. The camera topples over as Cliff thunders past. The episode ends on a sideways shot of their feet scuffling side to side as they wrestle pathetically, their distorted shouts and warnings providing the end credits soundtrack. Randy performed on *Shut Up and Listen!* every week after that and always tried to sell something.

I created a new episode of *Looking For Trouble* every other day with no end in sight thanks to our continually amassing footage repository. We hoarded the episodes and rolled them out weekly to continuously up the ante and keep viewers interested. Cliff berated me less frequently, as it seemed the show was catching on with male viewers in its 11 p.m. slot. Since we had no DataScrute numbers of our own to analyze, Cliff simply made estimates from the Network datasets he pilfered through Megan's account. He assumed any dip in Network numbers meant our shows were stealing viewers in those time slots. Network's high budget primetime programming saw viewership numbers unattainable by Cliff's Edge, but their pitiable late-night programs never performed well, mostly because the shows were simply repackaged daytime content with an edgier host and different commercials. Network's lack of interest in late-night viewers granted Cliff's Edge a sizable sandbox for building fresh and disturbing properties.

"Network may have sponsors and shareholders to worry about," I said to Cliff and Todd as we ate midnight breakfast burritos in the basement and pored over that week's DataScrute numbers, "but it's senseless to keep doubling down on weak programming in the late hours instead of actually producing something with more bite to it."

"Speaking of bite," Cliff said, tearing into a second burrito and wiping his greasy fingers on my shirt, "how about you concentrate on eating that burrito, so your mouth stops making stupid words fly out of it."

I rolled my eyes and took a bite. "All I'm saying is—"

"A bunch of worthless prattle, and I already told you to stop it." Cliff flattened his burrito wrapper across a dented snare drum, a remnant of the abandoned Power Cream and Jive drum set, and tightly rolled the remainder of the burrito, tucking sausage bits back inside. "All that matters is Network is ignoring an obvious void and we're filling it, so we win. I'm not interested in primetime, and they're free to produce any daytime crock of schlock they want. All that useless drivel being lapped up by those glossy-eyed morons in their antiseptic living rooms. It makes me want to swallow my own tongue and shove sharp objects into my eyes and do the same for everyone else in the world to spare them from the humiliation of living in a reality where that passes as entertainment. Now shut up and eat that and stop talking and shut up." He reached for my burrito as if to take it, but then smashed it against my chest as I turned away from him. I held out my shirt, wiped the dried eggs into my palm, and tossed them in my mouth.

"Big talk coming from a guy whose most popular show wasn't even his idea," I said and tossed the foil wrapper at him.

"Finally, the puppet fights back!" Cliff clapped, sticking his foot out to trip me as I walked past. I caught myself on the snare drum and pantomimed an epic slow-motion collapse, twisting and knocking over everything in sight, the effect of which was greatly enhanced by a falling crash cymbal.

Todd slowly balled up his wrapper and chewed the last bite of his burrito. "So, you don't care about any of the daytime programs I've made here," he said flatly. "You only keep me around to legitimize this dump. I guess I knew that already, but on some level, I thought..."

Cliff sat up and tapped a finger on the snare head. "Woah, woah, woah. Do I pay you to whine like a little baby with an ear infection, or do I pay you to create programming? Regardless of your answer, your head's about to hurt real bad."

"That makes me like...the cleaning lady, or something. Is that the way you see it?" Todd said. "That I just take out the trash and do chores?" He repeatedly squeezed the balled-up wrapper under his thumb like a malfunctioning detonator. "I do all my own scheduling, shooting, editing. It's like at least half the business here. Did you even know my documentary piece on the teacher's union was up for an award last year?" Todd asked.

Cliff glared at Todd, picking at his fingernails. "Sounds like it didn't win, so maybe it's best to let it go and stop living in the past, Todd."

"And a Network headhunter called me up. I had met her at the awards banquet, she was really nice." Todd stared at the floor and sounded like he was hallucinating. "She asked me if I'd like to work there. I told her I'm happy where I am."

"Well, apparently, that was a lie, so maybe you should watch out before you lie your way into an early grave." Cliff folded his arms, scanning each edge of the low basement ceiling like he was checking for bugs. I sat quietly and daydreamed about winning money on a game show.

Todd stood up and lobbed the wrapper in a high-arching hook shot across the basement as he walked toward the concrete stairs that jutted out irregularly like crooked teeth. After we heard the front door squeal shut, Cliff screamed, "Good talk, Todd! See you on Monday!" then turned to me and said quietly, almost earnestly, "It is what it is." He flung a cymbal across the room, and it stuck in a small, damp door that couldn't be opened because of its rusted antique handle. Cliff bit his bottom lip viciously, frothing and hissing. "Buddy, there's a new scripted comedy on Network that's been killing the past few weeks." He jiggled his wrist and looked at his watch. "The late-night repeat's about to start. Crank up that screen, and let's see what the fuss is all about." I wiped my hands on my shirt and knelt to switch on a TV that sat atop a bulging stack of moldy phone books.

The screen flashed to life just as the *Two Dudes and Another Dude* logo faded, sucker-punching me with the words "Created by Chibbs Ticonderoga." My jaw churned in figure eights as the characters Brody, Cody, and Jody were introduced in a painfully commonplace opening sequence under the pounding beat of some insipid beer-commercial jock rock. I wriggled my tongue against my teeth as if to remove a bad taste.

"Wait, isn't that your buddy from the sports place? Right, *Buddy*? Hahaha!" Cliff picked up a cymbal and doodled his fingers across it, then tossed it in my lap. "If you were mature enough to have feelings, I bet they'd be hurt right now!"

"We go back farther than that," I said woozily. "Went to school together. He helped me get that job at The Commoner way back when."

"The job where you made groundhog documentaries and played with Tom Goober-Booger's hacky sack? Yeah, you really owe him your life for that one. Have you made Chibbs executor of your estate yet?" He leaned over and grabbed the cymbal from my lap, put in on my head, and spun the rim. I jumped up and hurled the cymbal at the monitor. It unsatisfyingly did not explode in a death bomb of manifested anger but simply stopped the cymbal with a futile *clink*.

"Why does he always get everything?" I croaked.

"Chibbs? He's probably more talented than you, and by probably, I mean absolutely without question."

"Every cool job opportunity is automatically set aside for Chibbs." I stood and held my hands behind my head like a prisoner being led to a firing squad. "You expect your friends to look out for you, but man…not in this business."

"Well, it would probably be different if you actually had skills or friends or weren't a total genetic mishap."

I grabbed the cymbal I had thrown and squeezed both sides to break it in half but only succeeded in scratching red lines into my palms. I blindly hurled it across the basement, where it hopped twice, rolled up the base of an avalanche of debris, spun a full rotation, then clunked to the floor, and tossed up a sprinkle of dust.

I watched the entire episode of *Two Dudes and Another Dude* in a bent-neck standing position, producing a steady muscle spasm in my shoulder that matched my shallow breathing. The show was banal but not terrible. Chibbs had obviously based the characters' dialogue on the brew crowd from The Sports Channel, which I found funny, but it also stung a bit. When the episode ended, I rocked the monitor onto its back with my foot and stomped the power button. "Anyone could've written that," I said. "Who cares, I'm going home."

"Have a nice sulk!" Cliff shouted, and drum-rolled his hands on the snare table.

.....

After a few months of steadily winning viewers in the late-night hours and feeling the initial tingles of a sense of accomplishment, Cliff and I were paid an unanticipated visit from a hapless Viewsful salesperson. He somehow looked even younger, twitchier, and less confident than the reps we had met at The Indie. His starched plaid shirt exuded "ventriloquist dummy" more than "respectable employee."

"My boss watches your channel like...religiously, and he thinks you could really…you know, like…benefit, you know? From using our DataScrute solutions package," he said, spreading his arms and holding out a business card Cliff refused to acknowledge as he barred the doorway.

"Your boss?" Cliff said. "Is that what you call the negligent babysitter who turned their back while you escaped?" The rep nodded and continued his pitch.

"So, with the…uh, you know, size of your station here…Well…" He swallowed and folded his hands. "DataScrute is the leading aggregator of trends and analytics. With our robust family of services, you too can stay ahead of this relentlessly demanding business we call the future. Now, imagine yourself—"

Cliff turned to me. "Woah, it's like the co-pilot took over during an emergency situation. Did you see that? He's an entirely different person." Cliff snatched the business card from the rep's hand and snapped it between his fingers, shooting it into the kid's neck. The card slid down his open shirt collar. "Hey, doofus. Where's the other guy I was just pretending to listen to?"

"With a small upfront investment, your returns will be immediate and abundant," he continued, unphased as he wriggled around and pinched the front of his shirt so the card could fall out. I picked it up before Cliff could tear it up in front of him.

"Thanks," I said. "We're familiar with DataScrute, but it doesn't fit our budgets right now."

"Stop pandering to this infant." Cliff tapped his finger against the kid's bony concave chest. "Don't want it, don't need it. I do things my own way here, and I don't need advice from some omniscient data monster."

"And now with deeper InsEYEghts from the finely tuned AnalEYEzer," the rep continued, "customers in broadcast are given specific actionable recommendations for future programming. Imagine having the data to support an idea before you've even had the idea! Fruitless hours wasted brainstorming are a thing of the past when you can auto-fill your weekly schedule with hot new properties developed by the AdvEYEser, DataScrute's robust ideation tool that gives you the power to create the next generation of groundbreaking programming with the push of a button."

Cliff rolled his eyes, put his arm around the rep, and walked him toward the street. At the first corner, he picked up a cardboard box, shoved it over the kid's head, and rattled both sides rapidly, screaming, "Viewsless!" The kid tilted the box back and offered us an information packet. Cliff stomped back to the door, shouldering me to one side. I thumbed the business card and looked at the rep. Because the Indie's low-end version of DataScrute only included its core services, I had never considered using the software as a means of developing new properties. I wondered if DataScrute could help me determine what to do with the extraordinary reservoir of footage we had barely tapped.

I went to the address on the Viewsful business card hoping to get a feel for the cost of their services before Cliff could completely shut out the possibility of using DataScrute's advanced features. A warm and polite office manager named Tuliah greeted me at the door and seemed genuinely impressed when I told her I worked at Cliff's Edge. "Oh, John will be so excited to meet you. Let me give him a buzz," she said and insisted on making me a cappuccino while we waited for him to finish a teleconference with international clients.

Tuliah asked a few softball questions about how much fun it must be to work in the entertainment industry, to which I chuckled and said, "Eh, it's a job." I nearly choked on the scalding coffee when I instantly recognized the dopey face that drifted into the lobby like the world's happiest hot air balloon.

"Wow, Buddy! Hey, you remember me, right? John Klemchky. I was on your show once." He shook my hand vigorously with both of his and grinned like a child at a presidential photo op. My lips fluttered but made no sound. "Buddy, look, let me tell you something, and this might not sound true, but I assure you, I'm being one-hundred percent honest with you: getting fired from Bladoodle was one of the best things that ever happened to me. Seriously." He stood up straight and inhaled deeply, resting his hands on his hips. Through a half-frosted pane behind him, I could see a few employees plugging away energetically at computer terminals and phone stations while others played hacky sack and ping-pong. "When I totally botched that brake pad project, I went home and beat my head against the wall. Not literally, but almost literally," he said, giggling and lightly slapping my forearm. "But I was really disappointed that I hadn't come up with a solution. You remember the brake pad thickness sensors and all that, right? It haunted me. Really haunted me. I couldn't pull together any two coherent thoughts and focus on it. My mind works like that; too many deep wells of thought to pull buckets out of, and I have no control over where my interests lead me from day to day."

He pulled a sympathetic face and bit his lip. "Well, after that I visited some friends at a similar company, you know, shamelessly begging for work. I ran the brake pad idea by them, and we got to work on a solution, but—and here's the beautiful thing—we didn't come any closer, but we devised a whole new application for those sensors: brake lights that change color depending on how hard the brakes are hit. You know?" He shook his head like a manic toy on a spring. I tried to sip my drink but only succeeded in raising and lowering the mug a few times as I tried to keep up with him.

"Think about it—you're on the interstate in stop-and-go traffic, the person in front of you keeps tapping the brakes, tapping the brakes, tapping the brakes, then suddenly *boom*! They slam on the brakes to avoid a collision. Now, how can you tell when to hit the brakes harder in a situation like that?" I scanned the room, trying to correlate whatever impulse had brought me there to whatever he was talking about. "Yellow for a soft tap, red for a normal decelerate-to-stop, shocking pink for a hard slam. Done." He wiped his hands, then held one up and gave himself a high-five.

"Yeah, John. I mean, that's…that's good, man." I once again tried to sip the drink, burning my tongue and dribbling a bit onto my chin.

"Thanks, Buddy. No, seriously—thanks. Bladoodle wasn't a good fit for me, and I was languishing from not being challenged in the right way. *Your Job in a Week* did wonders for me—really. It freed me up to pursue the deeper concepts I'm more passionate about. Like this! It led me to this!" He motioned around the office and giggled. I saw the Viewsful logo on the wall behind Tuliah and realized it had been updated since my days at The Indie. The W in Viewsful sat cleverly in the center of a dodecahedron. I coughed, and my head spun as I noticed the enormous overhead lighting array in the same shape.

"I bought Viewsful! Well, so, my friends and I on the brake light project started a company with the tech we created, and things moved really fast, and I was getting left behind. I'm not business-oriented, I'm idea-oriented, you know? So, I let them buy me out. It was for the best, and we all agreed on that. Well, I've always been fascinated by numbers and how data can move and connect in so many ways, like drawing lines between points in space, forming three-dimensional shapes that never stop morphing. And geometry, right? It's a reflection of the cosmic balance, the underlying structure and spirit of the universe." He looked at the lighting array above us and described its shape with mystically wavering hands. "Well, I was watching a show one night and during a commercial break thought to myself, 'Who knows I'm watching this? Do they know if I'm enjoying it? Do they know if I've changed the channel?' Think about all those data points and how they can...*harmonize* to form detailed models of consumer behavior. I put feelers out to some industry friends to see if they were interested in pursuing data aggregation and analysis. Turns out Viewsful was already on it, so I used my buyout cash to buy *them* out, you know?"

I shook my head, then nodded, then shrugged and took another lip-scorching sip. I thought to myself, "So you still don't really *do* anything," but instead said, "What a crazy story. That's insane, you know?"

John nodded eagerly and placed a hand on my shoulder. I gritted my teeth and fought the instinct to brush it off. He squeezed lightly, smoothed out my shirt, and tapped my chin. "Speaking of idea people... What kind of groundbreaking TV madness have you gotten yourself into lately?" He spoke into his fist like a microphone. "He revolutionized the modern workplace with *Your Job in a Week*, changing the course of human history, and now..." He held the fist-mic toward me; I couldn't help but lean in.

"Well, uh...for the past year...two years? I don't...Uh, I've been working at Cliff's Edge—"

"I knew it!" he bellowed and clapped his hands, spinning in a circle with one leg raised. "I watch that channel religiously. It's all so well done, and I had this great idea while watching the firecracker show."

"*Heads Up, Dummy*," I said mechanically.

"It's all fake, right? Staged? Well, that was only my gut reaction: if this were real, nobody would watch it, right? Except, what if there were some people who would still watch it? Every viewer has distinct tastes, but popular shows shoot for the area where those tastes overlap, right?

Smartographer—that's the new software we're running full-steam ahead with right now. You know, like 'cartographer,' except it's mapping viewer trends and habits, you know? You'll love this, I just know it."

Tuliah handed him a stapled stack of marketing material. He flipped through a few pages, then held up a section too close for my eyes to focus on. "Each viewer is shown like a three-dimensional object full of points—like the planet's geodetic datum, you know? And we see how those points connect to each other in various ways and match up to form a profile of likes, dislikes, and potentials for both." He tapped an illustration I couldn't quite make out, then handed the papers back to Tuliah. "Plug a Smartographer map into the DataScrute AdvEYEser, and you get reliable suggestions for new programming. Run those through the AnalEYEzer, and you can see what level of viewership numbers to expect before the show has even been created. I know, I know; idea people like us don't need that kind of help, but for all the non-creative people out there, it's going…to…change…everything." He smacked the marketing booklet and held it out to me.

"Yeah, John, you know..." I glanced at the ecstatic television viewers on the cover of the booklet who were high-fiving under a subliminally faint dodecahedron. "Honestly…" I hadn't had an original idea since *Your Job in a Week*, and the notion of begging for ideas from a person I had lampooned on TV for having none of his own was beyond ironic and pathetic. "We had a rep of yours come by the other day, and it got me thinking…" I said, nodding and flashing a contemplative face at the marketing deck.

"Thinking—yes! That's always a good thing, right?" He elbowed my ribs and clicked his heels. I thought I should leave before he started dancing.

"I'm definitely going to look into this. I'll run it by Cliff."

"Wait, there's actually a Cliff? Who knew?"

"Well, John, it's been, uh, great talking to you."

He nodded solemnly and placed both hands on my shoulders. "Buddy, from one idea man to another: I could use more people like you here, and the door's always open. Always." John flicked his wrist and conjured a business card like a cheap magician. I took it and immediately felt nauseous. As I left, he clapped my back and shouted, "It's all data, Buddy! Throw a lasso around it and make your own shapes!"

Cliff immediately noticed the Viewsful marketing booklet I stupidly held in plain sight as I walked in. I didn't even remember John handing it to me and felt he'd somehow conveyed it there through telekinesis simply to embarrass me. Cliff grabbed it, fanned through the pages, then rolled it up and stabbed it into my heart.

"Buppsen, seriously? That's so pitiful. You're admitting you're terrible at coming up with ideas, so you're stepping aside to let the robots create them for you?"

I snatched the pages and tore a few off, throwing them at his chest, where they fluttered limply and slid down. "Are you kidding me? Ideas? Where are yours? You had to bring me in here because you're all out of ideas, too. The only original idea you ever had was *What Makes You Think You're So Special?*, but wait a minute—that idea wasn't even yours! You stole it from Arbie's friend in that pitch meeting."

"Prove it. And even if you could prove it, shut up and die. Just because a great idea bubbled up out of some idiot's subconscious doesn't mean he ever would've had the guts to use it. So, who really had the idea there?"

Face to face, we panted like greyhounds watching the rabbit escape through a tunnel. Cliff firmly yanked the marketing booklet from my hand and began shredding the pages into strips. "Numbers. Data. Projections. Statistics. None of that pseudoscientific hokum matters if you know your material is good. We have no sponsors to appease, no shareholders to massage, no feet to kiss. We are completely unrestricted, unrestrained, and totally, one-hundred percent liberated. When will you ever have this opportunity again? If you want to make visual baloney for the daytime crowd, be my guest, but I have a distinct feeling you won't be happy."

"Cliff—"

"Shut up and listen. See, there's an idea I had!" He pinched my cheek and jiggled it side-to-side. I swatted his hand away. "I confirmed my gut feeling about the viewership of our shows by peeking at some Network numbers. That's all we needed, so we're officially done with numbers." He tore one strip into tiny pieces and blew them into my face like a magic powder. "That stash of footage we have downstairs is waiting for you to mold into whatever slaps the audience in the face hardest. If you're not here to do that, then who are you and why are you on my property and you should get out of here before I call the cops."

The increased tension between us encroached on my editing decisions. Every episode I touched came out angrier and grimier, ultimately untethered from any semblance of decency. I collected every shot I could find of people getting punched in the face for a "very special" episode of *Looking For Trouble.* The pace of the cuts increases over the first few minutes until an explosive symphony of repeated smacks, jabs, and howls are all timed up to a lightning fast industrial metal soundtrack. In new episodes of *Heads Up, Dummy,* chaotic but unrelated footage of explosions and panic suggest the firecracker fiend is a nefarious supervillain bedeviling a hopeless city. I assembled a *Shut Up and Listen!* best-of collection called *Shut Up and Watch This!* that solely consists of Randy Rain being injured, ridiculed, and spit on by Cliff and Snake Karma's assorted drummers. It closes with the final shot from a performance where Randy plays so hard and loud that an enormous chunk of plaster falls from the ceiling and knocks him out cold.

Cliff's scattershot animosity began its acceleration into fever pitch when he saw the name of a new show listed in Network's upcoming DataScrute forecast: *Cruisin' For Losers,* scheduled in a Friday late-night time slot in direct competition with *So You Think You're Tough?* We watched two minutes of doofy teenagers lazily driving a convertible through a suburban neighborhood while hurling insults, slurs, and glass bottles at passers-by. Cliff kicked over the television and screamed with the power of a jet engine at peak propulsion, outraged by the familiarity of the premise. He quietly shut off the computer that collected the DataScrute feeds and hauled it into the basement. A moment later, I heard a muffled crash as it met its end at the bottom of the pit.

"They think they can rip me off again," he said as he huffed to the top of the stairs.

"Well yeah, think about it," I said "They have the same information we did, so they saw the late-night gap and finally decided to fill it."

"They think they can rip me off again." He leaned against a door frame and clawed out chunks of moldy drywall.

"You ripped off someone at The Indie and then turned around and ripped yourself off with your current show, so what's the big deal? What makes you think you're so tough or special or whatever you want to call it?"

Cliff tore a strip of soggy wood out of a window sill and launched it at me. "People like those shows the way I make them. Anything else is a cheap imitation."

"Oh yeah? Prove it," I said, mocking his whiny tone. "If it's all so cut and dry—sue them."

The intensity of his devilish grin momentarily collapsed my lungs and corkscrewed them into my stomach. "Buddy, you good-for-nothing glob of membranes in a skin wrap," he said. "As always, I'm way ahead of you."

.....

I lumbered up to my apartment one evening and broke into an immediate sweat when I saw a note taped to my door. In a flash, I thought my foster parents had come to their senses and cut me off, ending my lease without telling me because I easily could afford my own place and rightfully owed them for the years of rent they shouldn't have paid. But the note was just a yellow index card covered in Megan Brambles' cramped handwriting.

Hi, Buddy. Is your phone disconnected? I wanted to let you know one of the ideas you pitched came up again during a recent thinktank (brainstorming session), and some producers here are excited about the new property they're developing from it. The weightlifting and karaoke game show idea—they're calling it Rockin' Jockaoke with Smokey Bluenote. *"Smokey" is a new stage persona of someone you may know: Buck Tarstick from The Sports*

Channel. It's more of a sleazy lounge singer character than anyone you would find at a gym, but the data supported it.

A large ink glob told me she had passed out there momentarily.

Anyhow, Buck recently re-negotiated his Sports Channel contract in an effort to expand his "worldwide personal brand"—his words—and he does odd jobs with Network now. We're trying to find a good fit. Thought I should let you know!

The dot of the exclamation point trailed across the page. I imagined Megan nodding off and headbutting the note when she was done, like stamping a wax seal.

My guts stewed and sizzled and sank and swam. Network wanted my idea. I didn't know what to do first: break the news of my resignation to Cliff or buy some respectable clothes for my new position at Network. I didn't think much about the lack of detail in Megan's note, and I reacted in my customary fashion of making uninformed decisions first and asking questions later.

Against all logic, I decided to have a sit-down with Cliff to smooth out my transition, fully aware that a calm and sober version of that scene was excluded from the realm of rational possibilities. I worked a few late nights to stay ahead of the scheduling curve, hopefully presenting the work as a peace offering. As I put the finishing touches on an episode of *Heads Up, Dummy* where the unseen firecracker fanatic launches bottle rockets into the open doors of friendly neighbors handing out candy on Halloween, Cliff stormed into the editing room, yanked the computer monitor's power cable from the outlet, and barked in my face. "Who does Todd think he is? Were you in on it? Don't you lie to me! Do you actually think you'll get away with it? You're *mine*!" He punctuated each insinuation by slamming his hands on my keyboard.

I feigned confusion at the suddenly non-working computer and swiveled around to face Cliff. "Oh hey, Cliff. What seems to be the problem?" I picked up the power cable with an "ah, there it is!" expression and plugged it back in.

Cliff reared back and cracked his knuckles. "Buppsen, you get one chance and one chance only to come clean with me. If I find out you lied to me, you're done."

I tapped the keyboard as the screen hummed back to life. "Look, whatever your deal is with Todd—I mean, I rarely saw him, so how could I possibly know more about what he's up to than you? Plus—"

"Todd works at Network now. Tell me you didn't know that."

The genuine shock on my face said more than any words could have. He hoisted me up by my shirt collar and snorted. His labored breath was a heinous mingling of salty nachos, eggs, and stale pizza. "Ok. Let's say I believe you. Either way, Todd's a traitor, and he's dead to us. Big deal; happens all the time." He slid his pudgy hands across my desk and blew a fog of dust against the wall. "With you, I thought ahead. You were the one I was iffy about, but I should've covered my bases with Todd, too. When people think they can push me down and walk all over my back, that's when I roll over with both guns blazing." He dropped a stapled stack of notarized papers in front of me and spun it around. "Here's a friendly reminder that your contract stipulates a two-year non-compete clause if you ever leave here, which you won't *because no one else wants you.*"

I was afraid to touch the pages, feeble and bewildered. "What contract?"

"The one you signed when I found you patrolling the grounds of your decaying apartment crypt like a pasty thin-skinned zombie. If you think for a second that you can quit on me or steal my ideas, you are sorely mistaken, and I will see you in court. If you aren't one-hundred-percent committed to my vision, then you should get out of this business for good and rot in a cubicle while you stare at spreadsheets and dream about Casual Friday." He slid the contract closer to me and tapped it. "You can keep this copy." I could clearly make out my signature scrawled across multiple pages; I simply accepted the situation as he presented it. He stomped out of the room, knocking me to one side with his swinging hips. After three sweaty minutes of staring at my screen without recalling what I had been working on, I called Megan from the editing room phone and told her I was coming right over. I hung up before she could respond.

Megan sat on a bench outside Network's revolving door where indistinguishable power-suiters spun through and greeted each other in generic platitudes. She held up a finger as I approached and thumbed through a few DataScrute spreadsheets before reordering them into a tidy stack, then patted the bench for me to sit next to her. "Buddy, I understand if you're upset—"

"You have no idea, but if he thinks he can force me against my will, just because of a contract—"

"What contract? Nobody is forcing you to do anything. You have plenty of options at this point, but in my opinion, litigation might not be—"

"Nah, I'm not interested in suing him. I want to move on and put all this behind me. I'm ready to start—"

"Him who? I think if you're willing to play it their way for now—"

"Who's they? I'm talking about Cliff. Look, I doubt whatever lawyer he uses—if he even actually has one—I doubt he stands a chance against the team Network must have for mediating contract disputes. I mean, megastars renege on stuff all the time, so it can't be that hard—"

"Whose contract?"

"Mine! What are you—"

"But you haven't signed anything with us, Buddy."

"Sure. Got it. I'll sign whatever whenever. Just hand me a pen."

"But they haven't offered you anything."

"You're right, you're right. Let's hash out the details first. Do they want to pay me out for the one idea? I was hoping I could upgrade that into a full-time position. But look, I'll do anything at this point—edit, write, produce, ingest footage all day—anything. This thing with Cliff, it might not be a big deal—"

"What thing with Cliff? Buddy, they haven't offered you anything. That is to say, they're *not* offering you anything."

"But then, what," I said, finally taking a breath and feeling jittery from an unwanted adrenaline rush flooding my body. "But you said...What was that note for if you weren't telling me...Look, you said they greenlit my idea—what else could you have meant by that? They want to work with me in some capacity, right? Have I gone completely insane?"

Megan folded her arms over the stack of datasets as if to restrain herself. She retrieved a black index card she had been hiding under the printouts and read like a forlorn cyborg lamenting its last human friend who died ages ago in the apocalypse. "It was a misguided courtesy, Buddy. I thought it might help your morale to know they greenlit an idea that sounds considerably similar to something you pitched once. Since you didn't ask them to sign a non-disclosure agreement before the meeting, and since so many ideas are similar to ideas from other sources anyway, it can be very difficult to know for sure, much less prove, where each inspiration originated."

I shook my head furiously and jumped up, tugging at my hair as blood blitzed my cheeks. "No, no, no, no, no. You and I both know…I mean, that's completely absurd to suggest…Why did you even bother to tell me?"

Megan closed her eyes and breathed deeply. She tucked her hair behind her ears and slowly drug her hands down the sides of her face. "I can probably get you a development credit on the show, but I'd be putting my reputation on the line for something that seems kind of frivolous. Meaning, it won't help you get a job here, not to mention there would be no money involved. But if it's that important to you..."

"Thanks, I really needed some words of encouragement. Those will do just fine; the meter's full now." I kicked the cement planter by the bench and squeezed my fists, imagining the shrubs being completely shredded and scattered in a swift eruption. "It's not that I think you owe me anything, but this feels malicious, and I've done nothing to deserve it."

Megan clenched her index cards and fanned them for so long, I couldn't tell if she had blacked out again. "You left that meeting so broken down," she said. "I thought you might want to hear they came around to the idea and found value in it, and that, even though it didn't work out for you this time, I hoped it might give you a boost of confidence and motivate you to work on some more ideas, to help you get back to where you were when you created *Your Job in a Week.*"

I scratched my ear just to feel something. "Maybe you should stick to your monotonous spreadsheets and leave the psych evaluations to all the doctors and kindergarten teachers who are obviously far more qualified in the field of human emotions. All you do is work; you don't know people at all."

Megan flipped over the black index card and read the last two lines. "Buddy, I promise I meant it as a courtesy. Please don't feel like you have to burn bridges in order to move on."

"You brought the matches and gasoline and pointed out which bridge to burn, and now you're telling me I shouldn't burn bridges?!" I leaned back and uppercut a shrub, scratching my knuckles and stripping a trivial quantity of leaves before I darted across the street like a petulant child.

5.

After an agonizing bus ride home during which I tallied the abundant litany of my past failures, I stood firm and held on to my integrity for about five whole minutes before I relinquished it all together and called John Klemchky from a payphone to accept without reservation whatever menial, humiliating position he saw fit to toss me into. He giddily insisted I come to his office immediately so that we could "get started on forging the future's future right now." I went inside and foraged under my creaky sofa for enough change to ride the bus back across town. I brought along my Cliff's Edge contract so I could give it a closer look than the half-hearted perusal I had started and stopped numerous times, but instead hurled it into a wire garbage can at the bus stop after straining to understand the same intentionally impenetrable lawyer-speak bloating every legal document in existence. Cliff was welcome to waste his time trying to reclaim whatever paltry compensation I had acquired from Cliff's Edge. I had no resolve and nowhere else to go.

Walking into Viewsful, I covertly sniffed my arms to determine if the source of a phantom odor was my body or the bus. Tuliah surprised me with a firm hug, somehow professional in its duration and closeness, and told me it was good to see me again so soon. "Buddy, you'll love it here," she said. "Everyone does. Everyone loves being a Viewsie." My eyes nervously darted around the lobby in hopes of locking in on some sure sign of repulsiveness that could facilitate an abrupt departure for reasons of principle or pride, but there were none and I had none. All I found was a comfortable interior exuding serenity and optimism, worthy of a magazine cover.

"We don't exactly have a staffing department," Tuliah told me as she opened a drawer containing various corporate information pamphlets. "John likes for everyone to feel free to be their own boss and do things their way without any, you know, typical oversight. But I'm happy to answer any questions you may have. Here you go." She handed me two thin brochures on company benefits and organizational practices. "They're really short, but read those at your leisure. John cares more about the work than the management side of things, so you'll have plenty of time—"

The main office door swung in and thudded against the wall as John pranced through, pumping his elbows and chanting my name. The demented contortion of his face was a mix of childlike glee and cannibalistic satiation. He leaned back on his heels at an impossible angle with both hands stretched over his head. Luckily, I guessed he was readying himself for a full-body high-five and was able to meet him halfway without getting knocked down. "Buddy! We're going to do great things together. Great things! I've got chills. Are you ready? Ready to live the life of a Viewsie?" He pretended to hold onto his belt buckle and square danced in place, knees thrusting high from side to side.

"Uh...Yeah, you know it."

"Of course, I know it!" He stretched back and double-fived me again, then Tuliah as well. I forced a tense smile and nodded, inhaling heavily through my nose and still detecting a trace of the phantom odor from the bus.

"Buddy, there are world-changing ideas exploding all over this cerebral drafting table of mine. Gears are spinning and wheels are turning and pieces are coming together and the future is ours!" He lunged back and tucked one arm behind him, quarterback style. I hesitated and did the same, following his lead as we slow-motion high-fived and mouthed silent screams. He finally clapped and dispelled the pageantry. "Let's get to work!"

I followed John to a cozy, quiet glass-enclosed office down the hall. He turned a dial I had assumed was a thermostat, and the walls became an opaque white. I expected to receive hands-on training in how to waste time and avoid responsibility, but instead was barraged with a diverging stream-of-consciousness diatribe on unrelated topics like mercury levels in swordfish, envisioning hyperspheres in five-dimensional space, the evolutionary purpose of bilateral symmetry in snake scales, and how the pleasure of imagining a future purchase usually eclipses the actual owning of the item. John eventually plopped down in a retro-futurist egg-shaped chair and wheezed sleepily. He grabbed a few DataScrute reports from a small orange shelf and arranged them in a grid on a desk, which otherwise held a small computer, a single permanent marker, and a pad of unlined paper.

"Look, this is the next step: I want to revolutionize television. I want to change everything, and you're my guy on the inside." He winked; I tried not to cringe. "You've created hit shows and you know all the ins and outs and angles and sides and vertices and contours, so I trust you to chart the best course for connecting all these dots."

"Uh, which dots are those?"

"Exactly. Exactly!" he howled. "Where to begin, right? Viewer habits, product placement, ad space...There are so many points of entry, and we'll have to weave a huge mesh of data sets, find the overlap, and drill down past the abstractions into something concrete, something revolutionary."

I nodded slowly. "Well, since Network uses DataScrute, can't you peek into their accounts and get ideas from that? Find what viewers might like and which gaps to fill with new programming?"

John stood up straight with his arms folded, his eyes expanding to a perfect roundness. "I'm not interested in what Network or anyone else is doing. That presupposes a bias that isn't entirely justified. Just because viewers watch certain programming doesn't mean it's what they actually *want* to be watching—what they would prefer to watch if given the choice. It's only the illusion of choice anyway, and I want to change that. I want to tap into their brains and syphon out all their preferences, so we can serve them exactly the type of experience they're craving. We have all sorts of data to play with here at Viewsful, and I'm sure you can make something radical out of it."

"Sure, I'm on board with that," I said without meaning it or even knowing what he was referring to.

"Oh, before I forget." He picked up a permanent marker and wrote on the back of a business card. "I always forget this. It's the first thing most people are concerned with, but the last thing I ever think about. I need to change that." He held up the card to show me what he had written.

"What's that? A date? A lottery number? What is that?"

"Buddy, it's…you know." He bent one ear to his shoulder and pulsed his neck up and down. "You know, it's…I need to know…if this will work for you, you know." He slid his thumb back and forth across his fingers.

My eyes narrowed, then blasted open. "Sa—" I gulped and leaned in. "That's my salary? Is that over ten years or for the rest of my natural life? Who do you want me to kill?"

John leaned his head back and lifted a limp hand to his chest. "Ok, that's a load off. I've heard salaries in your field can get pretty crazy, so I wanted to make sure it was competitive. So, that'll work for you? No problems there?"

"Problems? Yeah, I'm worried my bank will assume I stole it from another bank."

John smiled and held his hands behind him. "Good. So that's one less thing to worry about while we forge ahead and kick the future into high gear." He overestimated my cognitive abilities; I tuned out the next ten minutes of his pseudo-philosophical onslaught and daydreamed about the practical reality of being able to pay my rent on time.

"Think you'll be happy here?" John spun the egg chair in a circle and motioned around the room.

"Well, the work seems...interesting enough. I'm still trying to wrap my head around—"

"No, no, no, of course, I *know* you'll be happy working at Viewsful. What I meant was, your office. Is this space ok for you?" With a hand on my lower back he guided me to the chair and sat me down.

I glanced around with my tongue hanging out as my neck and shoulders relaxed naturally, easing into the exceptional comfort of the egg chair. "Seriously? I assumed this was your space."

"Oh, I don't have an office—keeps me on my toes!" John threw his head back and barked. He spun me around to the datasets and tapped each one like he was playing a song. "Look, no pressure. I know ideas take time to gestate, and I have no firm expectations for the first year, other than you think about this stuff—all these wild pursuits my departments have thrown themselves into. Something substantial will start to emerge. Patterns, trends, waves, dimensions; there's a lot to absorb, and I know these things take time."

I sunk deeper into the chair and could feel my heart rate slow to a reasonable pace for the first time in my career. "Sounds good. But where should I start?"

"Totally up to you. I mean that. Let your mind go wild with innovation." John turned to leave and looked at his watch. "I'm sure I'm late for a meeting somewhere. See you around, Buddy."

During my first month, the other forty or so Viewsies each came by my office to introduce themselves. They comprised a diverse mix of backgrounds, industries, and lifestyles, but each seemed satisfied with the types of projects to which they devoted their time. Through them, I learned that DataScrute software sales and licensing deals brought in more than enough money for John to run other departments at a loss, allowing for exploration into any field they found interesting with no care for profits or results. This setup made for eager, happy employees who spent their days diving into their passions without typical work-related stress or strain.

Each group had an official title but were usually referred to in a military-sounding shorthand, like the Division of Communication, a team of eight psycholinguistic researchers everyone called DivComm. They often sat in a semicircle watching short television loops and shouting out the first word that came to mind. They sometimes chanted a single word in unison with their eyes closed in such mindless repetition that the word often naturally morphed into a different one entirely. Their freeform studies touched on language, philosophy, and neuroscience, largely focusing on speech patterns and rhyme schemes that most piqued alpha brain waves.

DivComm had earlier won John Klemchky's eternal gratitude with *Animal Sounds on Human Grounds*, a scholarly article published in a major linguistic journal that legitimized the department's ongoing research as well as John's indiscriminate interests. The impetus for the research paper was John's sudden appearance in a DivComm rhyming-word-chant-together to ask, "How do you spell the sound a dolphin makes?"

Unperturbed at being interrupted, one researcher responded, "Which sound? The click, the squeak, the moan, or the trill?"

"And do you mean to spell it with the standard alphabet or the phonetic alphabet?" called another. After a long stare-down, John simply said, "Huh," and left the room. A few days later, he returned with a video crew and some high-speed cameras to record extreme close-ups of team members pronouncing the human language equivalent of the accepted, standard animal noises for thirty different species. He then sent the crew to several zoological research and conservation facilities to record animals making those same sounds to determine if watching the animals' muscles and jaws move in slow motion could assist in determining how humans could more accurately recreate those sounds with their closest approximate mouth parts. The paper highlighted discoveries like cows no longer voicing a simplified "moo," but instead a "prolonged rounded vowel accentuated by the constricting of the abdomen to produce a deeper bellow, often culminating in a brief guttural lilt." As with most research papers, I could hardly understand why a team of geniuses would focus so intently on something so esoteric and specific, but many linguistic journals treasured the findings and lavished awards and accolades on the DivComm team.

The Consumer Tendencies department studied and analyzed all the DataScrute information aggregated by media clients, which was, by contractual default, shared with Viewsful. When combined with mobile phone data, GPS tracking, and retail transactions, the team could mostly determine which television shows and experiences successfully led customers to the purchases they made. One of the team's researchers, a constantly giddy giant with telescope-lens bifocals named Clinch Dehavers, would regularly rush into my office in a state of asthmatic excitement attempting to explain their progressing research into manipulating the brain's "default mode network," some sort of system that runs the show when a person is idling and daydreaming. ConTen's investigations into mood alteration included subjecting test participants to various colors, images, phrases, and sounds to achieve a desired response. Clinch's explanations were as indiscernible as a magic spell in a dead language; to me, the research just sounded like the study of cult indoctrination and mind control. Our chats usually ended with me saying, "Wow, that sounds great!" despite whether I could understand anything he'd said. Clinch would puff up his chest, hook his thumbs under his armpits as if wearing suspenders, and parade triumphantly out of the office.

To appear busy, I often stopped by "The Forum" to check in on Brian Vohangliss's team of ethics and standards debaters called The Bureau of Conduct, or BuCon. One afternoon, I ate an entire bag of popcorn while listening to two team members trade impassioned counterpoints on the morality of barring classes of people from cultural experiences they usually ignored.

"If this identified group of people—poor education, high unemployment, little chance for upward movement—if they aren't interested in these experiences in the first place, why bother pretending this whole branch of culture is actually available to them?" said Minke, a tiny dark-haired woman whose colorful outfits usually reminded me of candy wrappers.

Breece, a full foot taller—and seemingly more so with his volcanic eruption of spiky red hair—took a step closer, their noses almost touching. "So, people aren't allowed to learn? An appreciation for the arts can be nurtured—"

"Show me. Show me the data proving that actually happens in a representative sample large enough to even merit discussion. It all rounds down to zero, so let's just officially remove it."

"The people?" cried Breece.

"No, this fantasy of availability," whispered Minke. "If you don't like the opera, you won't stop to look at a billboard for an opera or watch a commercial for an opera coming to your town. So, in that space and time when the idea of going to an opera is being pushed on them, what is their response? What are they doing?"

Breece rubbed both sides of his face. "Idling. Non-engagement."

"Exactly. They're forced to tune it out. How is that beneficial to anyone? It's a waste of space, time, money, and brain power. It seriously dilutes the function of the arts," Minke said loudly, holding her hands out for approval. "Plus, when you factor in government funds—the public's money—being spent on these things—"

I stopped chewing my popcorn and looked around, irrationally alert at the mention of government grants, as if the job John gave me was actually a sting where undercover agents would swoop in and shake me down to retrieve the government's money I had squandered by going to school and working at Cliff's Edge, The Indie, and The Town Commoner.

"So, what's the solution?" Breece said. He sounded like he was crying now. "Close the museums and libraries in impoverished communities and give them a stipend for guns, tattoos, and strip clubs? What are you saying?"

"Why do people gravitate toward certain experiences and shun others?" Minke asked. "I'm more interested in investigating those deeper implications. Would some people be more productive members of society, whatever that means, if they felt their personal tastes were being taken into consideration by the arts? Is it possible to remove the adverse stimuli from their field of vision so they aren't forced to ignore something that wasn't made for them?"

"You'd first have to define 'the arts,' then the purpose of engagement on a person-by-person basis." Breece rubbed his upper lip like it was a magic lamp the answer would spring from. "Is it motivated by detachment and boredom—a simple pressure release valve for alleviating life's day-to-day monotony? Or does engagement with the arts inspire them to be better people—well-rounded, open-minded, interested in new experiences?"

"Do they seek engagement for a higher purpose or simply to get a fix?" Minke said and took a step back, both their stances softening from the attack dog mode that had thrust them together.

"That's what I'm asking." Breece nodded.

A Viewsie who had been sitting cross-legged on the floor with a laptop during the debate stood with her hand raised. "What's this?" she asked and turned her screen toward the rest of the room. I had assumed she was keeping notes on the discussion, but she had been watching a new episode of *Zero's Sum*. She pressed play, and the room was subjected to a few corny lines of typical daytime drama shallowness, before a horse head hand puppet reared up over the footage, flapping its lips and overpowering the program that continued beneath.

"Reeeeee-houyhnhnm houyhnm. Howdy, folks! In this here episode, Frank Zero doesn't run off with that sultry widow from down the street and none of his kin actually gets murdered neither, no matter what all them commercials led you to think. There sure are a lot of meaningful glances and commercials for adult diapers, though. Well, the pasture's a-callin' and it's time for me to mosey on out. Tell your friends! Who's your source? Spoiler Horse!"

The horse disappeared, and the program resumed its original volume. Most of the Viewsies palmed their faces in shocked laughter. Brian Vohangliss raised a single eyebrow and shook his head disapprovingly. I bit the inside of my cheek to neutralize the agony of being the only person in the room who could unmistakably identify Randy Rain's voice. My innate ability to create facial expressions went on hold as my synapses burst out in a smattering of simultaneous directions. Had Cliff found a way to override The Network's signal? Did he use Megan's login credentials from DataScrute? Was Todd's sudden resignation really a ploy to get a man on the inside?

Although Spoiler Horse wasn't directed at me, sensing Cliff's continued presence in my life's periphery was chilling enough to force my ego into retreat, burrowing into a tiny cave to endure the impending turmoil. In hopes of seeing more horse shenanigans, the team collectively finished the episode of *Zero's Sum* (Spoiler Horse's plotline reveals were absolutely correct), as well as the first few minutes of a new program it led into: a scripted dramedy about a married couple attempting a trial separation while having to maintain the outward appearance of being happy co-owners of a popular local coffee house. It was called *Grounds For Divorce.* The opening credits offered no surprise when the line "Created by Megan Brambles" faded in. Incorporating every possible television cliché, the first scene began with a limp joke about the job having lost its perks. To be fair, I thought the show should also acknowledge DataScrute as co-creator. I relaxed a bit when a Viewsie switched the program off and the group returned to their studies and arguments, signaling the end of the day's brief interlude provided by Spoiler Horse.

.....

I dreamed I was walking through a dense primeval forest and came upon a rotted oak stump. It pulsed with life from the mass of termites teeming inside it. I idly kicked the stump with my boot as I passed. A horde of tiny pluses and minuses billowed out and crawled across the uneven earth to infest a nearby poplar. I recoiled and held up my hands. When I peeked through my fingers, the tree had vanished, the swarm assuming its shape. The ground rippled as a mass of zeroes and ones. The entire tree canopy flowed as an interconnected throng of letters and symbols. My initial terror calmed into a warm, comfortable embrace of purpose and affinity with the universe. My hands had become clusters within clusters of undulating numbers. I pointed to a tree, and data shot from my fingertips into the roots. The tree grew and grew until it overtook the canopy and obscured the sun's light from all other plant life. The tree swelled into a magnificent titan of the forest while the lesser plants withered and blew away, leaving flea-like bits of data hopping and swirling in the dust. The mighty tree finally drooped under its own weight and toppled with a quaking boom. As it disintegrated, its data flow merged with the rest of the collapsed and devastated forest. An ominous wind whispered across the landscape and scattered the once-beautiful site into oblivion, the remnants of a bygone civilization annihilated by the desolation of time.

When I suddenly woke up, I grabbed a notepad and wrote down "A SHOW ABOUT TREES???" before scratching it out, tearing the sheet from the pad, and going back to sleep.

John stopped me as I walked into Viewsful one morning. He asked if I could drop everything I was doing and pivot to another important project he needed help on. I was proud of myself for not laughing in his face at the suggestion that I had previously been doing anything at all.

"Network's been getting loads of outrageous complaints about the content of their shows, and I'm worried it reflects poorly on DataScrute," he said, guiding me to the spaceship egg chair in my orange creamsicle office. "You've got to help me. I'm out of my league, for once."

"John, man, you know, the numbers stuff," I said. "I'm still trying to wrap my head around—"

"No, no, no, I got you, I got you." He nodded rapidly in a nauseating blur. "But you know television much better than me, and if the suggestions DataScrute generates aren't working for them, I need to know how to change that—pronto. If DataScrute goes down, the whole company goes down. But not to worry—I never worry. My head's too full of ideas to worry. It's physically impossible to fit anything else in there; trust me. I want to fix the Network thing before it's a problem. They're a big client, and they're a media company—a customer-facing company—so there's high visibility with that."

"Well, what kind of complaints are you talking about?" I picked up a marker and pad of paper, hoping for something worth writing down, visual proof I was concentrating on a project and making progress.

John swept his arms overhead in a rainbow arc. "Everything. This show's too corny, that one's too violent; the commercials are too boring, the commercials are too edgy; there are too many commercials, there aren't enough commercials. And another thing—the commercials. A while ago, ConTen developed more progressive commercial standards and guidelines, and Network has data to show that spending is up." John draped an arm around me and pointed toward some horizon, like following the path of a distant wagon train. "We can roughly track where viewers spend money and what they spend it on after a show airs, within a given timeframe. All the data out there talk to each other, and it isn't all that hard to piece them all together. But I'm worried there's something missing, you know? Something obvious." John curled his fists on top of each other and peaked through like a telescope. "We can objectively target a good idea—a type of show that's proven to be popular, matched with the right kind of commercials—and Network can put it on air. We can watch the numbers go up and validate DataScrute's suggestion, but we still get complaints. So maybe there's more to it than that? A personal touch of some sort?"

I tapped my pen to the pad, hoping it indicated my total understanding. "You might be onto something there."

"Yeah, I'm onto something all right. You." His eyebrows danced in time with the curling edges of his lips. His fingers fluttered as if casting a spell.

"You're onto me?" I croaked and dropped my pad.

"You're my guy! Mister breakthrough TV idea guy!" He rubbed the sides of my head and fluttered his fingers some more. I stared at the ceiling as the motion went on about five seconds longer than was necessary. "All I'm asking is that you look at this study Network sent me—it's only about fifty pages—and tell me what you think is missing," he said. "It's interesting because they refer to a focus group study that seems to support everything they've used from DataScrute. All the suggested program alterations worked out well, the new shows are returning promising numbers, and so forth. But all the complaints fly in the face of that and tell a different story. So, something isn't right—and you've got a brain for that sort of thing—so just take a look and tell me what you think." He lunged back for our customary slow-motion high five, handing off the document as our hands met.

I skimmed the document a few times before homing in on a short section with enough graphs to make it seem more palatable than the dense, wordy parts. It was a summary of the focus group study John mentioned. The charts presented projected numbers for *Firth Thing This Morning (with Fay Firth)* after DataScrute's suggested content changes. The show was revamped to include a newly constructed, muted lime green set which allowed Fay to stand instead of sit. Modernized hairstyles were fashioned for all on-screen talent, including the routine cast of sugary-voiced baby-talking correspondents, and more mentions of animals, jogging, and brunch were worked into each episode. The projected viewership numbers matched the actual numbers to a hundredth of a degree after just two new episodes—an incredible return that would typically take far longer to achieve.

ConTen's in-show advertising suggestions were also paying dividends. Fay's show experimented with what ConTen called "show-me marketing," wherein no products or sponsors were specifically called out, but the actions and phrasings of Fay and her cronies suggested a certain lifestyle which could only be supported by specific brands and retailers. It sounded impossibly subliminal, and ConTen's explanatory gobbledygook was more inscrutable than ever, but Network had pooled their "data targets" with sponsors and found the sales upticks to be objectively attributable to the adjustments in Fay's show. The bottom-denominator shows like *Cruisin' For Losers* and its new lead-in *Hey Fatty!* only seemed to advertise tacos, skateboards, phone plans, and bail bonds during their commercial breaks, leaving me to wonder if those ads actually appealed to the viewers or were merely suggestions based on biased assumptions of that demographic.

I thumbed through the rest of the document again. Toward the end, I found another section full of colorful and digestible charts, but I momentarily froze when I saw they highlighted viewership comparisons between Network and Cliff's Edge programs competing in the same time slots. Shockingly, no Network late-night show garnered anything close to the viewership numbers at Cliff's Edge. I tore those pages from the stack and ripped them into shreds, exercising the same futility as burning a report card to make the bad grades go away. Before I filed the rest of the report away beneath the carpet under my desk, hoping to never think about it again, I looked through the viewership report for *Zero's Sum*. Its numbers had leveled off in a respectable range but suddenly spiked and continued a slight increase each week with nothing in the report to explain it. I looked at the calendar and counted back a few weeks, snorting in disbelief when it seemed that the unexpected appearance of Spoiler Horse had helped the show win viewers.

"Do people prefer to already know what's gonna happen on a show?" I asked the empty room. "Or is it just the weirdos who like to see a stupid horse puppet ruin things?"

As the weeks went on and I continually digested never-ending chunks of research from each of Viewsful's branches, I felt as if there were a funnel wedged in my mind, out of which some malevolent force siphoned any thought particles that nearly merged to form a coherent or usable idea. Adding Network's issues to the mix further diminished the likelihood for focus and accelerated my mental depletion to a soul-draining slurp. I let John continue believing I was making progress, which I only regretted when he told me he'd scheduled a consulting meeting with some Network executives.

"Don't worry about having all the answers today," he said, sticking a Viewsful name tag to my shirt, which I immediately tried to pluck off. "I want them to rest easy knowing I've got my best guy on it and we're steering down an actionable course. And if by some chance you *do* have all the answers today, even better!" I forced a laugh and felt my stomach overtighten. With absolutely no time to prepare, I grabbed every stack of research I could find before leaving Viewsful, hoping the appearance of thoughtful deliberation could distract from the obvious fraudulence of my supposed qualifications. My second incorrect assumption was that John would be joining me in the meeting. He said he would only get in my way, and for once I wished he would.

As I sat in the Network lobby hoping not to lock eyes with the distrustful custodian who was certainly lurking behind some pillar, I couldn't help but eavesdrop on a conversation between a younger producer and Camelo Balivernes, the actor who played Brody on *Two Dudes and Another Dude*. Coming in from a cigarette break, they argued over the value of a softball daytime show called *Bark if You Love Dogs*, which I assumed was a retooled version of the "people and pets" show *It's the Leashed You Could Do*.

"Who are you to say that?" the producer said, adjusting her skirt and brushing off a bit of ash as they crossed the lobby. "Your opinion isn't any more valid than anyone else's. Just because you're an actor doesn't mean—"

"No, no, listen. I *do* know," Camelo said in a sultry voice that was nothing like the high-pitched idiotic screechings of his *Two Dudes* character. "The show is lame no matter how you look at it. The people aren't interesting, the pets are ugly, the commercials are dumb. It's a big goofy mess, and it's embarrassing. Get rid of it and put anything—*anything*—else in its place before we lose people."

The producer pulled an expression of mock concern and placed a consolatory hand on Camelo's arm. "Hey, this might be a surprise to you, but there are plenty of people who don't watch *Two Dudes*."

"*Pfft*. Yeah, they're called morons." Camelo shrugged and rotated his shoulder back to disengage her hand. "The show is amazing, and we're already talking spinoffs. It's hilarious and lighthearted; what's not to like?" Camelo pressed the elevator button and crossed his arms.

"You could say the same for *Bark if You Love Dogs*."

"No, you couldn't. It's terrible. Terrible." Camelo tilted his head back, flaring his nostrils in theatrical insubordination.

"Well, you know what?" the producer said with a huge fake grin. "Just don't watch it. Obviously, that show wasn't made for you."

The door closed, and from the adjacent elevator surged the hunched, lumpy rhinoceros form of Murk Torquins, head of Network. His bulbous head was topped with crinkly gray hair like a desaturated fern, ribboning up and behind him with every jerky motion. I flinched at the sudden sensation that he might mow me down and charge through the walls straight into the street.

"Buddy. You're here. Let's go." He motioned behind him, like lobbing a brick down a tunnel. I barely had time to grab my stacks of research papers and jog to the elevator before the door closed. At the top floor, I followed Murk down a blinding all-glass hallway into an enormous conference room that could have housed the entire governing body of a small country. I scanned the room for something recognizable to latch onto. All around me, folders and notepads slid around and flipped open.

I had considered starting off with a sly mention of *Rockin' Jockaoke*, my karaoke weightlifting game show idea that Megan told me had gotten the green light, but, thankfully, Network Vice President and Chief Marketing Officer Breff Kholkers, who looked even more like a wide-nosed pale-faced gangly swamp critter than I had remembered, spoke up first. He began detailing the problems with a few recently aborted programs and wedged in a quick mention of the karaoke show's failure to make it past the pilot stage.

Apparently, all three *Rockin' Jockaoke* pilot tapings were prematurely shut down when multiple contestants required serious medical attention. I hadn't considered how far some people would push their bodies to win a competition and was dismayed to learn that multiple thick-necked weightlifters only stopped singing when confronted with embolisms and blackouts. The show was too dangerous for further consideration and had been axed from the upcoming Network schedule. The tentative replacements were *Who's Special Now?*, a flip-flopped spinoff of *What Makes You Think You're So Special?* where targets from previous episodes tracked down their attackers to reverse their roles, and a *Your Job in a Week* "where are they now?" follow-up show called *One Week Later*. Even by Network standards, they sounded hollow and uninspired.

Breff prattled on long enough for me to have completely forgotten that my presence in the meeting suggested my intention to speak. I glanced around the room and blinked a few times as Murk patted the table in front me. "Buddy, your guidance? Out with the old, in with the gold?"

I gulped and nodded. "Yes. Of course. That's exactly the thing to do." The crowd's scribbling frenzy indicated I had just greenlit whatever they had been talking about.

"Cleared for duty." Murk nodded as if trying to loosen his head from his shoulders. I removed my hand from the top of my paper stack, where it had left a damp off-white imprint. I shifted that report to the bottom and smiled at Murk. He limply twisted his fleshy wrists like swatting invisible flies. "I see you have some research with you. Why don't we start with that?" All the pens in the room rose to their ready positions.

I nodded solemnly and grabbed a data report with plenty of charts from the middle of my stack. "Yes, let's do that." The analysis I had grabbed was titled "Indeliberate Side Effects of Insalubrious Prose Neglect." I momentarily went cross-eyed and held the paper up like it was vanishing. "Uh...So...*Ahem.* This one...Well, we have a team that looks into language and things—"

"We're all aware of DivComm, Bonny."

"Do they think changing the words we use will solve our problems?"

"I have a thing or two to say about that."

"And DivComm knows a better way to say it!"

I glanced around like hornets were descending from every direction. "Well, their research is very...uh...detailed and..." I flipped through the report looking for any one phrase that might be worth uttering aloud, hoping some ambitious underling in the room would pounce and mold it into something meriting discussion. "You know what? Let's come back to that one. I know BuCon has some interesting reports on getting the right shows in front of the right people."

"Oh, the *right* shows!"

"We've been going about this all wrong!"

"Then what is it *we* do?"

"We listen to reports on how we're not doing it right."

"And then keep on not doing it right."

Everyone in Network upper management seemed to be a laboratory creation optimized for impossible combinations of ruthless intent and calm indifference. I gazed into the stupefying BuCon analysis and tried to make up a meaning for it on the fly. "It seems that…If there's a reasonable market for a show, and the numbers support it, the show gets made. But…how do we know there's a market for it if…I mean, which comes first: the show or the market? Where does the idea for the market come from?" I tried to ignore the parallel paper cuts that had materialized on my thumb like tally marks scratched in the wall of a prison cell. "What I mean to say is…We should be making shows specifically for the audience they're being made for."

"Very wise."

"Got it."

"Yeah, just keep doing what we were already doing."

"Very insightful."

"Worth every penny!"

Murk had sat so still for so long, I nearly forgot he was there. He placed a meaty palm atop my facade of incomprehensible reports and muttered a low brassy grumble as he surveyed the room. "We're taking hits from all sides and don't need this friendly fire. Let's hunker down and circle the wagons. Sit up and listen tight. Here it comes." He elbowed the stack toward me. I slid two reports side by side and pulled phrases from each in a frenetic jumble as I prayed for a coherent thought to emerge.

"BuCon's data shows certain groups feel 'alienated beyond expectation' when there's a block of shows they don't want to watch," I began. "And it…'spreads with the magnitudinous velocity of a communicable disease.' These groups avoid certain programming blocks so often that we have little hope of winning them back, and it's almost…'stubbornly unethical?' Because we're 'knowingly and willfully isolating' groups of people. ConTen's reports make it look extra bad because it affects their spending habits 'in an adverse exponent.' It can even alter their mood so badly that they 'overrule their resolve' about making purchases they wanted to make. So, it's like…if each demographic group only got exposed to the things they already like, things that…'validate their personal legitimacy with authentic experiences,' like commercials that pertain to them and shows they'll definitely be interested in, then there will be a 'positive ripple effect of specific, desired inclusiveness.'"

I looked up, and the pulse in my neck briefly hesitated before galloping double-time through a wave of nausea. I had spoken uninterrupted for more than a few seconds, and it almost threw me off. "Well, I guess what I'm saying is…I'm suggesting, to cut down on complaints, that we find a way to…avoid letting viewers see things they don't like. Make them feel like...*everything* they see was made for them. That should cut down on complaints and keep the numbers up." The dizzying effect of everyone nodding in unison made me squirm.

"Simple as that, huh?"

"Genius."

"The tides are turning, I can feel it."

"The undertow!"

"What a momentous occasion."

"We're all so honored to have been here for it."

"I have to go call my wife and tell her our kids can finally be proud of their father."

Murk turned his yellowing, watery eyes to me and placed a hand on my shoulder, dragging it down slightly as he nodded. He swiveled my chair away from the table and motioned to the door, then addressed the crowd. "Field cleared. Guns loaded. Line up the next thinktank."

The suffocating tension of that meeting lessened over the weekend and a few days later was all but forgotten, sunk beneath endless waves of the Viewsful data tide. John never stopped me to ask how the meeting went, further proof of his distressingly misplaced trust. Because of the constant crushing terror of being found out and unmasked as a total phony, when he appeared in my office and tossed an envelope on my desk, I assumed it contained an official letter of termination. Before I could mumble any of the half-formed apologies or excuses ricocheting across my mind, John said, "Your consulting fee from Network. See it as a bonus. You earned that, Buddy." He crossed his arms, eyebrows popping up and down like an over-caffeinated gymnastics team. I drooled a bit when I pulled out a check for almost half of my annual salary. "Buddy, Murk loves you—*loves* you. Whatever you did for Network in that meeting has him all charged up and ready to roll, so pat yourself on the back, and then pat yourself on the back with the other hand. Crack your knuckles, kick off your shoes, lean back, and enjoy a mandatory week off."

.....

I hurried to the closest strip mall and bought an enormous television set, sound system, and leather recliner so that I could waste my time off in a record-breaking bender of excessive aimlessness. Only when I had kicked out the footrest and scanned through the channels did it occur to me that I had no remaining interest in watching anything other than game show reruns.

The days smudged together in a looping montage of the same three or four scenes; I may have showered twice the entire week. On Friday, I surrendered and switched on Cliff's Edge, nearly choking when I saw the same gasoline-fountain episode of *So You Think You're Tough?* that had introduced me to the channel in the first place. By the end of the weekend, I had watched nothing but Cliff's Edge, unconsciously reverting to a diet of pizza and burritos. The daytime shlock was gone, and the channel aired twenty-four hours of its abrasive, offensive material previously relegated to late night.

John's hands-off approach reached a new height when I didn't see him for two or three more weeks after my vacation; I nearly forgot there was a superior I supposedly reported to. He unexpectedly appeared along the edge of my peripheral vision one day, grinning like his lips could force his teeth into the back of his head. I was babbling along with DivComm during a post-lunch chant-together focused on food words beginning with fricative sounds (f and v, which I only remembered because they appeared in the word itself, although I still managed to forget that and screw up the chant more than once). I assumed John was trying to get my attention and followed him out of the room. I walked down three different hallways before finding him in the lobby, where he handed me an espresso in a thimble-sized cup.

"I like to cut to the chase, so here it is." He pounded his fist on a mountainous internal document from Network. The first page was a non-disclosure agreement awaiting my initials. "Network is up to something big, and I told them you're the guy to head up our new division. I met with Murk and Breff and some others over the past few days. They really wanted my input, but I told them I don't want to step on your toes. Whatever it is they're happy about, it's your brain-baby and you should be the one to nurture it in the right environment."

I burned my lips three separate times while he spoke and could feel the heat transferring into my fingertips from the thinness of the cup, so I shot it back and grunted as my throat was singed and lacerated. "*Gack*! Well thanks, John, that's uh..." I nodded thoughtfully as my chest and stomach warmed like an iron-melting furnace. "That's really exciting."

John pounded the paper stack again, turning to high-five Tuliah, then me. "Don't I know it. You hire the right people. It's as simple as that." I smiled, wondering if the old Bladoodle crew felt the same way. As I initialed the highlighted pages, he ripped them out and backhanded them to Tuliah. "Sorry I can't prime you on everything, but basically they commissioned us to write up some terms and guidelines, something about new techniques for standardizing ethics. It's all here in the document. They're setting up a whole new way of programming with that idea you gave them, something about showing different things to different people."

"Starting some new channels? That might be cool."

"No, no, no, no, no, it's much bigger than that. You'll see. I don't want to hold you up." We both assumed slow-motion high-five ready positions and followed through with half-hearted explosion sound effects. I glanced at the second page of the document as he sprung away; a trademarked phrase printed at the bottom read "Beyond TV: TVC." Next to it was an illustration of three human heads on one body watching three television monitors connected to the same base. Each screen showed a single enormous eye looking back at the mutant viewer. One eye winked seductively.

A few days later, I finally got around to skimming the Network document. It contained almost no charts, graphs, diagrams, or other visual stimuli. I fanned the pages back and forth, poking my finger in the middle and selecting a page at random to start with. I read and reread the same baffling paragraph on "enacting direct viewer motivation for favorable encounters" five times before flipping forward a few pages, stopping when I saw the TVC illustration again beneath the header "TransVariCast (Transmitter: Variegated Broadcast)." The body of the page was far too technical for any human being to successfully digest, but the gist seemed to be that Network was experimenting with broadcasting multiple versions of their channel simultaneously, each with different programs and commercials. Which feed entered a viewer's home depended on data gleaned from their viewing and spending history. The service was automated; if a viewer's habits began trending in a different direction, the feed would alter itself to a different version, unbeknownst to the viewer. Network claimed to already have five feeds up and running with five more anticipated by year's end. The TVC method only presented viewers a world within their predetermined comfort zone while leading them to believe they were still watching the one actual "Network."

Dozens of pages detailed a wealth of evidence cobbled from BuCon and ConTen studies that supported and led to the TVC idea. They found that most viewers sought a "predetermined set of desired stimuli" and, as consumers, were loyal to a small subsection of brands and companies, rarely swayed by "outlier options." The research showed if eighty percent of programming and advertising on one feed appealed to a viewer, tactics of "delicate manipulation for desired persuasion" could effectively coax viewers into embracing the remaining twenty percent to adopt "total system conformity." A more stable and quantifiable viewer base was easier to appease with the cultural experiences they desired, a practice which BuCon deemed an "essential ethical practice devoid of waste or exclusion." TVC simply created viewer archetypes and rounded everyone up to one of those standards instead of forcing viewers to split their attention across a perceived variety of choices.

I shrugged it off and went about my routine of popping into other departments' meetings, trying to imitate an actual goal-oriented working person. One day, I got a call from Murk's assistant asking when he could expect the verbiage for the new ethics terms and guidelines. I told him the meticulous density of the research was overwhelming and sorting all the necessary considerations couldn't be rushed.

"We understand that," he said, "and Murk of course expects it to be a five-star decorated thing of beauty, so let's say a week from tomorrow. How's that?"

I opened my mouth and worked my jaws around, expecting some sort of mature response to slip out, but I just hummed and tilted my head side to side.

"Great. I'll send Tuliah the meeting details, and we'll see you then."

I gripped the phone and nodded drowsily while a multitude of possible disasters congested my already sluggish mind. I grabbed the Network report and thumbed through it until I felt like I was going blind. I plopped down and nearly toppled the space egg chair when a horrendous nightmare ambushed me in the last few pages of the report. "Oh, please, no," I mumbled, scanning the paragraph where I saw the name Cliff Montagna printed next to the title "Provisional Consultant."

My knees buckled. The space egg chair tilted to one side and shot out from underneath me, dropping me on my tailbone. A partly redacted internal document stapled in the report detailed Cliff's efforts to sue Network over what he claimed were copycats of his Cliff's Edge creations. Network had done the math and found it was far less costly to simply pay him the undisclosed sum he deemed adequate compensation, avoiding an indefinite trial that could have halted production of at least four programs. After the meeting with Network arbiters, Cliff somehow slithered his way into a one-year contract position for program development. Instead of continuing the losing battle against the Cliff's Edge late-night numbers, Network wanted to horde his creations under their banner, which made perfect business sense until you factored in the volatility of Cliff's shameless temperament. I could only hope our paths wouldn't cross in meetings at Network, which, of course, was exactly what happened when I arrived for the meeting the following week.

I begged the Viewsful departments for help on the ethics terms and guidelines, an undertaking I had very little understanding of. Each Viewsie who had a moment to browse the Network report was astonished at the provocative implications the station sought to explore and, contrary to my passive approach, were thrilled to sideline their current pursuits to work on mine. In an hour, I had assembled a team who delighted in defining "The Elemental Ethics of Targeted Encounters for Apportioned Market Convergence," a snappy title they agreed on before I left them to sort out the rest. Astoundingly, Clinch handed me a rough outline the next morning, and the final draft the day after that. The team comprised members of every department, each of whom voluntarily worked late hours because of their excitement over the uniqueness of the project. I tried to imagine what sort of passion project would encourage me to work like that, but could only picture myself lying in my recliner, scanning through channels until I fell asleep. I gave the final report my usual non-perusal and tucked it away until the meeting. Since the Viewsies left it to me to devise a sharp name for our new department, it floundered at "The Commission," which was simply how John referred to the original contract request from Network.

I was given a laminated Network access badge with my face and name on it when I checked in for the meeting. I wasn't sure when they had taken my picture, but I flashed it mockingly at the condescending custodian who had been eyeballing me before I even made it through the revolving door. I rode the elevator up and strode across the blinding glass hallway to the same conference room where I had first met the Network executive team, practicing my fake smile as I rounded the corner. I froze with a horrified grin when I saw the only occupants of the room were Murk Torquins and Cliff Montagna, engaged in a fierce standoff at the main table.

"Buppsen, take a seat," Cliff said indifferently. "Then hit yourself over the head with it, throw it through a window, and jump out after it." He sharpened his gaze at Murk. "Jerk and I are off to a great start. Can't wait to see where this leads." Murk's slack face noticeably twitched, but he said nothing. Cliff hooked one arm over the back of his chair and tapped the conference table with his fingers, dancing them around as if performing a puppet show for Murk's enjoyment. Cliff's watch beeped. "Well, that's all the time we have for today. See you tomorrow, Jerk." I stared at the ethics report in my hand and pretended to search for something as Cliff stood and pushed past me. He stopped outside the door, then leaned back until his face was just within my peripheral vision. He came close, as if to whisper a secret, then yelled, "Stampede!" The doors on the opposite end of the room burst open, and the executive team poured in, politely fighting for the seats closest to Murk. I squatted to pick up the stack of reports I had accidentally tossed when Cliff screamed, then looked over both shoulders. Cliff was gone.

"Thanks, everyone. I'll make this brief." I trembled as I passed out misshapen piles of reports in both directions. One stack stalled in front of Murk. He stared straight ahead and rocked his head to one side as he breathed, the only indication that he was still alive. Two lackeys had to lean over and pull the papers in their direction to maintain their circulation around the table.

"Our team at Viewsful really jumped on this one," I said, "and, well, it's pretty self-explanatory. They defined what needed to be defined for the TVC initiative." I scanned the room just above eye-level to give the appearance of making eye contact with everyone without really doing so. Megan Brambles lifted her hand in a curt wave as my gaze passed her. She kept her hand up and froze as the reports reached her space at the table, her hollow raccoon eyes and sudden scowl betraying her brain's total shutdown. Breff Kholkers glanced at her and coughed politely while kicking the table leg to wake her. Megan shrieked; everyone pretended not to hear and continued passing the papers around.

I swallowed and took a deep breath at the same time, sounding like I nearly drowned. "As you can see, they're calling it 'The Elemental Ethics of Targeted Encounters for Apportioned Market Convergence.' That pretty much says it all. They've got it all worked out—the most efficient ways to sort of mold viewers to the ideal version of their demographic." I concluded my visual tour of the room at Murk, who rocked his head and breathed steadily. Everyone in the room looked at him and not me. I cleared my throat. "Well, I know you need time to read over everything and digest all the ins and outs. Any questions should go directly to the team lead, Clinch Dehavers." I nodded to both sides of the room, then smiled weakly at Murk, who was still gazing into some quiet personal oblivion. I had expected the typical back and forth hysteria of my previous Network meetings, but something elusive and oppressive hung in the air. I spun toward the door and gasped, remembering Cliff's ominous exit and worrying the moment had arrived for my comeuppance. The air conditioning clanged on, and the walls rumbled as if the room itself sought to end the tension and purge the phantom vibe.

"I'm sure it's an era-defining work of art," came Breff's voice from across the room. "Thanks, Buddy; we're all stoked to the extreme." He clapped and smiled smarmily, but a few Networkers stood rigidly, straightened their ties, and marched away in an expression of defiance.

A throat-gripping moment passed before Murk sat up and held out his palms. "Anyone else?" he said in a muddled mixture of sympathy and extreme sarcasm. No one moved. Murk rapped the table and stood, slinging his jacket over one shoulder to button it. "These advanced tactics and maneuvers are the new modern warfare. You'll be digging the trenches, loading the mortars, and leading the blitz. The outcome of this war will be strictly measured by the sweat off your backs and the heaps of bones you leave behind." He pounded the table twice and hustled away. The other Networkers exchanged worried glances as they rose hesitantly. Megan gathered the reports forsaken by the angry executives who had stormed out, banging her head on the edge of the table in what must have been her quickest power nap blackout ever. I glanced at my watch without reading the time and hurried out the door.

I stepped out of the elevator and immediately backpedaled into it. I smashed all the buttons with an open hand, clutching the leftover reports to my chest as Chibbs Ticonderoga grabbed the door to hold it open. "Come on, don't slink back into your shell," he said. "I know you're the most feeble creation ever to slime around this world and you have absolutely no purpose for being alive, but it's not like…Well, I guess it *is* that bad, now that I hear it out loud." Chibbs's angled smirk suggested his expectation for time to have made amends on our behalf.

I stared blankly for a moment, then said, "Ok, I thought of something nice to say: I'm glad you aren't Cliff." I slapped a copy of the report into his hand as I edged past.

"Look, don't…" Chibbs began, reaching toward me with the report. He glanced at the title and thumbed through it, then rushed to catch up to me. "Oh, ok, so this is you? This is how you're getting back at us?"

I jogged backward toward the revolving door, knocking against the custodian as he crept around a column by the entryway. I handed him a copy of the report and slapped his back. "Nope, I'm more of a glorified delivery boy. I can't say I had nothing to do with that, but I basically had nothing to do with it. I've heard it's a compelling read, so maybe it'll compel you to learn how to read so you can read it and be compelled."

Chibbs curled up the report and drummed it against his thigh. "Why would you want to…" He glanced around and lowered his voice as he came near me, yanking the papers from the hands of the unamused custodian. "This is what you'd rather be doing? This analytical data nonsense that doesn't prove anything?" He draped his arm over my shoulder and led me outside. "Do you have any idea the extra layer of frustration this kind of stuff adds to my job? To *all* of our jobs?"

"No, actually," I said. "I've never had a real Network job, so it would be unfair for me to pretend like I know or care. See ya!" Chibbs grabbed my forearm and spun me around as I tried to leave. His face hung forlorn, almost pleading.

"Look, just so you know, I've brought your name up more than once to these people when they're asking for ideas, but they're all a bunch of robots with faulty wiring. It's like where an idea comes from has more of an impact on their interest level than the idea itself. I don't understand their blind faith in this DataScrute stuff."

I folded my hands together like a thankful beggar. "That makes up for everything. Thanks again, but I have to go."

"You don't get it," Chibbs said. "Because of all these reports, they give us constant notes for changes we're supposed to immediately address, and then those notes conflict with whatever notes they gave us the day before. And then—like with *Two Dudes and Another Dude*. Here I am running a hit show for a couple of seasons, and they tell me they're thinking about changing the title. What in the world? *Why*? They say they have some data that shows viewers who hate low-brow comedies are more likely to give one a chance if it has a high-brow sounding title. Like it lets them off the hook because it's ironic or something? The real irony is hiring someone because you value their input but then you tell them what their input should be."

"But the title is the only thing *Two Dudes* has going for it!" I said. "Aside from the easily predictable plots and cookie cutter characters and endlessly recycled jokes and terrible opening sequence and obvious ad placement."

Chibbs hacked an unexpected laugh. "Agreed. The alternate title they asked for was *When Brothers Dwell in Unity*. Can you believe that?"

I squeezed my face with both hands and hissed a fake scream. "Well, actually, once you say it a few times, it really grows on you. I don't know, they might be onto something. I'm sure it'll be a hit on at least one of the feeds."

"See, that's exactly the problem. They split up the demographics into all these little factions, but now they're demanding 'crossover hits'—shows that ignore those boundaries and appeal to more than one group. So, what's the point? They're saying two conflicting things at once."

I shook my head. "Yeah, create a show that appeals to a specific group, but also make sure it appeals to everyone else, too. Make it broad but narrow." I flipped through the ethics guidelines but saw nothing pertaining to that issue. "That must be you guys. We didn't suggest that."

"Ok, so who's 'we?'" Chibbs leaned against a concrete planter and crossed his arms.

I exhaled and let my upper body droop forward. "Viewsful. It's ok. It's a job."

Chibbs elbowed me. "Oh, I've heard good things about that place—from nobody, because I just lied."

"Well," I said, "I get paid a lot to do nothing, so it has *that* going for it."

"Sounds like the ideal situation for you. You don't have to drain the economy by applying for unemployment, but then you also can't screw anything up because you aren't given anything to do. Congrats. You've achieved equilibrium."

"It's not where I ever saw myself, but then again, the jobs I thought I wanted keep dumping me somewhere I don't want to be. So maybe if I have a job I don't want, it'll lead me somewhere good?"

"That's airtight logic, Buddy. You should be a lawyer. Or instead of a lawyer, someone with nothing to do and nothing expected of him. Kind of like whatever it is you do now."

I saluted Chibbs and gave him another copy of the ethics report. "For your service. Don't spend it all in one place."

"I'll make sure it gets a proper burial, sir." We held the reports up and slammed them together repeatedly like gladiator swords, laughing hysterically as Network employees emerged for their cigarette breaks, confused and annoyed.

.....

The Elemental Ethics guidelines were an immediate success at Network. Drastic changes in programming and advertising saw huge increases in viewership and revenue, and Viewsful reaped the rewards of its first multimillion-dollar client. The Commission team, instead of disbanding after the initial report, doubled down and sent weekly updates to Network on trends, habits, and market shifts for each TVC feed's specific guidelines.

Using a fusion of Smartographer, AdvEYEser, and pseudo-ethics, the Commission team exercised more control over programming than the show creators at Network. The reports detailed hyper-specific techniques for how advertising should be placed within each show, all with specific timing for when the ads should appear for maximum engagement by the audience.

I usually delivered the new reports to Network myself, where I was seen as a hero and trailblazer, once I stopped sweating and stuttering through the intimidating executive meetings. Network accepted every tweak without question, honoring the reports as holy writ, glorifying and enforcing the gospel over the objections of any producer or showrunner, most of whom were nonplussed by sudden and relentless changes to their work.

When the *What Makes You Think You're So Special?* showrunner abandoned a location shoot out of protest over some frivolous and contradictory Network notes, the crew was left with two days of paid work but nothing to do while awaiting instructions at the state fairgrounds. Todd Gherkin, who was working as a cable wrangler and boom mic operator on that crew, picked up a camera and wandered through the sea of people lined up for rides and funnel cakes. Like a carnival barker, he shouted, "Who can take a punch? Come on down, folks. Show us your face, and we'll put knuckles in its place." A crowd formed like bugs around a zapper to see who would be the first to take a punch on camera. A goblin-faced older man sporting a skin-tight crew cut announced his intention to show up all the "lily-livered young folks standin' around gawkin' and waitin' for a real man to show them what's what" as he muscled his way through the throng, elbowing and ear-flicking everyone he found worthy of insult.

Todd hadn't considered who would deliver the punch and was thrilled when a craggy fist tore through the crowd and popped the provoker square in the nose. His head snapped back, blood sprayed up, and the crowd roared. Determined young men wishing to be the next punchers and takers jammed together and clenched each other's throats, baying like feral dogs. Todd pacified the crowd by flashing some overhead lights and yammering like a tobacco auctioneer, then set up a booth with waivers to sign that essentially asserted "whatever happens to you on camera is your own fault and may or may not be used in a television program." Todd edited the footage himself, mocked-up a graphic intro with the obvious title *Who Can Take A Punch?*, and took the first episode directly to Megan. She ran queries through the AnalEYEser, checked the output against some prior recommendations from AdvEYEser, and used Smartographer to determine commercial placement. Megan had carte blanche to approve anything supported by DataScrute, and the show was greenlit for four TVC feeds starting that weekend. The popularity of *Who Can Take A Punch?* surged and, as it expanded to more feeds than originally anticipated, Murk recruited Todd as his new frontline infantryman in his exhausting stalemate with Cliff. Murk gave Todd control over *What Makes You Think You're So Special?* as well as *Cruisin' For Losers* and *Freak Seek* (yet another clone of a clone), maneuvering one step closer to either carpet-bombing Cliff off the battlefield or triggering a doomsday device of mutual devastation.

In a few months, most TVC feeds were crammed wall-to-wall with programs of acute similarity. For some, this was a welcomed trend, as if those viewers demanded the same experience from every program; for others, a balance was necessary as viewers became disenchanted by the lack of real variety. When one feed jumped from nine daytime courtroom shows to ten, viewers began turning away from the three most recently added of those shows, not just the newest one. During a meeting at Viewsful on those issues, attempting to be helpful, I stupidly blurted out, "But how same is exactly the same?" Regardless of what I meant to say, Clinch and Breece were galvanized and shared a spiritual moment that led them down an exploratory path ending in ten new tiers of TVC feeds, each winning increased viewership as they replaced inferior feeds. It seemed they had discovered a new formula for providing an authentic illusion of choice on some of the more unstable feeds: intentionally providing viewers a few shows they had no interest in watching simply to reinforce their commitment to those they did. This contradicted their updated definition of ethics and was only used on intermediary feeds for viewers whose total persona had yet to be succinctly mapped by Smartographer.

Clinch thanked me for pushing them in a new direction; I laughed in his face. Luckily, John Klemchky walked into the room doing his impression of Spoiler Horse, and we all laughed.

Even after the boom of the Elemental Ethics doctrine, no Network feed's late-night numbers came close to competing with the reruns that still aired on Cliff's Edge. Cliff claimed he had no control over what aired there anymore, that Network would have to wait out the remainder of the five-year government grant until someone else took over and changed the lineup. Knowing Cliff owned the broadcast antenna transmitting the Cliff's Edge signal, I could've poked holes in his fabricated excuses and made trouble for him, but like with most things Cliff, I decided to steer clear and hope the better equipped powers of nature would deal with him later.

As predicted, Breff and Murk pressured Cliff to create shows flagrantly similar to everything he had created previously. He argued that since he retained all rights to the Cliff's Edge programming, he would also have to outright own anything he created for Network; otherwise, they risked infringing on his intellectual property and he could sue them for making copycat shows. Murk wouldn't budge on the issue, insisting that every Network show was a co-creation with the majority rights owned by Network. This made for supremely awkward conferences, with Murk and Cliff staring each other down while a roomful of professional adults shuffled their feet, hands, and papers, counting the minutes until they could escape. This provided further credence to my theory that Cliff only accepted the position to make Murk miserable, watering down Network's efforts as a means of bolstering his own tenacious spite toward its apocalyptic ideal.

The one creation Cliff wouldn't claim credit for was Spoiler Horse, but once his consulting position began, the horse suddenly appeared more frequently, and the scene he interrupted would freeze until he was done revealing plotlines, often mentioning specific products, brands, and marketing buzzwords in his rants. The frequency of puppet intrusions in any TVC feed depended on how tolerant those viewers were of the quasi-comedic disruption, ranging from once per week to once per program; on the lower end, Spoiler Horse would usually get chased off by "the stable boy," an overall-clad bumpkin chewing a wheat stem and wielding a metal rake.

Soon there was the standalone program *Horse Business*, a flashy Spoiler Horse "review roundup rodeo" of new shows, movies, and products. The show appeared on most TVC feeds in an early evening slot as a palate cleanser between the lighter daytime fare and the more substantial evening spread. It seemed Randy Rain had been dismissed as puppet operator, as Spoiler Horse's voice dropped an octave and exuded a slightly more polished air in *Horse Business*. He yelped goofy lines like, "Howdy folks! Time to check the feedbag! *Num num num*," as he stuffed his muzzle into the stable boy's burlap sack and snatched out strips of paper with his oversized puppet teeth. These were suggestions for reviews, which he rated on a scale of "Neigh" to "Hay." The sarcastic program interruptions were eschewed for sponsored tie-ins, and the diluted Spoiler Horse experience became an everyday fixture in many households.

Chibbs Ticonderoga was brought in to workshop further *Spoiler Horse* properties. He was partly responsible for *Workhorse*, a mildly popular scripted comedy where a down-on-his-luck Spoiler Horse works lamentable temp agency jobs. He's constantly picked on by co-workers, who drop apples and sugar cubes around his desk along with irritating comments like, "Why the long face?" Chibbs ultimately had his name removed from the credits. I told him to put mine in its place, since some of the plotlines were conspicuously identical to temp agency horror stories I'd told him years before. The show ran its natural course after two seasons. On some TVC feeds, it was spun off as the police horse action thriller *Call the Clops!*, which broke up the typical crime show drama with an excessive number of chase scenes; on others, it became the loosely related office dramedy *Past Temps*, wherein an over-stressed clerical worker undergoes a psychotic episode and wakes to find himself repeating his first temp agency position from a decade before. Condemned to relive all his previous work experiences and daily failures, it was more depressing than funny and didn't last an entire season.

.....

When I wasn't popping into various department meetings at Viewsful to add nothing of value, I leisurely whiled away the working hours as a hired consultant in programming audits at Network. I let them draw their own conclusions to Commission notes built around research I had nothing to do with. Megan, whose frequent open-eyed blackouts were expertly ignored by every Network executive, offered recommendations gleaned from data projections, but Murk always sought my approval before "giving the troops marching orders." All I really did was give a thumbs up to whatever Megan had the data to support. I perfected the thoughtful nod, giving executives and producers the confidence they needed to feel they were making the right calls. Megan could likely see right through the charade, but considering her job also hinged on DataScrute's continued usefulness, she was forced to tolerate my hierarchical authority.

Lounging through a Network discussion on rebooting *Happy Throw Lucky*, a knife-toss game show that had been "impermanently retired" (Murk's preferred term for cancellations because "the word canceled implies we engaged in the incorrect procedure, which we are incapable of doing"), Breff Kholkers addressed me directly and asked my opinion on a potential viewership issue. "Needs to be dangerous, but not too dangerous. Buddy, how do we kick something like that into high gear?"

I folded my hands, waiting for someone to speak up. "Oh, me? Uh..." I leaned over some DataScrute printouts I hadn't bothered reading. "Let's see...Do we have data on that? What do you mean by 'dangerous?'"

Breff smiled and waved the question away with the flick of a wrist, rattling the links of his watch band against each other like the clatter of rolling dice. "No, no, Buddy. I'm asking *you*. You created *Your Job in a Week*, right? Well, I'm thinking *Happy Throw Lucky* could benefit from that show's balance: a little funny, a little serious, a little dangerous, but not too much of any one of those things. *Your Job*'s not really a huge hit anywhere anymore, but it performs just fine on an average number of feeds."

"Thanks, but you already have one spinoff of that show, and that's more than enough," I said. I hadn't thought about *Your Job in a Week* in years, and in doing so, I imagined John Klemchky's dopey face stretched across a dodecahedron, bouncing on a spring.

"I'm only asking how we can harness that magic for *Happy Throw Lucky*," Breff said. "Loads of people don't watch game shows, but maybe we can entice them if there's an edge to it. Viewers who *do* watch game shows might not want to see someone get hurt, which happened a little too often on the original *Happy Throw Lucky*. Like, 'every episode' often. Well, if we incorporate a little of everything and keep it balanced…A funny side, a serious side, a potentially dangerous but not *actually* dangerous side…"

I massaged my temples and murmured words that bypassed my conscious mind entirely. "A goofy but intelligent host, a scientific analysis of angles and trajectory, demonstrations on how to throw different types of knives. Money and prizes, personal stories from the contestants…Yeah, that could work."

Breff clapped softly. "Buddy, it sounds like you've already got it all figured out. I think *you're* the guy to head up the reboot. What say?"

The incredulous management horde burst into commotion.

"He doesn't work here!"

"Then where does he work?"

"Who says he works?"

"He's allergic to hard work."

"Call a doctor!"

"Just let him have my job, too."

"Buddy or the doctor?"

"Either one would be more effective than you!"

"Give him a week to learn your job, and we'll send you packing."

"Sounds familiar."

"Yeah, let's find the guy who created *that* show."

"We've got him here, but he doesn't create shows anymore!"

"He's a no-show!"

"He's a show pony for Viewsful!"

"*Reeeeee-houyhnhnm houyhnm*!"

Breff coughed, rattled his watch, and hushed the rabble by addressing the head of the table. "As a consultant, Buddy's reach can extend as far as Murk allows it. Murk?"

Murk, who had flatlined for most of the meeting, stared straight ahead and turned his palms up, then swung his head toward me reverently. "Buddy, you've scuffled your way across similar battlefields and emerged victorious with your enemy's entrails dripping from the tip of your spear. If you've still got that fire in your guts, you can lead our troops and prove your worth, by blood or by blood. Will you answer the call? Will you raise high the flag and lead the charge on this knife show?"

I looked around the room and grinned like a schmuck. "Sure. I'll take a stab at it."

Happy Throw Lucky was far less work for me than expected. John Klemchky encouraged me to spend as much time on-set as necessary to maintain the favorable relationship between Viewsful and Network, but everyone on the show—the studio crew, set dressers, floor directors, camera operators, and audio recordists—executed their roles flawlessly without my supervision. Pretty soon, I was just another warm body standing in the studio or sitting in meetings.

.....

One afternoon, Cliff unexpectedly disrupted his usual pattern with Murk by firing a total curveball. Networkers filed into a development meeting in their standard shoe-staring subservient mode to find information packets at their seats detailing *Invisipeepers*, an unsettling hidden camera investigation show from the point of view of an unseen voyeur who simply spies on people in their homes without their knowledge. Cliff claimed it was all staged, but the photos in the information packet looked real enough to me. He offered to screen an episode during the meeting, but Murk declined, plus there were no screens for viewing programs in the Network conference rooms. I had always wondered if the executives even watched the shows they greenlit.

Cliff had gobs of DataScrute spew to support the potential success of *Invisipeepers* and agreed to produce original episodes with the stipulation that any Cliff's Edge copycat shows airing on Network be immediately "retired." Murk greenlit the show before Cliff finished speaking—perhaps just to stop him from speaking.

Hey Fatty! and its sister program *Hey Fatty! Where You Goin'?* were immediately dropped, along with *Cruisin' For Losers* and the *Freak Seek* spinoff *Freak Seek: High School Chess Team.* The core *Freak Seek* program stayed on the air despite Cliff's objections.

Later that week, Cliff had six *Invisipeepers* episodes ready to air, which surprised everyone but me. I always assumed that he not only hoarded heinous material regardless of its potential to air, but that he intentionally held some back from Cliff's Edge in case he ever had a larger platform for shocking audiences. Only twelve of the forty-six TVC feeds initially carried *Invisipeepers*, but after four episodes, it was the most-watched program on all of them.

Focusing on a new property for a few months did nothing to allay Cliff's animosity toward Murk and Todd. Cliff had taken to sitting next to Murk in every audit meeting, staring at the side of a head that refused to turn and make eye contact. He constantly demanded *Freak Seek*'s cancellation and Todd's removal as showrunner of any program, calling him a fraud and a puppet. Cliff argued the late-night schedule was too cluttered with inferior shows and this kept him from doing his job, giving him adequate reason to sue Network over breach of contract. When Todd and Cliff attended the same meetings, no one spoke unless singled out by Murk, and even then, a shaky apprehension would prevent them from saying anything of worth.

"That ridiculous punching show is an embarrassing rip-off," Cliff said in a meeting he hadn't been invited to, derailing plans for yet another revamp of *Firth Thing This Morning (with Fay Firth)*, "and it squanders an important lead-in time slot for *Invisipeepers* on most of the feeds where it airs. It's more like we're punching ourselves in the face, which is something all of you should do until you understand just how terrible you are at your jobs," he boomed. "It has to go, or we'll lose all the momentum we've been cranking up in those hours. These numbers prove just how detrimental it's become." He snapped his fingers at Megan. She snored loudly, gargled, and shrieked, then circulated a stack of DataScrute reports that stalled in front of Murk. It seemed he neither heard Cliff nor noticed the heap of papers blocking his line of sight. Cliff leaned over and toppled the stack, pouring copies into Murk's lap.

"Bleh, bleh, bleh, you big fat blubbering baby," Todd said, staring Cliff down while bouncing on his heels against a wall. Todd held his arms behind his back and never sat during meetings. "There's DataScrute charts that say nearly anything you want them to say depending on the angle, you dope. That's no reason to change anything."

Cliff blasted an invisible death ray from his fingertips. "It's a flagrant copy of *So You Think You're Tough?*, and you know it. Targeting people on the street for physical violence; it's exactly the same thing!"

"Nope. My show asks people to target themselves for violence, so *there*. It's different."

"It's the same thing!" Cliff roared and yanked at his hair with both hands. He flung a DataScrute report toward Todd; it glided across the table and fell in between two executives who backed away, horrified, refusing to touch it.

Todd picked at his fingernails as if the conversation distracted him from something more important. "Why don't you just run up a tree and film someone dropping a load on the commode, you big creeper?"

The childish back and forth continued for the duration of the meeting, ending only when Murk raised a hand for silence. He pointed at me and asked, "Buddy, how should we deploy the troops?" In an exhausting meeting prior to that one, I had received a barrage of self-contradicting notes for fixing *Happy Throw Lucky*. Its second season numbers were plummeting, so my mind was elsewhere. I suggested moving *Who Can Take a Punch?* up an hour to retain viewers between primetime and the late-night block. This would open space for Cliff to test out a new creation, contingent on its projected viability in DataScrute. Murk nodded and waved me away. "Cliff, what's the plan of attack?" he bellowed, looking at the wall.

Cliff edged toward him, eyebrows raised in lunatic glee, and said, "Seriously? That's what you look like?"

The room was a vacuum of deafening silence as Murk finally turned to Cliff. "Son, you choose your next words very carefully. That's all I'll say to you."

Cliff let the tension reach its peak, then slapped the table. "*Seriously, That's What You Look Like?S.T.W.Y.L.L.* Network! Tonight!" Out of thin air he revealed a new pile of DataScrute reports for the *S.T.W.Y.L.L.* idea, a reality show solely consisting of a camera operator rushing up to people on the street, shoving the camera inhumanly close to their faces, and shouting rude comments about their degrees of ugliness. The AnalEYEzer predicted *S.T.W.Y.L.L.* to be a success on a few feeds in the newly opened time slot between *Who Can Take a Punch?* and *So You're Think You're Tough?* It did in fact air that same night, Cliff once again having stockpiled his demented curios until they became useful for agitating someone else.

The vastly retooled and excessively overbalanced *Happy Throw Lucky* was moderately successful on a few TVC feeds, but ultimately stagnated sooner than anticipated, barely lasting to the end of its second season. Viewers tired of sitting through drawn-out scientific commentary on knife throwing techniques before a contestant hurled a brand-sponsored knife at a rotating board of brand-sponsored balloons, each containing a prize, another throw, or black confetti. Some episodes were crammed with so much technical explanation, contestant backstory, and marketing moments that only enough airtime remained for one actual knife toss.

However, my stint as showrunner was semi-successful, mostly because all I had to do was tell other people when to do their jobs, when to stop, and when to clean up. The experience bought me enough clout to be summoned by Breff for another Network pitch meeting. I yet again squandered the opportunity by overthinking potential ideas until they all seemed bland and awful. After timidly stumbling through two terrible scripted drama ideas whose geneses I didn't remember, I smashed my temples together and moaned. "Ok, then. A table with money on it. People try to grab it. *Cash Grab*. A game show. Contestants run into a room and grab money and run back out." I threw my hands up in surrender and slumped feebly, embarrassed that relying on my years of industry experience to provide a nuanced intuition only got me a partial concept for another gimmicky game show. The swell of nodding heads and Murk's flick of a wrist gave the vague premise a preliminary green light to move forward to the next development phase: a vigorous DataScrute scouring to grind it down until it was smooth and shiny.

6.

The rules for *Cash Grab* were simple. Twenty contestants had thirty seconds to race across an enormous warehouse to a concrete slab holding one million dollars and collect as much money as they could carry back out before the buzzer sounded and a hangar door slammed shut. The AdvEYEser spiraled through a profusion of nearly conflicting requirements to make the show as broadly appealing as possible, and one strangely unconventional rule it developed was "no physical contact between contestants." If a player unintentionally collided with another, both would be disqualified. DataScrute's projected numbers suggested the rule would be a masterstroke for orienting the show toward its goal of innocuous perfection.

I brought in Brian Vohangliss from Viewsful to decipher The AdvEYEser's suggestions and assist with "ethics consistency," the DivComm phrase for making everything bland enough to be rendered inoffensive to the touchiest of people. The real data-driven genius was the addition of commentary by Buck Tarstick and Pete Pamselle. I was surprised when a DataScrute report recommended using them to host *Cash Grab*, but the AdvEYEser pointed to the duo's popularity from co-hosting *Game Changers* on The Sports Channel, the short-lived misplaced footage rehash from a few years before. At least something positive came out of a highly visible mistake that insisted on coming back to haunt me. I only had to endure sly remarks from Buck about why he didn't see me around the Sports Channel food trucks anymore.

I was the de facto head of *Cash Grab*, but I still had to submit to any Commission suggestions that came in, maintaining the appearance that Viewsful's involvement with Network properties was necessary and beneficial.

To have a fighting chance at staying on the air, I needed to ensure *Cash Grab* was a crossover hit and attracted stable primetime viewership in nearly every demographic. The Commission's wealth of research probes into "competition reality programming behavioral economics" concluded that younger males were the most likely to act aggressively during a high-energy competition whereas middle-aged females demonstrated a better potential to conduct themselves in a manner appropriate to the situation, regardless of the prize at stake. To provide a favorable tone for the series, The AdvEYEser proposed we only enlist married women over forty-five for the first episode. For simplicity, I always yielded to its guidance, but the only real certainty in human behavior is the constant of surprise.

In our initial pilot episode run-through, the first two contestants to reach the cash pile suddenly turned and attacked each other. The other contestants stopped abruptly, squeaking shoes echoing throughout the warehouse like a malfunctioning conveyor belt. Most of the crew members lurched and teetered in a series of ambiguous stop-and-start moves, extending a hand forward as if to lend it in help but then leaning back on their heels to prevent their bodies from moving in any direction. One camera operator managed to utter a full-on "Hey!" but it was precisely timed with the bridge of one woman's nose being split by the other's elbow and went unheard by anyone. The audible crack of her nasal bone forced me out of my transfixed astonishment and I hit the buzzer. A thunderous alarm sounded. Both women immediately threw their hands up and whipped their faces toward the mezzanine-level control room where I stood with my face in my hands. The more damaged of the two contenders, a fifty-something middle school office manager and mother of three, now with a lopsided nose and tectonically shifted cheekbones, looked horrified not at being caught fighting, but at the prospect of forgoing her chance at the money.

I choked back a windstorm of swears and ground my teeth until they squeaked. My face curled into a demented smile as I hissed like a punctured tire. Buck Tarstick clicked his tongue and patted my shoulder lightly. "Buddy, it looks like you have a *hit* on your hands."

I swatted his arm away and took a deep breath. "Thanks, Buck. Keep up the jokes, and one of these days I might actually laugh my way out of renewing your contract." I turned to give him a serious, reproving look, but he quivered his bottom lip like a scared infant and glanced nervously side to side. I gurgled a nervous laugh and sponged the oily sweat from my forehead with the cuff of my shirt, a stiff and itchy high-class button-down I had bought the day before. Buck stood straight with his hands at his sides and bowed in multiple directions to an invisible crowd, fluttering his hands regally.

I barely registered a knock at the door. Brian Vohangliss appeared in the control room and handed me some papers. "Here are two forms for each of those contestants to sign—I assume you're replacing them? The 'Consent to Termination of Assured Recorded Appearance' agreement and the 'Presumption of Confidentiality deal.'"

I gently plucked the forms from him as if they were on fire and slowly turned to Buck. "Ok, mister personality; you want the honors?"

He flashed his best innocent country boy grin and performed some sort of hoedown hand jive. "Can't nobody stay mad at this face, Bud." Buck winked and snatched the papers. He snapped his fingers like a musical theater backup dancer and slunk away toward the warehouse interior he had spontaneously christened "The Bargain Basement" earlier that day.

The production coordinators corralled the remaining contestants as the studio crew reset the warehouse. After breaking the news to the disqualified contestants, Buck returned to the control room with Pete Pamselle, who had been interviewing contestants in the "Contender's Corner" alleyway behind the warehouse. Pete's deadpan commentary offered a more traditional on-screen presence than Buck's relentless homespun vigor. Buck shuffled across the room and clapped like he was channeling a lively spirit during a religious revival. Pete rolled his eyes but grinned despite himself.

"So, they're *not* supposed to fight?" he said. "I'm so confused. What show is this, and what am I doing here?"

Buck slapped Pete on the back and fired a finger-gun at him. "I think there's still a few garbage cans need emptyin' out back, Pete, if you're lookin' for somethin' to do. What else you been doin' down there all morning?"

Pete pulled a confused face and rubbed his ear. "Well, sir, I met some enthusiastic people in the alley out back, and they told me there was money stashed somewhere in this building. Say, you want to help me look for it?"

"Shucks, Pete. We'll be lucky if we walk out of here today with any money at all, right Buddy?" He nudged both of us with flapping chicken wing elbows as Pete mimed digging through the floor with a shovel.

I coughed into my fist and spun my hand in tight circles. "I think they're ready, so, can we…you know."

Buck spun an imaginary lasso over his head and hollered, "Loud and clear, have no fear! Bucky's here to spread the cheer! Let's crank this baby back up and see what she can do!" I surveyed the area the cleaning crew had restored by the cash slab and gave them a thumbs-up as I led Buck to the mezzanine stage, shaking the jitters from my arms. Buck strapped on his headset and tapped the mic, then grinned and stretched his arms out wide as he addressed the crew and contestants like a phony prophet on a hillside.

"Howdy, howdy, hey, hey, hey, everybody. We gathered here today to have some fun and go home with some money, did we not?" The production coordinators clapped exaggeratedly from their perches over the contestants and mimed huge smiles as everyone returned to their starting positions. Buck cocked back and belted out a convincing wolf howl. The contestants roared in affirmation. One, a gymnastics instructor, unleashed a cascade of backflips and shrieks, further heightening the excitement but doing little to allay my fear that the second run-through would produce the same result as the first.

"That's the spirit!" Buck screamed and pumped his fist into the air. The coordinators lined up their contestants shoulder to shoulder along the hangar door, each giving a thumbs-up to an external camera feeding back to a closed-circuit monitor. As I slid shut the false wall of the control room behind the mezzanine stage, Pete waved to get my attention. I leaned my head out worriedly and angled one ear toward him. He pointed at the cash pile and mouthed, "I think the money's over there." A coordinator frantically waved him through the hangar door and pulled it down behind him. Buck brought his hands together in a solemn look of prayer, then arched both eyebrows and sneered devilishly. "On my cue. Get ready. Get greedy. Now grab that *cash*!" The hangar doors whooshed open, and the contestants flocked in.

What really made the show unique was its unanticipated comedic value. Overriding the instincts to push and fight forced contestants into a realm of hurried but over-the-top politeness. Voices were hushed, breathing delicate refrains of "sorry" and "excuse me," while bodies twirled and twisted in opposite orbits. The subdued chaos came across like the first rehearsal of a synchronized dance where each performer had been given the wrong cues.

In the second run-through, the entire group of contestants reached the cash slab almost simultaneously and halted. They seesawed on their toes as if confronted with the rim of an abyss, then all spun counter to each other and ducked to avoid contact. "Watch out, folks. We nearly had some flaky elbow skin scrape together there," Buck's commentary began. "Nothing humorous about that. And now this whirling dervish is getting ready to roll and spin out of control! Like the gears of Father Time's eternal clock, these women are turning, turning, turning!" Eight contestants made it out of the warehouse with a combined total of almost forty thousand dollars.

Buck's absurd observations were an instant highlight, and in the next round, he fell into a motif of soup-related analogies, possibly from the visual of people mixing together. "The pot was simmering, and now it's heating up fast to a *rolling* boil," he said as the women circled the money but hesitated to get too close for fear of contact. "This cash slab is a honey of a ham hock. The contenders are a harvest bounty of potatoes and carrots swirling in its savory eddies." Two contestants were booted when their backs touched. Buck shouted, "Jambalaya! Booyah-baisse!" The round ended with only two women making it through the doors before they closed, each with a thousand dollars. In a post-round "Contender's Corner" interview, one winning contestant, out of breath and shaking, explained her strategy to Pete by saying, "I just tried to grab the money and leave without touching anyone, you know?"

The crew struck the set and left the warehouse. Our original plan for the day was to reap two salvageable rounds of *Cash Grab* for the first episode, and we were luckily right on schedule, even with the total loss of the first run-through.

"Boy howdy, it sure is funny, Bud," Buck said as we decompressed in the control room after the rollercoaster first day. "Bodies flying and spinning all over, eyes bulging, tongues lolling like a bunch of starving puppies. Some of them looked like they forgot what they're even doing there, like they blacked out and woke up at some kind of demented aerobics class."

"I had an idea earlier, when those two were ejected for making contact," Pete said, sipping lukewarm coffee from a paper cup. Buck clenched a dry bagel in his mouth and stood in front of him with his hands up in a timeout signal.

"Sorry, Pete, but Buddy Buppsen here is the idea man. Network only pays you to talk, so maybe stick with that."

"With you around, it's impossible to get a word in," Pete said flatly and pinched Buck's cheek.

"Oh, I got the gift of gab, mister you-so-drab. There's cash to grab from that big ol' slab, and it'll be fab to slap it on my tab." Buck clutched his hands to his hips and gyrated around in self-satisfaction.

"So, what's your idea, Pete?" I said, unbuttoning my shirt collar and massaging the crease it had furrowed into my neck.

"We should interview contestants after they've been disqualified for illegal contact and we'll call it the *Cash Grab* Crash Gab." Buck threw an arm around Pete and convulsed in silent laughter.

"Thanks," I said. "I'll give it serious consideration after DataScrute tells me to. Too much filler, and this show might get tossed quicker than *Happy Throw Lucky*."

"Well, I hope the folks at home have as much fun with it as I am," Buck said, wiping away a tear. "What with all that DataScrute hooey gettin' shows axed and retooled, you got to hit the ground runnin'."

Pete raised his palms submissively. "That data hooey suggested bringing me along, so you won't hear me besmirching its good name." He turned to me. "Buddy, does the data say I can go home now?"

"That data don't mean so much; they just like to hide behind it, is all." Buck said. He stiffened his back and wagged his finger at me with a haughty frown like an overbearing school marm. "You see, the sociocultural importance of such programming has been thoroughly substantiated by Network's tremendous efforts to ensure every viewer receives exactly the experience they want. Those courageous folks's only goal is to achieve total satisfaction and psychological equilibrium for the entirety of mankind, God bless 'em, and if that means crankin' out a thousand shows that are all ninety-nine percent the same, well I'll tell you, that one percent that's left over—therein lies the soul." He slapped Pete's arm and smirked knowingly.

Pete elbowed him. "Now *you're* doing Buddy's job."

"No," I said, "my job is only to remind everyone else to do *their* jobs. But I'm off the clock now, so feel free to keep wasting each other's time."

"You're the boss," Pete said, throwing his hands up in a full-body yawn and scratching under his arms.

"But what's with all those shows that got the ax recently?" Buck said. "Never seen anything like it. Plus, they're so similar, who decides which ones stay and which ones get chopped? *Cruisin' For Losers*, *Hey Fatty!* What was the other one?"

"*Hey Fatty!Where You Going?*" Pete said tonelessly.

"Now how's that any different?" Buck pretended to straighten his tie. "Call me old fashioned, but give me nice people racin' to grab money from a pile and I'll be just fine, thank you very much."

"Do you even have much free time to watch TV after a full day of talking to yourself in the mirror?" Pete said.

"Shoot nah," Buck snickered. "That knucklehead likes to argue too much."

Pete thumbed through a tray of stale pastries, delicately picked up a muffin, and rotated it to check the sides. "So, Buddy," he said, offering me the muffin, "were those shows canceled because Network got too many complaints, or is it really just the data reports? I'd like to know what we're up against." I took the muffin and handed it to Buck, who swatted it across the room, landing it precisely on top of an overfilled garbage bin.

"Game on," Buck whispered as he grabbed an armload of Danishes and started catapulting them at the bin, dislodging a tower of carelessly piled plastic plates and crushed cardboard boxes.

"Well, the new ethics guidelines have helped ease up the flow of complaints a bit," I said, and chugged a cup of water. I immediately started to refill it, jiggling the plastic faucet of the water cooler and leaning the jug forward to edge out the remaining drops. "Some of those cancellations were, eh, an unfortunate byproduct of political fallout, I guess you could say." I tried to sip a second cup of water but closed my eyes and mindlessly drained it.

"Did Cliff Montagna create all the ones that got cancelled?" Pete asked.

I took a deep breath and collapsed my shoulders as I exhaled, like forcing the last bit of air out of a blowup mattress. "They were all copycat shows. So, I guess you could say he created all of them and none of them."

"I'd heard Murk's gunnin' to take that little troll's shows away from him," Buck said, shadowboxing in a dark corner and kicking garbage at the wall. "What's that all about? Cliff cranks out a bunch of hit shows, and they want to punish him for it?"

"Weren't you just trash-talking those shows a minute ago?" Pete asked.

Buck looked back over his shoulder, perplexed. "You expect me to remember anything I say?" He snapped his fingers and clapped. "Sakes alive, what was that last one he did? Cliff, I mean."

"*S.T.W.Y.L.L.* or *Invisipeepers.*" I said and checked my watch, instantly forgetting what time it showed. "I don't remember which."

"*Seriously, That's What You Look Like?* How is that even an idea for a show?" Buck said. "Plus, it's hard to say—*stwyll.*" His backcountry accent forced it out like "*stwuhl.*" "Just raw footage of bitter, hateful people runnin' up on uglies and ugmoes and scarin' 'em half to death with nasty comments about how awful they look. And those people doin' all the criticizin', well, they ain't exactly prize pigs themselves. I suppose all that pent-up anger and frustration has to go somewhere, like a transference of energy." Buck extended his hands and waved gracefully as if reaching for the cosmos and tracing the paths of stars. "You understand what I'm saying?"

Pete looked at him dumbfoundedly and shrugged. "Not quite," he said, "but if you keep talking, maybe I can keep ignoring you."

"Well, I'm glad we're marchin' to a different tune with *Cash Grab*, that's all," Buck said. "It's more diversified, if you will. Kudos, Bud." He offered me a bagel, but then side-armed it across the room.

"Yep, it was all my idea. You're right to thank me," I said, thumbing through the Commission reports I had brought along for a quick refresher. I had trouble focusing on any one of the unnecessarily grandiloquent paragraphs on viewership tendencies I was supposed to know well enough to successfully implement on *Cash Grab*. The charts only seemed to suggest that viewers like to watch the shows they like.

"Now that we've all had a nice lungful of fresh air from up here on our high horses," Buck went on, turning to Pete, "you see the one last week where the nightclub singer was crying into the piano with her hair on fire?"

Pete winced and held his nose in mock pain, nodding.

"That big old songbird's in there croonin' her oversized heart out," Buck said, "and that lanky, googly-eyed girl storms in from the back room, blaming her for what? Basically everything bad that's happened to her the past twenty, thirty years? She comes in stompin' those spiky heels across the stage, strikin' kitchen matches, and flickin' 'em at the singer right there at the climax of the song. Things really started to sizzle!"

"What a showstopper. I almost called for an encore," Pete said.

Buck slapped his knee three times and barked a raspy laugh, his voice surging up an octave. "The singer's hair must've been so full of product—it goes up like fireworks, and the crowd is stunned. *Stunned*," he said. "You'd've thought someone would've stepped up to help her—to at least pat down the flames—but nobody moved! Like it was part of the act! Even the piano player stayed rooted to his seat."

"He should've broken into a fast number. 'And now to heat things up a bit, ladies and gentlemen,'" Pete suggested.

Buck leaned against a wall to keep from falling over, chest heaving. He steadied himself with one hand on Pete's shoulder. Tears trickled down his cheeks as he tried to go on. "Oh, but the best part. The best part was that lady's voice!" Buck struggled to finish. "When that fire caught, her voice went higher and higher like she was practicin' some scales."

"You mean warming up?" Pete snorted as his lips trembled.

Their faces were both beet-red and dripping sweat. Buck's geometrically precise pompadour haircut unwound itself and began a slow landslide down his brow. "And then the piano," he wailed. "She ducked her head in—why? To smother the flames? To look for a way out?"

"Well, Buck, she decided to call it a night and closed the lid on the whole thing," Pete said.

Buck doubled over and slapped his hands together, gasping for breath and fully crying out of both eyes. They fell into each other's arms, Buck smacking Pete's back in a steady rhythm as their laughs thinned to a high-pitched wheeze. Their impromptu rapid-fire routine gave me further hope for *Cash Grab*'ssuccess, but my anxiety over the next morning's call time considerably impaired my mood. I held up my Commission notes and saw that I gripped them so tightly, the ink had smeared into the creases of my palm, outlining a confluence of rivers on a topographic map. I twisted the papers into a wrinkled tube and wedged them under the pile of stale leftovers in the garbage bin, then picked up the fallen trash and stacked it on top. I heard most of it slide back down as I walked out.

.....

The first week of taping yielded enough material for four solid episodes, each with three rounds of *Cash Grab* padded by contestant backstories, slow-motion instant replays with analysis, and post-round celebrations. In the "Contender's Corner" interviews, contestants demonstrated their talents and relayed the highlights of their life stories to Pete, who intuitively explored and presented the narratives that made them all relatable and seemingly television-worthy. Buck hosted the "Cash Count" after-parties in the karaoke room left over from the short-lived *Rockin' Jockaoke* show (DataScrute had suggested "depicting contestants engaging in fun, communal experiences" to lend a positive tone for the show, but it had the opposite effect on me since the karaoke show reminded me of the one time I almost presented a decent idea in a pitch meeting). Each episode would include twenty minutes of fluff and three minutes of real action.

The editors quickly assembled and delivered rough cuts to the Network executive team, who responded with only a few notes. While they seemed pleased with the upbeat tone we had cultivated, mostly thanks to the hosts' naturalism with corny puns and overly precise replay commentary, Breff's marketing enclave was more enthusiastic about the "deep potential for synergistic opportunities in promotional realms," or marketing tie-ins and advertising space within the show.

The lead editor snorted as I read that comment aloud in the editing room. "Yeah, maybe they'll modify lyrics in popular songs for the karaoke room, and the contestants will belt out tunes about sweaters and vacuums," she said. After what I had seen go down on other Network shows, she wasn't far off the mark.

Some showrunners had received notes regarding the "abrupt viewer disengagement derived from sudden lapses in narrative flow, causing momentary disorientation and undesired focus on the antithetical natures of storytelling and advertising." It seemed that having any sort of overt break in some programs put too much emphasis on the commercials being *commercials*, resulting in many viewers automatically tuning out the paid-for messaging and experiencing "acute cerebral discord." Sponsorships and promotions needed to be cleverly woven into each show in hopes of having a more persuasive effect on viewer habits, matching the tone of a program while somehow not attracting direct attention from viewers. A character in a scripted show could open a can of soda and drink from it as long as the act appeared natural and secondary to the narrative focus of the scene, but if the character smacked their lips and smiled at the can in satisfaction, that action provided "unduly accentuation" and would have to be revised as per The Commission's ever-mutating guidelines.

I was overseeing what I thought were the final edits of *Cash Grab*'s pilot episode when Chibbs Ticonderoga stopped by the editing room to vent about a Network revision request he had just dealt with. In a new episode of *Two Dudes and Another Dude*, Cody ("the main dude") was compelled to engage in a heart-to-heart with Brody ("the roommate dude") regarding the apparent use of Cody's toothbrush by a party other than himself. The Network's grievance against the episode cited a marketing analysis from a recent Commission report:

> *"The character Brody states (quote)* 'Co...I would never put something that looks like that into my mouth! Bro has standards, for real though.' *A clearly visible logo on the prop toothbrush in the scene negligently provides a derogatory reference of one potential sponsor, as emphasized by the character Brody, leaving other eminent toothbrush manufacturers as those to be 'approved for use' by Brody and, by extension, the viewing audience. This unfortunate wording could be construed as brand slander, and the undesired exclusion of potential sponsors necessitates removal of the offending scene."*

The episode was anchored by the resulting conflict over the toothbrush, mentioned continuously by multiple characters, so removing it from the narrative would have entailed a total rewrite when there was neither the time nor the budget to do so. Instead, Chibbs quickly reshot the offending scene and eliminated the negative reference to the toothbrush. He had Jody ("the neighbor dude") enter the room and complain that his imminent intestinal distress required him to make use of their toilet, as his was in dire need of repair. Brody and Cody reluctantly flee the bathroom, and the remainder of the episode stands unchanged, generating only a minor gap in logic that likely went unnoticed by most viewers. Chibbs told me that in any instance where a Commission note forced him to alter a scene on *Two Dudes*, he would simply bring the Jody character in to make a reference to scatalogical bathroom activities because, in his words, "that's basically all they're doing to me."

Along with the toothbrush request, Chibbs received his first *Two Dudes and Another Dude* "Comprehensive Ethics Analysis" from The Commission, whose perception of the show's unsophisticated and borderline vulgar humor was surprising.

"At some point in the past year, they conducted a pretty sizable focus group study to determine the value or non-value of the show. It's obviously more to do with its attractiveness to sponsors than the material itself, which is ridiculous," Chibbs said as I slid the editing room door shut and leaned against it, stretching my arms over my head. "I mean, we got so many sponsor booking requests after the pilot, I had to extend the first season by three more episodes so we could accommodate them all."

"Is that why there were suddenly so many Jody moments mid-season?" I asked. "Wait a second—that one where Brody and Cody were hiding under a bed the entire episode because they thought a prowler had broken into the house and it turned out to be Jody stumbling around suffering from an allergic reaction to the pine nuts on a slice of pizza—are you implying that one was hastily written just to pad out the season, Chibbs?"

Chibbs stared me down for a moment, then pretended to quickly draw a pistol from a holster. He aimed it at my heart and shook his head slowly. "This town ain't big enough for the both us, Bud." *Bang*, he shot me.

I tossed the report papers up into the air, threw my head back, and clutched my chest. "Oh, you got me. I ain't long for this world," I moaned in my best rugged cowhand voice. "Befores I drift on to the other side, mister, please tell me, how could Jody afford that house he owned next door to Brody and Cody? He was sorrowful unemployed. And how come we never actually saw his house, huh? Was that on account of budgetary constraintments or just plain old laziness?"

Chibbs fired again, then grabbed my shirt collar and mimed pistol whipping me.

"Oh mister, please," I cackled, "I can't help but point out your gaping plot holes and inconsistent character traits. Even an illiterate cowpoke such as muhself could see them flaws a mile off."

Chibbs bit his lip theatrically and shook his head. "Those Netjerkers wanted a crossover with *Invisipeepers*. That's where the prowler storyline in that one episode came from. I said no way and had to fix that one on the fly, too." He pretended to pull a bowie knife from his belt and held it to my throat. "Now I'm gonna do to you what I shoulda—"

Abruptly dropping the act, he said, "Oh, you know what? Originally, I had written in a little backstory where Jody had some winnings from a lottery ticket, like just enough to buy a modest house, cash," he said, smoothing out my collar and sheathing the invisible knife. "The joke being that he thought buying a house was the mature thing to do, but he had no money left for basic necessities, hence all the mooching. It was only a throwaway line in the first episode. Even though most viewers aren't exactly hyper-perceptive of conspicuous omissions like that, I wanted there to be *something* funny that explains him living next door. But, oh man, Network's issue with it—get this—they didn't want any mention of a character winning the lottery, in any amount, unless the lottery authority specifically bought ad time in the show. One of our account managers reached out to the lottery people, but they weren't interested. We waited to hear back until it was too late to write anymore—the first episode was halfway through production—so we cut the mention of his house from that scene. In one of those go-nowhere leadership meetings, that accounts guy tried to apologize and said something like, 'We were unable to secure the lottery funds,' and I said, 'Yeah, it's a gamble!'"

I let an ultra slow-motion smile distort my face. "Oh, I get it—lottery, gamble. Good one. I'm proud of you! Since when did you get funny, Chibbs?" I said. "Must've been that exact moment. I think we've pinpointed it."

Chibbs rolled his eyes. "Anyhow, everyone started shouting out suggestions for alternate backstory ideas, and I cut them off. 'No, no, no, we're good, Bruce or Brad or Brett or Branch or whatever your names are. I think we're good, we can handle it.'"

"So, they held up production for that, and when it didn't work out, it was up to your team to fix it and keep moving."

"Yep. Even their mistakes aren't mistakes," Chibbs said. "They're like the cream that always rises to the top, except instead of cream, they're dead jellyfish."

"*Mmm,* jelly and cream. Chibbs, you're making me hungry for a doughnut. Did the ad guys pay you to say that?"

"Choke on it, Bud," he replied, grinning.

I picked up the focus group papers I had tossed and motioned toward them. "So, this magnum opus of toilet humor you concocted—The Commission's report found actual value in it? That's funnier than anything you've ever written."

"Oh, it gets funnier, mister do-nothing know-nothing worth-nothing. In that study there, they determined that males in the core demographic are less likely to engage in 'non-social behavior' like vandalism and arson, I guess, if they're…what did they call it?" He grabbed the study from me and flipped through the pages. "Oh man, here it is," he laughed, pointing to the appropriate passage. "How they could even gather data on this sort of thing is beyond me. I guess that's why I'm on the creative side."

"Creative? *You*? Slow down, I'm still getting used to the idea of you being funny."

Chibbs sighed heavily and flipped through a few pages. "Ok, ok, here's the real joke, right here. '*The aforementioned demographic subsection is proven to be stricter adherents to societal norms and unspoken principles of behavior when routinely engaged with suitable material for escapist cognitive projection, becoming adequately pacified by the vicarious experiences of characters in programs viewed.*'"

I laughed silently. "Wait, so, jokes about bodily functions help keep them off the streets?" I asked, bewildered. "Wow, that makes you some sort of humanitarian. You might be next in line for Murk's job."

"You got it, Bud," Chibbs snorted and continued reading. "This is the best part: '*Viewers of the program demonstrate a heightened arousal to the positive benefits and reinforcement of constructive societal attributes. This program successfully encourages this subgroup to congregate more frequently and in greater quantities than other programs in this subgenre, thus achieving a farther-reaching impact and providing vital intellectual stimulation for its target demographic subsection.*' There you have it. *Two Dudes* helps young men achieve enlightenment." Chibbs gently placed his palms together and bowed.

I had difficulty processing the absurdity of what we had both just learned. "So, your show caters to a specific audience of young males who might be prone to delinquent behavior and, in some way, they're so placated by the experience of *Two Dudes* that they become better people? And that's magnified when they gather in groups to watch the show?"

"That's the gist of it," Chibbs said, throwing his hands up. "The meeting I had yesterday with the two Network execs—they were already hitting me up for new show ideas before I had a chance to read the report. It's insane."

"Keeping potential delinquents off the streets by catering to the lowest of brow and commonest of denominators, giving them feeding tube portions of recycled dreck to stupefy them into docile geniality," I joked. "You're not keeping at-risk youth off the streets; you're just giving them a reason to stay in front of their screens and be exposed to more advertising. *Two Dudes* shows them what they really want to watch, which is apparently 'ethical' in some weird way I still don't understand, and when they gather together to watch..." I grabbed a corner of the report and squinted to read the fine print under a chart. "It '*forces significant notice amongst their peer group.*' And nobody wants to be left out, especially young people, so a popular show like that helps...'*condense behavior patterns into predictable models.*' So they say."

Chibbs folded his arms. "Uh-huh. Is that how they try to justify all the late-night programming?"

"Uh, there's different metrics for that kind of stuff."

"I bet there is," Chibbs said. "But isn't Network responsible for encouraging viewers to—How do you watch something like *What Makes You Think You're So Special?* without thinking it's ok to go out and pick fights with people in public? And there used to be a *Freak Seek* spinoff solely about roughing up teenagers? I mean, have you seen *Invisipeepers*? Come on, are we going to normalize hidden surveillance?"

"Cliff is Cliff," I said, looking over both shoulders to the opposite ends of the hallway. "He wasn't raised in polite society, and no gutter is too grimy for him to crawl inside."

"Sure, that's him, but Network is hyper-focused on that type of material right now. Just because some people are willing to watch stuff like that doesn't mean we should air it, right?" Chibbs said.

"I think I've heard people say that about *Two Dudes*," I said.

"Oh ok, so as long as the data supports it, who cares what it actually does to society?"

"Still sounds like you're talking about *Two Dudes*."

"Well, as per usual, I can count on you to suck the life out of the room," Chibbs said. "At least you're consistent."

"Backhanded or not, it's still a compliment, and I thank you." I bowed diplomatically.

"Har times three, you sharp-tongued, flat-faced mental sloth."

I patted Chibbs on the shoulder. "Enough with the pep talk, coach. My head's big enough as it is." I checked my watch without actually reading the numbers it displayed. "But look, the late-night thing—there's an audience for it, and they're pursuing it. Simple as that."

"But with all the notes I've gotten, trying to appeal to everyone at once..." Chibbs closed his eyes and beat the report softly against his face. "I just don't want to get too cocky or complacent with things as they are, you know? Do you think there's a chance *Two Dudes* will get retooled into something awful?"

"You mean it's not already?" I held my hands up in a calming gesture of surrender. "I think it's worth sticking with what you know because trends are so finicky, plus—"

"Who would mess with a cash cow?" Chibbs nodded. "That's what it comes down to. I hope."

"Exactly. *Cash Cow*—now there's your next show. A cartoon cow shoots money from its udders when you squeeze them." I snapped my fingers as my eyes shot open wide and my jaw hung slack in a look of divine intercession. "I can see it now. The cow roams through troubled inner-city neighborhoods and poor rural communities to assist the neediest of the needy like a modern folk hero. 'Don't worry, kids. *Cash Cow* has your milk money!' Why aren't you writing this down?"

"Hmm, let me kick that one around with the guys upstairs. Yeah, they said thanks but no thanks." Chibbs smiled and shook his head. "So, you don't think—"

"I don't think at all. I thought you knew that. Wait, I mean I *didn't* think that."

Chibbs stared blankly and thumped me on the forehead with his middle finger. "In your completely unprofessional opinion, should I be worried about *Two Dudes*?"

"I really doubt it. You're running a hit show, and as long as you let Network call the shots on marketing, you'll keep them happy," I said. "That ethics report is plenty of reason not to worry, plus you've got that *Cash Cow* idea in your back pocket in case things turn south. Think about it."

"No thanks, I'll cash out on that one," Chibbs said. "But now that you've said it out loud, someone's bound to make it."

"I'm pretty sure it was your idea, regardless of who said it. *Cash Cow*. Yeah, that sounds like a Chibbs original. I think it would hold up in court."

Chibbs smacked my elbow and winked. "You keep sucking the life out of the room, Bud. It's your legacy."

.....

The editors finished the recut of the *Cash Grab* pilot, leaving room for marketing moments to be filled in later. While awaiting those data-driven decisions, I was asked to attend a mid-season audit of *Seriously, That's What*

You Look Like?. I reluctantly sat in the corner of a cavernous Network conference room and kept my mouth shut. *Cash Grab*'s impending premiere date provided all the tension I needed to render me indefinitely sleepless, and listening to Network goons slice and dice another creator's work only wrung more sweat from my glands.

Cliff gaily strolled to his seat and cracked his knuckles, obviously thrilled at the prospect of another fight. Todd and Megan walked in after him, each carrying a stack of DataScrute reports. Todd had pored over numbers from thirty TVC feeds and found that whereas his and Cliff's shows were equally popular when taken as averages, there were ten feeds where *S.T.W.Y.L.L.*'s numbers had started to lag. That tiny slump hurt viewership of both *Who Can Take a Punch?* and *Invisipeepers*, as well as their allure to sponsors. Always quick to panic, the executive team called an emergency audit regarding "dynamic program reconstruction for aggressive resolvement of desired viewer engagement," Network speak for overhauling a show against the creator's wishes and bombarding them with negative feedback veiled as "endeavoring to achieve the optimum upward thrust for a program's legacy." Legacy was spoken of in hushed, reverent tones, a subtle deceit reinforcing the expendability of every crew member and producer.

Instead of arguing for Cliff's termination, Todd simply suggested he take over *S.T.W.Y.L.L.* himself, allowing Cliff time to retool his other creations to attract more viewers. "My shows are all bigger crossover hits than his ever were," Todd said, "Give me control, and I'll turn things around."

The *S.T.W.Y.L.L.* audit boiled over in record time when Cliff screamed at Todd, "I'm going to grab you by your crooked teeth and drag you through the street until there isn't enough of you left for the cops to identify as a body!"

Breff Kholkers snapped his fingers and shouted, "'*Whose Body Was That?* Network—Tonight!' Now, Cliff, that's the kind of fresh idea we'd expect from you."

Cliff knuckled down on the table, seething and shaking like a gargoyle in heat. "Breff, I swear on your mother's forgotten pauper's grave, if you make one more suggestion, I'm going to—"

"Well, have you considered doing anything with unsolved homicides?" Breff said innocently. "Unidentified victims, unclaimed bodies. 'What are your police doing to solve these heinous acts of aggression?'" he said in a baritone commercial announcer voice, which all Networkers randomly lapsed into like irregular fits of demonic possession. "I could really see the home audience getting hooked on it, trying to piece together clues and solve an actual real-time mystery. Not ages-old cold cases; I'm talking current, immediate, right here and now. You know, real gritty stuff."

Another executive sputtered, "*Get there before the cops.* We assemble a team of ambulance chasers with police scanners, souped-up sports cars, and handheld cameras."

Breff slammed a notepad on the table and popped his lips. "We could even air it live!" They all leaned back in petrified awe, a collective gasp whooshing through the room. I stared at my shoes, trying not to think of the impending restructure of *Cash Grab.*

Breff raised his hands like summoning a spirit during a séance, then pumped his arms forward and back in small circles. "Cliff, let's get this train rolling. Full steam ahead. Woo wooo!"

"What do you say, Cliff?" grunted Murk Torquins. "Want to pursue the unsolved murder idea?"

Cliff flared his nostrils to maximum expansion and licked his lips suggestively. "Sure thing, birdbrain. Meet me outside, and we'll get started." He stared down Murk and growled hoarsely as he stomped out of the room, leaving the door open. Just as Breff opened his mouth, Cliff appeared in the doorway, screaming, and slammed the door full-force before yanking it open and slamming it twice more, pulsing his shriek like an astronaut training in a centrifuge. He stormed over to Murk, grabbed his jacket collar, and leaned in close enough for their noses to touch. "Seriously, that's what you look like? What makes you think you're so special? So, you think you're tough? In case you didn't catch the subtle subtext of my last comment, allow me the opportunity to make this plain: let's go outside so I can murder you, and we'll air it live to see if anyone watching at home cares enough to solve the mystery! *Network! Tonight!*"

Cliff howled and kicked a rolling chair down the length of the room in a dizzying whirligig. The chair stopped a foot from me; I glanced around the room, trying to avoid all eye contact when Cliff pounded the wall and pointed in my direction. On his way out, he punted a small trash can against a wall, then slammed the door again.

The crowd hushed and swiveled their necks toward the center of the room. This unfocused trance was their precursory posture for the loose-form babble that overcame them when they were completely void of the most basic of ideas and simply "talked it out." They discharged a blind toss brainstorm mortar shelling Murk Torquins called the "thinktank." The Networkers' disconnected voices spiraled around the room in a concentrated echo chamber where every shapeless thought was blurted at maximum volume in hopes of a centralized theme materializing around which to focus subsequent rounds of incoherent chattering, often evolving into a bizarrely sing-songy cavalcade. An alarming number of Network shows had been workshopped in this manner.

"Whose body was that?"

"Look at all the blood!"

"Solve the crime before it's too late."

"Solve the crime before it happens to you!"

"These heinous crimes!"

"These painful times."

"Use the clues."

"The evidence is all around you. Do you have what it takes—"

"We raise the stakes. Do you have what it takes—"

"We kick down the door and force the grim reality of the slums into your home."

Megan Brambles coughed deliberately into the crook of her elbow. "We should stay on track and settle these *S.T.W.Y.L.L.* issues before—"

"Lies! Corpses. Cadavers!"

"Bodies. Bullets and bodies. Dead bodies."

"Blood clot. Body rot."

"Clotted blood and body crud. Gristle. Meat. Bones and giblets."

"Some scum from the slum bumped off some bum just for fun."

"Come downriver, we deliver cadavers with splattered gray matter."

"Nameless cases. Desecrated faces."

"Streets choked with marrow."

Megan shuffled and stacked some Commission reports.

"The staggering loss of life."

"Whose body—"

"He lost his buddy."

"What did he look like?"

"Is *that* what he looked like?"

Breff knuckle-rapped the table in a thundering barrage. "*S.T.W.Y.L.L.* Yes! Megan, Buddy—what's the proper action course for this *S.T.W.Y.L.L.* problem and, secondarily, how do we get this red-hot crime scene show up and running?"

Megan cleared her throat and laid two Commission reports side by side, gently patting them. She nodded off with her eyes open for about two minutes before speaking; by that point, the Networkers were used to it and just stared at her for the duration of her nap. "DataScrute suggests Cliff is spread too thin, manpower-wise, and that we should transfer control of *S.T.W.Y.L.L.* to another producer, like Todd Gherkin, so Cliff can focus on his other properties before their ratings suffer. Buddy?"

I rubbed my temples and gazed at the jagged loop of a loose carpet thread, wondering why some small part of me wanted to sympathize with Cliff. For better or worse, *S.T.W.Y.L.L.* was wholly his creation; he had always shot and edited it himself with practically no overhead costs. I slid a copy of Megan's report in front of me. "Well, it looks like overall viewership of *S.T.W.Y.L.L.* is only slightly down," I said. The executives nodded together, as if their faces were drawn up and down by the same strings. "Like these reports here show, all the considered factors must...*stabilize within the boundaries of available resources and optimal viewership targets*. And—" I breathed deeply and held the papers in front of my face. "Yeah, just let Todd run the show for now. He can handle the remainder of the episodes that've been ordered. That should do the trick."

Murk flicked his wrist in my direction, confirming his approval. Everyone in the room folded their hands like clergy readying for prayer. I glanced sidelong at Megan; she held her reports firmly to the table and stared straight ahead, her bottom lip drooping to one side and twitching.

"Thanks, Buddy," said Breff. "We'll inactionate that plan immediately. And we'll set up another meeting to thinktank *Whose Body Was That?* so hard, there'll be bodies everywhere!"

A few Networkers rose from their seats and waited for me to leave before sitting back down, a routine action I speculated to be some sort of tactic demonstration of my subservience. Todd traipsed away whistling bird calls. I shuddered as I left the room and looked both ways, half-expecting a flying elbow from Cliff to knock me down. A receptionist at one end of the hall called out, "Don't worry, he's gone," without looking up from her terminal. "But he left you a note."

I tiptoed to her desk and slowly reached for the folded napkin, still warm to the touch. It was slashed and smudged with Cliff's telltale spiky, angular handwriting, like it had been stabbed and left to bleed out in an alley on the wrong side of town. "*I'm giving you one last chance to do the honorable thing, Buppsen. Kill yourself, or I'll be forced to do it for you.*" I grit my teeth and forced a smile. The receptionist mirrored my strained face and held out a hand as I absentmindedly wiped my forehead with the napkin. "Oh, here," I chuckled nervously and reached to hand it back to her before realizing what I had done. I stared at the thick streaks of ink on the napkin and momentarily wondered if Cliff actually had the power to remotely conjure pranks like that.

"The closest bathroom is just down the hall," the receptionist said as she grabbed the napkin and threw it away.

The Network executive team responded to our second draft of the *Cash Grab* pilot with more notes than I'd anticipated, some of which contradicted editing suggestions from their first batch of notes. "I usually take half of the editing notes and throw them out," the lead editor told me as I followed her out of the editing room. "If you do everything they tell you to do, then they just think you'll do *everything* they tell you to do." I assumed she was heading to a quieter space to discuss the notes with me, but as I turned around, she closed the door in my face and went back to work. I dropped my head against the wall and sighed. Overseeing the re-edit despite her objections was the smart thing to do, so instead I left to go bother Chibbs in his office. The career-affirming elation he felt after The Commission's ethics breakdown of *Two Dudes and Another Dude* had waned some since I'd last seen him.

"When the Netjerkers brought up the potential for spinoffs, I was on board, but it's like they just want different versions of the same show. Why would I be involved with that?" he said, leaning his chair back against a cardboard cutout of the three dudes high-fiving.

"Well, you did set the standard for rudimentary storylines and scripted comedy clichés," I said. "Oh, do a spinoff where the dudes all work at the town dump and call it *Recycled Garbage*."

"Best idea I've heard all day!" We saluted each other and shook hands. "The first one they pitched—that's the thing, *they* pitched ideas to *me*. What's that all about? I thought I was the creator."

"Woah, I know you have a massive ego problem, but thinking you're a deity might bump you up a level of the dementia tax bracket."

Chibbs tossed a *Two Dudes* branded koozie in my face. "Shut up and kneel, blasphemer. Their first idea was the exact same show but set in a different city. They called it *Dude B. Cool*, and it had Brody's cousin—who's never been mentioned on *Two Dudes*, by the way—in the same living situation. Two roommates and a moochy moron next door. They basically asked me to rewrite the first episode of *Two Dudes* with different character names."

"Sounds like too much work for you. Pass."

"Up next was *Dudes Be Friends*, I think? Some uninspired attempt to flip the formula by showing a younger, more responsible version of Jody living by himself with two moochy moron neighbors next door."

"Well, we've established your audience looks right past plot holes and obvious filler, so that at least frees you up to write whatever you want without worrying over consistency," I said.

"You consistently disappoint even the most degenerate of people."

"Write that down. That can be the opening line of the *Dudes Be Friends* pilot."

"I'm on it," Chibbs shouted. We both stood and saluted, then sat back down. "But their last pitch was a show for older kids that was only slightly related. Brody's nephew Brad—who's also never been mentioned on *Two Dudes*—is a timid middle schooler, and everything he does is awkward and embarrassing. They want to call it *That's Too Brad!*"

I shook my head. "You're right. Such a great title shouldn't be wasted on your sophomoric drivel."

"It's like they come up with a title and then try to write a show around it. Either way, why me? Why a *Two Dudes* spinoff? If they have the ideas, let them line up a producing staff and do things their way. I'd rather branch out."

"They're not paying you to branch out; they're paying you to make them money," I said. "And really, it's just your name they want. I saw a report on behavioral studies a while back; if I'd bothered to read it, I think it would've said something like viewers who like your show are accustomed to seeing your name in the credits whether or not it registers in their conscious minds. So, having 'Created by Chibbs Ticonderoga' at the beginning of a show, as terrible as that sounds, actually piques some people's interest on a subliminal level, like through basic familiarity."

"So, it's just another marketing gimmick?" he said. "Put my name and the word 'dude' on it, and the same people will watch?"

I gave him a thumbs up. "Dude-a-Scrute approved. See, what do you need me for?"

"I don't. I keep saying that."

I shook my head and pointed to my ear. "White noise. It's all white noise."

"So, if I walked into a room and kept saying, 'Steve, Steve, Steve, Steve,' and then the people in that room had to choose between two candidates named Steve and Jeff..."

"Jeff doesn't stand a chance," I said. "Basic familiarity is all it takes, Jeff, I mean, Steve. People choose things they're familiar with. Again, I think that's what the reports would say if I read them."

Chibbs shook his head and massaged his neck. He leaned back and pressed against the *Two Dudes* cardboard cutout until it bent in the middle; the dudes leaned over him like they were eavesdropping on some juicy gossip. "This is the price you pay for being good at something, not that you'd know what that feels like. They keep saying, 'Thanks! What else can you do?' but then they pigeonhole you back into doing the same thing over and over."

I held out my hand and grinned like a buck-toothed idiot. "Trade ya."

He slapped a *Two Dudes and Another Dude* sticker into my hand and pushed me out of his office. "Not on your life, Buppsen."

.....

I made my way to the main Network conference room knowing I was early for a meeting to discuss the third recut of the *Cash Grab* pilot, but I had little else to do besides worry, sweat, and worry about sweating. I stood outside a moment before Murk swiveled his head around like a psychic owl and homed in on me. He motioned for me to join them, his fleshy wrist bending across his chest in a gesture of self-flagellation. The vast hall echoed with the chaotic shouts of countless executives, showrunners, producers, and lackeys.

"Chuckle Buttons."

"Bucky Chubbles?"

"What did you call me?" I asked helplessly as I walked in. "I'm Buddy Buppsen."

"Chumble Bubs."

"Bumbling Crumbs?"

"Buddy Buppsen! Now *there's* a clown name."

Murk shoved a rolling chair toward me with his elbow. "Buddy, take a seat." Murk wheezed, staring at the ceiling. His mouth seemed to continue moving after the words had been spoken, like a poorly overdubbed movie. "You remember Chubby Buckles? The clown from the Saturday morning show *Russ Gus's Superfluous Circus*?"

"Yeah, I do," I said, flooded with scarred childhood memories of the most ridiculously spastic show ever made.

"Chubby retired this year," Murk said, "and that loathsome old goat took the name with him. He'd been around long enough to own the copyright, so we're thinktanking a new name for the clown on Rus's show."

"I didn't know that," I said. "That's too brad, I guess. I mean, *bad*."

"Chuckie Butts?"

"Troubled Bubbles?"

"Amble 'n Scram."

"Scrambled Ham."

"Scribble Drips."

"Pickle Chips."

"Sit tight, they're almost done." Murk nudged me with his colossal elbow, leaving it pressed against my arm. "Soldiers, we're losing the favored rhyme scheme DivComm gave us," he shouted, pounding the table. "Ubs, ubs, ubs, remember?"

"Rub-a-Dub Scrubs!"

"Chunky Bunkum!"

"Buncha Hokum!"

"Skunky Punks!"

"Monkey Chunks!"

The meandering clamor finally dwindled to the scratching of pens and heavy breathing. Murk held his hands high and rose, staring at the gawdy tentacled light fixture in the middle of the ceiling as if it spoke to him. A hush spread over the room. "We're almost there." His monstrous fists slammed the table, rattling my teeth and threatening to topple a pile of Megan Brambles' DataScrute reports. She also stared at the light fixture and drooled out of one side of her mouth. I wondered if that was why she had taken to wearing scarves year-round.

Murk slid his palms to each side like a card dealer clearing the table. "Moving on. *Cash Grab*." The room mostly cleared until the remaining dozen or so Networkers shifted down the table next to Murk. Megan straightened her stack of papers and plucked two from the top, sliding them toward me. Her eyes were yellow and rolled around in tiny circles.

"The editors are almost done with the new draft; should be ready this afternoon," I said, rearranging my posture in various swirls and angles but never quite getting comfortable. "We're pretty happy with it, and we're still on track for the premiere date." Megan cleared her throat and tapped one of the reports in front me: Vicarious Stimulation in Show-Me Marketing Opportunities.

"Oh ok, so we need to talk about the marketing notes. I thought maybe we could cut a minute or so of each episode and fill the gaps with more commercials?"

Murk shook his head. "First things first. Megan." She thumbed through her copy of the Vicarious Stimulation report and folded the pages back to an outdated photograph of some sort of dinner party where a group of plastered-smile freaks threw their hands up around a man with a microphone. The other Networkers flipped to the same page in unison.

"Buddy, the marketing group solicited marketing opportunities for the karaoke room," she said. "There is substantial interest, and DataScrute suggests moving forward—"

"Oh no, do they want contestants to sing advertising jingles? Please, don't do that to me," I croaked.

"Of course not," Megan said, her body hunched over the table, head swiveling between Murk and me. "Many of the sponsors' parent companies also own music licensing businesses, so they're interested in contestants singing paid-for songs during the program."

"*During* the program?" I looked around the table. Everyone was hypnotized by the living room karaoke picture as if trying to mimic the grotesque mannequin faces. "Ok, ok. Maybe for future episodes, but we need to settle on a final cut of the pilot before we even begin to…There's already so much filler—"

"Due to the *likelihood of abrupt viewer disengagement during explicit marketing moments in reality-based competition game shows,*" Megan said, somehow reading from the report even though her eyes never stopped spinning, "DataScrute suggests *agile approaches to sponsor inclusion through methods more ethical to the desired viewer's standard of acceptance.*"

Murk pounded the table. Megan shrieked and scattered a few papers. Murk, as if he hadn't heard her, patted the table and pointed. "Breff and his team also had a gold medal idea. Breff."

Breff appeared beside me, beaming like he had just returned from a near-death experience ready to divulge the secrets of the afterlife. "Buddy, we had a breakthrough."

"That's wonderful," I said, failing to hide my irritation.

"We found a way to offer marketing moments throughout the entire episode without hindering the action at all." Breff's gaping smile seemed to include twice the normal number of adult teeth. "*Cash Grab.* Let's be honest: it's a race. A *race.*"

I raised my eyebrows, waiting for the breakthrough part. "You know what, Breff? I think you might be right."

"Mm-hmm. And how do we normally work sponsorships into races?"

I bit my lip and tried not to sneer. "Something tells me you're the guy who knows the answer to that."

"Oh, you bet I am. Here's what we do: decals, badges, bibs, stickers." Breff ticked off each option with an upward thrust of a finger, the act made unnecessarily lewd because of the raw satisfaction on his face. "Whatever the race, the competitors are proudly sporting the sponsors' logos."

My mental faculties hiccupped, and I stared at Breff for an uncomfortable duration. Megan groaned and snored, then yelped like a small dog. "Ok," I said, "we can get future contestants to maybe wear some shirts or something? Once we've got the pilot episode in the can—"

"We had the design team mock these beauties up. They'll look out of this world in the pilot." Breff tossed me a black and green checkered stock car racing jersey with the *Cash Grab* logo on the front. I was taken aback by the polished quality of the design, but it was spoiled by gaudy logos on the sleeves for Cheap Shots discount liquor stores.

"Breff, yeah, this looks great. Really, I'm speechless. But—"

"One more thing," Murk said, thrumming two fingers down one side of the report in front of him. "The contestants aren't running fast enough."

I stroked the side of my face, worsening the color shift I could feel swelling up. "Ok, well...How am I supposed to fix that? A firing squad?"

"Bigger warehouse."

"What?" I coughed. "The warehouse set we're already using has this intricate state of the art audio-video infrastructure. It took *weeks* to build it, we can't just...And the cameras; so many cameras. No square inch is hidden from view. It's just—"

Megan cleared her throat, moaned like a lonesome ghost, and tapped the other report she had slid in front of me. "A bigger warehouse means the contestants have to sprint harder to reach the cash. This DataScrute report shows—"

"Let me guess," I said. "Farther distances take longer to run. Is that it? And it saves on costs because if people have to run farther they don't have as much time to grab the money?" I hovered my hands over the paper like it was a priceless treasure I was afraid to touch. "We definitely needed a report to clear that one up. Thank you."

"The data supports these changes," Megan said, "and suggests a much higher potential for *viewer engagement and return engagement.*" She let out a long high-pitched screech like a hawk swooping down for an attack, teeth bared and eyes narrowed, then abruptly smiled and tapped the report.

"We'll stripe the new interior with sponsor logos, like a regular sports field," Breff said. "Logos in every shot. That'll get sports fans to tune in, too. Even more marketing opportunities! I've got chills." Breff quivered his hands to signify the truth of that statement. Megan made gentle sputtering sounds like an old tugboat entering a harbor; her head rolled in circles.

"I just don't know how I feel about all of this," I said, my voice involuntarily rising in pitch, which made me even more nervous. "Those are pretty major changes, and then for the crew, and the editors, and the laborers who built the warehouse set—all the technology that has to be torn down. We've already shot four episodes worth of material. We have another week of shooting scheduled and—"

"The data supports these changes," Murk said. "Don't worry about the time or cost."

"The time! That's another thing. We've been airing commercials for six weeks! Viewers are expecting to see something. We've promoted that date and now to suddenly move it—"

"The premiere date isn't changing, Buddy." Murk took my copies of the reports and stacked them back with the rest. Megan purred and bit her bottom lip repeatedly. "The new warehouse is being fortified for battle as we speak," he said. "Should we bring in Todd Gherkin to lead the charge instead? If nothing else, he's decisive."

A barricade of blank faces turned toward me. I looked at my hands, spread my fingers wide on the table, and pushed my palms down. "I'll go tell the crew."

.....

When Todd took over *S.T.W.Y.L.L.*, heimmediately doubled down on the amount of content per episode, giving each a reckless fever-dream pace verging on subliminal and epileptic. He brought in doctors and plastic surgeons to provide freeze-frame commentary on the specific facial feature peculiarities that amounted to each victim's supposed ugliness. This leant a bizarre pseudo-scientific credibility to the show, a somewhat educational factor in breaking down what characteristics generally determine attractiveness, like symmetry and mathematically average proportions.

Todd complied with every Network advertising request and found simple ways to include sponsor logos during *S.T.W.Y.L.L.* confrontations by having onlookers wear branded shirts, hats, or jackets and stay just within the edge of the frame. In one episode, a pockmarked, moon-faced intern walking out of his uncle's law firm gets hit with the classic "Seriously, that's what you look like?" line, and a bystander yells out, "You wouldn't look half as bad if you'd use Clearion Acne Cream, you dopey donkey!" The insult was doubly clever as Clearion's commercials always ended with its mascot, a disheveled donkey, hobbling past their logo and braying, "*Clear-EE-AWN.*" I started watching *S.T.W.Y.L.L.* regularly after Todd took over, ignoring the core material but appreciating the sick humor in its marketing ingenuity. It was the antithesis to the forced and obvious sponsor tie-ins being crowbarred into *Cash Grab.*

Without *S.T.W.Y.L.L.*, Cliff Montagna focused his efforts on *Invisipeepers*. Each episode featured a single uninterrupted thirty-minute shot of an oblivious person being recorded from outside their house by a concealed camera operator billed as "The Curator" in the closing credits. His unsettling commentary was voice-modulated to mask his identity, making it impossible to prove whether Cliff was behind the camera. When asked about this, Cliff would look at the ground and say, "I know a guy."

With most of the footage being too blurry or distant to recognize who was being filmed, *Invisipeepers* miraculously skirted any criminal proceedings that came near, and neither Cliff nor The Network were formally charged with a single offense. A local upper-crust socialite pressed her lawyers to threaten Network arbiters with potential legal proceedings over her supposed likeness in one episode, but the matter culminated in a stalemate over the proof required to dispute that the show wasn't simply "*an exceedingly well-produced scripted drama transporting viewers into the mind of a serial voyeur.*"

The ominous snippets of footage shown in the *Invisipeepers* commercials left me too creeped out to ever consider watching an entire episode. The low-pitched heavy breathing alone gave me nightmares, but many viewers were ok with becoming desensitized to the idea of spying on people because it was an above-average late-night hit and ran for two whole seasons before it was the target of a Network audit for its continued lack of sponsorship opportunities.

Being a marketing issue rather than a logistic puzzle for DataScrute and The Commission to solve, Murk and the executives beckoned Cliff without me, sparing me for one more day from the consuming flames of Cliff's hysterical outrage. They summoned Todd as a "peer mediator," since his shows continuously harvested healthy ad revenues; referring to Todd as Cliff's peer was far more damaging than giving Cliff unwelcome feedback on his show. To momentarily ignore my tense anticipation of *Cash Grab*'s looming premiere date while the pilot was being frantically reshot in the new warehouse, I looked for Todd to hear news of the hour-long *Invisipeepers* audit, hoping for some clue as to what Cliff might be planning next. Cliff had left me a note at reception reading, "Audit my show again, and you'll be in for a big surprise," but I hadn't seen him in a couple of weeks.

I found Todd leaning on a wall outside the Network's production truck loading dock, where he often threw dice with various crew members to determine who bought lunch.

"*Invisipeepers* is just thirty minutes of dead space to Murk and them," Todd said, sniffling and wiping his nose on the wrist of his denim jacket. "No ads means no revenue; doesn't matter how many people tune in. I guess you could see it that way, but a popular show is a popular show. Anyhow, they tell Cliff he has to find moments in each episode to include some sponsored material. You can imagine how that went over." Todd shook like a wet dog in slow-motion and adjusted his ball cap repeatedly, shifting the bill up and down in a jackhammering stammer. "I went in there thinking it was the end—they were finally shutting him down and sending him packing. But nope. *Advertising*. That's all they care about." He shrugged and picked at a scab on the back of his neck.

"Hmm, if only I had undergone some recent experience that would allow me to relate to that story," I said jokingly, trying to ignore Todd's grimace as he dug a little too deeply into the scab. "Maybe I should take a cue from Cliff and play the scorched earth card."

"Man, whatever," he said, stretching and pushing a palm into the small of his back. "He accused me of ripping him off, but his shows…I mean, he's one of the least original people I've worked with. He's just lucky people like shady stuff on late-night TV right now. Tides change, he could be tossed out just like anybody else." He turned and spit into a pothole filled with stagnant oil-streaked water, lifting his cap as he did so like a pump handle activating a water fountain statue. "It's crazy how those executives don't care what you've done for them. They're all 'thanks for keeping millions of people watching every night, but what have you done for us lately?' And they can only react to things—like you have to show them a finished idea before they can think they had that idea. TV's a visual medium, but those people can't seem to visualize anything." Todd snorted like a rusty gear and hocked another wad of glop into the pothole, where it looped and coiled around the slick oily ribbons. He threw up his arms and started walking away. "Just do what they're paying you to do and shut up about it. What else are you gonna do?"

An assistant editor jogged around the corner of the loading dock and waved us down. "You guys want to see something really crazy?" We followed him to the editing room, where he queued up the newest episode of *Invisipeepers*—the first scheduled to air after the audit. Near the beginning of the tape, which the editor had simply found on his desk that morning, a hand drifts into frame holding a half-opened candy bar. The Curator fumbles the camera briefly, attempting to cradle it in his neck to free up both hands for wrenching open the rest of the wrapper. The Curator gnaws off half of the king-sized bar, smacking and chomping obnoxiously. The swampy voice purrs and delights in the sweetness of the candy as well as the prime vantage point, about twenty feet high in a forested common area in a newer-construction neighborhood.

The camera swings down and zooms toward a middle-aged couple sunbathing in their fenced-in backyard. The Curator becomes louder and more excited as the candy bar disappears in chunks. His chocolate-covered fingers smear the edge of the lens. The other hand swoops into view clutching a lump of tissue; he attempts to clean the lens but only makes it worse. The gruff voice growls a few expletives at a dangerous volume. The sunbathers both raise their heads from their deck chairs and look at each other in confused alarm. The man shields his eyes from the sun and scans the tree line but can't seem to spot The Curator. He chuckles softly and holds the candy wrapper up to the camera, ensuring the logo is visible.

"Thanks, Flav-O-Treat," he says. "That gave me just the energy boost I needed." The camera blurs in a twisted spiral as The Curator falls from his perch, slamming branches and wailing like a wild boar before suddenly catching hold of a dirty knotted rope ladder with one hand. The agitated voices of the sunbathing couple become louder. The Curator slides down the last few feet of a thick oak tree and crouches. The camera whips to one side as the man opens the gate in his privacy fence, wrapping a towel around his waist. "Come and get it!" shouts The Curator as he takes off into the woods. His pursuer gains some respectable ground on him, but The Curator charges ahead in a burst of sudden stamina, taunting a small group of neighbors who have joined the chase. They follow him through the woods on the undeveloped land adjacent to the neighborhood as he continues filming and vanishes into the dense late afternoon shade. The Curator hides in a ditch obscured by shrubs, the camera gently rising and falling in time with his labored breathing. He pushes aside a wooden pallet covered in leaves, revealing a crude hole in the earth from which he hoists up a burlap bag full of smoke bombs and what look like bear traps.

I reached over and hit stop on the video controller.

"Nope. Not interested," I said. Todd chuckled and pulled his cap down low.

"It's a two-parter," the editor said. "This is only the first tape."

"I really don't need to see this."

"But the tape stops before...It ends on a *Cliff*-hanger, get it?"

I waved my hands in the editor's face. "Look, I don't need to see what Cliff does next. I already have enough anxiety over him materializing at any moment to exact his revenge on me for—"

"Buddy, it's funny you should say that," Todd said as he leaned over the editor, rewound the tape to the candy wrapper scene and paused it. He pointed to the smooth, skinny nail-trimmed fingers that bore no resemblance to Cliff's beefy hair-choked gorilla knuckles. "That ain't Cliff."

My heart skipped a series of beats and then sped through a compressed drumroll. "And that's somehow worse," I said. I turned off the video monitor and flashed a sarcastic smile at the editor. "Thanks. And by 'thanks,' I mean holy crusty giblets, please don't show me anything like this ever again."

The editor grinned. "You almost have to hand it to him, Buddy."

"No, I don't!" I yelled as I left.

I blew the rest of that afternoon wandering around the other editing rooms. I settled on watching a rough draft of a new episode of *Bark if You Love Dogs*, an intolerably sweet daytime program that served as a welcome divergence to the horrifying parade of mankind's worst impulses exemplified by Cliff.

I did a double-take as I left the daytime program editing suite, surprised to see Chibbs Ticonderoga watching over an editor's shoulder and giving her notes. I approached the window and watched what looked like an ordinary roundtable discussion program on the video monitor. I tapped the glass and pretended to fall asleep against it. Chibbs and the editor must not have heard me and continued working, so I tapped the glass harder and pretended to sleep again. Chibbs confusedly slid the door open and told the editor to take an early lunch break.

"What are you doing, peeking in all the windows?" Chibbs said. "Have you finally reached the level where you have so little to do you have to watch other people work to remember what it was like?"

"Yeah, it's for the new season of *Invisipeepers*. Maybe we'll change the name to something like *Hall Monitor* or *Insecurity Camera*."

"How about *Workplace Jerkface*?"

"Sure, but are you ok with us using your legal name like that?" I said.

"Speaking of *Invisipeepers*, did you hear—"

"Heard it, saw it, traumatized by it, ready to move on," I said and motioned to the video monitor. "Let's talk about whatever new flavor of boring you're whipping up in there."

"Branching out, Buddy." He pointed to the four stuffed-shirt fossils on the screen. "Got the greenlight for this last week: an intellectual current events panel discussion program called *Topical Brainforest.* It's really exciting. I mean, it's not—it's basically visual anesthesia—but it feels great to do something outside of the Dude-iverse for once."

"Playing both ends against the middle, huh?" I said. "I guess that's one way to atone for unleashing the unforgivable awfulness of *Two Dudes* on the undeserving world."

"Check out the logo Breff's minions mocked up for me." He held up a glossy sheet with an illustration of brains growing atop a thicket of tall trees, stylized in the manner of a clinical biology textbook.

"Ok, that looks way too cool for whatever those nerds are discussing. But do they get to wear racing jerseys covered with logos? That's the next step, Chibbs. Get ready for it."

"Nope. Believe it or not, we're reaching for a higher purpose with this one."

I put a hand on Chibbs's shoulder in consolation. "You should probably stop telling yourself that so it won't hurt so bad when they retool this snooze fest into another *Two Dudes* spinoff."

Chibbs pushed me away and slid the editing room glass door closed. He pointed to his ear and mouthed, "Sorry, I can't hear you."

I took a deep breath and walked down the hall to the primetime show editing suite. I found a door with a handwritten sign taped to it reading "*Cash Garb*" and knocked. When the lead editor finally glanced over, I raised my eyebrows and a hesitant thumbs up. She spoke plainly without opening the door or moving to get up. The thick glass muffled her voice, but I believe she said, "They only gave me two notes this time, so I threw one out and did the other one." She waved me off, and I gladly left for a change of scenery. I trudged back to my apartment, the same shoddy place I'd lived in since I finished high school that my foster parents were still paying for because I still hadn't found the time to move out.

.....

On the morning of *Cash Grab*'s premiere date, I received a note at Network reception. Murk Torquins requested my assistance in mediating an emergency audit of *Invisipeepers*. Apparently, the appalling open-ended tape I was shown somehow made it to air, but no one was willing to accept the responsibility of having scheduled it. I imagined a surreal scenario where Cliff urged The Curator to include sponsor tie-ins on the show, only to realize The Curator also reacted adversely to feedback, and instead of adding marketing moments would rather ramp up the show's intensity by nearly getting caught. Then I imagined how Cliff might turn around and vent that frustration on everyone at The Network, making what I had assumed to be my maximum level of queasiness soar to new heights. I had enough on my mind without Cliff's looming deathblow, and the audit summons was like adding injury to injury. All week I had slept poorly, eaten terribly, and considered not showing up to watch the *Cash Grab* premiere with the crew. But once I was there, it all felt so inevitable. I hung my head and trudged over to the conference room, where I waited an hour for the meeting to start, like a criminal offender showing up a week early for a lengthy jail sentence, resigned to my fate and ready to get it over with.

Megan stumbled through the door and thrust a stack of audit reports against my chest, then fell into a chair next to me, whimpering. I waited a moment for her to come to, as accustomed to her daytime eye-opener blackouts as the Network executive team, but when I looked at her, I was startled to see that her eyes were closed. Instead of nodding off in typical horror-catatonia, her body had finally forced her to sleep. I wheeled another office chair next to her and gently nudged her arm with my elbow. She slid over and curled up across the two chairs. The first executive to walk past her rolled his eyes and whispered, "Wish *I* got to sleep on the job." I handed him a report and told him to feel free to go sleep at the other end of the table.

The report detailed Network's grievance with the *Invisipeepers* episode where The Curator falls from a tree and runs off into the woods, luring his pursuers toward some violent encounter. Before falling, The Curator made direct mention of Flav-o-Treat candy bars and showed the wrapper on-screen. Flav-o-Treat's parent company Omni Nom Noms didn't sponsor *Invisipeepers* or any Network late-night program, so the show was audited for "*improper placement of sponsored content.*" I assumed Murk would use this to crush Cliff into the ground once and for all.

Thirty or forty Networkers filed into the room, a delirious sweatbox anticipating the total annihilation Cliff would bring. One lackey excused himself and could be heard retching outside. We all sat panting in unison until Murk signaled his assistant and screeched, "Send someone over to Cliff's Edge and drag his sorry butt out of there. I'm sure he's just hunkered down there, is all. Too scared to watch the bombs drop." One executive mistakenly took this to mean the meeting would be postponed; he stood to stretch and collected his things. Murk slammed the table with both hands. "We're in a holding pattern. You walk out that door, you'll be considered a deserter and shot on sight." The same lackey excused himself again and became sick as he stumbled through the door, catching some of the spew in his hands and holding it to his chest. Todd leaned against a wall, whistling softly.

An hour of jittery silence later, Murk's assistant returned with a message: Cliff was gone.

"Gone," she repeated, as my heart pounded and my stomach rose into my throat. "He left town two weeks ago."

"Two weeks ago?!" Murk thundered. He stood and sat and then stood again, like being yanked through an involuntary aerobics routine. "How is that even—" He leaned on the table and snapped his fingers at me. "Buddy, quick, when did we last see him? When was that audit?" All I could think of was how new tapes for his shows had still been piling up in the editing rooms.

"It was three weeks ago," Todd said, chuckling. "Buddy wasn't there, but I was."

"Has anyone seen that bozo since then? *Anyone*?" Murk's bewildered gaze surveyed a wave of shaking heads. Breff mopped his sweaty forehead with a tissue, flailed his hands as if considering how to offer any insight, and then, smiling psychotically as always, left the boardroom. A few Networkers followed.

"Mission accomplished," someone shouted glibly as the door closed. Murk fell into his chair and slouched onto his bent elbows, clawing at his scalp. "How is this possible?"

His assistant struggled to fill in the gaps. The underling who had driven to the Cliff's Edge building found a notice of condemnation hanging on a heavy chain blocking the main door, which was also padlocked and crisscrossed with caution tape. Not to be deterred, the resourceful underling went to the government office listed on the notice and talked his way into obtaining Cliff's home address—a swank apartment a few blocks away at the epicenter of Cliff's Edge, The Indie, and The Network. No one answered his aggressive knocks, so he found the building superintendent and was told Cliff and his wife had moved two weeks ago.

A collective gasp squeezed the room. "*His wife*?!"

The assistant went on to explain what the super had told the underling. "His wife was the manager of one of those organic grocery stores; she was promoted to regional manager, so they moved to where the company's based."

"Wow," one Networker lamented. "Not even Spoiler Horse saw that one coming."

The executives filed out, laughing, either from long-awaited relief or the sight of Murk's sagging jowls that deformed his face beyond recognition. "I never back down from a fight," he said. "Never. But this...This..." He skimmed his hands across the table, fixated on its galaxy of swirling wood knots, looking for some benevolent spirit to soothe the disillusionment of an unwinnable game being concluded without his say-so.

Todd stretched his arms wide, then yawned and cracked his back. "Well, I guess little Cliff finally took all his toys and went home."

Murk never spoke of Cliff again.

.....

Invisipeepers lapsed into impermanent retirement. Todd continued to churn out episodes of *S.T.W.Y.L.L., Who Can Take a Punch?, What Makes You Think You're So Special?* and *Freak Seek* at high speeds, but the unfiltered reruns on Cliff's Edge, still playing regularly despite being housed on a server in a condemned building, lorded over late-night viewership as if nothing else was on. That frustration led Todd to spearheading a commendable original project: *Who Was The Curator?*, a ten-part miniseries that teased the unmasking of the *Invisipeepers* voyeur through extreme attention to his perceived habits as well as testimony from his supposed victims, none of whom were actually proven to have been in episodes of *Invisipeepers*. It added up to nothing more than a "best-of" rehash of the original program's two short seasons. Todd then moved on to the DataScrute-approved real-life crime scene exposé *Whose Body Was That?*

Chibbs fought to wriggle out of the Dude-iverse, but his presence in any Network meeting ensured chatter about trite comedic situations in which the various dudes could find themselves. Three *Two Dudes* spinoffs were produced without his involvement, and Megan's and Veena's *ManDates* was rebranded as *BroDudes* on some feeds, picking up a respectable number of viewers who otherwise would have avoided an honest look at modern male friendships.

Halfway through its first season, *Topical Brainforest*, although roundly acclaimed by critics for its unflinching engagement with complicated social issues, lagged disastrously in viewership numbers. To curtail any undesired retooling recommendations from The Network, Chibbs brought in the actor Jay Ugee (who played Cody on *Two Dudes and Another Dude*) to lead each week's panel discussion and offer uncultured commentary from the mindset of an average simpleton. The program was thus renamed *Dude...(Seriously)*, and its ratings immediately edged into acceptable territory. Jay Ugee's only contributions were delightful but vacuous comments like "Woah..." and "I know, dude" and "But that's just...Woah..." It was a minor crossover hit, which of course hastened unnecessary retooling from Networkers based on their flimsy interpretation of Commission notes. On some feeds, the show was retitled *A Fool Becomes Wise*, and on others, *Dwell On These Things, Dude.*

Megan slept for two days in the office chairs where I left her. Numerous meetings took place around her; two programs were created and retired before she woke. She quietly gathered her things and walked out during a marketing discussion on yet another *Two Dudes* spinoff called *Three Dudes and Two More Dudes*. Chibbs was the only person who noticed when she tiptoed back in, dropped a pile of index cards in a waste basket, and left.

Murk wasn't at all worried when he received Megan's resignation letter thanking him for the opportunity because he was confident I could handle all the DataScrute analysis for the whole Network. I gagged on the stomach acid bubbling up into my throat when he told me this and had no chance to refute him before he slapped me on the back and marched away.

Megan and Veena Chumbley applied for and were awarded the government grant funds previously used by The Indie and Cliff's Edge; they simply called the station Public Access. They created new shows that interested them, cast their friends and any members of the public who wished to be on camera, and paid no attention to data or ratings. Network's suddenly declining daytime numbers had executives scrambling for ideas; one massive thinktank concluded with Megan's creations *Zero's Sum* and *Grounds For Divorce* being merged into one mega soap opera extravaganza called *The Perfect Blend* on some TVC feeds and *Trouble Brewing* on others.

The crossover potential of the retooled *Happy Throw Lucky* reached fruition on *Cash Grab*. The hilarious excitement of the competition part of the show, where players rushed to the cash pile but then politely wobbled and swerved to avoid contact, was complemented by the relatable contestant backstories and spirited pre-competition singalongs in the karaoke room. The contestants' unique jumpsuits and sponsor-branded running shoes were extremely popular with viewers; by the midpoint of the season, Breff's marketing team made the uniforms available in athletic retail stores with customizable options for colors, logos, and branding packages. Breff was promoted to Senior Vice President, a position whose only perk seemed to be that he got to sit directly next to Murk in meetings.

I sailed through *Cash Grab*'s first season miraculously well. The only revision request from Network I received was for the season finale holiday special. In that episode, the warehouse interior was converted into a North Pole workshop scheme. The floor was resurfaced with a synthetic ice-skating rink polymer, and the money was left in an enormous "Santa's Sack" atop a pile of fake snow. This increased the difficulty of grabbing the money while avoiding contact. Naturally, the contestants dressed as elves, and vertical poles striped like candy canes were scattered throughout as obstacles. The poles were the object of Network's concern. The report read, "*The upright and shaft-like nature of the festive poles may be borderline objectionable to some viewers. This visual is exacerbated by contestants colliding with and struggling to remove themselves from the poles, creating an impression of evading undesired insertion. The seasonal appropriateness of the festive poles is unfortunately counterbalanced by the aforementioned grievance.*"

I oversaw the re-cut without making much of a fuss. Thirty shots had to be altered, half of which we simply replaced with alternate angles. The remaining shots were cut, leaving a one-minute gap in the required episode length. I had the hosts record a short "Thanks for watching!" holiday greeting for filler, which Buck warmly referred to as "good old-fashioned yuletide slop."

The assistant editor took the footage we removed and assembled a two-minute highlight reel he titled *Christmas Penetration*, which was also the name of Network's holiday season market analysis report. I caught wind of his plan to sneak the video into one of the TVC feeds and convinced him there was nothing funny about losing your job over a juvenile inside joke. I showed Christmas Penetration to the *Cash Grab* crew at the end-of-season wrap party, then asked the editors to delete it and all the excised footage from the Network servers.

Cash Grab was the first show since *Your Job in a Week* to feature the credit "Created by Buddy Buppsen," but considering my paltry contribution against the tidal wave of DataScrute suggestions, that felt like an outright lie. It wasn't a hit because it garnered impressive numbers on any one TVC feed, but because it performed just well enough on almost all of the seventy-five feeds. In that regard, it was the first major TVC crossover success, establishing the benchmark future shows would be measured against. Because *Cash Grab* cost relatively little to produce and brought in a wealth of advertising money, I had essentially conjured a perpetual motion machine freeing me from ever having to work again. Even if I sabotaged Murk's blind trust in me and squandered my lucrative consulting fees, I'd still have my cushy Viewsful job where John Klemchky treated me like a hero.

.....

I had just finished moving to a new apartment in the middle of downtown when Murk Torquins's assistant told me the old half-demolished building that once housed Cliff's Edge was finally scheduled to be fully demolished. I walked a dozen blocks in surreal anxiety to watch the heavy machinery that would finish the job, almost expecting Cliff to show up with a tank or sniper rifle to wipe the slate clean on both sides.

The hazy late morning sunlight beamed between two distant high-rises onto the site, a hard-edged ray terminating in a luxurious glow around the decaying brick like a showpiece under glass in a museum. I ate an apple as I approached the temporary fence surrounding the building and allowed my tortuous memories to resurface in hopes of teleporting them into the cellar to be consumed and buried in the forthcoming rubble. I was so overwhelmed by the distorted passage of time that I started giggling and spewed bits of mashed apple through my clenched teeth.

"Mind the spray, Buddy," came a voice from behind me. Todd Gherkin adjusted his ballcap and savored the splendor of the demolition crew as he sipped a tall can of off-brand malt liquor. "So, you had to come watch them finally put an end to this mess, huh?"

I nodded and wiped my chin. "Something like that. Do you ever have dreams where you wake up and Cliff's in your bedroom pointing a gun at you or shaking some kind of voodoo stick?"

"I used to, for sure. That's partly why I had to move on; I guess it finally got to me. Oh well." Todd finished the can and crushed it between his palms. He lobbed it at a mud-caked bulldozer as it hobbled across the loose bricks and broken concrete left over from the previous attempt at demolition.

"I want to know what happened in his life to make him hate people so much," I said. "Did his dog die when he was a kid? And afterwards he was determined to never feel that pain again, so he kills everything off before it can die on him?"

Todd cocked an eyebrow in my direction. "You know what he'd tell you if you asked him that?"

"That I should shut up and go kill myself?" We both grinned and nodded.

"Well, Cliff didn't sue you when you broke your contract and left this place," Todd said. "Honestly, that's as close as he could come to saying he likes you. Plus, you let him call the shots and take all the credit; that's all he ever wanted, so in his mind, you're probably square."

"Still, I'd rather never see him again. It's creepy enough that some of the Spoiler Horse clones and offspring are still around. *Son of Spoiler Horse: Foaled Again*; that one just came to me. Maybe I can pitch that next week as a reboot or an origin story."

"Spoiler Horse? Was that him too?" Todd winked and cracked open another can, draining half in one swig.

"Speaking of mysteries," I said, "did you know Cliff was married?"

Todd started to take a sip but nodded and lowered the can, smiling. "I assumed everyone knew that, but somehow I must've been the only one. Yeah, they've been married as long as I've known him. Whatever her name is, she sometimes dropped him off at locations when his car was getting work done, otherwise I wouldn't...When I first started working for him, he'd threaten to shut down productions if he didn't get his way because his wife made enough money for the both of them and he was just doing this for fun."

"For fun? Oh man, that's…that's…I don't know *what* that is."

"Unclear motivation; yep, sounds like Cliff to me." Todd tilted his head back, finished the second can and hooked it over his head, nearly making it to the building's steps as it clunked in the dust. "You know what's really funny? On my home TVC feed, *Your Job in a Week* is a daytime reality show. A fluffy day-in-the-life kind of thing. A crew follows people at their jobs for a week just to show what their daily lives are like. Somehow that's supposed to be entertaining?"

I laughed until I coughed up some apple I thought I'd fully swallowed. "I guess I should've known that, but they don't pay me to pay attention."

A smoke-belching excavator lifted its bucket and began leveling one of the upper-floor turrets. Todd pulled two more cans from his bag, offered me one, then looked at his watch and stuffed them back in. "Gotta get back to it." He slung his bag over one arm and gave me a sarcastic salute. "Have fun doing whatever it is they pay you to do."

I looked back at him as he passed. "Do you like where you are, Todd?"

"You mean at Network?" He looked over his shoulder, then turned back to me. "Yeah, I enjoy the work. It's fast-paced but never boring, and I get to do a little of everything. Most days, I don't feel like blowing my brains out, and there's something to be said for that." Todd dropped his bag, sighed, and crossed his arms. "I guess now I'm supposed to ask if you like where you are?" He heaved an open-mouthed burp into the crook of his elbow and smacked his lips.

I forced a nervous laugh that sounded more staged than I'd hoped. "It's strange," I said. "I have a great boss, but I don't like him; I get paid really well, but nothing's expected of me; I have the power to make big decisions, but a computer makes them for me. I have—"

Todd cleared his throat and burped again. "Sounds like you've reached the pinnacle, Buddy: show up for work, do nothing, get paid. I'd say you've won." He shrugged as he kicked over a dirt clod and stomped it. "What's not to like?"

The last remaining wall of the old building was suddenly bulldozed away. I shielded my eyes from the jolt of sunlight blasting my face, just making out Todd's blurred-edge figure hustling off around the corner. I panicked, anticipating the horror of hordes of blind beetles swarming out of the cellar to overtake the city. I whipped my head around, blinking furiously. My blown-out vision gradually returned as my pupils adjusted. I squinted fiercely and could just barely make out some silhouettes two blocks away that had been obscured by the building. One raised an arm and began a slow, dramatic side-to-side wave, like deserted islanders flagging down a passing boat. I instinctively mirrored it and smiled, then realized I was waving at Tom Geiger-Beef and his group of freelancers outside The Town Commoner. Tom lifted his captain's hat, shook out a hacky sack, and tossed it over his shoulder. Play resumed, and I walked back to work.

Acknowledgements

I would like to thank Andy Newton and Marty Dundics at Humorist Books for giving this novel a chance and for their astute suggestions that made it more streamlined and readable.

Thanks to my parents and brothers for putting up with me for so long. I'm blessed to have been born into a family of funny, unpretentious people who enjoy each other's company.

To my wife and kids—you are all amazing and special and I love you so much.

Thanks to all the kind and hilarious people I've had the good fortune to work with at the jobs I've had. You make work suck less. And a sincere thanks to all the humor sites who have accepted and posted my short humor pieces. You also make work suck less by providing anonymous weirdos an outlet for their ridiculous observations on important topics like parenting, cheese, leaf blowers, and snakes.

And finally, thank *you* for picking up this book. I hope it made you laugh or consider quitting your job.

Made in the USA
Coppell, TX
20 March 2022

75274558R00149